W9-CYD-612

for the win

a gaming the system novel

win

AUTOGRAPHED by the author

brenna aubrey

Enjoy the "win"!

FOR THE
WIN

A GAMING THE SYSTEM NOVEL

Best,

Brenna Aubrey

Brenna Aubrey

Silver Griffon Associates
Orange, CA

Silver Griffon Associates
P.O. Box 7383
Orange, CA 92863

Publisher's Note: This is a work of fiction. Names, characters, places, and incidents are a product of the author's imagination. Locales and public names are sometimes used for atmospheric purposes. Any resemblance to actual people, living or dead, or to businesses, companies, events, institutions, or locales is completely coincidental.

Trademarked names appear throughout this book. Rather than use a trademark symbol with every occurrence of a trademarked name, names are used in an editorial fashion, with no intention of infringement of the respective owner's trademark.

Book Layout ©2014 BookDesignTemplates.com
Cover Art ©2015 Sarah Hansen, Okay Creations
Cover Photography: (c) Lindee Robinson Photography
Cover Models: Destiny Mankowski and Ahmad Kawsan
Content professionally edited by Eliza Dee, Clio Editing.
Line and copy professionally edited by S.G. Thomas

For The Win/ Brenna Aubrey. – 1st ed.
First Printing 2015
Printed in the USA
ISBN 978-1-940951-09-6

For the wonderful not-so-little men in my life. You are the world to me.

ACKNOWLEDGEMENTS

There are so many people to whom I owe all gratitude for the invaluable part they have played in helping to bring this book into being. To my first readers, Kate McKinley and Sabrina Darby who never hesitated to pull their punches and push me to make the story better. To those who helped me with research: Mia Kayla, Kate Pearce and Mr. Pearce, Mimi Strong and Jennifer Lewis. To my production team, who make it all pretty and shiny: Sarah Hansen, Lindee Robinson, Chasity Jenkins-Patrick, Eliza Dee and the amazing S.G. Thomas. Thank you to my lovely ladies in the moral support department: Tessa Dare, Courtney Milan, Carey Baldwin, Leigh Lavalle, Natasha Boyd, and the awesome chicas in the Fast Draft Club ™.

Huge thank yous go out to all those who blog and review and spread the word about my books. I would not be able to do this without you. I'm so humbled that you love these stories and characters as much as I do. Your e-mails and tweets and posts on Facebook and on my blog mean so much and I cherish your kind thoughts and words.

The last acknowledgements go to those who sacrificed the most while I was producing this book—my family. Sorry, Mom for the sudden lack of phone calls and thank you for being so understanding while I was under deadline. It's hard to have a long distance relationship with those you love so much and yet have the work cut what little time we have. To my wonderful, amazing partner in life. I rolled the dice and hit a Nat 20 when I found you. I love you so much sweetie. Thanks for making it possible for me work my dream job. And many big thanks and kisses to my two not-so-little guys who haven't seen much of me lately. I promise it will only be for a little while longer and you'll soon be wishing you could see less of me. P.S. stop growing so darn fast, please! xoxox

1
APRIL

"**A**PRIL, WAKE UP *NOW*. YOUR BUTT IS ON THE INTERNET." Sid's panicked voice cut through layers of fuzzy sleep to reach me.

I groaned and buried my head under my pillow. Yesterday, I'd asked my roommate to make sure I got out of bed on time this morning using any tactic necessary, short of ice cubes. I had no idea she'd resort to nonsense phrases.

"Sid, go away."

Her hand was on my shoulder, shaking me. "No, seriously, you need to see this."

"Don't touch me," I mumbled. "I can sleep five more minutes."

"No, you can't. April, there is a sex video from Comic-Con and I'm pretty sure you're in it."

I sat up, blinking, my vision blurry. "What the *what?*"

I'd gotten next to no sleep over the weekend, and with all the overstimulation, drinking and debauchery, I was flat as a pancake this morning, exhausted.

And I had to start my new position at Draco Multimedia *today*.

My eyes narrowed, cutting to my roommate. I'd accuse her of playing a joke, but Sid would never get so elaborate. Nor would she *ever* frivolously use the S-E-X word.

"Okay, back off and speak slowly. It's before coffee o'clock."

Sid sighed, obviously frustrated with my grogginess. "I was on Tumblr following the tag for Comic-Con, and this video of people having sex kept popping up. I kept closing it right away because— icky—who wants to see that? But one time I got a closer look at the girl dressed up in what looked like *my* elf costume—the one *you* borrowed." Her voice was shrill like she was excited or panicked. Almost as effective as ice cubes for waking me up.

I swung a foot out of bed, still half asleep as her words rushed over me like a flash flood. There was this sick sensation in the pit of my stomach, and I had a feeling it had nothing to do with my rough weekend.

"Please tell me you're joking."

With wide gestures, Sid stalked over to her computer screen and angled it so that I could see. She pointed at the frozen figures. A woman, her back to the camera and naked from the waist down, was straddling a guy who sat on a chair. She had a distinctive tattoo at the small of her back, a hideous skull and snake motif.

Suddenly, my insides froze. *My tattoo.* My fit of rebellion from years ago now staring back at me from the screen, mocking me.

"So is that not you?"

I gulped. "Uh."

"Holy Spock on a cracker! Apes, it's *everywhere*. There are hundreds of reblogs on it. It's on Twitter, Facebook, *all* over."

I jumped out of bed, comforter and sheets falling on the floor and twisting around my legs, almost tripping me. "Nooooooo!"

Sid would be the last person I'd ever show this video to. She was pure as the driven snow. I was almost one hundred percent sure she was a virgin, and the girl sang—*sang*—while cleaning the house like Cinder-fucking-ella. And I bet when I wasn't looking she got little animals to push her broom for her, too.

Unlike Sid, I *had* had sex before, though I was no expert at it. And the one time I'd ever done anything on the wild side to prove I could be a bad girl—like anonymously hooking up and making a video of it—somehow it ended up everywhere. What the hell was up with that?

My body came alive with panic and fear, adrenaline coursing through my veins and nausea twisting my gut. This couldn't be happening! Not today! Not any day, but definitely *not* today. Without my asking her to, Sid clicked on the play button and I was treated to an unobstructed view of the hottest sex I'd ever had in my short twenty-two years.

I stood rooted to the floor as I watched the entire thing play out. I'd been drunk, but not so drunk I hadn't realized what I was doing. My judgment suffered greatly when I drank, as evidenced by this crazy sex tape and the aforementioned tattoo. With tears prickling my eyes, I vowed I was never going to have another drop...*ever*. Because next time, with this progression, the world would probably cave in on itself if I drank.

Or maybe just *my* world.

I put the heels of my hands to my temples, my fingers threading into my hair.

"Earth to April...did someone revenge-porn you or something? What's going on?"

I took in a shaky breath, unable to believe what was happening. "Oh God. Oh God. *Oh God.* This is a nightmare."

"Did you have sex at Comic-Con, April?"

I turned and gave her the best "duh" look I could muster. Her mouth formed an 'o' and her brows rose. She sniffed with disapproval and adjusted the heavy black frames of her glasses. "Uh, who was it?"

Crap, my answer was only going to make things worse. My mind grasped for purchase on anything I could possibly think of. "Uh...um." *Think fast. Come up with something, damn it!* "It was...he—"

"You don't know, do you?"

Oh God, I was the worst "bad girl" ever. I swallowed bile as I waved a wild hand at the computer. "Delete that!" She was the geeky one, after all. She spent *hours* in front of the computer. She'd know how to make it go away.

Sid frowned. "I can't."

Now the sickness inside was bubbling up. Sid wouldn't lie about this to teach me a lesson. "What...why? Why the fuck can't you?"

"Because, potty mouth, it's not my account. It was uploaded by someone else and tagged #ComicCon. I've been following the tag since, um—you know, unlike *you*, the undeserving non-geek—*I* didn't get a chance to go. And that's a good thing, because it seems like a den of iniquity!"

Uploaded by someone else? How in the hell had that happened? Had I accidentally uploaded it to the cloud? What the hell was "the cloud" anyway, and how did it work? Had someone hacked me like those poor actresses who'd had their naked pictures spread across the Internet?

I was going to vomit. Projectile puke everywhere.

"Did I...did I upload that from my phone?"

"So it's *your* video? April! Why would you video yourself having sex with some random guy? And how could you not know who he was?"

"He was dressed up as that bounty hunter guy from the game—"

"Falco."

"Yeah—whatever. Anyway, he had that armor on, and the helmet. And...and..." My stomach churned. "Oh hell, I'm going to barf."

"Too much alcohol, April!" Sid shouted after me as I bee-lined it to the toilet.

Vague memories filtered in. It was the last night of Comic-Con, a mere two days ago. Even in my drunken haze, I remembered that the sex had been incredible. Heated breathing, sweating through my elf costume, the feel of skilled hands sliding under my clothes, squeezing my hips so tightly they'd been sore the day after. He'd only spoken in whispers and that had made it all the hotter.

That steamy encounter, along with the alcohol, had helped me forget for a while. Before that night, I'd been miserable the entire time because of the awful news I'd received the day before. I blinked stinging eyes and pushed it out of my mind.

Damn it. I gripped my belly, waiting, but nothing came up. Instead, my guts were cramping into tighter knots. It was my first day working as an assistant in the CFO's office, and I had to start under these circumstances? What if people at work had seen the video? What if those who knew my costume figured out it was me? The questions swirled in my mind, making me dizzy. How would I even be able to concentrate today?

I stumbled to the sink to splash cold water on my face, and icy droplets soaked my temples, running down my neck and into my nightie. Then I confronted myself in the mirror, examining the blotches on my pale skin, complete with new dark circles under my blue eyes. Above the eyes, there were perfectly arched eyebrows, thanks to my makeover before the Con. I combed through my dark brown hair. I looked like hell. Felt worse. How had I gotten into this mess?

Oh yeah, I'd gotten drunk to drown out the humiliation and had let that affect what little good judgment I had—*yet again*. Alcohol and April clearly did not mix and were a dangerous combo. They led to ugly tattoos and anonymous sex with a helmeted man who had a ridiculously large penis and the hardest abs I'd ever felt against my body.

I'd been at Comic-Con because of my job, and he'd been some Dragon Epoch-loving nerd that I'd picked up because that's what *nice, boring, docile little* April would never do. She'd never go find some random dude in a costume and fuck his brains out. But drunk April was no *nice girl*.

I was like Dr. Jekyll and Miss Hyde when it came to booze, apparently.

Ten minutes later, after jumping in the shower and toweling off, I went back into our bedroom. Sid was still at her computer, gaping open-mouthed at the monitor.

"Umm," she mumbled when I stopped next to her. She was watching the goddamn thing again.

"Shut it off. That's just getting creepy with you looking at it over and over."

"This isn't the video—this is a gif that someone made from the video."

I knelt in closer, staring at the animated gif of my pelvis gyrating over the guy's muscular legs as he dug his fingers into my hips—on repeat. A flash of heat went through me as I recalled how amazing he'd felt. My remembered pleasure evaporated the second oscillating letters appeared above us, reading, "Cosplay geeks mating in the wild."

Shit...this was getting worse and worse.

I straightened. "Close that goddamn thing or I'm going to put a Trojan virus on your computer!"

Sid gave me a pitying look as I turned and headed to my closet. "It's a Trojan *or* a virus—not both."

"Whatever. Now please tell me you have some ideas about how to get that thing off the Internet."

"How on earth would I do that?"

I froze, my hand on my smartest business skirt and matching crop sweater. "You mean, you can't?"

"April, the thing has gone *viral*. There are memes, gifs. It's all over social media. Were you not listening? It's *everywhere*. There's no way I can get it off."

I sank to my bed, still wrapped in my towel. My stomach took a nosedive toward my ankles. I rubbed my forehead, trying to stave off a stress headache. "Shit."

Sid swiveled her desk chair around to face me. She was petite and cute as a mouse, with olive skin, dark hair and eyes like polished onyx framed by dark glasses that overpowered her face. She folded her arms across her modest chest and raised a thick, dark brow at me.

"You know, it really isn't *that* bad. No one could possibly know it's you. You're dressed up as Princess Alloreah'la from Dragon Epoch— purple wig, pointy ears, thick glitter makeup on. I doubt even the guy you...um...*you know*...even knows who you are. And he has a helmet on, and you both have most of your clothes on—except for your butt. So the odds of people knowing who it is are slim."

"Well...thank God for that. But still..."

With my leg, I scooted aside a stack of economic theory books—my latest passion—laid the outfit on my bed and went to my dresser. Doubtful my friends who knew about the cheesy tat were the type to follow the #ComicCon tag on social media. I may have been "*bookish*" and "*boring*," but I wasn't a video game geek. And I usually kept the damn tattoo covered up. I was biding my time until I got the courage to get the hideous thing lasered off.

Biggest mistake of my life...

Okay, maybe *second* biggest mistake of my life. I sighed.

"So...how long does it take stuff like this to blow over?" I asked, bending over to grab a fresh pair of panties and a bra. I held the panties up—dark blue lace—and decided against them, shoving them back into the drawer and pulling out a thong. This skirt showed every single panty line. So weird that my mind was grasping, beyond the panic, to find some sort of normalcy, nitpicking every item I chose to wear. But I knew I had to try to shove this cosplay humiliation behind me somehow and hope against hope that this would soon fade away.

Scarlett O'Hara always said, "*Tomorrow is another day*," but for me, "tomorrow" was going to start in about thirty minutes. I had to get my shit together, or at least act like it was together. Being moved up to work with an officer of the company was a huge honor for an intern. I needed his recommendation to get into business school, and I wasn't about to blow it. Not now. I'd worked too hard for too long.

"No. More. Alcohol. *Ever*," I intoned to myself as I sat on my bed and pulled on my clothes.

Sid snorted from where she sat behind her computer. "I've heard that one before."

I stuck my tongue out at her, though she couldn't see because her back was to me.

"Who knows what STD you picked up on this escapade?"

I grimaced at her. "He had a condom on, idiot."

"Oh, well then. I guess that makes it all okay."

"Sid, please," I begged, pulling on my boots.

She spun around again on her chair, hands on her hips and affecting that motherly tone that she liked to use. "April…walk me through this, please, because I'm really confused. Doing something like this is so *not* you. Did aliens abduct your brain? Because, ya know, Comic-Con would totally be the place for that."

I blew out a breath and leaned back against the wall. "My mom called me while I was there."

Her face fell. "Oh, criminy. And what did the Wicked Witch of the West Coast want?"

I clenched my jaw, fighting off the renewed feeling of hurt. "She was calling me from Las Vegas, actually. She got married. *Again.*"

Sid's eyes widened. "Oh, holy poop. For the fourth time? You barely had a chance to meet the last husband before it was over…" Then she seemed to remember one key detail—thank God, because I had no desire to spell it out for her. "Oh no…please don't tell me… she didn't—"

"She and Gunnar are now man and wife," I choked out. "Isn't that just *sweet?*"

Sid's face reflected pure pity. It would have made me utterly furious to be on the receiving end of that look from anyone but her.

Yeah, I was *that* loser. The one whose ex-boyfriend married my mother—that same mother who didn't have the wherewithal to figure out that it might hurt my feelings, nor would she care if she *did* realize it.

The term "mother" could only be applied to her in the most scientific of ways, in that she carried me for nine months and then gave birth to me. Jennifer Alden probably hadn't had two thoughts together in the same day about me from that point on.

"I'm sorry, Apes. He's such a—such a—"

"Cock smooch?"

"Bad person! I hate him. And your mom sucks too."

I raised my brow. My sweet Sid was *very* pissed to have used such vulgar language. Or maybe it had been my bad influence. April Weiss, the worst "bad girl" ever was now corrupting the purest, sweetest person I'd ever known... I blinked, suddenly overwhelmed again, my eyes stinging.

Her head tilted. "Oh, Apes. Please don't cry. Ugh...if I were the violent type, she'd be in trouble. I've always hated the way she uses you. Like when she takes you on shopping sprees and pressures you to pick up the bill. She's so gross."

I forced myself to swallow the unshed tears and started stuffing essentials into my new Kate Spade bag—my laptop, phone, wallet and, of course, my e-reader for break time.

Sid watched me with concerned eyes. I could feel the weight of her gaze. When I straightened, my eyes met hers. She spoke with soft, sympathetic tones. "So after she called you...you went to the bar, got wasted and picked up Falco the Bounty Hunter?"

"Not...exactly."

She raised a brow, wordlessly encouraging me to continue with the whole sordid story. I figured I'd better let it out now. Like ripping off a bandage—get the pain out all at once. I sighed in surrender. "I was at the bar downing one vodka gimlet after another, and the other interns wanted to know what was wrong."

"The 'other interns'...meaning Queen Meangirl?" We shared a look. Sid had met Cari once and they had *not* gotten along. It was understandable. Cari was an acquired taste. And many didn't acquire it. Sid continued, "She *is* a mean girl. I don't know why you hang out with her."

"I've told you, it's for survival purposes. She's the type of person I'd rather have on my side instead of against me. Besides...I think some of that is just her own issues. I feel sorry for her because her twin brother was killed. It's so horrible."

Sid nodded. "Nobody deserves that, I agree. But sometimes I don't understand why you put up with her behavior."

I looked away, heat rising to my cheeks. A good half of the time, I wasn't proud of how I'd behaved when I was with Cari. I'd done things that I wish I hadn't done. Things I'd like to make up for. This was one of those times.

"Anyway, with all the alcohol in me, I spilled to Cari why I was upset, and she was consoling me and even said Gunnar didn't deserve me. Then she said I was a bit too goody-goody and that's why I couldn't hang onto a man."

"That was not consolation, that was a taunt. And I'm guessing that in your drunken stupor you thought it would be a good idea to go out and prove to the world that you aren't a goody-goody?"

Her accurate assessment of the situation showed how well she knew me. Though we'd attended different schools, we'd been friends throughout our high school years and had roomed together the entire four years at college, as well.

Sid had been a bit of a loner at her high school. She'd had a small group of friends, but they were picked on often. *I*, on the other hand, was a social chameleon who'd had a knack for appearing to fit in without actually fitting in. I'd adopted it at an early age—a child who never fit in anywhere needed that special tool in her kit in order to survive. But it turned out that fitting in often meant not being true to myself.

"Yeah, she irked me. And yes, it was probably on purpose, but I was feeling low anyway and there was this hot guy at the end of the bar in a full costume and helmet."

"How could you tell he was hot?"

I rubbed my forehead. "He could have had a gorilla face under the helmet, I don't know. But his body was pretty smokin'. He was tall and solid."

"Did you talk much?"

I shrugged, trying to shove aside the panic and reason through the events of that night. I experienced again the cold thrill of sitting and talking with him, planning out what would happen next—anonymous sex, so unlike me, so dangerous. I'd rebelled against Cari's words because they'd so closely echoed my mother's words six months before. *I hope my relationship with Gunnar isn't weird for you...we're just having fun. If anyone knows how to show a guy a good time, it's your MILF-mama.* More bile burned my throat at the humiliating memory of her words over the phone, of the tears I'd held in until she'd hung up.

"A little. We talked over drinks. I got silly and giggly, and then I invited him back to my room."

"Why?"

I rolled my eyes. "To play charades. Why do you think?"

"April..."

I grimaced. "I hadn't had sex in a long time. A woman has her needs. Please don't get judgy or I won't tell you what happened."

"Well, I think from your starring role, I can see plain as day what happened. What I don't get is why you recorded it."

Sighing, I gathered my dirty clothes off the floor and tossed them into my hamper. "Because somewhere in my drunken stupor, I was all horny and hot for this guy's bod.

And...I was *excited*, you know? I'd never ever done something like that before. So I thought, what could possibly make this encounter even *more* exciting? And it just popped into my head. I set my phone down and hit record. Then I attacked him where he was sitting in the chair."

"You recorded the entire thing? Because the video is only five minutes long, and even I know that...well, that it must have gone on longer than that."

"He said something about wanting to lay me down on the bed. I got up and turned the phone off."

"And how the heck do you have no idea who it was? He never took his helmet off?"

"He was going to take it off, but I told him not to. I didn't want to know who he was. It was more exciting that way. Then...when we moved to the bed, he laid me facedown, turned off the lights and took off the helmet. I didn't look or try to figure it out. That's the whole point of anonymous sex."

Her eyes bugged. "Uh. If you say so. Was it...more exciting that way?"

Heat rose to my face at the memory of the weight of him, his hands and mouth at the small of my back, the feel of him pushing inside me. "It was."

"Do you think he knew who you were?"

God, I hoped not. He'd be one more person to deal with over this viral video catastrophe. But there was no way...

"I was wearing the purple wig, and my face was all made up with that glitter paint you gave me. I'm pretty sure he'd never be able to pick me out of a crowd."

"And he knows you recorded it, right?"

My stomach dropped and I stared at her, reluctant to admit it. "Uhhh..."

Her face fell. "Criminy, April. You made a sex tape and didn't tell the guy you were doing it?"

I put my head in my hands, mostly to avoid her scrutiny. "I told you my judgment was crap. But I swear to God it wasn't meant for anyone to watch. It was just a flight of fancy, like buying a cheesy souvenir after an awesome vacation. I planned on deleting it later."

Her lips pursed like a disapproving grandma. "Too late for that."

I straightened and looked at her. "Any thoughts about damage control?"

"The mean girls saw you hook up with Falco, didn't they?"

I blinked, blearily remembering walking by the booth where they were sitting. I was holding hands with Falco and waving to them. "Yeah...if they see the video, they'll know it's me. But I think they'll cover for me."

They were my friends...at least on the surface, they were. I could count on them to keep my identity secret, couldn't I?

Sid left her chair and sank down next to me on the bed, slinging an arm around my shoulders. I looked at her, my throat feeling prickly. What the hell was I going to do?

"You've got to stop letting her get to you like this." I knew she meant my mom and *not* Cari. "And Gunnar—"

"Gunnar can suck it. I hope I never see him again."

"But you probably have to now. Thanksgiving, Christmas, Chanukah—or do you do that one with your dad?" Given the choice, I'd do them all on my own. I stared into my lap, feeling utterly alone. Her arm tightened around my shoulders. "Gunnar is *nothing* to you— just brief, ancient history. You only dated him for like, what? A few months?"

"A year." I'd met him at the end of my sophomore year and we'd dated through my junior year. My sorority and his fraternity were closely linked and people thought we were a cute couple...

She made a cutting gesture with her hand. "Okay, whatever. You weren't even all that into him."

"Did I—did I ever tell you what he told me when I broke up with him? That I was a boring little bookworm and too vanilla in bed. Asshole."

She took a deep breath and let it go, likely grasping for something to comfort me with. "He was probably covering for his own insecurities. Your mother is the worst culprit in this. She should have realized—"

"She has no sense of anyone else's feelings but her own. Even if I had said something, which I didn't, she would fool herself into thinking that I'm totally and completely cool with her newest marriage." And I knew that if I had said something, she would have called *me* selfish for intruding on her happiness. "I'm such a coward," I groaned.

"You're a *peacekeeper*, April. A child of divorced parents. It's common, given your family situation. You never wanted to rock the boat because you felt like their love was conditional."

"My mom's 'love' is completely conditional. Dad's just...never there. Thank God I have a friend like you." My mouth tightened and I leaned my head on her shoulder. "You're the bestest. I love you."

"Love you too, chicken butt."

"Stop calling me that."

"Never."

I brushed some lint off my skirt. I had to get up, get some makeup on and get going, but I was feeling really unmotivated at the moment.

Sid screwed up her mouth as if she'd eaten a salted lemon. "So...this makes Gunnar your step-dad now."

That bad taste in my mouth was back. Our girlfriend moment was over. "Shut the fuck up, Sid."

She shuddered.

I leaned forward and put my face in my hands, my elbows resting on my knees. "God... I need to get my head in the game. I have to start this new position at Draco today."

"That starts today? Oh, suck an elf! I just remembered that. Could the timing be any worse?"

"Not really," I mumbled into my hands. Working with the CFO was my dream position. A good evaluation from him could help me into any school I wanted to attend. Harvard...Stanford...or my first choice, UCLA. "I don't think I'm going to be able to think about anything else but this..."

"Why don't you concentrate on how jealous I am that you get to work at the place that makes my very favorite video game." Sid was a gamer to the core, and had not stopped talking for *days* when I'd arranged for her to have a tour of the campus a few months ago. She played Dragon Epoch constantly and filled me in on the goings-on of the game even though I'd never really done much beyond dip my toe into the gaming environment. My interests lay elsewhere.

"You can keep your joysticks, Sid. I've got my books."

Sid laughed. "Silly. Dragon Epoch isn't played with a joystick!"

"Yeah, yeah. Whatever. I gotta get going. Please, if you can find a way to deal with this...?"

"I have no idea how it could have gotten uploaded unless you synced it to the cloud and someone hacked you."

I sighed, wondering if I'd pressed the share button the one time I'd played it back for myself. Now that it was out, it was spreading like wildfire. My gut clenched with nausea again. Ugh. Uggity ugh.

I guess it no longer mattered how it had happened because the *why* it had happened was due completely to my own stupidity. Aside from the abstention of alcohol, I'd add getting a "dumb" phone to the list of things I had to do in order to atone. No more videos. No cameras. And no social media. Not anymore.

I stood and went into the bathroom to finish my makeup.

***

I pulled into the parking lot at Draco Multimedia Entertainment a good forty-five minutes early. The best way to show enthusiasm for the new job was to show up early, smiling and eager to get to work. And the harder I worked today, the more I'd be able to force the negative, panicked thoughts from this morning's events to the back of my head. They nagged at me, swarming around my brain like gnats at dusk, and no matter how much I tried to swat them away, they came right back to aggravate me even more.

I'd been working at Draco for the past six months as an unpaid intern but had recently been given the opportunity for advancement—probably due to my hard work in marketing. And this position was primo. Rumor had it that the company would be listing for its initial public offering (IPO) soon, so I'd get to see a big part of the process from inside the office of the financial officer. Adding that accomplishment to my résumé would have the business schools bowing down and begging for me to attend.

Draco was situated in a unique castle-shaped glass structure lined with mirrored windows from the ground up. I liked the design, as it reflected the company's mission—to provide a complete fantasy environment as the backdrop for its game. Inside was bright and airy with tall ceilings and an open-space floor plan divided by department. After entering the foyer, decorated with elaborate displays from the games Draco produced, I walked through my old division. Only a handful of the marketing people were there at this hour. There was no one I really knew, and most especially not the other interns, who usually slid in the front door a few minutes before the start of business.

I shook my head at the thought. They'd all been very good-natured but visibly envious of my new appointment. It felt good to be the subject of their admiration.

Usually it was me trying so hard to fit in that I went along with whatever the herd did. Especially Cari, the self-appointed leader of the group. Fortunately, she was nice to me, likely because my daddy was richer than hers.

Not that I really cared about that. I would have preferred a less-rich dad who'd spent more time with me and didn't foist me off on my narcissistic mother. But people like Cari cared about that sort of thing, so I'd had an in.

The trick was all in the appearance of belonging, because I was never "in" anywhere. Social chameleon, always changing to blend into the scenery. That was me. But chameleons had a major flaw—they didn't stand out. And in business, particularly in this new position, I would have to do exactly that. Make a name for myself so I could receive that coveted recommendation.

I pushed through the double doors that led to the wide atrium in front of the offices for the company executives. It, too, was quiet except for another intern assistant—the nerdy guy who worked for the CEO of the company, ultra-beautiful boy wonder, Adam Drake. Adam, like my new boss and most of the other officers of the company, was young, driven and mega successful from the start. At my age, he was already heading his own start-up company, which, within four years would become a multimillion-dollar business well on its way to going public. Hearing about his accomplishments often made me feel like a slacker.

"Hey, Charlie," I said, stopping at his desk.

"Uh, actually it's Charles," he corrected, straightening his black hipster glasses on his nose.

"Oh, I'm sorry. I think I've been calling you the wrong name for months."

He shrugged, sliding a slow gaze over my chest. I folded my arms to cover my breasts. The thought of being exposed in the video for all to see was still shaking me to my core. Every time it threatened to jump to the forefront, I had to put my head down and concentrate on the *now*. It was almost impossible to do.

Charles finally remembered where my eyes were. "It happens. But I figured since you're going to be working up here for a while, best to set you straight now."

I glanced in the direction of the CFO's office. "Is, um, Mr. Fawkes in yet?"

Jordan Fawkes, my new boss, was even younger than Adam and had partnered with him to create the company. It was strange that I'd be more intimidated by them than if they were older, perhaps because their wild success served as a reminder of my own inadequacies.

Charles smiled condescendingly. "First off, none of the officers go by anything but their first names. It's all casual here. And business casual dress," he said with a pointed look at my smart skirt and sweater set.

I shifted where I stood and pushed my long hair back from my shoulder. "It's the first day. There's no such thing as making *too* good an impression," I said, murmuring one of my ever-present aphorisms. I pinned quotes and truisms from my books all over bulletin boards and on sticky notes stuck to my computer monitor and bathroom mirror. They helped. They were like guideposts. My books were the mentors I'd never had in my parents.

"Anyway, Jordan usually gets here early, but since it's the Monday after Comic-Con, you'd be doing yourself a favor to avoid him before noon. He'll probably send you out to get his lunch for him. I have his standing Subway order."

I tried not to scowl. Of course I said nothing, because in situations like this, I knew it was better to never show irritation or any other negative emotion. *Grin and bear it.*

But lunch errands? I wasn't aiming to be a diner waitress. I needed good, solid business experience to write about in my admission essay. And I'd heard that Jordan Fawkes was a shrewd and savvy businessman. Word on the street was that the company owed as much of its success to him as it did to the CEO's ingenuity at programming and virtual innovation.

Nevertheless, I was eager to please, and if I had to start with Charles and his condescending attitude to get by, then so be it. My new boss couldn't possibly be worse than this little jerk.

"So should I do something? Maybe go in and straighten up his office or—"

"Dude—do *not* touch his desk or his stuff unless he asks. Just…wait over there." He pointed to a waiting area with a comfortable-looking arrangement of deeply padded chairs meant for visitors and clientele while they waited to meet with the bigwigs. "You report to Susan, his paid assistant, and she isn't in yet."

I looked back at him. "Can't I do something for you?"

He raised his brows. "Yeah, as a matter of fact…" I leaned in, anxious to get to work and impress my new co-worker. "I take my latte with skim milk and two sugars. And don't go to our café. They suck. There's a Starbucks down the street. Extra hot, mmkay?"

I straightened, resisted shooting him a glare, and with a bit of resignation in my slumped shoulders, turned around to carry out his orders. There was a pecking order here, and clearly Charlie-boy considered himself above me.

I returned twenty minutes later with his coffee and one for myself. This time, when I walked through the front, the marketing department was populated, and some of the interns I'd worked with waved and smiled. Cari raced toward me, her massive mane of blond hair trailing after her. She was wearing a provocative outfit—plaid, pleated mini-skirt that hit well above mid-thigh paired with a tight white blouse and knee socks. She'd referred to this outfit as her take on the "naughty school girl." Professional it was *not*.

She took in my sweater set with a nod of approval. "You're looking very grown-up today for your new position! How are you doing? Want me to help you carry that?"

I smiled, a little uneasy as I remembered Sid's comments about her this morning. "I'm good, thanks."

She threw a curious glance at me out of the corner of her eyes as she pushed the double doors open. "So, um, nervous? Everything going okay?"

I hesitated a moment and returned her look, slowing my pace. "Why do you keep asking?"

She grimaced. "I, um…well, I was going through my timeline this morning on Facebook…"

My hand carrying Charlie-boy's *ultra-hot scalding with the fire of a thousand suns* coffee shook and a bit of it spilled out the top, burning the back of my hand. "*Shit,*" I said, but didn't know whether it was because of the pain or the fact that Cari knew it was me in the video.

"Um. I don't want to talk about it," I muttered.

"I, uh…why is it on the Internet?"

"I don't know. I must have pushed a button to upload it to the cloud or something. I have no fucking idea. And did I mention I don't want to talk about it?"

I turned and started back to the atrium and Charlie's desk, anxious to get this blistering cup of simmering lava out of my hand.

"So, what are you going to do?"

"I'm not sure there's much I *can* do," I said bitterly. But maybe there was... If I got Cari on my side, her loyalty would prevent anyone else from talking about it. So as much as her behavior of late had been distasteful, I was going to have to be her bestest buddy ever. Cari was fast becoming one big gnat I couldn't bat away. I'd have to sweet talk and kiss up to this gnat, in fact.

"Can I, uh, ask you to cover for me with the others?"

Cari smiled. "Ingrid was the other one with us at the bar, and she was so drunk she doesn't even remember that was you. I won't say a word. I know you must be stressed out. I'll do whatever I can to help. Let's get together for lunch, okay?"

The feeling of relief came as a rush—I was almost giddy with it. Thank God I had Cari on my side for this. "That sounds great," I said.

I didn't fully trust her—had never fully trusted her. But she had no reason to rat me out, and she was smart enough to know it could backfire on her to do it. I'd find a way to keep the loyalty I'd won in her. Time for the chameleon to change her colors again.

Cari quickly peeled away from me before I entered the atrium, where I all but slapped that cup of white-hot neutronium on Mr. Hipster's desk. I shook my hand out the minute it was free.

"Mmm, piping hot. The same way your new boss likes it," Charlie chimed. "He's *here*, by the way, and the first thing he grunted at me was a demand to get him a venti triple espresso, no cream, no sugar."

I froze. He had to be fucking kidding me. But there was no cheeky smile incoming. Charlie jerked a thumb toward Jordan's office. "Better hop to it, girlfriend. He's hungover from partying all week at Comic-Con and not in the best of moods."

Shit. Shit. Shit. This was already proving to be a fantabulous day. Goddamn it. I spun and walked back out the door, taking a long pull from my now tepid cup of coffee. Fantabulous and long-ass day.

Seriously, how could it get worse?

2
JORDAN

I T WAS WELL INTO LUNCH HOUR, BUT I'D LOST MY APPETITE.
Instead of eating, I paced beside the back wall of my office, staring
out the floor-to-ceiling windows at the greenery and that weird,
giant, marble, sphere-shaped fountain in our inner atrium garden.
While I'd been called into an impromptu meeting, my new intern had
left lunch on my worktable, complete with a little message scrawled
on a sticky note, punctuated with a smiley face. I'd promptly crumpled
it into a ball and hurled it across the room. No one was fucking smiling
in this room, nor in the offices next to me.

I strode to my desk and opened up my laptop to watch the
incriminating video again. I'd been so shocked when Weston, our PR
guy, had shown it to us fifteen minutes ago, I'd hardly had a chance to
take note of any telling details. Nor had I been aware of exactly how
viral it had gone.

And sure enough, all it took was a Google search of "Comic-Con
Cosplay Sex" that showed as the first hundred hits. On every social
media platform imaginable. *Holy fuck.*

I hit play and sat back, taking in the background and foreground of the non-descript hotel room—standard furniture and few personal belongings. Forcing myself to ignore the passionate couple in the middle of the screen, I scoured for any detail that my boss might be able to take note of and use to figure out our identities. He'd already spotted my employee badge in the corner of the frame with the name blocked out. Thank God for that, because my ass was on the line here. Adam would crap bricks if he knew it was me. He was already pitching fits about it to begin with, and now I was in the unenviable position of lying to my best friend to save my own miserable skin. Helpless rage burned again.

But hearing the sounds the girl was making on the video was also starting to turn me on, and hot anger soon mingled with lust. I couldn't sit here and listen to those delicious noises and *not* get turned on. It immediately brought to mind the feel of her skin under my hands, the way her body had felt against mine. I clenched my jaw, trying to get a hold of myself.

I studied her tight little ass again and that weird tattoo. April Weiss, one the hottest in our latest crop of silly college interns, now was the bane of my existence.

What the *hell* had I been thinking?

I hadn't been thinking. That was the problem. I'd been drunk and enjoying my anonymity at the bar. No one had known who I was in the armor and helmet, and while I'd been getting a perfect buzz on, that delectable intern in her skintight leggings and halter top had plopped down next to me, assuming I didn't know who *she* was.

And I'd tapped that.

Because hell, why not?

Except she was an intern at my company, and the interns, my boss had warned, were strictly off-limits. But as we sat drinking at the bar, she'd told me that she'd fantasized about having anonymous sex. And I was a guy who had fulfilled a few fantasies in his lifetime.

I was giving and selfless like that.

Well, okay, not *entirely*. I had to admit that I'd wanted a taste of her since the minute I'd laid eyes on her last fall. But because she was out of bounds, I'd restrained myself. In my drunken state, I'd rationalized that if she never knew, I could get her out of my system and we'd both move on, no harm done.

Only now it was safe to say that harm had been done. I didn't know what to make of the video's existence. I could only assume *she* had made it. But why? And why not tell me she was doing it?

I'd been into what was going on and pleasantly buzzed, but I would have liked to think I'd notice something like *that*. Unless this was some kind of sting operation. Unless she'd known exactly who I was and wanted something to hold over my head...

I shook my head, trying to figure out what to do, my mind racing. Should I fire her immediately? Should I get a private investigator on it? What about legal takedown notices? Since it was a video of me, I could do that, but I risked exposing myself. Not gonna happen.

My fist closed in frustration, pounding on the desk. All hell was about to break loose because of this damn video. I needed a plan and I needed it fast.

As if hearing my thoughts, Adam, my best friend and boss, busted through the door without knocking, clicking it closed behind him.

I slammed my laptop shut with a grimace, suppressing a streak of guilt.

Now Adam only looked a hundred degrees of pissed off, instead of a thousand. His face had returned to a normal shade rather than the deep red he was sporting earlier. He moved toward my desk and sat on it, leaning back with his ankles crossed and arms folded over his chest.

I avoided his eyes, massaging the stiff muscles at the back of my neck. "Five minutes isn't enough time for me to figure out how I'm going to handle this, you know," I said.

He clenched his teeth and looked away, appearing every bit as frustrated as I felt. "Just tell me how bad this is—for real. You've been working with the investment bankers through all of this IPO stuff. What is this going to do to our bid?"

I bit down the first—and most honest—response that flashed inside my brain. *It's going to fucking tank it.* Investment bankers and their army of underwriters were a skittish, superstitious bunch. The minute they got wind of a sex tape involving Draco employees going viral, they were going to pull out faster than an eighteen-year-old during sex with his underage girlfriend.

I cleared my throat and formed a more careful answer. "I don't know. We need to come up with a plan for damage control. They don't like scandal, especially sex scandals." I took a breath and then released it. The manure I was going to have to spread in order to smooth things over with Adam was about to get thick.

"We need to find out who the guilty party is immediately. My next phone call will be to that Internet security firm I use—"

I held up a hand and tried to stifle the panic. "Whoa, pardner. I told you I'd handle it, and I will. Just leave it to me, okay? I'll take care of it all. But...we also have to be careful about throwing accusations around before we have any solid proof. We don't want to be guilty of sexual harassment. Might be time to contact our lawyer, too."

Adam scowled. "Jesus Christ. Between last year's murder-suicide case and this one, I'm going to have to start bankrolling him."

I blinked, surprised that, in my panic, I hadn't looked at this in context with last year's events. A devoted player of our game had, in a fit of rage, driven over to his girlfriend's house because she had meddled with his in-game progress. He'd pulled out a gun and shot her and then himself. The parents had blamed his actions on his addiction to Dragon Epoch, using the media to tell anyone who would listen. And, of course, they'd filed a lawsuit. These events, along with others, much deeper and more personal, had shaken Adam to the core.

And now this, which was *my* doing. What kind of shitty friend was I to add to his load?

"That might be a good idea, actually. You might just want to see what you can do about employing Joseph full-time," I said.

He shook his head. "At least it's not too late for us to pull out of this deal. We could wait 'til all the shit blows over...hold out for a better time. We've filed the S1 form with the government, but companies back out of an IPO all the time."

Over my dead body would we be pulling out of this.

Every muscle in my body tensed. I rocketed out of my chair and stalked to the window to stare out at that goddamn fountain. Long, deep breaths. In with the good—out with the bad.

I'd been working on this project for years, keeping meticulous books and documenting everything the company had done since its inception. This had been my goal since the beginning, and it had taken me at least a year of begging and cajoling Adam to go along with it.

Lord knew the last thing a control freak CEO wanted to do was to slice off a portion of his corporate pie and hand that power over to a board of directors. For the longest time, he'd wanted no part of it, even though the day we'd open on the stock exchange he'd become a billionaire.

But then he'd fixated on a new pet project—one he needed the liquidity in order to develop. And I'd seen that as my chance to swoop in and win him over. Finally. *Finally*, he'd agreed. Trust Adam to be motivated by his own ingenious imagination rather than fattening his bank account. It was an admirable trait, but one that I didn't share with him. Which explained why we worked together well.

I had to play this carefully. The bankers weren't the only ones who were skittish.

I glanced at Adam. "Can I ask you to give me some time to come up with a plan? I've been meeting with these bankers on a regular basis for *months*. I've been schmoozing, wining, dining, and charming the hell out of the lot of them. I don't think that things are that dire."

Adam raised his brows at me and his dark stare never wavered. Yeah, he'd known me a long time. We'd been good friends since our freshman year at college. He knew when I was full of shit, and today I was full to overflowing with it.

"You've got two weeks and I'm yanking everything if it doesn't look good."

I almost howled in frustration. "How about a month? There're a lot of bankers...some of them are *not* located nearby."

He continued to stare at me, and I knew what his next words were going to be before he even said them. "Two weeks, Jordan. And then I'm pulling the plug."

Fucking hell.

Adam straightened, unfolding his arms. I clenched my jaw so tight my head ached. Without another word, the boss turned and left the room, firmly shutting the door. I picked up the legal pad on my desk and flung it in the direction where he'd left. It slapped against the closed door then slid to the ground.

Goddamn this. It got worse and worse with each minute. It had started as your ordinary shit hangover Monday and devolved into this crap situation. I was now an anonymous Internet star featured in a sex tape that had gone viral and was about to tank my company's biggest project since it had been founded.

All because I'd gotten shitfaced and then, in my stupor, decided it would be a *great* idea to bang the hot intern in the elf costume.

I was never drinking again, damn it all. Glaring at the door that Adam had shut, I jumped at a sudden knock. That meant it wasn't Adam returning to dump any more ultimatums on me.

"Come in," I growled.

Tentatively, the door cracked open, and then, inch by inch, it slowly widened. A dark head poked in. And there she was, the author of this miserable situation—Miss April Weiss.

Her silky dark hair hung over her shoulders as she gave me a timid look. This morning I'd been staring at her ass, remembering how hot it had been to do her that night, drunk or not. Remembering those deep-throated husky moans in my ear and the feel of her—shit. I didn't know whether I should be turned on or pissed off. Right now, it felt like both.

Because she had *recorded* it and uploaded that shit to the Internet.

Those dark blue eyes met mine, a question in them. "Hey, Jordan. Just checking to see that I got your lunch order right. Charles said you do Subway on Mondays."

Her gaze flicked to the untouched meal and the door widened. Now she was *in* the office, wearing that form-fitting skirt and that thin, tight sweater that clung to her lush breasts. My fist tightened at my side. Two weeks ago, I'd fucked a cover model—eight times in a three-day span. This girl was nothing special, hot hookup or not. I looked away and swallowed.

"I wasn't hungry," I growled. I was so goddamn pissed off I couldn't even look at her.

She almost tripped on the legal pad that I'd thrown at the door. Her dark eyebrows pinched in a frown as she scooped up the pad and moved to the table, her shoulders slumped slightly—as if somehow my rejection of the goddamn sandwich reflected upon her performance of her new job. My eyes went back to her face again, drawn like magnets. She was beautiful—fresh, glowing skin, shiny hair and those blue eyes. Perfect features. Christ, the lady in HR in charge of assigning interns must have been smoking crack when she put this one in my office. Like throwing chum in a shark tank.

I'd known she would be my assistant and that it was risky to do anything, but the moment she'd said "anonymous," it had been too tempting to turn down. Anonymous, yeah, but broadcast to billions. I studied her serene features, attempting to find evidence of a cold-hearted conspirator underneath.

Slowly, April started tucking the food back into the bag. "I'll clear this out and put it in the fridge in the break room for later."

I blew out a breath, stood and stormed out of the room without another glance at her. I headed straight for Adam's office. Maggie, his assistant, tried to wave me off, but I barreled right past her and entered.

Weston, the publicity guy, was there, showing him something on his tablet. Adam was poring over it. Weston looked up, clearly offended that I'd interrupted his private time with the boss. He was not my biggest fan and the feeling was mutual. Tough shit. I needed some private time of my own. Adam must have seen that in my face immediately, because he straightened and handed the tablet back to the now dejected-looking Weston.

"We can go over the rest later. Thanks, man," Adam dismissed him.

Weston glared at me until he passed by my shoulder and I shrugged. When the door shut, I began by clearing my throat. "Two weeks isn't long enough—"

"Well—" he began to cut me off before I held up my hand to stop him.

"*But*...if you insist, then please, for the love of God, send me some *real* help and yank the intern? My assistant is pregnant and sick all the time, and I can't babysit an intern. We *are* a multi-million, possibly *billion*-dollar corporation. We can afford to hire me a professional to get through this—"

"I'll get you whoever you need, but the intern needs to stay there for now."

That brought me up short.

Shit. I *had* to get rid of this girl, but I couldn't raise any suspicion that it was anything more than her being a waste of my time. "I'm going to be too busy to teach her anything."

Adam looked away as if already bored with the conversation, which irked me, and had I not been semi-panicked, I would have said something.

"I owe her dad a lot, okay? He hired me at Sony Online. She wants to get into business school and having experience working in your office will be a golden opportunity for her. I have good reasons. Trust me on this, okay?"

I fought the urge to roll my eyes at him. *Typical.* Adam had his own mysterious reasons for doing what he did and only occasionally shared those reasons with lesser beings—even his goddamn friend and business partner.

I gritted my teeth. "I'm not here to entertain spoiled little rich girls. Besides...you never even knew her name. You just called her Snow White. Now suddenly she's your old boss's daughter?"

Adam shrugged. "She looks like Snow White... Look, David Weiss, her dad, emailed me last year, asked if his daughter could intern here. I said sure and referred her to human resources. I had no idea until last winter, when I saw him at the Congressional hearing in D.C., that Snow White was his daughter. Which is kind of funny because Weiss means 'white' in German."

"Yeah—hilarious—now about getting rid of her—"

He tensed. "I'm not going to do that. I know this situation has us all stressed out. I'll hire whoever you need, okay? Just let her...I don't know...shadow you, make you coffee, work under you for a while."

Oh, that was rich. *Work under me...right.* There were several things I could think of that I would like her to do *under me*, but work wasn't one of them. I studied him for a moment, taking in the way he gripped the edge of his desk. It was sometimes hard to read Adam, but I knew him well enough to know he was tense. It would be better not to push it.

"Fine, but I don't have to be nice to her."

Adam shrugged. "You're a rat bastard. Everyone knows that."

I flipped him the bird, and for the first time since seeing the goddamn video, he actually cracked a smile. Meanwhile, my mind was racing, trying to figure out how to worm my way out of this mess.

But another part of my brain wondered if this might not be a good thing. If April worked in my office, I could keep an eye on her, figure out her purpose in taking the video. If I had sway over her with a business school recommendation, then I had some leverage to keep her from using it for blackmail. At least I hoped. And that hope was the cold, sick ball of lead in the pit of my stomach.

I took a deep breath and let it out. "Fine, whatever. I promise you I'm going to handle this, but you have to have a little faith in me."

His jaw tightened and he nodded. "I do. I will. Just…talk to the bankers. Get the lay of the land and find out if they are going to throw us under a bus or not."

My arms stiffened with resolve. "No one's throwing us under a bus. Over my dead body, anyway."

He raised a black eyebrow. "*That* doesn't sound promising."

"Yeah, that was a shitty choice of metaphors."

Adam checked his watch. "I've got a meeting with programming right now. But I need you to meet me over at R&D later—the new prototype equipment arrived. We're testing it out and doing a little demo."

"Ain't nobody got time for that," I quipped. "I've got fires to put out here."

"Well, since you are going to be talking to the bankers, and this is the stuff we are trying to raise the capital to buy and develop, it would be good for you to see it in action."

That was something that might actually be useful to my cause. "That's a really good idea. I should get some pictures, maybe a little video. We could add it to the beauty contest."

Adam frowned at me. "I don't speak 'business.'"

Ours was a partnership of Adam's brilliant mind and imagination and my know-how with business. But I was as fascinated with the prospects of our new advancement as he was. It might not have been my sole motivator like it was his, but things like this still excited me—*when* I didn't have the weight of the world on my shoulders.

"It's just what we call the phase where we show off the company to the underwriters, try to convince them why our corporation is a great investment. Now would be a really good time to wow them and get their minds off of, ah…other things."

"Okay, see you over there at four. Bring Snow White."

Oh, for Chrissake. Was I really stuck with this girl?

He followed me out of the office, and I turned and went into mine while he headed to his meeting.

The minute I rounded the doorway, I stopped in my tracks. Snow White—uh, my new intern—was bent over, her round, delectable ass in the air, dragging a heavy box stuffed with files across the floor.

After taking a split second to admire the view—complete with yellow thong peeking up over the edge of her skirt—I noticed that her short-cropped sweater had ridden up, revealing the tramp stamp tattoo. I'd traced that tattoo with my tongue. It had tasted delicious, that very distinctive tramp stamp. A very memorable—*incriminating*—one.

I slammed the door shut so loud the entire wall shook. The girl almost jumped out of her skin, stumbling on her high-heeled boots and staring at me, her beautiful blue eyes widened in shock.

"Uh. Oh, I'm sorry, Jordan. I just noticed this file box on the floor over there and it looked really messy, so I figured I'd—Oh, but now I remember that Charles said I probably shouldn't touch your stuff."

My eyes narrowed. What kind of game was she playing? Was she flashing that tattoo at me on purpose—trying to taunt me with it and the dirt she had on me? A small ball of rage flared up in my chest.

I spoke between my clenched teeth. "Do you have any idea what's going on in these offices today, Miss Weiss? Why the officers seem in an uproar? Have you picked up on any of that?"

She frowned, her hands clasping each other nervously. "Um...people have said there's something weird going on, but no one knows what it is."

"Well, thank God for that. But you know what? I'm going to tell *you* what it is, and you aren't going to breathe a word to any of your little intern friends, got it? Because there's a viral video out there on the Internet right now featuring people dressed up like characters from Dragon Epoch, and at least one of the *participants* is an employee of this company."

She froze, going white as a sheet. Truly living up to her nickname now. To say it didn't feel good to see her terrified half out of her mind would be a lie. As pissed off as I was at this moment, I wanted to scare the shit out of her. She wasn't messing around at the sorority anymore. I could play hardball, and I wouldn't be swayed by a pretty face.

"You wouldn't...know anything about that, would you, Miss Weiss?"

She glanced at me and then away, starting to shake and appearing as if she might faint.

I walked toward her slowly, but she didn't look at me. Her eyes shifted to the floor and her head bent forward, her long, dark hair falling forward to curtain her face. I circled her like a predator. She visibly swallowed, utterly petrified.

Good.

"I—" she began shakily.

"Shh. Say nothing. You are going to do everything I say and you are going to do it *yesterday.* The first thing to remember is that the dress code in this office is business casual, and it would be in your best interest to make sure that tattoo of yours stays covered up. Got it?"

She jumped, her head snapping up. "Y-yes. Yes."

"And the other participant in the video...?" I breathed. I was standing behind her now, speaking over her shoulder. It was as intimidating as hell, I was sure. But I did it mostly so she wouldn't see my face. I had to be *certain* that she didn't know it was me.

April was silent for a moment—a *tense* moment—while I waited behind her, feeling the warmth of her body close to mine, smelling the scent rising off her hair, her pale neck. She smelled sweet, like honey. It drifted to my nose and I remembered—again—burying my face in that soft hair, that neck. Even looking down at it now, I was fascinated by the white skin, the delicate lacing of blue veins underneath, the tiny dark freckle just below the hairline. My entire body was reacting to her. *Christ almighty.*

"I—I have no idea. He was...some guy at Comic-Con." Her voice was shaky, nervous.

The relief that washed over me in that moment almost floored me. Thank God. At least there was that. I still had to mop up this mess, but at least it wasn't *my* ass on the line.

"I should fire you right this second," I growled.

She faced me. "*Please.* I don't know how it happened. I just—"

"Shh—" I held up a finger to her mouth. Her lips were dark pink, full, soft. How amazing they had felt wrapped around my—

Goddamn it. I took a step back. "I want that box of files organized, indexed and out of this office with a full description of *every* slip of paper in them before you leave today. Got it?"

She blinked. "Uh, yeah. Yes. Sure."

"Then do it. *Now.*"

With a jump, she turned back to the box, about to bend over again. "Get a damn cart to wheel it out of here. Christ."

She walked out of the office on shaky legs without even looking at me.

I rubbed the back of my neck, determined to be gone when she got back. She was too quick for me though and re-entered a minute later, pushing the cart dejectedly across the office to the box.

I growled again. "You need to meet me in Research and Development at four. Other than that, you are working on this until it's done and you don't go home until then."

Without missing a beat, she nodded. "Yes. Yes, sir. I'm—"

"Save it. Just get it done." I turned and stormed out, heading for the cafeteria to grab some shitty food to eat while she cleared out of my office.

3
APRIL

O H SHIT. *SHIT*. GODDAMN. FUCK. I WAS SCREWED, SO VERY screwed. More screwed than I was that hot night at Comic-Con. Shit. Goddamn. *Fuck*. The sex had been the best I'd ever had, but it had *not* been worth this.

The best sex in the world was not worth it if it ended up ruining your life. Now Jordan knew I was the one in that video and he could reveal that at any time. And who knew? He might do it if I screwed up badly or if he decided it was in his best interest to do so.

How had this workday degraded so quickly? This morning I'd been so eager to put the viral video craziness behind me and start my new job. I was excited and raring to go, eager to please my new boss—my very hot, young, new boss.

I'd had to remind myself several times not to stare at him when I'd first brought him his coffee. It would not do to develop a crush. In fact, it could be downright detrimental.

He'd looked up at me, kind of bleary-eyed from an obvious hangover. But he was so gorgeous even with glassy eyes and a slightly greenish complexion. With his light brown hair and hazel eyes that sometimes looked green, sometimes brown, sometimes gray. I wondered if they changed color based on his mood or the clothes he wore. I spent at least an hour contemplating his eyes after I'd left him alone.

That was before all Hell had broken loose. Then he'd spoken to me like he wanted me gone *yesterday*.

Hours later, when I was elbow-deep in the files, I determined that I should resign on the spot while I still had my dignity. There was nothing they could do to me after the fact...right? I'd be safe if I resigned.

But if I quit this internship early, my counselor at the university wouldn't be able to find me a new placement because I'd already graduated. I'd been placed here before finishing my studies and stayed on for the opportunity to get the coveted recommendation.

So I couldn't quit and kiss that goodbye.

My hands trembled and I'd all but given up before I murmured my old adage to myself. WWSD? What would Scarlett O'Hara do? She'd never give up. She'd fight with her last breath. She had. Over and over.

But I wasn't like Scarlett. I didn't have courage. I gave in repeatedly. Because it was easier. I blinked back tears of frustration and kept at my work until Charles called over to me from his desk. "Hey, April. You're wanted in R&D."

Oh, shit. I glanced up at the clock. It was quarter after four. Damn it! Jordan had said to be there at four o'clock and now I was late. He'd surely fire me now. He already hated my ass. Why, really, was I even still here?

I contemplated that as I walked the route from my desk to Research and Development, which was on the other side of the complex. Somewhere along the line, Cari and Ingrid, another intern, fell into step alongside me.

"Hey, superstar," Cari said with an obnoxious wink. "How's your first day in the big leagues going?"

I shrugged. "Okay." I stepped up my pace, glancing at my watch. Damn. I was *so* late.

"Where're you off to in such a hurry?" Cari asked, speeding to keep up.

"I'm supposed to be at R&D right now. Jordan is meeting with other officers about some new equipment that just arrived—"

"Other officers?" Cari perked up. "You mean like Adam? Is Adam going to be there?"

I suppressed a sigh. While I agreed with her that the company's CEO was ridiculously good-looking, I was starting to get weirded out by her constant fixation on him. It used to be all in fun. We'd make comments about what clothes he was wearing or how great his ass looked in jeans on casual Friday, but it started feeling wrong when I found out he had a girlfriend—and that that girlfriend was someone we had all worked with for months, Mia Strong.

Cari had refused to accept this because she'd always felt entitled to him in some bizarre way. I'd thought it was an innocent crush at first, but after his relationship with Mia had been revealed, she'd become enraged that Mia had swooped in and "stolen him right out from under" her.

I doubt it had actually happened that way, but Cari had become progressively unstable in the last year since I'd met her. I assumed this was due to the loss of her brother mere months before she'd started her internship, but it was hard to say because I didn't know her that well to begin with. Either way, her fixation on Adam was growing into a determined hatred of Mia.

While we'd worked with her, Mia always kept to herself, but I never disliked her. Then she got sick—*really* sick—and I opened my big mouth at a party and said some stupid stuff. Cari had been nitpicking Mia's appearance and I'd agreed with her. Mia had heard what I said and I felt mortified, but she handled it with grace and strength. When that happened, I'd wanted the ground to open up and swallow me on the spot. Not unlike the events of today, to be honest.

In answer to Cari's question, I shrugged. "I don't know. I don't even know if Adam's in today."

Her head jerked toward me in obvious shock. "You mean you work right in front of his office and you haven't seen him? I'd be stalking his ass constantly if I worked up there."

I wasn't surprised by *that* admission.

"Nope. I've had too much to do. I'm there to work, not scope out the men." Besides, personally I found Jordan hotter than Adam. There was something about his smolder, the gleam in those hazel eyes. The man oozed sex appeal. When he stood close to me today, though I'd been terrified, naturally, of the information he'd been conveying, I was also incredibly aware of him on every level. The smell of his subtle cologne. The feel of his hot breath on the back of my neck. His imposing height and solid build towering over me. I'd almost dropped to my knees to beg for mercy for reasons other than my job. I swallowed, wondering what was going on with me. My libido was in overdrive, and I had no one to thank for it but the hot mystery man of Comic-Con.

Alas, I personally hoped that wouldn't be the best sex I'd ever have in my life or I'd have to box up all my sexy lingerie. Maybe I'd have to resort to running through the convention next year with a Falco helmet, trying it on every guy like Prince Charming had done for Cinderella with her glass slipper.

"I'm coming with you," Cari squeaked.

"Me too!" Ingrid echoed, clapping her hands together.

"I'm not sure this is something you guys are allowed to come to."

Cari shot me an unreadable look and then shrugged. "They can throw me out then. Better to ask forgiveness than permission!"

We walked through the double doors into R&D, which was set up like a giant warehouse with various terminals and stations. This area was used for testing new software and hardware. Since there had been talk of prototype equipment, I guessed in this case it was hardware.

A group of people huddled at the other side of the warehouse, and I spotted Jordan's tall form among them. I rushed along while at the same time trying to walk so that my heeled boots wouldn't echo loudly across the floor. When I'd almost reached the group, he turned, speared a look at me and glanced pointedly at his watch, scowling, before turning his attention back to the demonstration in front of us.

Adam Drake was standing in front of a giant screen in what was called command central—a huge video monitor that allowed a number of people to watch what was going on. The video game displayed was, of course, Dragon Epoch.

Near Adam, two play testers were perched atop circular platforms, wired into some strange-looking equipment with harnesses around their waists. Each woman wore goggles and matching tennis shoes with, as Adam pointed out, special sensors on them to track their every movement in the virtual world. I recognized one of the play testers as Adam's fiancée, Mia. The other one was shorter, with a red braid dangling down her back.

Behind them, their characters were displayed on the screen. As the women walked, ran, or gestured on their platforms, their characters mirrored them in real-time. When Mia would swing her arm in a giant arc to the right, her character, Eloisa—so the name said above her head—would do the same thing on the screen before us with an almost undetectable delay.

Adam explained to the small crowd. "These sensors allow the game to interpret signals from the player's body language to give commands to the character in the game, so that instead of using a keyboard or game controller, the player can use this equipment and their own gestures. What the players see on their goggle display is a three-dimensional depiction of the game environment. In this particular scenario, Mia is a spell caster and Katya plays a healer so their spells are different." He turned to Mia. "Cast a fire blaze," he said.

She made a wide-circled gesture with her right arm and then flicked her wrist. On the large screen in front of them, the character did the same thing and a giant ball of fire appeared between her hands. She hurled it, like a beach ball, out in front of her.

"Katya, as a healer, will use that same gesture to get a different effect." Katya was the girl with the braid who kind of reminded me of a red-haired version of Katniss from *The Hunger Games*. She made the exact same gesture as Mia, and her character's hands started to glow with pure green energy (I presumed meant to heal). Mia's character became bathed in that energy. A sentence appeared in the dialogue box at the bottom of the screen: *Eloisa has been completely healed!*

The group murmured, summarily impressed. Even *I* was impressed and I wasn't a gamer. To imagine people being able to communicate their intentions through movement in an online gaming forum was amazing. It held stunning implications for the future of gaming.

Adam held up a set of goggles much like the ones the women were wearing. "While we are watching the action on a two-dimensional surface, eventually, once the prototype equipment is universally implemented, players will see the in-game environment around them as three-dimensional. Players of melee classes—like warriors and mercenaries—will have representations of their weapons to carry and wield as they fight. As with spell casting, certain moves and gestures will equate to special fighting moves for those characters."

We continued to watch as Eloisa and Persephone—Katya's character—proceeded to duel each other. Adam explained that these two had been gaming together for over two years, since they'd met in the beta version of the original game. It had never occurred to me that Mia was a gamer.

I watched her as the demo played out. She seemed healthy and happy, swinging her hands and gesticulating while she kicked the crap—virtually—out of her friend. In the end, she ended up winning the duel.

The group clapped. Mia and Katya pulled off their goggles, appearing as if they'd gotten a bit of a workout. The crowd started to either disperse or talk among themselves, but I was too interested in what was happening in front of that video screen. Mia was grinning up at Adam and he smiled back, watching her with a look I could not describe as anything other than sheer adoration. There was this gleam in his dark eyes and he never took them off of her. She said something, cocking an eyebrow and tilting her head cheekily, and he laughed, curling an arm around her waist and whispering in her ear. Whatever his reply had been, it had made her both laugh and blush furiously.

This was like the last time I'd watched them together—at that same party where I'd made the awful remarks. The way they looked at each other was as if no one else in the world existed but the two of them. Like the entire world could pass them by, and as long as they had each other, they would be fine. They would be happy.

My heart pinched in my chest. Someday, I wanted a man to look at me like that. And when I looked at him back, I'd have those same feelings in my heart. My throat tightened.

Cari leaned in conspiratorially and muttered, "Ugh, she makes me sick."

I straightened, leaning away from her. I knew exactly who she was talking about. On a regular basis, she picked apart Mia's clothes and looks, though it was ridiculous because it was obvious that Mia was a beautiful woman, even while she'd been ill.

Cari's mockery had grown since they got engaged. She'd spent hours raging to me about the size of Mia's engagement ring. *It's at least three carats; it has to be. Shit, why do the brown-haired mousy girls get all the luck? I want a gazillionaire. I want that gazillionaire,"* she'd ranted.

"She looks happy. Healthy," I replied neutrally, reminding her that, up until a few months ago, Mia had been sick with a life-threatening illness. But she'd pulled through and Adam had stood by her through it all. He appeared to be a top-notch guy and it seemed like she deserved him. Apparently, others didn't see it that way.

Ingrid was agreeing with every word out of Cari's mouth, just like the rest of the herd did. Just like I'd often feigned to do. I wondered how many of them *really* agreed with her or how many of them, like me, were too chicken to speak up and disagree, lest she turn her wrath on one of us.

"What's so special about her, though? Why would he pick *her*?" Cari whined.

I fought rolling my eyes and Ingrid leaned in. "She's not so great. She's tall and thin and pretty, I guess, but she's so flat-chested."

My mouth dropped and I felt ill. The poor woman had survived breast cancer. Who knew what surgeries she'd had to endure, and they were taking pot shots at her figure? Women were so cruel to each other sometimes, and these two were gross. And I was gross for having gone along with them as long as I had.

"Excuse me, I'd better check with the boss and find out if he wants me to do anything," I lied.

To be honest, approaching Jordan at this moment was extremely low on my list of things I wanted to do, considering our previous confrontation and his revelation that he knew I was the person in the wretched video. But I needed some excuse to get away from this conversation that was now making me feel icky.

Cari's eyes narrowed and I suspected she'd figured out I was getting bothered. I sent her my trademark hide-everything grin, hoping that would cover for me, and then I crept up to Jordan's side.

He hadn't noticed me, as he was having a discussion with someone next to him. Cari was watching me, so I figured I'd better at least *appear* as if I were talking to Jordan. I cleared my throat. "Excuse me."

Jordan glanced over his shoulder at me and then turned and continued his conversation. I raised my eyebrows and gritted my teeth. I'd stand here until he acknowledged me, then, damn it all.

He spun suddenly and said, "Weiss, take some pictures of Mia and Kat wearing the equipment. I got video of Adam's demo, but I need still shots. Go up there and ask them to put it on again and model it for you."

"Uh. Okay..."

"You've got your smart phone on you, I presume? You seem to be a big fan of your smart phone..." he said with extra meaning layering his voice. My face and neck heated and I avoided his eyes.

Then he raised his hand and snapped his fingers inches in front of my face. "Quick, get up there before they leave! And email me the photos. Then get back to your filing job."

Did he just snap his fingers at me? I was so mortified—and, to be truthful, terrified—that I couldn't speak, even when I opened my mouth. He'd already turned back to his companion, who happened to be a *very* beautiful woman—designer suit, Jimmy Choos, expensive highlights and lowlights in her blond hair. She was *all* decked out. Who was she? I'd never seen her before. Maybe his girlfriend du jour?

I fumed, pulled out my cell phone—the very one that I'd used to tape mystery-man and myself having sex—and walked toward the big screens and the trio standing in front of them, still joking around.

They stopped their conversation, then turned and looked at me when I appeared. "Uh, hi."

"Hey, April," Adam said.

Mia glanced at me and then away, clearly remembering my offensive words about her a few months ago at the party. "Hey," she muttered.

Adam pointed to the red-haired girl. "April, this is Kat. She works in playtesting. April is Jordan's assistant now."

Mia turned back to me, her thin brows raised. "Oh really? You're working for Jordan? God be with you," she said, making a mock sign of the cross as if she were a priest, blessing me.

Kat sputtered a laugh. "Yeah, how'd you screw up to get that position?" I bit my lip. So apparently I hadn't gotten the memo that

Jordan had a rep for being a hardass at the office. Kat and Mia seemed to know a lot that I didn't.

Adam gave them both warning looks. "I worked with April's dad at Sony for a little while. She's been in marketing for so long, I figured she could use a change of scenery."

My mouth opened, shocked. I had no idea. And now I realized why I was working in the CFO's office. Not through my own merit. I'd been deluding myself to assume it had been my own hard work that had gotten me here.

I wondered if my dad had something to do with this—maybe asked Adam to move me up. I knew that he felt guilty nowadays. Maybe he didn't feel his generous monthly allowance was enough to absolve him of it.

Dad and I hadn't connected in any meaningful way in a long time. He was lost in his work, and what little time he had left was spent with his new family. It always seemed like I was an afterthought. So instead of attention, he lavished me with money. And now, I guessed, pulling strings.

I glanced quickly over my shoulder, hoping that Cari hadn't heard Adam's comment. But no, she was carefully watching this interaction and appeared to have heard everything. I was uneasy with her knowing any more of my weak spots. She already knew more than enough to sink me.

"Uh, Jordan wanted some photos of you two wearing the equipment, if that's okay?" I held up my cell phone. "I promise to get only your good sides."

Adam turned to them and quietly explained something that I couldn't hear. Both of them nodded and pulled on their goggles before once again stepping onto the platforms. Kat posed like a comic book super heroine, doing arm curls and hulk-like poses. Mia laughed and teased her, dancing in front of her with her dukes up like a boxer while I snapped photos.

"Okay, look up, please, and smile."

They posed, their arms around each other's shoulders. Mia raised her fist and said, "Girl Power!"

"Word," Kat agreed.

Jordan and the blonde approached our group. Adam turned to Jordan's lovely companion and smiled. "Hey, Lindsay, glad you could make it."

"That's some pretty impressive stuff you were just flashing there, Drake. I've got my checkbook out. Where do I sign on to invest?" she laughed. "And you're looking gorgeous today, Mia. How are you doing?"

Adam, Mia and Lindsay continued to chat briefly. They all seemed to know each other so well that I really did wonder if this Lindsay woman was Jordan's girlfriend. She looked older than him by about five to seven years. Maybe the bad boy *was* settling down. They appeared to make an attractive couple, though that thought irritated me so I didn't dwell on it.

After a few minutes, Adam said something to Mia, kissing her on the cheek, and then he, Jordan and Lindsay moved away to talk to a couple of guys from developing.

I turned back to Mia. She was a very pretty woman, tall and thin with short dark hair and brown eyes. Those eyes suddenly fixed on me as she seemed to realize that I was still there, waiting.

"Hey, Mia," I started nervously, tucking my phone into my pocket. "Could I—um…"

"Hello, Mia..." Cari said, bumping up against me. She threw an arm around my shoulder and I stiffened. "April and I were just talking about you."

Mia's lips thinned. "Funny, I didn't feel my ears burning."

"I think—" I began.

"Yeah, we were saying that you look so good, considering. I mean, you are looking a lot better than you were."

My face burned, and Mia and Kat exchanged a long look.

"Also, I wanted to get a close-up glance of your *gorgeous* ring. You are so *lucky*. Can I?" She reached out her hand.

Mia paused and then hesitantly held it out so Cari could get a closer look. "Wow, Mia. Just *wow*. You sure are living the dream."

I stared at Cari, mouth open, and pulled away from her. Mia was already turned toward Katya, and they began to walk away with their heads close together as they talked. I took a step forward and Cari put a hand on my arm. "Hey, April. We should hang out. Maybe tonight..."

"I have the project from hell to work on—for the boss from hell." I glanced in Jordan's direction. He and the blonde were leaving the warehouse, and Adam was going off in a different direction with the developers.

I grasped at that in order to get rid of Cari. "Oh, look at that, Adam's leaving..."

Cari spun and waved for Ingrid to join her. "Gotta go! See ya." She and Ingrid fell into step behind Adam and his group, as I suspected she would.

I watched her go and my heart sank. I'd let Cari spoil my opportunity to apologize to Mia. And I'd thought up all the things I wanted to say, too. About how I shouldn't have said what I had, how

I was so sorry I'd hurt her feelings. I clenched my teeth in frustration and turned, dejectedly making my way back out of the warehouse.

Taking responsibility for my bad behavior toward her would have felt good, even if it was scary. I had no idea if Mia would reject my apology or laugh at it or whatever. But I was angry that I'd allowed Cari to railroad my attempt so easily. I also knew that, deep down, I was too chicken to stand up for myself. I didn't make waves. It had always been like that.

Having to go from one reluctant parent to the other every other week while growing up had taught me that if I wanted to fit in, I'd have to tell them what they wanted to hear and show them a smile while doing it.

What was worse was that this might have been my only chance to apologize to Mia, since my job future was extremely uncertain. It occurred to me that I owed Jordan an apology, too. Maybe this was one I could find the courage for.

During the entire walk back to his office, I rehearsed what I was going to say to him. By the time I arrived there, I had a beautiful speech all planned in my head. It sounded poetic and perfect, like another of my favorite book heroines, Anne Shirley from *Anne of Green Gables*.

When she'd practiced her lovely apologies, she'd charmed the old town gossip, Rachel Lynde, who had been prejudiced against the new orphan girl in town. I could do that. My words, like Anne's, would need to be heartfelt. I could *definitely* do that.

It was only with a slightly shaky hand that I raised my fist and knocked on Jordan's closed office door. He grunted for me to come in.

Anne liked to get down on one knee to profess her apology. I wouldn't go that far, but I made sure to stand front and center before his desk. Luckily, this time he was sitting down—he was much less intimidating that way. I clasped my hands in front of me.

"Well? Did you get the photos?"

"Yes, they're already in your inbox. I just—"

"And the files? What about those?"

"About halfway done. I'll stay late and finish them, but—"

"Then what are you standing here for? Get back to them. It's five, for Chrissakes."

"Um, I wanted to say something first, please. If you'll let me get a word in."

He stood, narrowing his eyes and clenching his teeth. He slowly came around the front of his desk, sat on it and folded powerful arms across his wide chest. So much for not feeling intimidated. I literally gulped.

He raised a brow and then held out his wrist to look at his watch. "You have three minutes. Starting now."

I blinked. Had Rachel Lynde timed Anne during *her* speech? In a panic, the words came rushing out of my mouth in no particular order at all. "I just wanted to say that I know you don't know me at all, but I've always tried to do the right thing. I've...um...I've had some judgment lapses lately and made some serious mistakes that I deeply regret, but I want to do the right thing and that includes this video situation."

I was rambling, I knew, but I couldn't stop myself. I took a deep breath to continue on. "I never do stuff like that. I'd never done anything like that. I mean, it was amazing sex—no idea it could be that good—but with all this trouble it's caused..." My voice faded out for a moment at the cocky smirk that hovered on his lips. Oh God, I couldn't believe I said that. I sounded so pathetic.

"I—I never set out to hurt anyone or the company. But I was in a pretty dark place at the convention. There was this thing—I don't want to get into it, but my family is kind of screwed up and I let it mess with my head and I did a really stupid thing. And I feel terrible that the company has been dragged into it so—"

"Time!" he said, cutting me off. He hadn't taken his eyes off his watch the entire time I'd been speaking. I swallowed.

"Weiss, you just said absolutely nothing to me. All I heard was 'blah, blah, blah.'" He held up his hand, opened and closed it like a quacking duck. "Get back to work."

I sucked in a painful breath. It had taken a lot to say all that. I'd spent twenty minutes summoning up my courage to get it out.

My cheeks heated. "I resign," I said.

His handsome features did not change in the least. "What?"

"I said that I'm resigning."

"No, you're not."

"Yes. I'm giving you my resignation, and all I ask is that you keep my identity secret as long as possible. So I might be able to find another position to intern somewhere else."

He stood and now towered over me. I was on the shorter side of medium height—okay, five-four. And he was at least six feet tall, probably taller.

"You're not interning somewhere else because you're *not* resigning."

"I just did."

"No, you said 'blah, blah, blah.'" He opened his hand again. I wanted to slap that damn hand. "Now get out here and finish my goddamn files."

"But—"

"And you are not allowed to talk to anyone about that video. Ignore that it exists."

I opened and closed my mouth several times, positive I looked exactly like a carp. He stepped up to me, standing less than a foot away. Then he bent and got in my face. He could have been saying anything to me, but all I could do was reel from how good he smelled. His scent was warm, like cinnamon, and dry like the white sage that grew in the Southern California coastal hills. My nostrils twitched.

His eyes narrowed. "Knock off the fish face and get the files done."

I closed my mouth, pivoted and walked out of the office. What the *what?*

He left an hour after our talk, not even saying goodbye, simply nodding in my direction as he walked by. I sat in a daze for several more hours as I finished my pain-in-the-ass task.

So, that was interesting. My Anne Shirley apology didn't work on him…or did it? Maybe he would have fired me otherwise? I wasn't quite sure. All I knew was that I'd divulged way too much information—information that it bugged me he now knew.

Maybe my apology had been so pathetic that he'd taken pity on me and decided against firing me for that very reason. Well, whatever it was, I still had my job though I'd likely never find out why.

4
JORDAN

GODDAMN, THIS WOMAN WAS MURDER ON MY BLOOD pressure. I'd felt like strangling her during that speech of hers—okay, except when she was talking about how good the sex was. So the not-so-poor little good girl had gone slumming and done a naughty thing. I knew her type. A woman who needed to tie one on and sow her wild oats, then cry and wring her hands afterward when she realized the consequences of her actions had hurt other people.

I knew that type *all* too damn well, as a matter of fact. I gripped the steering wheel on my drive home, tense with anger. It didn't help that she was so goddamn beautiful—that hot body, that angel face, those blue eyes. I told my brain to stop noticing it, but my body hadn't gotten the memo yet. Every time she walked in the room, instantaneous reactions would hit me between the eyes—that fine ass, those hot tits, that shiny hair. And I'd remember how one quick hookup had only given me a taste of what I could no longer have.

Instead of getting her out of my system, which had been the original plan, I now wanted her more than I did before.

I rubbed my forehead forcefully, trying to shove her out of my thoughts.

And goddamn but if I didn't have a shit-ton of work to get done tonight. I would have liked to blow off a little steam, but I couldn't afford the time or energy.

Something had to give. *This lifestyle* had to give. The empty hookups. The drunken parties. The rock star way of life. Was it worth it? Was it even doing anything for me anymore? It all felt so hollow and unfulfilling. Or maybe I was just getting too old.

It was dark when I got home, but I grabbed a bottle of beer and went out onto the back patio of my house, which opened directly onto the sand of the primest stretch of famed Newport Beach surfing real estate in Orange County.

I always liked to end my day to the sound of the sea. Though I had hours of work yet, I needed this now. This evening was busy with people strolling by on the paved bicycle and walking paths that paralleled the shoreline. I was hidden to them, tucked away in my covered patio. Their conversation grew and faded, but the ever-present rhythm of the ocean was what calmed me.

My phone chimed and I checked it.

Hey lover. Haven't heard from u in a while.

It was Lyla, the cover model I'd recently "dated." Her text was accompanied by a nice shot of her very lovely rack. I smiled, licked my lips and actually considered it for a few minutes. A good roll in the hay with her might be a welcome diversion from thoughts of the unattainable and unbelievably frustrating intern.

Lyla was the type who wouldn't mind getting down to business and then letting me get back to mine. I had to admit that I was sorely tempted. But before I could allow myself any more of those thoughts, I keyed in my reply.

Sorry, beautiful. Have a shitload of work to do. Maybe another night?

Her reply came less than a minute later.

But I'm horny tonight. :(

Well, shit. So was I. But my careless actions this past weekend really had me thinking. I'd fucked up. *Literally.* And somehow that had ended up all over the Internet.

Because of that, I'd had to lie to my best friend—the best friend who had gone through some major crises in the past year. Now my stupid move had added to his already heavy load. With a deep breath, I suppressed the guilt that had me second-guessing myself and my persistent goal to get the company on the market.

I miss my fav set of rock hard abs.

I humored her, pulling up my shirt and snapping a pic for her then hitting send with the message:

This will have to do for now. Sorry babe.

Her reply made me grin and *almost* had me hitting the call button to get her over here.

I just licked the screen. Don't judge.

Before I could even control it, the image of that intern licking me flashed into my mind—her dark head moving across my chest. It had been hot sex, but I'd kept my clothes on the entire time. I really could have stood for her to lick my chest. And my—

What the *hell* was I thinking? Had I learned nothing from the past twenty-four hours?

I was starting to doubt myself—to the extent that I was considering the unthinkable. To punish myself for my stupidity, I was going to abstain from random hookups—and for getting drunk, for that matter. Hell, if the CFO thing fell through, maybe I'd join a monk order or something.

With a sigh, I went inside and pulled out my laptop to bury myself in the paperwork I'd brought home with me. I had to go over the legal documents that had been filed by our investment bankers to see what loopholes they might try to exploit. I also had to call my Internet security guy and find out what he could do about this viral video, if anything.

Once something went viral, though, it was like pissing into the wind to try and stop it. There were recourses we could take, like the takedown notices. But the risk of exposure made those recourses of questionable value.

The fact that she didn't know the identity of her sex partner got me off the hook, but I had to wonder again if she truly didn't know or there wasn't a way she could find out. And if she found out, what would she do? Why had she uploaded it in the first place? But if I asked her that directly, she'd realize I knew it'd been her that had done it and not the other party. She wasn't stupid—that much I'd pieced together—and could probably figure it out. I couldn't risk that. I'd have to get to the bottom of her reasons for doing it in a more roundabout way.

After about an hour of poring over legalese, I fixed myself some dinner and hit the 'call back' button from the voicemail app on my phone. There were other women in my life that I couldn't keep putting off.

"It's about time you return my call," was the first thing Hannah said when she picked up.

"I do have a life, you know. I'm not your personal homework helpline."

"I know where the bodies are buried, Jordan. Don't mess with me."

"More like you know where I used to stash my joints and that's what you used to blackmail me, you pain in the ass."

"Whatever. I need help with this. I emailed you the problem. Just give me a hint?"

"How is college going, anyway? You've already been in two weeks and I haven't heard a word from you since you started."

She paused for a moment before answering in a too-loud, too cheery voice. "It's going great!"

Hmm. That concerned me, but I knew better than to ask her directly. Hannah always liked to project that everything going on with her was perfect—even when it wasn't. Unfortunately for her, she wasn't the greatest actress.

"Meeting a lot of new people? Any guys I need to go beat up?"

"Ha, ha. I'm concentrating on studies, thankyouverymuch. But this economics class is the bane of my existence. Already."

I flipped open my laptop and pulled up her email again. "So this question is pretty basic, Banna." I used the old nickname, just to mess with her. Big brother's prerogative.

She blew out a breath on the other end. "The class is for my general education requirement, but we weren't *all* managing multiple stock portfolios from our earnings at the surf shop at fifteen."

"Too bad you can't be a genius like me. Sibling rivalry is such an ugly thing. Try not to let it eat you up inside."

"Whatever. Speaking of the surf shop...Mom told me something she found out from Ms. Nolan. "

"Ah, how's Ms. Nolan doing?"

"Mom's been driving her to her treatments. She seems to be doing better. But this last time, she told Mom that Cyndi's getting a divorce."

I paused. The name stopped me first. The news, second. I had no idea what to do with that information. I actually had no idea how I even *felt* about that information. Deep down, I should have felt some sort of satisfaction to hear about her unhappiness, but I didn't. Did that mean I'd moved past all that—past her?

"You still there?"

"Yeah. Not sure why you chose to tell me that."

"Dunno. Thought you'd want to know. She *was* your girlfriend for a zillion years."

"About a zillion years ago. I've had a lot of girlfriends since then."

"Oh, so that's what you call them? I'm sorry, but if you sleep with someone for a couple weeks, she's not your girlfriend. You need to maybe think about settling down."

"Why the hell would I do that? I'm twenty-five and I live like a rock star."

"Ah yes, pissing away your youth and your filthy, ill-gotten millions."

"Has Dad been spewing his *Das Kapital* bullshit again?"

She sighed. "Okay, I tease but…this is getting ridiculous. When are the two of you going to sit down and talk?"

I ground my teeth, tensing. She knew better than to get into this subject with me. Then again, I'd screwed up by bringing the old man up in the first place. "We've got nothing to talk about. So, about that homework problem…"

"Dude, speaking of problems…I almost forgot. I saw a viral video on the Internet. People dressed up as characters from Dragon Epoch—"

Uh, no. Just no. The thought that my little sister had seen me having sex brought on a sudden rush of nausea. "I'm not talking about that, and neither are you if you want help on your homework, missy."

"Fine. But do you know who it was?"

"So your email says that you needed to know about market elasticity, right?"

"Even from two hundred miles away, you're still a dork."

"Don't bite the dork that helps you with your homework."

"Yeah, yeah."

We spoke for another twenty minutes before I hung up then stared at the phone for a long time trying to process the conversation…the news of Cyndi's failed marriage, the crazy events of the day in general. My head hurt, but I had hours of work of ahead of me yet.

I called my Internet security guy and made one other phone call to my information guy. I had to find out what April Weiss was up to—

what made her tick, and why she would be motivated to record herself having sex and then upload it to the Internet. And if she had dirt on me, was she the type of person who would use it?

So I asked him to gather information on her. I had to make sure I had dirt in return. Because I *was* the type of person who would use it to get what I wanted. And what I really wanted was her tempting, mouth-watering body out of my radius. But since I couldn't have that—yet—I needed leverage. Just in case.

No hookup—not even a damn hot one—was worth this shit. Or that was what I kept telling myself.

At least my last sexual encounter before this newly established period of abstention had been a damn fucking hot one. After she was gone, I'd take time to savor the memory. Until then, I had to shove it out of my mind and not dwell on it.

In the meantime, I could enjoy myself by making her life a living hell.

5
APRIL

I WOKE UP THE NEXT DAY AMID A PILE OF SHOPPING BAGS FROM MY late-night shopping spree. Sid, who had gone to sleep before I'd gotten home—as usual—and arisen long before me—also not unusual—had not been apprised of the complications in the viral video situation.

When I finally woke up, she was eager for me to fill her in.

"No way... he *knew* it was you?"

I sighed. "He saw my tat and recognized it from the video."

Sid shook her head. "Girl, that is one mistake that has come back to bite you in the hiney—literally—and who knows when it will happen again?"

"Yeah, yeah, I'll get the laser thingy done when I have time. I have to psyche myself up for it."

Sid waved a hand toward all the shopping bag debris. "So what's all this? Retail therapy?"

"Hah, no. These are new clothes—all very long shirts and sweaters that won't ride up in the back and a couple of body suits. I'm not taking any chances. It's bad enough that Jordan knows it's me and is still, for some reason, allowing me to work there. I'm sure if anyone else found out, there would be hell to pay."

"But the mean girls know it's you, right? Do you think any of them will say anything?"

I shook my head. "Cari told me she has my back."

Sid frowned. "Do you think…did anyone else have your phone this weekend besides you?"

"No way. I may be an idiot, but even I know not to give someone access to my phone. I don't even give *you* access to my phone."

"Well, that's good to know. They are not nice. Especially Cari—that chick is like Regina George."

"Who?"

Sid rolled her eyes. "You need to see more movies, Apes. You read too much."

"There's no such thing as reading too much!"

"*Anyway*…Regina George was the head of the mean girls in the *Mean Girls* movie. Cari reminds me of her."

I got up and started pulling tags off my new clothes, grabbing the trashcan to toss them into.

Sid rubbed her eyebrow thoughtfully. "After class, I spent a big part of the afternoon rewatching that fracking video."

I scrunched my brows together. "Why? Do you really need the sex education that badly?"

She glared at me. "I was looking for clues…like I know how the officers figured out it was an employee in the video."

"How?"

She went to her computer and cued up the horrid thing again. But instead of forcing me to watch it, she froze the frame soon after it started. "See here? You set the phone to record after you took off your underwear, it looks like... and the phone is right next to this badge right here."

I leaned in and my eyes followed where she was pointing.

Holy. Shit. She was right. Sure as anything, that was a Draco badge. The kind we all used to get into the building and move around anywhere on the campus. It was tied to the company's security system. They required us to wear them in conjunction with our industry passes at the Con. I leaned in more closely to get a better look. If my name was on that thing...

"The name is blocked out—ironically, by your underwear. But that's how they know. They saw your badge."

I straightened. "Ah..." I said to express understanding, but I was still confused. Because that was *not* my badge. My badge looked a lot like that badge, but the company logo and name and everything else was printed in blue on my badge to denote my status as an unpaid intern. Regular employee badges were printed in black lettering with a black logo—like that badge showed.

The guy dressed up as Falco the Bounty Hunter. The man with the hot hands and the huge cock. That guy was a Draco employee.

I took a deep breath, held it and then let it go. Holy crap. I was so fucked. This thing got worse and worse the more time that passed.

Because that person was probably angry as hell that a video of him having sex was posted on the Internet. Sooner or later this guy would find out who *I* was and want to know why the hell I'd jeopardized his job for no good reason. I'd have to find him before it came to that. But I had no idea how.

"Speaking of having access to your phone, it was completely dead so I plugged it in for you this morning when I woke up. The notification screen said you had five missed calls and two voicemails from your mom."

"Yeah, I know."

Sid paused. "You aren't even going to listen to the voicemails?"

"No. I'm deleting them. Whatever she wants, I'm sure her new hubby can take care of for her. Gunnar is a trust-fund brat so he can buy whatever her little heart desires. She only calls me when she wants something. And I'm not in the mood to argue with her."

"You *never* argue with her, April. You just put up with it."

"See? This is a good way to avoid the entire mess. If she never gets a hold of me, then I never have to feel disgusted with myself that I didn't stand up to her—yet again."

Sid nodded. "Good point. Hey, my mom wants to know when you are coming over for dinner again."

Sid often took pity on me when speaking to me about my mom. She liked to offer her own mom, who was an amazingly sweet lady, as a surrogate.

"Oh, that sounds amazing. I could go for some more Persian food, but I don't even know when I'll be able to break away from this hellacious job to do more than eat and run. And that would be so rude to her."

Sid shrugged. "I'm sure she'll be filling up our freezer soon anyway."

"Yum. Hope she makes that great stuff with the pomegranates and walnuts again."

"*Fesonjān.* I'll put in the request."

I got up, and with rounded shoulders opened up my laptop to check my email. Speaking of mothers...there was another one from Rebekah in there. I still hadn't answered her last one.

This one had the subject line: *Israel Birthright Info.* My stepmom was concerned about my dire lack of education with regard to my heritage and had made it her personal mission, of late, to get me on board with the family plan. My half-sister, Sarah, was going to have her Bat Mitzvah in a few years, and I was sure Rebekah had visions of one big happy family gathered together in the synagogue to celebrate.

Or maybe she thought I was a crappy role model for her daughter to look up to. And Sarah did idolize me. Despite the fact she was only ten, it felt good. At least someone on this planet thought I was pretty great. Nevertheless, I sighed as I contemplated how to respond to Rebekah's question of whether or not I'd go to temple with them. It seemed that religion was yet another barrier between them and me. It set me apart, made me different from those I should have called my closest family.

With a sigh I sat back, opened another browser and Googled the program in question. Maybe I could take off on a trip to Israel, and when I got back this damn video would be wiped from the face of the Internet forever.

When it snows in the summer, as my German grandmother would say. Or *when pigs fly*, as I would say.

After a quick breakfast, I dressed for work, making sure to wear clothing that would keep me adequately covered. Given this second chance from a grumpy, yet remarkably understanding boss, I'd make every extra effort to be the best assistant *ever*.

But the boss got surlier with each passing day. And he nitpicked every single goddamn thing I did. I fought hard to maintain a smooth exterior—to never show my emotions, my self-doubt. People like Jordan Fawkes could smell fear, and so I knew I had to try my best to hide it.

Meanwhile, when I wasn't stressing about job stuff, I was agonizing over the Falco question. Vital questions like 'who was he' and 'did he know who I was' and—more importantly—'was he ragingly pissed off at me' plagued my mind.

And despite all the trouble it had caused, I couldn't seem to shake the thoughts of that night. I wasn't sure whether it had been because of any special skills or, ahem, equipment on his part or the illicitness of the affair, but it had been *so damn good*. Who knew a Comic-Con cosplay nerd—and Draco employee, apparently—could be so incredible in the sack? Or maybe the handful of guys I'd been with before this had been *that* bad.

Every day I spent at Draco, I found myself idly wondering about male co-workers I passed in hallways or delivered random items to— had it been him? Or *him*? The only thing I knew about the guy was that he was tall and filled out a Falco the Bounty Hunter suit very, *very* well. And he'd sounded so sexy when he whispered low in that flat, toneless voice.

Oh, and that his manhandle had been huge. I hadn't forgotten that either. How could I?

The boss from hell, along with the constant worry over Falco, was driving me insane. Therefore, it should have come as no surprise that one particularly awful day, a week later, I almost broke down right at my desk. Susan had to call my name several times to get my attention.

Finally, I blinked and sat up straight.

"Hey...what's wrong? Are you okay?" she said.

I turned to her. Susan was a plain-looking but sweet and funny lady in her mid-thirties. She had short blond hair and green eyes. And she wore quirky earrings for, what seemed, every day of the year. I hadn't seen her repeat a pair yet. She'd explained that she chose them to reflect her mood for the day. Currently, they were two miniature baby pacifiers—one pink and one blue. Yesterday, she and her husband heard the heartbeat for the first time and she was ecstatic, showing everyone unreadable pictures of her ultrasound.

"I don't know how much more of this I can take..." I said in a shaky voice.

She sighed. "Well, he's generally not very easy on the interns, if that makes you feel any better."

It didn't.

"Last weekend, I don't think an hour went by that he didn't text me for something. Forwarding stuff to him or researching something he could do himself with Google and a few keywords."

"Hmm. Maybe he just wants to make sure you're learning everything you need?"

I bit down the frustration. Every hour, practically on the hour? "Does he usually have you take his car to get washed, pick up his dry-cleaning and scream at you if the coffee you bring him isn't hot enough?"

Susan frowned. "He's never asked me to do any of those things, but he probably feels it's his responsibility to make sure you have lots of things to do."

I gulped. The other morning, he actually pulled out a kitchen thermometer and took the temperature of the coffee I'd brought him. *"One hundred forty, Weiss? What is this, a cool, refreshing summer drink? I told you extra hot. No stopping to chat with your BFFs on the way in here while you are holding my coffee. Jeez, why don't you just throw ice cubes in it while you're at it?"*

I'd bared my teeth in that now familiar 'I want to kill you dead' long-suffering smile, picked up the coffee and exited the room, tossing it in the nearest trash can. Blinking back tears, I'd rushed out the door to go back to Starbucks. I'd had to run in my heels to get it back to the office fast enough and even that hadn't worked.

Then on the rush back the second time, I broke my heel mid-run and the coffee—and me—went flying. The third time was the charm, but after that, I had to lock myself in the bathroom to cry for a good half-hour.

From that day on, I packed a pair of sneakers in my desk especially for coffee runs and developed a special run-jog so the steaming liquid wouldn't slosh over the top and burn my hands. *Note to self: bring gloves to pack in desk alongside sneakers.*

"You look exhausted, you poor thing," Susan continued.

"I've been staying up late preparing the files on each investment banker."

She frowned, fiddling with her anti-nausea wristband. "What files?"

"Well, Jordan wanted me to create files with contact information on all the investment bankers, the legal terms of their contract agreements—"

Susan looked at me like I'd grown another head. "He has all that already." My face clouded and she seemed to be hurrying to cover for him. "But...maybe he's afraid his info is incomplete and you are double-checking everything for him. Rumor has it the IPO thing isn't going well because of this sex-tape scandal."

My eyes grew wide and my stomach dipped. "Uh. Really?"

Susan nodded and her baby pacifiers danced at her earlobes. She lowered her voice. "Yes. Word on the street is that Adam had a shit-fit when the scandal broke and wanted to pull the plug on the IPO. Jordan's been working on this for *years*. Adam gave him two weeks to see if he can make it work, so obviously Jordan's pretty upset. I think you may have just gotten caught up as the target for his frustrations."

I looked away guiltily. It made sense that I'd be the target—and not for the reason she thought—but there was no way Susan could know that. I swallowed a ball of lead and blinked back some new tears. This was not good. Not good at all.

I knew from my business education that it took a huge expense and at least two years of hard work to get a company ready to go public. And it was tough to get bankers on your side, especially for a young and relatively inexperienced CFO like Jordan.

"Yeah, and the bankers aren't too pleased that there is a company employee involved in this mess. Since they are the ones who would underwrite the initial stock shares on the day the company goes public, their financial risk is pretty hefty."

I nodded. If things didn't go perfectly in an IPO, a company could take a huge hit. It had happened with some big and successful companies very recently. They'd been valued at a certain price and then their shares dropped in price the second the company went public, losing them millions—sometimes even billions.

And that could happen to Draco, all because of my stupid sex video. *Shit.*

No wonder Jordan looked at me like he wanted to literally eat me alive.

I leaned in. "So that's why he's been out so much for meetings and taking so many conference calls? I was—"

"I hate to break up this gossip session, but would you two mind getting some work done?"

We both jumped and found ourselves face-to-face with the subject of our discussion. My eyes slid down Jordan's powerful form.

He was dressed in suit and tie—as he was pretty much every day since the return from Comic-Con. And he looked as exhausted as I felt. Not that it made him any less hot, curse him.

He dumped a pile of outgoing mail on the desk in front of us, spun and entered his office.

With shaky hands, I reached out and started sifting through the envelopes. "These need addresses..." I snatched up a lavender envelope that was blank. A love letter?

There was a sticky note attached, on which he'd scrawled, "*Mom.*"

"Oh yeah, I forgot it was his mom's birthday this week! I didn't even have to remind him," Susan said, pulling up the address on her laptop.

I grabbed a pen, ready to address it. "Does he have you buy his cards and gifts for him?"

"Sometimes for his dates. He goes out with so many different women that he probably can't keep up. But he never has me do it for his family. He does all that himself." *Sometimes for his dates.* Huh, that figured.

I thought of the blond woman he'd been talking to in R&D. "He was chatting up some blonde at the demo last week. Lindsay. Is she his girlfriend?"

Susan laughed. "No, no. Not even. She's Adam's friend. Jordan doesn't really stay in a relationship long enough to have them even be called 'girlfriends.' He might be a bit shallow and misguided, but he really is a sweet surfer kid at heart."

My lips thinned. She read off the address and I wrote it down on the envelope. His mother lived in San Luis Obispo, about two hundred and fifty miles north of Orange County.

"He's really close with his family, actually. Except for the dad. There's something weird going on with his dad." She shook her head. "Anyway, just give it some time. I'm sure he'll calm down soon."

I hurriedly addressed the rest of the mail while nervously keeping an eye out for his door to open. God forbid he needed another coffee.

Somehow I made it out of there on time, for once. That gave me hope that he might leave me alone for the weekend.

That hope was dashed, however, when Susan called me late Saturday afternoon.

"*Please*, April. I've been puking all day. I'm so dizzy I can hardly stand up straight, let alone drive."

I took a deep breath and let it go. "Susan, I have plans. I'm going out with some girlfriends tonight."

"Hon, I promise it won't take you more than a half-hour to run to the office, grab the paperwork off my desk and then run it over to him. He lives really close. He's in Newport Beach—the Wedge."

I knew the area. It was at the tip of the Balboa peninsula in rich man's land. I took a deep breath, wanting desperately to refuse. But it just so happened that my plans for the evening were going to take me to Newport Beach. It would be a simple matter of getting the file and then stopping by. Having to deal with the beast boss on a Saturday night was the real problem.

I wanted to say no, but my mouth—like always—said the opposite. "Fine. It's going to be a few. I need to get dressed."

"It's not a huge rush. Thank you *so* much. I owe you, April!"

I hung up and then started to get ready. Sid came home not long before I left, tossing her book bag on her bed. She turned to take me in with a wolf whistle.

"Why are you all gussied up?"

I had on a cute little black dress and my shiny, patent leather Christian Louboutins.

"I'm meeting the Phi Kappa girls at a club. But wish me luck. I have to run some paperwork over to the Beast."

Her brows rose. "Dude, he's making you work on a Saturday night?"

"It's a favor, for Susan," I sighed.

She gave me a knowing look, but thankfully said nothing about my inability to say no.

"We're meeting down by the pier in Newport. Why don't you come with?"

"I dance like a duck. It's too embarrassing." Sid had been raised in a pretty protected home environment. Her dad was Middle Eastern and very traditional, and therefore Sid had not been allowed to date in high school, which then led to an awkward social life in college—even more awkward than mine.

"Well, I'm going for an hour or two to hang out with the girls and do a little dancing."

"No drinking?"

"Hell to the no," I said. "I told you. Alcohol will never touch my lips again. Alcohol is apparently my kryptonite, but instead of turning me weak, it makes me dumb as a fencepost."

I grabbed my everyday purse, snatched out my wallet and tucked both it and my phone into my Louis Vuitton clutch.

Sid waggled her eyebrows. "You look foxy. Maybe if you stay sober, you'll meet a *nice* boy instead of a jerkface."

"Likely I'll end up bored after fifteen minutes of dancing and sit in the bathroom reading an e-book on my phone."

Sid laughed.

"You can laugh, but I've actually done that before and then slipped out at an acceptable time."

"Why not just say you don't want to go?"

"Oh"—I waved my hand and checked myself one last time in the mirror—"you know me. I go with the flow and make it appear like I'm following the crowd, then do my own thing."

"Maybe you need a new philosophy."

I sighed. "You're probably right." Then I walked out the door to, once again, follow the crowd.

It took me the full thirty minutes to drive over to Draco, get security to let me in, find the paperwork that Susan had described to me, and drive over to his house. I'd followed the GPS app on my phone to direct me down the narrow streets at the end of the peninsula, where the houses butted up against each other and looked out over the crowded and popular beach.

I knocked on his door at quarter to seven and he answered a minute later. I had to fight to keep my jaw from dropping because Jordan was in his swim trunks—long, colorful board shorts that hung low on his hips—and nothing else. No shirt. No shoes.

No breathing—on my part.

He. Was. Magnificent. Muscular, well-developed chest. I could see the indentations to every crease and rise. He wasn't overly bulky, but every muscle was firm and clearly defined, even that delicious little valley that separated his six-pack from his hips, dipping below the waist of his trunks. There was a light dusting of hair on his taut pecs and trailing across his flat stomach. He had a surfer's bod, complete with a light tan, a smattering of sand on his shin and damp hair.

My mouth went dry. I was about to start panting like a puppy at any moment. I wanted to lick him like a puppy, too.

I hated him, but I wanted to lick him. He was licktacular.

He was also staring at me with a completely confused look on his face. "What the hell are you doing here?"

I flushed hot, realizing that I'd been standing there for half a minute, staring and gaping at his beauty. He was Adonis, surfer-style. On top of that, he hadn't shaved today, so he had light scruff along his jaw, making him *that* much yummier.

Speechless, I shoved the envelope at him, afraid that anything coming out of my mouth at this moment might sound a bit like, "Duh, der, uh, uck, errrr."

Jordan took it from me without even looking at it. "Where's Susan?" he snapped.

"She's sick. She asked me to drop it by. Well—goodbye then!" I stepped back.

He stepped forward, running his eyes down my little black dress and my legs. Where his eyes touched me, I could swear it was almost tangible, his hands sweeping down over my body. His gaze wandered back to mine very slowly, lingering on my cleavage. I was hot everywhere those eyes stroked me. "Where are you going all dressed up like *that?*"

I cleared my throat, trying hurriedly to work some moisture into it. "Some friends are at a club near here. I'm going to meet up with them now."

I had to forcibly pull my eyes from the tribal band tattoo of stylized ocean waves that seemed to ebb and flow around his bulging bicep. Lord, he was beautiful. No wonder the models all wanted him.

He shifted his stance, shaking his head. "Nope."

It took me a minute to pull myself from the mental drooling. I jerked my eyes to his, frowning. "Wait, what?"

He waved a hand in front of my face. "Earth to Weiss, come in, Weiss. You're staying here and helping me with this."

"But you didn't—"

"I didn't *have* to. I'm the boss. What I say goes. Got it?"

My jaw dropped. What a. Fucking. Fucker...fucktard.

Oh my God. I hated him so hard right now. "But my friends are waiting for me."

He stood back, widening the door but not backing down. "Your friends don't write your business school recommendation." My stomach dropped and my shoulders slumped. He won—before the battle had even begun.

I stepped into his beach house and followed him to his living room. I could see the shimmering water of the Pacific Ocean out the sliding glass door that led directly onto one of the most famous beaches in Southern California. The waves pounded relentlessly and there were surfers out, riding beneath the last rays of sunlight. Jordan's board was propped askew against the back wall on the small patio. That explained the swim trunks.

The house was not big—most of the ones in the Wedge weren't— but it came with a price tag well into the millions. Jordan gestured for me to stay put while he went out to the covered back porch, grabbed his surfboard and stuffed it up on a ceiling rack alongside a standing paddleboard and a kayak. I watched the muscles in his back roll under his skin as he performed the action.

My throat was constricted, dry. I ordered my lust to calm down. The prettier they were, the more dangerous and detrimental they could be. I forced myself to remember Gunnar. He'd been like that.

Not as gorgeous as Jordan, but still a catch and the envy of most girls on campus. Until he'd utterly humiliated me in more ways than I could count.

There would be no more trusting those warm, wiggly feelings I got in my lady parts when laying eyes on a hot man—particularly a half-naked one. I was over the pretty boys. *Never again.*

Chances were that my mystery man, Falco, also of the hot bod and rock-hard abs variety, was a sweet, mild-mannered and nerdy Draco employee. Maybe he was a playtester or a programmer. Definitely not a playboy like Jordan with a fast lifestyle.

Jordan adjusted the surfboard and reached up to straighten the paddle for the kayak. Clearly the man liked his watersports, and judging from his body, he actively engaged in them. I looked away, irritated with myself, and pulled out my phone to text my friends that I wouldn't be coming. I hit send about two seconds before he came back inside and gave me an insolent stare.

"Did you text your boyfriend and tell him you weren't going?" he asked in a flat voice.

I tucked my phone away with shaky hands, trying to contain the helpless fury and rage I felt at that moment. I had to give up a semi-fun evening with the girls to do this jackass' bidding all night. He could have been a little nicer, at least. "I don't have a boyfriend. But I did text my friends."

"Ah. So he broke up with you over the sex video?"

I blushed. "I believe you have ordered me never to discuss that— whatever it is you're referring to."

He raised his brows. "Very good. You *do* listen."

"Will that be going into my business school recommendation?"

"It might be."

I shook my head and peered up at him. "You really thought I had a boyfriend? And that I'd cheated on him with Falco the Bounty Hunter?"

His features were unreadable. "You're a nice girl, Weiss. Exactly the kind that should never be trusted." Then his square jaw tensed and his eyes narrowed with some renewed fury or slight. "Make yourself comfortable. You're going to be here a while. And I'm going to put some clothes on."

"Oh, thank God," I muttered quietly to myself.

"What was that?" He spun before hitting the stairs.

"Oh, nothing...nothing. Just talking to myself."

He frowned, shook his head and left.

With a long sigh, I leaned back against the big, white couch. I looked up at the cathedral ceiling, complete with airy skylights. The room was decorated beautifully and professionally, with white-on-white, glass and chrome and tiny splashes of color here and there, a deep blue loop carpet and understated beach-themed paintings and décor. As nice as it was, there was little personalization to it that I could see. It could very well have been a high-end rental.

I gazed at the flawless blue sky that was darkening with each passing minute. How was I going to survive months of this? Was every aspect of my life his until he wrote me the recommendation—*if* he wrote me the recommendation?

Was it really worth all this pain and suffering to put up with this cocky jerk? Jane Eyre had done it. Her boss, Mr. Rochester, had been an utter jackass, too. But stupidly, she'd fallen in *love* with him.

Well, there was no chance of that in my case. It was more likely I'd murder him if I could figure out a way to hide the body. That solid, perfectly toned body with just the slightest hint of a tan. He must have worn a lot of sunblock, because he wasn't as tan as I'd expect someone who was outdoors as much as he appeared to be—

"And what the hell are you daydreaming about?"

I jerked back to reality to find him standing right in front of me. He was dressed in jeans and a t-shirt that stretched across his broad chest and sturdy shoulders. I could see the edge of his band tattoo peeking out from underneath the tight left sleeve, waves stylized in three different shades of blue.

"Earth to Weiss. What are you thinking about?"

Flustered, I tore my eyes away from his arm, unable to even look at him now. "Sunblock," I blurted.

"Sunblock?"

"I was—well, just wondering why you aren't more tan."

He raised his eyebrows. "Because I hardly get a chance to hit the waves anymore. Today was a rare exception—for the forty-five minutes that it lasted."

"Ah," I said.

He bent and scooped up the envelope I'd brought him. "I have reports to finish, and I had to have these brought to me because the meeting was changed to first thing Monday morning." He shot me a hard look. "If I have to spend the time mopping up your messes, then the least you can do is help."

He had a point. I was, after all, responsible for all this emergency crap he was being forced to deal with. I leaned forward and grabbed an empty legal pad and a pen that were sitting on the coffee table, ready to take notes as he went through the pages.

"Why didn't you fire me?" I finally asked, after a long moment of working up the courage to question him with the one thing that had been burning in my mind for the past two weeks.

He looked up from his paperwork after a long pause. "Maybe because I believe a person can be competent in spite of fucking up— *literally.*" He fixed me with his intense hazel eyes that glowed almost amber. The hand resting atop his muscular thigh closed into a fist. "That being said, maybe you should have thought about the possibility of losing the internship *before* you went on your little sexcapade and decided to record it."

I opened my mouth and then shut it. I wondered how he knew that I was the one who'd recorded it. Then I remembered the brief part at the end of the video that showed me turning to grab the phone and switch it off. I guess that had been a pretty big clue.

"It was really bad judgment."

"You need good judgment if you want to succeed in business, Weiss. You can't let the heat of the moment take over. Even if it was *the best sex you ever had,*" he said with a strange look on his face. He looked like he was reveling in my discomfort.

My cheeks flamed and I nodded, feeling like a chastened schoolgirl at the front of class, about to have her knuckles slapped by the schoolmaster's ruler. Rochester had yelled at Jane Eyre so many times, but she'd had the courage to speak up to him and they'd become friends.

I didn't have that courage, and I doubted I'd ever become friends with Jordan Fawkes. But I was determined to make things right—if I could.

"There's something you might not know about—about that thing I'm not supposed to talk about."

His expression was completely neutral, but his eyes looked wary. "Oh? And what is that?"

"The guy—I'm pretty sure he was an employee too."

Did I imagine it or did the color drain out of his face? "But if you don't know who it is, how do you know that?"

"Because of the badge in the video. That's not my badge. It's the wrong color."

"So you think it's his?"

"It has to be. I'm sure he has no idea who I was either. And he has no incentive whatsoever to step forward, so I think the secret is safe. I just—just thought you should know."

"So is that why you uploaded the video? You thought it would be safe because no one would know who either of you were?"

His question stunned me. "Actually...that was an accident." *Ugh, April...way to prove to your boss that you are even more of a fuck-up than he previously thought.*

"How the hell do you upload a video on accident?"

I chewed my lip so ferociously it started to hurt. "I, uh, I have no idea. I'd had a lot to drink that weekend. I think I might have shared it on accident. I'm so non-tech savvy that it's a miracle I haven't accidentally launched a nuclear missile by hitting the wrong button in the wrong app."

He continued to watch me, that unwavering stare unsettling me. I tried not to fidget. Finally folding my hands in my lap, I stared at them instead of allowing myself to be distracted by Jordan's underwear model good looks.

"Wow, Weiss. That's, uh...I have no idea what the fuck I'm supposed to do with that information." He looked down at the paperwork in his hands and then said, "Shit...I left my laptop upstairs. Go grab it for me."

I opened my mouth and then shut it, confused and angry yet again. This man pushed my buttons constantly. He stared at me, as if expecting me to reply. I stood and made my way toward the stairs. "Which one is your room?" I asked.

He frowned, studying my heels. "Take off your shoes. You're going to be here a while."

"That's okay. I prefer to keep them on," I said between my teeth.

"First room on the left at the top of the stairs."

I climbed the stairs and slipped into his room, flipping on the light. This room was the complete opposite of the rest of the house. His bedroom had a lot to say about him. There were pictures of him on the wall, posing with a surfboard as a teen with numerous ribbons and trophies. He had a line of books on a shelf above his desk, mostly related to the stock market and business but some econ theory books as well. I made a mental note of the ones I hadn't read.

His bed was neatly made and surprisingly tame-looking. Not what I had been expecting from the playboy millionaire. No mirrors on the ceiling or flashy disco ball. No kinky bondage equipment. Maybe he had another room set aside for that. I almost snorted at the thought.

I wandered over to the desk where his laptop sat amidst neatly arranged and precisely labeled folders and binders going back at least five years. As I scooped up the laptop, I paused when I noticed the family photo sitting on the corner of the desk. There were five in the photo, including Jordan, in a picture that looked like it was taken at his college graduation from Caltech. His mom and dad stood on either side of him, his dad grim-faced and his mother smiling so wide that you could barely see her eyes. Two other people were in the photo, a teenage boy and a preteen girl with golden blond curls. I bent to get a closer look.

"Did you find it yet?"

I straightened with a jerk and threw a guilty look at the doorway. How long had I been up here? And more importantly, how long had he been standing there watching me snoop in his room?

He studied me with hooded eyes, and my face burned with a furious blush. We held each other's gaze for a long moment before he broke it to glance over the room, as if making sure I hadn't swiped something.

"Sorry. I got distracted," I muttered.

Blank-faced, he held out his hand for the laptop and I brought it to him. He took it from me but did not move from the doorway, signaling for me to go ahead of him. Maybe it was because he didn't trust me in his room alone for another moment.

I brushed by him, acutely aware of the heat of his body, the smell of the ocean on his skin. My chest briefly grazed his and I paused, glancing up at him. He swallowed visibly. I was barely able to breathe in the tension-thickened air. We were now inches from each other.

My heart drummed in my throat, but I didn't know if it was from his nearness or my fear of his reaction to my snooping.

Slowly, I licked my dry lips. "I—I'm sorry about that. There—"
He stiffened. "Just go, Weiss. Downstairs, *now*," he said in a voice like steel. I suppressed a yelp as I spun and tripped down the stairs like a panicked colt.

6
JORDAN

I LEANED AGAINST THE DOORJAMB AND WATCHED HER GO, scrubbing a hand over my face to break contact with her ass. Apparently, I had an unwavering fascination with the damn thing. And that slim waist...the way the graceful curve at the small of her back rose to the swells of her round ass in that sleek, black, form-hugging dress. God, she was a knockout. For the umpteenth time I questioned my sanity for keeping her here tonight.

I called out to let her know I needed a pit stop and I'd be right down, then set aside the laptop and strode with purpose into the ensuite bathroom. It always took forever to take a piss when my dick was hard. And fuck it, her brief brush up against me and the sultry licking of those pink, puffy lips was all it took.

Hell, having her in here standing within three feet of my bed was a bad idea. When I'd come into that doorway, the first thing I wanted to do was push her down on the bed and pin her underneath me.

Squeezing my eyes shut, I finished my business and washed my hands, making sure to splash some cold water on my face. It would have to do instead of a cold shower. It had been two weeks since I'd decided to abstain from sex, and it was not proving to be easy. Especially with a little sexpot intern as my captive for the night.

It was an idiotic decision to force her to stay, but how the hell could I let her to go out looking like that? She'd have to beat the fuckers off with a stick, and as long as I had any control over it, that was *not* happening. As long as I was her boss, I *did* have control over it.

If I couldn't have her, no one could. At least while she worked for me. If I had to suffer from lack of getting any, so would she. After all, this was her mess to begin with. Accident or not.

And honestly, who the fuck uploads a recording without realizing it? She could have hit a share button while she was drunk, but she'd find that on her profile later—unless it was on a platform that didn't tolerate indecent material. Then it could have been deleted by the provider.

But content like that spread faster than a STD at a frat party.

I frowned, drying my hands. Whether or not she meant to upload the video remained to be seen, but she deserved the deprivation for all the trouble it had caused. And I was just the one to inflict the punishment. I looked at myself in the mirror. Adam was right—I *was* a rat bastard.

Minutes later, with certain body parts now completely under my control—for the moment, anyway—I settled back on the couch in the living room.

She was standing at the sliding glass door, watching the sunset, and I kept my eyes away from that alluring backside by snatching up my forms and gathering them on a clipboard. I looked up when she turned and walked toward me, still teetering on those ridiculously

high heels that made her legs look spectacular. *Eyes averted, Fawkes—*
goddammit!

"Those shoes can't be comfortable. Take them off."

She slipped into the chair beside the couch. "I don't want to take
them off." She flicked a glance at me, as if testing my reaction. Then,
to emphasize the point, she crossed her ankles and wiggled the foot
on top. Oh, so it was going to be like *that*, was it?

"I insist."

Her brows rose. "I'm afraid you're going to have to be
disappointed. The shoes stay on. All night."

All night. She was sending me a crystal clear message. She didn't
trust me…like somehow keeping her shoes on would protect her from
my degenerate inclinations. But I knew damn well that Snow White
wasn't as pure as her nickname might imply. Underneath that cool
reserve she showed everyone, there was a she-devil waiting to be let
loose again—with my lips, my hands, my tongue.

If only I could make that happen again. I sighed, shifting,
frustrated with myself. "I need you to look some shit up for me on
Google."

Her dark brows twitched, and she picked up the laptop then
opened it. It immediately came alive with the login music to Dragon
Epoch. I'd left the program open again.

When she realized what it was, she laughed. "Taking your work
home with you in a very literal way, I see…I didn't realize you play
Dragon Epoch."

I leaned back, unable to tear my eyes away from that wiggling foot.
"Of course I do. First rule of business, Weiss. Know your product.
Know what it can do. Know about the people who use your product."

Her mouth twisted. "Comic-Con nerds and pimply geek boys."

I shook my head, laughing. "Maybe in the eighties that was the case, but with our game, nearly half of the players are female. And they are of all ages, too. We have players in their tweens, teens, all the way up to retirement age. There are young married couples who can't afford to get out, so they play the game for entertainment and to spend time together. College kids with too much time on their hands, even entire families who play with their kids or family who live long distances away."

"Wow. And...and all the officers play?"

"Yes. Why not? It's a fun game. You should try it before you knock it, Weiss. Like I said, know your product. Didn't you ever log into your trial account we give the interns?"

A slow stain of color crept across her face. "Umm. I may have...misplaced that login code somewhere. I have to confess..." Her voice trailed off and then she shrugged.

My eyes darted from her cleavage down her shapely legs, back to that goddamn wiggling foot. "You're full of things to confess. What is it this time?"

She sent me an almost fearful look, as if whatever information she had to share with me would somehow spell her doom—like everything else I had on her wasn't quite enough, but this admission would finally cause the axe to fall.

"I'm, um, not much of a video game player."

"Well, as your boss, I'm telling you to *start*. On top of that, I want you to design and come up with three different options for a project you're going to work on. I'll choose from the three which one I want you to do."

Her mouth worked and she shifted uncomfortably, her eyes dropping to the notepad on her lap. She merely nodded and started taking notes, then ripped off the top paper and folded it.

I shifted, pulling my eyes away from those delicate ankles, wondering how much she actually knew. She'd admitted to me that she knew her sex partner from the video had been an employee, and she seemed on the level with the fact that that was all she knew. Either that or she was a damn good actress.

But who could trust a woman who would video herself having sex without letting the man know he was being recorded? The now familiar heated feeling of resentment and guilt bubbled up. That sex tape had almost ruined everything—still might ruin everything. All my hopes and goals were now balancing on the edge of a knife.

And yet…I still wanted to fuck her again. God, how I wanted to fuck her. As my eyes skimmed down the tedious forms and documents and I continued to bark commands at her, a lower, baser part of me was picturing her bent over the back of my couch or spread out on my kitchen counter…or anywhere, really. Naked. Writhing. Moaning my name.

I hadn't even had the chance to see her fully naked, either. I'd pounded her breathless and yet I still hadn't touched those full, soft tits. Hadn't tasted them.

Goddamn it. My eyes squeezed shut and I rubbed them through closed eyelids. She yawned loudly and I heard her stand. My eyes snapped open. Although I really didn't need her here, there was no way in hell I was letting her leave now, internal repressed sexual torture or not. But whether I needed her here didn't matter.

Tormenting her? That was another thing altogether. Because now it had become a game to me. I wanted to push her—see how far I could bend her until she broke. Until that cool demeanor, that pleasant façade shattered and the hellcat underneath showed herself again.

In fact, it was becoming my newest mission in life.

"Do you have something to drink? I'm falling asleep."

"There's bottled water in the fridge. Some energy drinks, too. And, oh—bring me a beer while you're at it." One beer wouldn't hurt...

Her mouth twisted and she gave me the evil eye. I almost snickered. *Good*. She turned to go and suddenly she stumbled, off balance and falling.

Before I could even think about it, I bolted out of my seat and caught her before she did a face-plant onto my glass coffee table. My arms closed around her torso, pulling her away from danger as she cursed. "My heel got caught in this goddamn loopy rug!"

As she steadied herself, my arms tightened around her instead of letting go. "I *told* you to take the shitty things off."

She tilted her head, looking into my face, eyes narrowing. With the three-inch heels, she was only about four inches shorter than me now, the top of her head reaching my nose. "No. I don't want to."

My mouth thinned and defiance formed in her eyes. As frustrating as she was, it was good to see her take a stand. She didn't do that nearly as often as she should.

Now we were staring at each other and it was getting awkward. She shifted against me and my asshole dick decided this would be a great time to perk up again. I could tell she noticed because the look on her face changed. Her eyes darkened as they dilated and her breathing suddenly quickened.

"You can let me go now," she said in a voice huskier than normal.

My arms flexed impulsively, as if rebelling at the thought of releasing her, unwilling to give up their prize. The feel of her pressed against me right now was just too good. Too much of what I'd been wanting all night.

"I can't do that."

"Why not?"

"Because I don't know if you're safe...not with those stilts attached to your feet."

She swallowed, and I was suddenly intensely curious as to how she would handle this. Would she rise to the challenge or would she give in? Could I break her this quickly?

Slowly, she shifted, deliberately rubbing her thigh against my erection. A bolt of lightning sizzled right through me, and the slow rise of those lips in a knowing smile told me she knew exactly what she was doing.

She was taking this situation and she was owning it, goddamn her. *Well played, Miss Weiss.*

I tightened my arms, pulling her against me. My hand moved to the back of her head as my head sank to hers. Now I was the one in control—or at least that was the lie I told myself as I pushed my tongue into her mouth.

7
APRIL

H E WAS KISSING ME. MY BOSS. THE MAN I LOATHED. THAT smoking hot dude in the swim trunks with the surfer's bod. *He* was kissing me.

My lips were bruising and swelling from the pressure he put on them as he forced my mouth open and slid his tongue inside. I squeezed my eyes shut, trying to resist that all-consuming tingling feeling that was starting at the back of my throat, slithering down my spine, coiling in my center like a traitorous snake. I may have been annoyed with him, but this kiss and his hold on me aroused me in seconds.

Jordan's arm remained locked around my rib cage, pressing me against him. The other hand traveled down my back, sliding along the silky material of my dress to fondle my ass. A low growl rose in the back of his throat and suddenly I was finding it hard to remain standing.

In my mind, I tried to summon up the memories of all those times he sent me back to the coffee shop. Considering it was almost every damn day, you wouldn't think it would be that difficult. But his smell—that hint of spice and sage and a salty tang—filled my nose, turning my insides into warm goo.

His breath was coming fast, and that mouth—those lips, that tongue—were doing wicked things to me. All at once I was aching, from my breasts to the dull throb between my legs. Aching with desire, hot, thick and heavy.

There was a fire in my belly that only he could put out. The feel of his solid abs against my rib cage, his hot arousal against my stomach. His mouth teasing mine and never letting up. Everything in my body trembled and everything inside my brain was taking a back seat to this new feeling of pure, seething lust.

My hands grasped at his t-shirt, pulling fistfuls before sliding up those perfect pecs to latch around his neck. Both his hands were on my ass and he nudged me, directing us to the couch. I stepped out of my shoes and went with him, ordering myself not to think about the irony that, by removing my shoes, I was giving him what he wanted. Right now I was ready to give him a whole lot more than that.

Without removing his mouth from mine, he pushed me down beneath him onto the couch. The weight of him on top of me felt so goddamn good. I wanted him to smother me, encompass me, press me underneath him and have his way with me.

His hand slid up my thigh, pushing up the skirt of my dress, and my legs cinched around his narrow, hard hips. He ground them against me and we both gasped in unison.

I tried to ignore the warning blipping at the back of my mind but it grew louder and louder, and I didn't have the excuse that alcohol was clouding my judgment. He was my boss. This was a huge mistake. If I went to bed with him—like my body was now *demanding* that I do—I would regret it. It would be as huge of a potential disaster as sex with the mystery man at Comic-Con.

But the other side of my brain was flashing the green light and sounding the bugle cavalry charge full speed ahead, hormones a-raging. I was about to get lucky with the second hot man in two weeks…

My hands stilled as my mind raced and his hand caressed the inside of my thigh. He wasn't saying anything, but his mouth was claiming mine, making the room spin. Every sense seemed to hyper-focus itself into a tunnel of sensation that was only him. His smell. His heat. His hands. His tongue. My body throbbed in time with the movements of his strokes across my feverish flesh.

I didn't just want this. I hungered for it—I *craved* it.

One hand stroked my chest through the satin of my dress. My nipples hardened painfully, ultrasensitive to his touch. His thumb brushed over my nipple, the pressure between my legs increasing to a near painful degree.

He pinched it and white-hot pleasure shot through my body and straight down to that coiled snake at my center. I let out a little cry, but he didn't relent.

"I want these tits in my mouth, Weiss," he groaned.

Those words almost made me peel my own clothes off my body. I wanted his mouth on my breasts. Sucking, nipping, licking.

I rubbed my hips against his, fucking him through his clothes. His hands slid under me to reach the zipper on the back of my dress. I arched my back to give him access and our mouths broke contact. His eyes opened and he stared into mine. We were both breathing like we'd just broken the surface after ten minutes of submersion. His warm breath bathed my face, his eyes almost black with lust.

"I got you out of those goddamn shoes," he finally said as he worked the zipper down. "But I don't give a shit. Because I want you out of this dress more."

My eyes closed as he pulled the strap down from my arm, his breath hissing through his teeth as he looked at my lacey, see-through bra. His head lowered to capture my nipple with his lips when suddenly there was a knock at the door.

His head jerked up, eyes meeting mine. He blinked, as if coming out of a daze, and then turned to take in the chrome digital clock hanging on the wall. It was a few minutes after nine p.m.

The knock came again and Jordan pulled back as if I'd sprouted thorns. "Shit," he mumbled.

"What? Who is it, your wife?" I joked.

He rubbed a hand over his mouth and jaw like he was trying to remove my lipstick. Luckily, my lipstick had worn off hours before and so the telltale evidence he feared wasn't even there. "Sit up and I'll zip you. Put your shoes on. It's Adam."

I sat bolt upright on the couch and did as he asked.

He growled at the door. "Just a fucking minute!"

"How do you know it's him?"

He stood and ran a hand over his hair, then adjusted his pants as if he could hide the sizeable erection straining against the fly of his jeans. I could barely tear my eyes away even though my heart was drumming in my throat from fear.

"Two reasons. The way he knocks, and the fact that it's nine and he's out for his evening run. He lives a mile and a half up the road."

"Is he checking up on you?"

Jordan bent and grabbed the laptop, snapping it shut and angling it in front of his crotch. "Grab that pad and pretend you're taking notes. And Jesus, don't let him see your mouth."

I rolled my lips inward to lick them. They felt bruised and swollen from his kisses. Another shot of desire speared me from breastbone to backbone. Jordan spun and strode to the door.

"What the fuck took you so long?" Adam's voice came from the open door.

"I'm in the middle of *working* with my *assistant* sitting right there." Jordan stepped back to let him in.

Adam was wearing running shorts and sneakers and a sweat-soaked t-shirt. I licked my lips again, feeling as guilty as if I'd been caught with a dirty book by a parent.

His eyes widened when he saw me. "Oh, hey April. Sorry about that," he said.

I assumed he was apologizing for his language. He took in my dress and shoes, frowning, then shot a look at Jordan. "I saw the email about the changed time for the meeting with the banker...thought I'd see if you needed any help with that, but I see you called in the cavalry."

"April brought me the file from Susan's desk and kindly volunteered to stay and help instead of going out dancing with her friends."

My face instantly heated. Wow...Jordan's casual lie to his best friend was so convincing that I almost believed it myself. And that was nothing short of scary. Who knew what other lies this man told on a regular basis? What did he say to women in order to get in their pants?

Although, with the way he looked, did he really have to *say* anything at all?

"Uh, yeah...we've been hammering away on the reports, trying to get the data together..." My voice faded as I got a glimpse of Jordan's expression, his frown telling me that he didn't approve of my not-so-suave attempt to follow his lead and lie.

Well, I sucked at lying so I didn't blame him for wanting to shut me up.

"How did you even know I was home?" Jordan asked Adam, shifting the laptop from one hand to the other while still managing to cover his crotch.

"I was running along the beach. Saw the lights on. Figured it was too early for you to have one of your dates back here yet..." Adam then glanced at me again, probably conscious that he didn't want to say much more with me here. But Jordan seemed even tenser than before.

"I was just about to send April home. If you want to take a look at what we were working on..."

Adam pulled out his phone and removed his ear buds, winding them up to set aside. "Sure."

Jordan, however, was trying to send me some sort of hidden signal with a furrowed brow and gritted teeth and overtly pointed glances at the door.

I had to admit, I really wanted to mess with him. So I pretended not to understand, looking away. I bit the inside of my cheek to keep from laughing. Now that the panic had subsided, I was finding this the most hilarious situation ever.

"So April was just going..." Jordan repeated.

I looked up. "Oh? I was? You sure you don't need me to help some more? Run some more searches?"

If looks could kill...

I smiled at him and he seethed. After an awkward silence, I stood. "Okay, well, the night's still young. I could probably still catch my friends over at the club."

Jordan scowled and I ignored him.

"Good night, Jordan. Night, Adam."

I grabbed my notes about Jordan's new assigned project and stuffed them in my purse, then nodded to them both. Adam went to the door and held it open for me. At least *he* was a gentleman.

But clearly I didn't *really* want a gentleman, because the wild animal who just had his hands and mouth all over me had been a lot more exciting. My body heat flared up again and the memory of him was causing me to sweat. Weak-kneed, I hobbled back to the driveway and my car.

His kisses had been amazing and my body was still aching with unfulfilled arousal. Goddamn it, his mouth had been inches from my nipple. I took a deep breath and then let it go. Now I'd never know what it would feel like. What *he'd* be like.

Sometimes at work, I watched his hands. They were large, strong hands. Masculine. I'd wondered if he was good in bed. He changed women like underwear, so it was evidenced—and even Adam had alluded to it. Jordan's dates were all six-foot tall, flawlessly beautiful size twos with glowing skin and amazing bone structure. He was an extremely good-looking guy and a millionaire so he had lots to offer, but he must have been pretty good in bed too. The angry ones often were...so I'd heard.

I sucked in a quick breath. Jordan was giving the sex god Falco of Comic-Con a run for his money in the hot sexual encounters department...and he hadn't even gotten to second base.

I clicked the alarm off on my car, shakily considering the consequences of what might have happened had we not been interrupted. I'd probably be naked and under him right this moment had Adam not shown up, and that could have been a disaster. Sex with my boss. Way to *really* screw the pooch, April. At least Falco the sex god was still a safely anonymous encounter that, God willing, would remain that way despite the notorious video.

I tried to shove the memory of Jordan's kisses and his hands out of my mind. I couldn't allow things to go any further. And judging from the look on his face, he probably felt the same way. We'd gotten carried away—that was it. No more being alone together. No more going over to his house.

When I arrived home, it was almost ten. Sid was in her fuzzy jammies and yellow Minion slippers huddled over her keyboard with a ridiculously oversized headset on that made her look like a helicopter pilot.

She was using a commanding tone of voice that she normally didn't use in her face-to-face encounters and saying things like, "Trash mobs just spawned! Hit your AOEs," and "No, no. Secondary heals only! You're drawing too much aggro."

It was like she was speaking a completely different language.

I followed her lead and changed into my most comfortable nightie. But instead of pulling out my e-reader and tunneling under the covers, I went to my desk beside hers and started running searches on Google.

As I skimmed over websites discussing Dragon Epoch, I tried to tune out Sid's laughing and joking with her friends. I only understood about half of it, but I could tell she was having a great time. They were chatting about the game but also about personal stuff, and it seemed as if she were from a different culture, relating to the world in a completely different way than I could. I was almost envious of it.

I glanced at her a few times and she frowned, curling a hand over her mic. "What are you doing home so early? You pooped out quickly."

I sighed. "It's a *really* long story. I got waylaid by the boss to help him with work stuff. Never made it to the club."

Sid's brows shot up and there was a look of concern in her eyes.

I went back to my search. There were approximately 35,754,632 hits that came back in seconds on a search for Dragon Epoch. I blew out a breath. Shit... I had a lot of homework to do if I wanted to know my product.

A short while later, I'd noticed silence from Sid's side of our work area. I glanced up and she was watching me, apparently having finished with her game.

"What?"

"So what *really* happened?"

"That's what really happened."

"He made you stay there and work with him on a Saturday night?"

"Yes." Her lips thinned. I shrugged at her. "What?"

"He didn't try anything with you, did he?"

I swallowed.

"April..." she said when I didn't answer. "You've mentioned before how young and hot he is. I know you already have a crush on him..."

"I don't have a crush on him. Sheesh." But I blushed. The thought of having a crush on my boss...okay, I thought he was hot. And after seeing him tonight in his trunks. That bod...and then the way he'd kissed me...

Shit. I had a crush on my boss!

"Apes, you need to be careful. You're in a very vulnerable state right now."

I turned away, embarrassed, and pretended to be engrossed in my search. "I have this project I have to work on," I mumbled, motivated to change the subject.

Sid angled her head to glance at my monitor, brows raised. "Just what are you trying to find?"

"I'm trying to get a better knowledge of the game so I know my product. I have no idea what project design I can come up with. And he wants three."

"Well, you could ask me for help, you know, since I spend approximately sixty-two hours a week playing it."

I shook my head. "Girlfriend, we have *got* to get you out more."

She shrugged. "I love my homies in the guild. We hang out virtually. It's a lot of fun."

"So all these people from all over the world who are logging into the game...how do you find people to play with and how do you make new friends?"

"Sometimes you just call for people to help you with a certain quest. If you end up grouping with cool people, you keep doing it again and again. Or you'll get invited to a raid or asked to join a guild."

I shook my head. "You might as well have just spoken Martian to me."

"Instead of sitting around Googling it, why don't you roll a character and start playing?"

"Hmm. Are there any good blogs or online magazines to look at?"

"What the hell did you do all those months you worked in marketing?"

I shrugged. "Mostly I made coffee and did some graphic design work for internal memos and newsletters and whatnot."

Sid rolled her eyes. "Okay, so...blogs. There are some really good ones. Unfortunately, my favorite, *Girl Geek*, is no longer writing on hers. Her stuff is archived, though, over at GameGlomerate. She's awesome...snarky. She blogs about feminist issues and gaming. Like...why the women are always scantily clad in chainmail bikinis or why male gamers have issues with women being as geeky as they are."

I pulled out a piece of paper and wrote down *Girl Geek*. "Why isn't she blogging anymore?"

Sid shrugged. "She cited life issues that have come up recently, although I think that it's because GameGlomerate bought her out. Her blog was by far the best, but there are some others that are still producing."

"Hmm. I'll find her blog and read her old posts then. But for now, I guess I need to form a character."

"*Roll* a character. Although it's not really rolling. They just say that because it comes from the old-school type of games where everything was randomly generated by a roll of the dice."

I frowned. "Uh, okay. Jordan gave me a key code I can use to log in."

Forty-five minutes later, after loading up the software, opening an account and downloading game patches, I was ready to create my own character.

"Are you sure you want to play a man?"

"Yeah. Why not?"

Sid shrugged. "I guess it doesn't matter. Most of the women running around in the game are played by guys."

"I can see why. They all look like Victoria's Secret Angels."

"Okay, so you want to be a male human. You get to choose features like hair color, eye color—"

"Medium-brown hair. Hazel eyes. Tall. Nice muscular body…"

"You have quite the clear picture of what you want him to look like."

I shrugged. *I get to watch him die. Over and over. Might as well get some enjoyment out of it.*

"Now you need to come up with a name for him."

Hmm. Jordan. Jordyn. Joldan? I shook my head. "I just want to call him 'Beast.'"

Sid gave me a puzzled look and instructed me to type the name in.

I admired him for a moment, dressed in a bland pair of brown trousers with no shirt. He didn't look exactly like his inspiration, but it would do.

"Okay, so now that I've created my own monster, aside from rubbing my hands together and shouting, *'It's alive!'* what do I do?"

Sid let out a long-suffering sigh. "You are really going to need me to baby you through this, aren't you?"

"Girlfriend, I upload sex videos to the Internet without even realizing it. I'm sure that if I press the wrong button on this game, all of Draco Multimedia Entertainment is bound to blow up. So, yes, talk to me like I'm a first grader."

"Like I don't already do that."

I smacked her arm. "I know where you live."

She laughed, nodding. "Okay, okay. Click that button that says *Enter Yondareth.* It will put your Beast into the world and then you can run around and get quests."

I did as she said. After a minimal waiting period, I was standing at the edge of a city gate. On one side of me was the entrance to the city, on the other side was a meadow. As I'd seen before in promotional artwork, videos and, most recently, the demo that Mia and Katya had run in the warehouse, the graphics were amazing. It really looked like I was standing in another world. Blades of grass shifted in the wind. Different bricks of varying colors were discernible in the city wall. Nearby, other figures stood, some elves, some dwarves, other humans. All different skin tones, hairstyles and features. Everyone had a name floating over his or her head.

"Now what?"

"You want to go up and talk to the NPCs—they're the game-generated people. The other avatars represent real people behind them. NPCs with quests have a shield symbol above their head. You complete quests to gain experience and items which help you gain levels for your character."

Not too long after, Sid left me to get ready for bed. She wandered into the room between brushing her teeth, brushing out her hair and her various other nighttime routines to give me pointers or nod approvingly at what I'd accomplished.

"This old elf guy in the kilt wants me to go pick a bunch of flowers for him. That sounds like a dumb quest," I said as she flipped back the covers on her bed.

"You have to do that quest. There's a whole big story behind it. It's so romantic. And it leads to other, higher-level quests. *Everybody* does that quest. It's like a tradition in Dragon Epoch."

"Ah, okay," I said, shrugging.

Sid let me know she was turning the lights out and going to sleep. I grunted at her, plugging my ear buds into the headphone jack so the sounds of the game wouldn't disturb her. I figured I'd play for another half hour or so before throwing in the towel and getting some shut-eye.

The next time I looked up at the clock, it was four a.m.

Four. Freaking a.m. And I had to get ready for work in two hours.

The game had sucked hours of my life in immersive amusement and I hadn't even realized it. At all. Man, this stuff was better than crack. No wonder so many people loved it so much.

Even when I lay down, though, it was hard to sleep. I kept thinking about what had happened between Jordan and me at his house. Though it had felt so good and my body had even begun to ache again with the memory of it, I knew I could never follow through with these feelings. I had to fight them.

But...I might have fantasized about him for a little while before I fell asleep. There was nothing wrong with a healthy fantasy, was there?

One way or the other, this job was going to be the death of me.

8
JORDAN

ONE WAY OR THE OTHER, THIS WOMAN WAS GOING TO BE THE death of me.

Adam had camped out on my couch for a few hours after she left, helping me go over the paperwork. At first he'd thrown me a few questioning glances, and for good reason. It looked bad...the time I'd taken to answer the door. The way she'd been dressed. Adam probably thought we'd been out on a date together. But up until the moment I'd kissed her, it had all been completely innocent...well, as innocent as not wanting her to go out and pick up some other guy could have been, anyway.

I buried the rest of my weekend in work—and working out—figuring that was the surest way to get that woman out of my mind. I was spending way too much time remembering the way she felt underneath me as I kissed her and touched her body. And it was a hard sell to get my own body to not react to it.

My Monday early-morning meeting with the investment banker was lackluster. He'd been fairly cranky about our current situation with the viral sex tape. But the good news was that he seemed to think there were steps we could take to avert disaster.

Adam wasn't going to like his suggestions, though. Regardless, I was going to do anything—*anything*—to keep this project going. And I was rubbing up against the two-week deadline he had imposed on me. I'd have to turn the charm all the way up on this one...and point it right at my best friend.

"Sexual harassment training?" Adam spun from his office window to pin me down with his black stare. "You aren't shitting me, are you?"

I held my hands out to him, palms up, an 'I give up' gesture. "He had a couple other stipulations as well. There's all this controversy now going on in the gamer community regarding sexist attacks against women—"

Adam nodded. "Yeah. Yeah. I've been following all that and watching it closely. We've got anti-harassment protocols in our *Terms of Service* and protective measures—"

"In the game, yeah, that's great. But with the employees—"

He sighed. "Of course with the employees. We follow the law of the land."

"He thinks we need to go the extra mile. We need to hire a consultant and go through a regimented training program. Every last employee, down to the janitorial staff."

Adam was staring at me like I'd grown another eyeball in the middle of my head. "How long does something like that take?"

"State law requires two hours every two years. But if we are putting our best foot forward and really trying to cover our asses—"

He shook his head. "God, no. Two hours is enough, Jordan."

"You should double it. And everyone attends. Even you. Even me."

Rubbing his jaw, he slid his hand over his mouth. "There are online programs for that."

"We should all do it together, as a company, in person. And the employees should see *us* sitting there—"

"*Policing* them?" He scowled. "I don't want this to devolve into finger-pointing, do you understand? We have employees who are married to each other or are living together or even just dating. There's nothing wrong with any of that."

I shrugged. "I agree."

"But then, any of them could have been the stars of our infamous video, I guess."

The collar on my monkey suit suddenly felt tight. "Yeah. It, um— it could have been anyone."

His black eyes flicked up to me. "Have you figured it out yet?"

I held up my hands. "Whoa, who the hell am I? CSI Irvine? I've got my people working on it, like I said. But the shit is viral and there was no metadata to find on the video. The person who recorded it had location information turned off." *Thank God for that.* "Though that could have only told us so much, and without a warrant, we can't get the IP address of the person who uploaded the original copy, even if we could trace the copies back to the original one...which my guy has told me is virtually impossible. It's like looking for a needle in a thousand stacks of needles."

His mouth thinned. "With the identifying information stripped from the video, I'd agree with you. Shit." He ran a hand through his hair and stared out the window again.

"Look... I've been putting out fires with the IPO attorneys, the underwriters, and the banker. Let's not expend our time, energy and resources on a witch-hunt. That horse has already left the barn."

"If we find out who it was, we could cut the culprit loose and show that we are taking care of the situation."

"Corporate training and some of these other things would do the same thing, to be honest. In the eyes of the Wall Street crowd, anyway."

"So the banker actually suggested sexual harassment training..."

"You think I'd make that shit up? And as for those other things..." Oh, he was not going to like these. I braced myself.

His eyes narrowed. "Out with it. What?"

"We release a statement about this whole gamer sexual harassment thing that's going on."

"But we have nothing to do with that," he huffed. "None of those people have any association with Draco Multimedia Entertainment or Dragon Epoch. It's a bunch of sexually frustrated, antisocial fifteen-year-old kids bullying women over the Internet."

"Other associations and companies have made their stand. We should too. Consider it a restating of our own *Terms of Service* against harassment and cyber bullying."

He waved a dismissive hand. "Whatever. What else are we doing?"

"Oh, some monetary donations, community service hours—"

"Community service hours? Doing what? Picking up trash on the side of the freeway?"

"I'll line up something—get us some good press. We're going to be earning feathers in our cap, that's all. We just need to keep our noses clean. I've got that TED talk next month. And we've got all those awards the game is up for—especially Game of the Year. *Entrepreneur Weekly* is featuring us on their cover. This is good shit. We can turn this around. We're a big company and everyone has their brush with scandal. This little thing isn't going to tank us. "

"*Yet,*" he replied, stuffing his hands in his pockets.

"Christ, Adam. You're always such a glass-is-half-empty kinda guy."

"I'm a realist, and it's my job to look down the road ahead to see what's in store for this company and prepare for it. And given our previous dance with scandal..."

Adam was still somewhat jaded from the legal run-in last year with the family of the murder-suicide victims. Our company had been embroiled in a struggle with our liability insurance company, which had refused to allow Adam to fight the case in court, insisting we settle instead. It had been a setback for us, a minor misstep in the early stages of my progression toward our IPO.

"So no bullshit here, but does he really think this is going to work?"

I nodded. "Yeah, he really does. He says the New York Stock Exchange is hungry for tech companies to open with them instead of NASDAQ, which is where the biggies like Facebook have been going for their IPOs. They *want* us, Adam. But we need to toe the line and keep ourselves distant from this online cyber war-of-the-sexes going on in the other gamer communities." I looked at him and then glanced out the window, unable to meet his gaze as I delivered the rest. "Besides, there's been a lot of doubt about whether or not that video actually even featured Draco employees or if that badge was a plant."

Adam actually laughed at that. "Wow, I don't know whether to feel threatened or flattered that someone would go to all that trouble to smear our reputation like that."

I shrugged. "You never know..." It felt kind of slimy to put this idea into his head, but better to take the pressure off me and let him fixate on something else.

He glanced at me and then away, stuffing his hands into his pockets. "I think it's best to apply Occam's razor. The simplest explanation is the most likely one. Which means that at least one of those two was an employee getting their freak on at Comic-Con," Adam said, raising a brow.

I paused, waited for a long moment and worked up the courage to ask him the big question. "So what's the verdict, oh illustrious leader? Are we going public or are we yanking our bid?"

Adam turned and looked out the window again, taking a breath and appearing deep in thought. He actually looked like he was still considering yanking the whole thing. I figured this might be a good time to remind him why we'd set out to do this in the first place.

"That prototype equipment is really amazing. Imagine the things you'll be able to do when you have the capital to incorporate that new interface into the game."

"Oh, I've already imagined it," he said. "But I'm not going to injure our bottom line because of my pipe dream."

"It's not a pipe dream, Adam. You've got the vision and ability to see this through. There isn't another MMO game out there that is using an interface like this—not even the mighty World of Warcraft. Just think what our game could do if you have the assets to acquire the company that makes that equipment. And you get to apply all that knowledge in your boy genius brain to develop a three-dimensional experience for players."

He shot me a look out of the corner of his eyes. "Laying it on a bit thick, aren't you?"

"C'mon, man. The players are going to eat that shit up. I saw how much fun Mia was having during the demo. If for no one else, you have to at least do it for the woman you love."

Adam barked out a laugh. "Man, you are so full of shit your eyes are brown! *'Do it for the woman you love.'* I can't wait to tell her that tonight. She'll wet herself laughing when she hears that came out of your mouth."

I shrugged. "Hey, I've gotta try, right?"

"You never cease to amaze me. All right. I have full confidence in you, my 'rookie CFO.' Go get 'em, tiger."

I felt a surge of victory. "You aren't shitting me, right? You aren't leading me on so you can squash my hopes like a bug?"

He rolled his eyes. "No, I'm not. We're still in for the bid. But I'm trusting you"—he brought his hand up and pointed at me—"to keep me informed of everything that is going on. And if you have a moment of doubt about *anything*, I want you to come to me with it, okay? I know how much you want this, but I also trust that this isn't going to come at the expense of our company."

I shook my head. "Never. I may not be King of the Geeks like you, my friend, but I love this company every bit as much as you do."

Adam's eyes grew shrewd. "You love the goose that lays the golden eggs."

I shrugged. "That too. There's no denying this company gives me a nice fat bank account, which I duly enjoy."

He laughed. "Yes, you do. What 'benefits' are you enjoying this week? Is it that blond D-list actress or the brunette *Vogue* model?"

I smirked. "Now don't be jealous just because you've doomed yourself to be a one-woman man. One woman...for the rest of your life...no variety...never changing..." I feigned a yawn.

"It's you I feel sorry for. But enjoy it while it lasts, man. I suspect when it's your turn, you're going to fall hard."

I shook my head. "Nah. You have to have a heart to fall in love, and I had that removed a long, long time ago."

It was Adam's turn to smirk. "Yeah...right. We'll see about that."

"What is it with dudes when they settle down? They're all about wanting to drag their friends down with them. Misery loves company, I guess. Besides—you're marrying your cousin. I just changed my ringtone for you to banjo music."

"Fuck you," he said, moving to his desk when his phone chimed. He picked it up to read the text message.

"Is that the little woman now? Or should I say, the little *cousin*?"

Adam didn't look up from the phone as he read but held up his free hand, middle finger pointed straight in the air. He wasn't too pleased about the fact that he and Mia were now related by marriage, since his uncle had married her mother a few months before.

"I'll just mention to her that you called her 'the little woman' and *she* can take care of you the next time she sees you. It was nice knowing you." Adam typed out a quick reply to the text message.

"I'd actually be scared, but you need me too much for this IPO."

He grinned. "That I do." Then he frowned as if something had occurred to him and flicked me a speculative glance. "So, ah, how's your intern working out for you? You teaching her lots of interesting stuff?"

I shifted my stance a little, stuffed my hands in my pockets and shrugged with one shoulder. Trying to act casual without looking like I was acting casual.

"She's okay." I hoped the façade worked, because I definitely did not feel as casual as I hope I looked. I was already starting to sweat under my collar at the memory of what had happened between us on Saturday night.

The feel of her curvy, feminine body underneath me on the couch. The taste of her. Those gorgeous tits that could bring a man to his knees. I clenched my jaw.

Adam frowned. "You okay? Did she piss you off or something?"

I resisted looking at him but surmised this was far from an off-the-cuff question. Likely, Adam had been suspicious about the whole thing since interrupting us the other night. And if he hadn't interrupted us? I knew I wouldn't have stopped, and I had reason to believe she wouldn't have either.

I swallowed. She still had no idea that we'd already had sex once. Now the guilt over this situation had a new layer added to it—as if it needed any more. The guilt about lying to Adam, jeopardizing the company and nearly ruining all our hopes and dreams wasn't enough. Add to that the guilt I felt over the fact that I had been all over her on Saturday night, and that if we had gone to bed, she'd have had no idea that we'd been together before.

I took a deep breath, knowing I had to play this cool. Adam wasn't asking me to make small talk. He didn't work like that. There was a purpose behind everything that he did and said.

And if I wasn't careful—because the guy was as observant as a hawk, too—I could get snagged by my own lies. "She's fine. I torment her, she hates me. It's a perfectly healthy boss-employee relationship."

Ah, yes, if I hadn't already been heading there, I was definitely going to Hell for that one. Now if I could ignore the fact that apparently I'd been the best sex of her life—and, well, she'd ranked up there in the top three for me.

Maybe top two, I'd admit—if begrudgingly.

I slid out of that meeting a few minutes later, mentally wiping my brow that Adam had chosen not to give me the third degree about the intern. I glanced across the atrium and saw April at her desk.

I'd already vowed to avoid her as much as possible from here on out. As much as I could, anyway. But it was going to be difficult.

Mostly because I really didn't *want* to.

I liked looking at her. She was beautiful, of course, but it wasn't only about looking at a pretty face, perfect, shiny hair and a fine ass. There was this inexplicable deepness in her lovely blue eyes that made it obvious there was a lot going on behind them. But she showed the world a serene, collected face even in the midst of the scorching humiliation and criticism I'd heaped upon her of late. Not to mention, I'd been almost obsessed with the idea of getting her to crack.

Over the next few days, I started noticing that April was avoiding me as much as I was avoiding her. She started getting to work earlier than me and leaving my coffee sitting on the desk in a special insulated cup before I'd get there. When I'd walk into the atrium and stop to talk to Susan, April would get up and leave her desk. In the break room, when I entered, she either left or sat on the other side of the room.

Soon it had become a game. I'd find an excuse to come out of the office a few times a day. Every time, she'd leave. I didn't have time for that shit—except that my brain, of course, thought it would be a great thing to fixate on.

I also wasn't above noticing how Adam's creepy little nerd assistant, Charles, had developed a thing for her, too. He was over at her desk a lot, and one day I even spotted him walking her to lunch. I began wondering if they were eating lunch together every day. Okay, so I'd prevented her from going out and picking up someone at a club one night, but that didn't mean shit, did it?

Only a few days later, I lost my resolve to avoid her because avoiding her meant I couldn't keep an eye on her. And besides, I rationalized, it was time to talk to her about her project.

After lunch, I entered the atrium where she sat talking on the phone at her desk and took the long way around so she wouldn't see me coming. I stood beside her, waiting for her to wrap up, but she didn't notice me immediately.

"I'm sorry, I didn't know the Beast was going to give me all this work today. It looks like I won't be able to make it." She paused, shifting in her chair and doodling on the pad of paper in front of her where she had scribbled down Le Chat Noir—the name of a martini lounge not far from here.

I wondered what she was talking about. I hadn't given her anything extra to work on for days...then it occurred to me that she was using work as an excuse not to go.

"Okay...well, I'll try then. Just give me the address. Yeah, yeah. I can find it using my GPS. You said it's nearby?"

She jotted down the address. At that moment, she became aware of my presence and nearly jumped when she looked up at me. I gave her my most convincing glare and frown.

"I gotta go," she huffed into the receiver and slammed down the phone.

"Who was that? Your little admirer?"

She gave me a wary look. "I don't have any admirers." I raised my brow in disbelief. Clearly, she was lying to me. Disappointing, but...did I expect anything else?

Her eyes flicked away nervously. "It was just my friends in marketing. They wanted to go out tonight."

"More partying? Maybe you need more work to do."

Her eyes narrowed. "Maybe I do."

"You still haven't come up with ideas for your project."

She turned her chair to face me, folding her arms across her chest. "Actually, I *have*. I emailed them to you this morning."

I ran my thumb along my jaw line. "Hmm. Okay, I'll have a look. Who's 'the Beast,' by the way?"

Her skin reddened like a fresh sunburn. She nervously tucked a long, silky strand of dark hair behind her delicate ear. I swallowed, my eyes tracing over the elegant line of her neck.

Christ. I shook my head. "Never mind. I think I can guess. Carry on, Weiss. You don't want to keep your little friends waiting. I'm sure you're all dying to get drunk and laid tonight."

She bit her plump, sexy lip and again I swallowed, ripping my eyes away. Pushing back from her desk, I went back to my office, disturbed at how I felt about her going out with the giggling interns to meet men. It was her prerogative, of course. It wasn't like I had any right to dictate what she did and didn't do. But damned if it didn't irritate the piss out of me anyway.

I was her boss, after all, so if she were to get drunk and go home with some strange dude, that would affect her ability to work on my projects and get things done. And damn it, she was responsible for this clusterfuck. So I was looking after my own professional interests when I called up Adam's cousin, William, who worked in the art department, asking him to go along with me that night to Le Chat Noir.

William was an unlikely wingman. I'd known him from the beginning days of the company when Adam had brought him in to work on early concept artwork for Dragon Epoch. We'd developed a full portfolio to take around to venture capitalists who would become our first investors to help us get the company off the ground. After we'd gotten the ball rolling, William had taken a job in the art department.

He was immensely talented but shy, quirky and more than a little awkward.

Right before Comic-Con, he'd come into my office unannounced. Plopping himself down on a chair with hands in his pockets and eyes on the floor, he'd asked me what my secret was for getting all the women.

If I hadn't known any better, I would have thought that Adam was punking me. I'd tried not to laugh. William was a great guy, but I'd been at a loss to explain to him 'when you've got it, you've got it' or the concept of *mojo*. William was autistic, and thus did not do well with abstract concepts like that.

So I'd promised him a demonstration when I had more time. And tonight, apparently, would be that night. He hadn't seemed too thrilled about going to a bar, but it was more of a lounge than a bar, I'd reasoned. It took some time to talk him into it, saying that this was how I met women—which was not exactly the truth. The women I dated I'd met at much classier places than this one.

Le Chat Noir was not a dive by any stretch. It actually tried its hardest to be a level above the typical meat market type of places these tended to be—especially in a college town like Irvine. The décor was muted purples and black. Jazzy music played over a sound system, though it appeared as if they had live music regularly.

William and I sat at a small table nursing drinks. William had ordered a beer and I had a rum and coke, minus the rum. I flicked a glance at my introverted companion; I hadn't accounted for his reserve to make this situation awkward. Oh well, we hadn't come for him, anyway.

After asking a few questions, I finally found out that there was a particular woman he'd had an eye on—one of Mia's girlfriends. I'd met her once—the blonde—pretty girl. He'd known her for over a year and still hadn't asked her out. Christ. This poor guy was probably almost crippled from blue balls syndrome.

Twenty minutes after we arrived, a group of young women from Draco—April among them—entered the room. No sign of that creep Charles. Good. However, I did notice a lot of male heads turn as they walked past. I knew what was going through their minds. They were categorizing each woman based on coloring, body style, height and looks. Some women had gorgeous bodies but so-called "butter face"— meaning she was hot, "but her face."

April was most definitely *not* in that category. She was shorter with a more petite build than her friends—the shortest one in the crowd. She trailed behind the other three, most noticeable because of her long, dark hair, which she wore down and to the middle of her back. I'd spent more time than I should looking at that hair, wondering if it was black or dark brown, studying how it reflected the light, wanting to smell it. It was silky, shiny and I wanted to run my fingers through it. Wanted to wrap it around my hands while I fucked her.

I jerked my eyes away, taking another sip of my unleaded drink. William was sulking, watching me with his dark eyes. As usual, he was dressed in mismatched clothing. He didn't have a knack for fashion—nor did he have a stylish haircut. Nevertheless, half the women on this side of the bar were checking him out and he was completely unaware. Figured. Although Adam had a better sense of style, the family resemblance was unmistakable and my best friend had a similar effect on women. What *was* it with that family, anyway, that made them women-magnets?

The group of Draco interns took a table near the other side of the bar from us, but in clear line of sight. Sometime after work, April had changed into a short purple dress that accentuated her pale complexion and her curves perfectly. Eyes followed her as she walked by, and I wanted to stab out every one of them for looking at her and thinking the same dirty thoughts that were going through my mind at this moment.

"I still don't understand the point of us being here," William said in his usual blunt monotone.

"Well, when you asked me how I talked to women, I told you it was hard to explain—that I'd have to show you. I figured I had the time tonight. I could show you."

He frowned. "I don't like this at all."

Over his shoulder, a blonde about thirty years old had not stopped staring at him. It was clear she was waiting for him to look up so she could meet his gaze and give him a 'come-hither' smile. *Good luck with that, lady.*

"Consider this practice. I have acquired our first target. There's a blonde on the other side of you who appears...interested."

William scowled. "This isn't what I meant when I said I wanted to learn how to talk to women. I already have the woman in mind that I want to talk to. I told you. I want Jenna."

"*Women*, William. Plural. You know what they say, there are a lot of fish in the sea."

He shook his head. "I don't like fishing."

I scratched at my chin then threw another glance at the interns from Draco. A couple of guys had joined them and were chatting them up, beer bottles in hand. April did not appear to be engaging with them but was staring intently at her cell phone.

Across from me, William harrumphed. "You aren't here to talk to *women plural* either. You've been staring at those Draco interns since they came in. Especially April Weiss."

I jerked my head back to William. "Listen, do you want to learn what I do or not?"

He said nothing, returning a heated glare at me, his eyes dropping almost immediately.

"Have you tried just, you know, asking her out?"

William kept his eyes on the tabletop. "I don't know what words I should use. That's why I was asking you. And after I ask her, if she says yes, I have no idea how to talk to her."

"Talk to her like she's your friend, or a member of your family. It might be less scary if you ask her to go out in a group—like, for instance, find something you like to do with friends and see if she wants to go along."

He appeared to be fixated on every word while staring at the tabletop.

"But while we're here, we can practice on these ladies…" I took another sip of my drink and slid off my chair. "Watch and learn, kid."

"We are nearly the same age. I am three weeks older than you. I'm not a kid. I'm not even relatively a kid compared to you."

I waved him off. "Relax, William, jeez. That blonde who's been staring at you? I'm going to go get her number for you."

Before he could protest, I made my way over to her table where she sat with her friend. As soon as she saw me approach, she said something to her friend and they both turned to smile at me.

"Hello, ladies, how are you tonight?"

"Hello there." The blonde and her friend both looked me up and down with a smile. They were prettier from a few tables away than they were up close, but they seemed nice enough.

The brunette next to her perked up, giving me a wide smile, and leaned forward, providing me with a nice view of her ample cleavage. "Hi! I'm Skyler. This is Avery."

"I'm Jordan, and my friend over there, the shy guy, is William. Would you like to join us for a drink?"

The ladies exchanged glances and the blonde nodded enthusiastically, her eyes fixed on William, who had pulled out a pocket-sized sketchpad and was writing or drawing something. At a bar. We'd have to have a chat about that.

The ladies joined us and I ordered another round of drinks, then proceeded to spend the next half hour in the most stilted, awkward conversation *ever* while attempting to get William to open up—he never did.

He kept his head down, answered questions in monosyllables and continued to sketch. This was going to be a long night. I found myself constantly checking the other side of the bar where men were on that table of nubile young interns like a fat kid on a Twinkie.

My blood pressure shot up every time one of them talked to her. *Fuckers.* If looks could kill, they would all be dead.

She spotted me not long after the women came to join us at my table for drinks. It was fairly amusing to watch her do a double take when she'd glanced over, recognized me and looked back, her eyes narrowing.

Not long after that, she started sending me her own looks of death. She did *not* appear happy to see me here. Tough shit. What was she going to do, order me to leave?

As the minutes passed, I became less and less aware of the people at my table and more and more fixated on the goings-on over at intern-central. The two women eventually finished their drinks and drifted away, but William's dirty looks were not lost on me. He continued to draw and I ordered another Coke, vowing to myself that I wasn't going home until she left the bar alone. If it took the closing of the bar to do that, then so be it.

9
APRIL

Y EYES FLICKED AGAIN TO THE BEAST, WHO WAS DOING his best to mad dog me from across the room. What was he trying to prove by being here, anyway? I shot him another set of invisible daggers across the room. He was sitting at a table with two women and a good-looking, dark-haired guy who looked really familiar for some reason. After puzzling it out for a moment, I remembered that I'd seen him at Draco. A fellow employee.

"So what do you think of my plan?" Cari was muttering to me on this end of the table, completely ignoring the two guys talking to Ingrid and Sheila at the other end.

"What plan again?"

"You know... about a certain devilishly handsome CEO we both know."

I poked my straw into the dregs of my drink, twirling it around the ice cubes. When she'd first proposed this absurd "plan" to me a half hour before, I'd finally decided she must be insane. Of course, I was too chicken shit to say it. I shrugged.

She scowled. "Come *on*, April. We were *all* in marketing working together last year. You, me and her. Why did he pick *her*...do you ever wonder that? Over you or me? What does *she* have? It's like...he was totally unattainable to all of us, and then one night at the employee party in Vegas, he started drinking and then dancing with Mia. The next thing everybody knows, they're a couple. Did she put Rohypnol in his drink or something?"

I suppressed rolling my eyes. "We have no idea what happened. They could have been dating before that, Cari." I licked my lips. "Anyway, it's crying over spilt milk now. He put a ring on it. He's engaged."

Her eyes were burning with a strange sort of intensity. "He *hasn't* put a ring on it yet. At least not the ring that counts. And even if he had... well...it wouldn't be the first marriage I'd broken up." She batted her eyes and swished her impossible amounts of blond hair. "My senior English seminar teacher, to be specific. His wife left him because of me."

I raised a brow. His job probably left him because of her, too.

"So you have a superpower?"

She tilted her head haughtily. "Why certainly, if I do say so myself. And now my sights are set on Adam."

"But you don't seem to have gotten very far."

She flicked her eyebrows up as if sharing a lurid secret. "I catch him checking me out sometimes."

I sighed. I highly doubted that.

"Why not? I've got more tits and ass than she had even before she got sick."

I pushed my cup of ice cubes in my face to hide the utter shock and disgust I felt at her words. She was a piece of work, and I wondered what had possessed me to join her and her cronies out here tonight.

Oh yes, it was because she had pestered me incessantly for two days straight and punctuated it with her pointed concern: "*I hope no one finds out it was you in the video. I'm so nervous for you. You must be stressed out. Can I buy you a drink?*"

There'd been a clear message there. Play nice with her or she could make trouble. I wondered how I could get out of this before she started increasing the pressure with more threats. As usual, I'd keep my mouth shut and play nice while trying to think my way out of the situation.

But there might not be an easy way. Besides avoidance. I could do that...I was an expert at it. My dad had been trying to get a hold of me for almost a month now. And my mom would be needing a PI soon in order to get a call through to me.

If they gave degrees in avoidance, I'd have a Ph.D. and everyone would be calling me Dr. Weiss.

"I'm going to get another drink."

"Is this one going to have alcohol in it?" she asked.

I slipped off my stool and shrugged. I was still honoring my vow to never drink alcohol again. She called after me as I headed to the bar. "When you get back, we are going to discuss the plan."

I resisted shaking my head, afraid that she would see. I pressed up against the bar and noticed the nearest bartender was talking to a pair of tall and very beautiful blondes. I gave the front of my dress a tug to show some cleavage and then leaned forward. Another bartender appeared in front of me in one minute flat. I smiled, shaking my empty glass. "Can I get another Shirley Temple?"

He frowned, apparently certain he'd misheard me.

"Yeah, you heard it right."

His brow twitched and he smiled. "Coming right up, beautiful."

I smiled. Even if he was milking me for a bigger tip, I didn't care. Tonight especially, I really needed to hear it.

The bartender turned back to me, placing the drink down on the bar. I handed him my money and he rang me up. But to my surprise, he didn't move on. "I'm Chris. How are you tonight?"

"April. Nice to meet you. Currently, I'm trying to avoid my psycho friend."

He flicked a glance over my shoulder. "The blondie over there? She does have a bit of the crazy eyes going on."

I smirked, pressing the drink to my lips. "It's not the only thing crazy about her."

He laughed and gave me the once-over. Okay, I'd already paid and tipped him, so I decided he wasn't just trying to snag a bigger tip from me. I gave him my best flirty smile.

"That's not the only crazy-ass thing about this night. My even crazier boss is over on the other side of the room trying to hit on women twice his age."

He threw his head back and laughed. "Well, who said we didn't have entertainment?"

I licked my lips and he followed the motion, his gaze lingering on my mouth. "So I'm off in an hour. You planning on hanging around?"

"I just might be." I flashed him another smile. He was cute. Not overwhelmingly gorgeous, but my track record with *those* types was not good. I swallowed as I remembered not too many days before when I'd had a heart-stoppingly gorgeous man all over me.

I flicked another gaze across the bar at him. He was chatting with the women at his table, but his eyes were on me. When our gazes met, his eyes visibly narrowed. What was he, my babysitter?

I pressed the drink to my lips again, this time clasping the glass so that my middle finger was visible to him, obviously positioned that way on purpose. When he saw, his eyebrows rose. With a wide grin, I put the drink down and shot the bartender another flirty smile.

"Be right back...where's the ladies' room?"

He pointed. "Don't lose your way back to me, lovely April."

Ugh. That was cheesy. But my grin remained pasted to my face as I slipped away from the bar and weaved between crowded tables toward the back of the room and down a dark hallway.

I twisted the knob on the scuffed-up bathroom door, finding it locked. Damn it. I didn't frequent this place at all, but if it was like other bars, there were probably people fucking in there. I didn't have to go to the bathroom that badly. It had been an excuse to get away, maybe spend fifteen minutes sitting in a stall reading on my phone. This whole night was proving deeply annoying, between Cari's "plot" to go after Adam—and somehow, vaguely involve me in it—and Jordan's unexpected appearance and subsequent social butterfly routine. Personally, I would never have pegged him for a place like this. I would have thought he did his woman-trawling at private parties for the rich and famous and incredibly hot model and actress hopefuls.

With a sigh of frustration, I stepped away from the bathroom door and pressed my back up to the fake wood paneling on the wall in the narrow hallway. Well, the good news was that, wherever I was—whenever I didn't want to be there—as long as I had my phone, I had an e-book I could read. And I was currently in the middle of the steamiest, most lurid romance novel ever, complete with a rotten-to-the-core motorcycle gang biker dude chasing after the virginal preacher's daughter.

I slid back along the wall when I heard someone coming toward me and flattened to make room for the person to move past. But the person stopped right beside me, and I had the sensation he or she was reading my phone over my shoulder. I looked up into Jordan's face.

"What the hell are you reading?" he asked.

I clicked the phone off, shoving it into my shoulder bag. "None of your business. What are you doing here?" I spun, facing him. Now that I was seeing him up close, I couldn't help but notice he looked particularly fetching tonight. He was wearing black jeans that hugged his slim hips and a dark green button-down shirt, open at the collar to reveal his strong neck. I swallowed and looked away.

"I was thirsty," he said with a mocking gleam in his eyes. He glanced around the narrow hallway then his eyes fixed on the back door. "What are you doing back here?"

"Waiting for the bathroom. It's locked."

"There's probably somebody fucking in there."

I turned and pressed my shoulder against the wall, folding my arms. "So how's the hitting on the old ladies going? Get any of them to take out their dentures for you?"

His eyes flashed dangerously. "The older ones know what they're doing. Sometimes better than the young ones."

His comment knocked the breath right out of me. That same old hurt from Gunnar and my mom. My mouth fell open and then I snapped it closed again, turning around because he blocked my way back into the bar. And I really didn't want to go back in there anyway, because tears were now prickling my eyes. So I turned and grabbed the back doorknob, gave it a twist and ended up in the alley behind the bar. I slammed the door behind me, but two seconds later Jordan pushed his way through.

It was dark and quiet back here. The only lighting came from a distant street lamp. Tiny puddles of gross water collected in dips of asphalt. And naturally, there was a distinct stench coming from the direction of a big green dumpster.

Jordan glanced around and then looked at me, eyes wide. "What the hell was that about?"

I turned my head away from him, quickly brushing tears away with the back of my hand. "That was about getting the hell away from you. Too bad you can't take a hint."

His eyes narrowed as he watched me, then his thumb brushed across my cheek as if to verify what he was seeing. "Are you crying?"

I gave a sniff and jerked my head away. "No. Go away now."

He ignored me, of course. "What's going on, Weiss? Did that bartender say something to you? I'll go fuck him up."

"No. I'm fine. *He* was nice. Nicer than any other guy I've talked to in months."

He didn't say anything in reply, just scowled. If possible, he looked even hotter when he scowled—it was an intense sort of look, with his eyes narrowing like darts that could punch a hole right through me. Then he cleared his throat and looked away. He pulled a bar napkin from his back pocket and handed it to me.

I took it without a word, blotted tears from my cheeks and blew my nose. "How much have you had to drink?" he asked quietly.

"No alcohol. I do stupid shit when I drink."

He frowned. "So what's with the crying then?"

I shrugged. "You're my boss, not my psychotherapist."

"Are you going home with that bartender?"

"Is that any of your business?"

He moved in close, standing right in front of me, bracing a hand on the wall above my head. My heart hammered in my chest. He ran a finger along the line of my jaw, giving me that intense look again. His Adam's apple bobbed as he visibly swallowed.

"I'm making it my business." Then his finger slipped down the column of my throat, over my collarbone and right to the deep cleavage of my neckline. Where his finger traced my skin, his touch burned. I felt it clear down to my bones. My chest squeezed tight. I couldn't breathe. He pissed me off and turned me on like no other man could. I froze as his head dipped so that his lips were mere millimeters from mine. I could feel his breath on my face. And I didn't smell alcohol like I'd expected to.

"You're a good girl, April Weiss. And those are the worst kind."

I frowned, completely confused. And then his hand was on my thigh, sliding slowly up my skirt. His eyes shot a challenge into mine. He seemed to be daring me to stop him. I didn't. Instead, I reached out and brushed my hand against his crotch, rubbing him through his jeans. He sucked in his breath and hardened immediately under my touch.

"Tell me to stop, April," he whispered.

I wouldn't. I continued to rub him until his erection was straining against his fly. His hand was now on my panties, lightly stroking me through the silky material. I let out a little whimper and the world spun around me. His fingers pushed aside my panties and then he was rubbing me along the seam of my sex.

When I gasped, it was into his mouth because it had sealed over mine, muting me. As his tongue thrust into my mouth, I pressed my chest into his. His entire body was hard—almost as hard as the wall behind me. I felt enclosed, hemmed in, disoriented. I was completely absorbed, as if he were weaving a spell around me with his hands and his tongue.

"Did he tell you that you were beautiful?" he whispered, his mouth kissing its way to my temple now. My eyes fluttered closed. Transfixed, I could only focus on what his hands were doing. One was now relentlessly rubbing against my clit, the other winding through my hair at the nape of my neck. I had one hand still groping him through his jeans while the other untucked his shirt and skimmed across his flat abs. He felt amazing. He smelled even better.

"Did he?"

"Yes," I moaned.

"Did he tell you how much he wanted to taste you?"

I didn't answer. I was being drawn under by his spell. That gnawing, deep want cutting deep to my core. My body was awakening under the touch of those magical hands.

"He wants to taste you. He wants his mouth all over your pretty tits."

His touch against my clit intensified, and I began to feel that familiar climb to climax. He was going to make me come right here in this back alley in no time. And I didn't care. I wanted him to.

Jordan's hand released my hair and skimmed along the neckline of my dress, tucking a finger underneath and hooking into my bra. With a light tug, my breast was free and feeling the cool night air for mere milliseconds before his mouth was on me, as he'd said. He sucked my nipple into his mouth as if he were starving, feasting on me. He let loose a growl at the back of his throat and bolts of searing lightning streaked right through me. I arched my back, pushing into him, and he pressed me down—hard—against the wall, knocking my breath from me. He sucked harder, and the impossible pleasure of his hand moving at my center began to spread over my legs and stomach, gorgeous heat washing over me. With a shout that echoed across the alleyway, I came in sharp, breath-stealing spasms of pure ecstasy.

Fuck, it felt so good I never wanted it to end. His hand stilled, but he kept sucking my nipple and I shuddered under him. His cock leapt under my touch, straining in his jeans. He pressed his crotch into my hold and he pulled his mouth free.

"He wants to feel you come when he's inside you, April."

"Yes," I breathed against his neck.

"And he really, *really* wants to fuck you."

"Jordan," I moaned.

He pulled away from me and cool air passed between us. He was breathing hard, and I was still awash in the afterglow of one incredibly intense orgasm. My limbs felt slow to respond, listless. Slowly, he took hold of my wrist and pulled my hand away from his swollen crotch, his eyes burning into mine.

I tucked my breast back into my bra. He watched me, his tongue darting out over his bottom lip. If we weren't in some dark back alley somewhere, I wouldn't have let him pull away, wouldn't have stood for him to not finish until he was inside me. I needed him inside me. No, it was more than a need. More than a hunger. It was like finding a missing piece of me and needing to fit it to fill the empty gap within.

I shook my head, dismissing that thought. It was way too deep, way too emotional. And I didn't do that anymore. I wasn't going to let myself get swept up again by a pretty face—fantastic, amazing hands or not. He'd only shatter me worse than Gunnar had.

This was all physical. And it felt good. So I was going to let myself enjoy it, but feelings weren't allowed.

I cleared my throat and tried to ignore that he was still watching me with that intense, narrow gaze.

"You're *not* going home with him," he said. A statement, not a question. And of course, he was right. I hadn't even been considering it before this, and now that Jordan had put his hands and mouth all over me, there was no way I'd be satisfied with a random hookup. But I didn't want him to know it.

I shrugged. "I can do what I want," I said.

His beautiful face darkened in a scowl. He opened his mouth, but before he could say anything, the door to the bar pushed open again and the dark-haired man that Jordan had been with earlier was now in the alley with us. Jordan backed even further away from me and turned a little away from him, still noticeably aroused. I pushed off the wall and brushed a hand down the front of my dress as if nothing at all had just happened.

Jordan's friend looked pissed. "What are you doing out here?"

Jordan ran a hand over his hair. "April was upset. I just wanted to make sure she was okay."

"She looks fine to me."

"Um. Yeah. Yeah, I'm fine," I said, clearing my throat. "I feel... very, *very* good as a matter of fact."

Jordan shot me a dirty look. "April, do you know William Drake?"

William was now looking uneasy, not meeting my eyes. He was tall, dark-haired and good-looking, if a little strangely dressed—blue khakis and a brown and green patterned knit sweater. He had dark eyes and a visible five o'clock shadow—probably one that appeared five minutes after he shaved in the morning.

"We've never met, no. Are you related to Adam?"

"He's my first cousin," William said.

"Oh. Oh, okay." I silently wondered if I should introduce him to Cari. Maybe it would distract her from her fixation with Adam. But I suspected that she was like a bloodhound after the first scent of the fox and that nothing would deter her, not even the good-looking and *single* first cousin.

"I, uh...I'd better get going," I said, attempting to push my way around Jordan to get to the door.

Jordan's hand closed around my upper arm. "William and I can give you a ride home," he said.

I shrugged out of his hold. "I drove myself. I'm fine."

"You're going home *now?*" he said, but it sounded more like a statement than a question. I wanted to argue with him, but I really had no desire to stay. I wanted nothing more than to climb into my fleecy PJs, wrap myself in my comforter and pull out my worn copy of *Pride and Prejudice* to lose myself in Mr. Darcy. *Another* incredibly hot man who was terribly full of himself.

I only shrugged. I wasn't going to give Jordan the satisfaction of agreeing with him.

His eyes hardened. "Well, just remember there's going to be a whole crapload of work on your desk in the morning. I have lots of notes regarding your project and I want that first draft before you leave. You need to be there at seven."

My eyes widened and my jaw fell open. I was about to protest, but he turned to his friend and said, "C'mon, William, let's go finish what we started in there."

Then he turned the knob on the door, snapped it open and was gone. I fell back against the wall with a sigh before realizing that William was still standing there watching me.

He bent and opened the door, holding it for me, indicating I should go through before him. I straightened. "Thank you, William. It was nice to meet you."

"We met already. You just don't remember."

"Oh...oh really? I'm sorry."

"You're sorry you don't remember?"

I frowned, rubbing my temple, and ducked in through the doorway ahead of him. He closed the door and we were standing in the back hall. At last, the bathroom appeared empty. Jordan was nowhere to be seen.

I stopped and turned back to William. He'd been watching me with a frown but jerked his eyes away when I looked at him.

"I don't want to go out there and finish what he started," William said, peering down the hallway.

"What did he start?"

"Well, he wants me to think he was here to show me something, but I think he was here to watch you. So if you're leaving, I have a feeling he will too."

"He was here to watch me? What for?"

William's eyes shifted from my left shoulder to my right shoulder, as if unable to connect with my gaze. "I have no idea. But hopefully you are going so he won't force me to stay with him."

I laughed, glancing down the hallway again. If I didn't have to be in to work at the crack of dawn the next morning, it might be worth it to hang out here late in order to spite Jordan. My fist closed. Damn it. Mr. Darcy and my fuzzy jammies beckoned.

"Don't worry, William. I'm going home after I visit the little girl's room."

William looked visibly relieved.

I decided against hitting the bathroom and instead followed him back into the bar. At my table, five guys sat talking to the three women. I made a quick excuse about a sudden migraine and then hightailed it out of there before Cari could say anything.

I didn't even chance a glance at the other side of the bar to see if Jordan had left. But when I was out in the parking lot headed toward my car, I walked by the big, flashy Range Rover that I once drove to the car wash and noted that there were two people inside.

A minute after I pulled out of my parking space, the Range Rover did the same. At least he didn't go full stalker on me and follow me home. He went straight when I made my first right turn.

I blinked, still completely confused about the goings-on of today—and beyond that, this entire week. Since that heated night when Jordan kissed me on his couch, I hadn't been able to get him out of my mind. And I'd failed miserably at avoiding him.

Apparently, I was an expert at avoiding everyone else, but when it came to Jordan Fawkes, I sucked at it.

Probably because...deep down, I didn't want to.

10
JORDAN

TODAY WAS SEXUAL HARASSMENT TRAINING. WASN'T THAT great? Last night I'd had my hand up my intern's skirt, making her moan while I put my mouth all over her, and now here we were. *Fuck.* I rubbed my sore neck as I watched another set of employees file in for the third such session today. Adam and I had to sit through all of them and—thank God—this was the last one. There was a dull ache in my head, tightness in my temples. I put my head in my hand, covering my eyes. I felt a nudge at my elbow.

"What's the matter, can't stand to suffer the torture you inflicted?"

I sent Adam a dirty look. "It wasn't my dumbass suggestion, it was the goddamn banker. Don't shoot the messenger."

"Can I punch him in the nuts instead?"

"Quit whining."

For the third time that day, Essie, from the outside firm we'd hired to come in and inflict this low-level torture, stood and gave her canned spiel about the importance of power equality in the workplace and maintaining a safe, harassment-free work environment. I resisted the urge to check my phone when the dumbass video started, staring blankly at it like a zombie—yet again. I ignored the whispers and the rustling behind me. Clearly, the employees hated this as much as I did.

And like before, we progressed to the goddamn Q & A session. But this time, when Essie opened it up to questions, you could have heard a pin drop and crickets chirp. There at least had been some healthy discussion before—enough that it had taken almost all of the time. Apparently, this last group was the rebel bunch and they were protesting.

"So no one has *any* questions at all?" Essie said, her black brows rising. "Maybe as a jumping off point, we should start the discussion with the viral video."

I sat back, trying not to cringe. This had only briefly been touched on in the other sessions, but now the gloves were coming off. "Now we know that at least one person participating in that video was an employee. But let's suppose they were both employees..."

"I fucking hope not," Adam muttered under his breath for only me to hear. "Wouldn't *that* just make it so much better?"

I pretended to be so enthralled by what Essie was saying that I didn't hear him.

"Is this harassment, per se? If two employees of the same company were engaging in a sexual act?"

"That depends," someone said. "Maybe they were dating beforehand."

"Okay." Essie nodded. "Good point. Previous relationships should be considered. But what if a couple that works together breaks up or the relationship changes...or what if the two people involved are not of the same rank within the company?"

"You mean like if one was the other person's *boss?*" a voice piped up. A voice I recognized. *My* intern. I clenched my jaw and a fist on the table, but I resisted the urge to glance over my shoulder at her.

"Yes, that changes the entire power dynamic, doesn't it? If one person works for the other, even if they are engaging in a consensual relationship, the power structure between them is inherently unequal."

I fumed under my collar at her pointed comment, given what had happened between us last night. Perhaps it was her way of telling me she hadn't wanted it? I frowned at that thought, suddenly brought up short. Maybe she'd been afraid to tell me? But she'd reached out and touched me, too. And I'd given her the chance to tell me to stop...

Of course, there were the liberties *she* had taken with her goddamn smart phone. I raised my hand. "What about the tape itself? Like, if one person filmed it without the other person knowing? Is that sexual harassment?"

There. Take *that*, Miss Weiss.

Essie nodded. "Very good question. Of course, filming without the other party's consent is a grave violation of trust, but beyond that, it is also illegal and a violation of basic civil rights. It's punishable in civil and criminal court."

I sat back, stunned. I'd only intended to give April a little grief, not scare the shit out of her. She still had no idea it was me. And she probably was wondering how I knew that the guy in the video didn't know...or hopefully, she'd just thought I'd guessed right.

Essie started droning on about legal codes, but I was hardly listening. Sure, I was pissed about the goddamn video. I would much rather it had never been made. Hot night of sex or not, I didn't need the type of reminder that threatened to blow my plans for my company sky high. Nevertheless…I didn't want April going to jail, either.

Adam stood in the middle of Essie's diatribe, interrupting her. "I think we are digressing a little from the discussion, don't you think? It's only supposition that one party filmed without the other knowing. And now that we know it's illegal, can we move on?" He shot me an irritated look and I glanced over my shoulder at April, who had paled to the shade of the wall behind her.

She had her hands folded in her lap, her gaze fixed on them. I'd sure showed her, hadn't I? But it didn't feel good. She looked petrified.

"Shall we do some role-playing, then? Any volunteers?"

Role-playing? We hadn't gotten that far in the previous sessions. There hadn't been time after the discussion. Clearly, Essie was reaching for material to fill this one. I doubted any employee here would volunteer when they couldn't even muster up a nonsense question. I nudged Adam with my elbow and nodded toward the front of the room. "It's your leaderly duty," I muttered.

He rewarded my sarcasm with one of his signature death glares. Unfortunately, sitting in the front row, my movements had attracted Essie's attention and she brightened, her gaze fixing on me. "Excellent, let's get one of the big bosses up here for role-play!"

The room burst into applause and Adam started laughing. Under the cover of the table, I flipped him the bird and stood. *Shit.* How much longer until I could bail on this farce?

I moved to stand beside Essie, facing the room, and the applause only got louder. April had finally looked up, still pale but a faintly amused smile touched her beautiful lips. I held up my hands to quiet the room.

"No applause necessary," I said. "I already know I'm awesome."

"I feel threatened by that statement," one of the smartasses from accounting said, and his buddies laughed.

A wolf whistle came from the back of the room and I pointed. "Hey! No harassing me." More laughter.

Essie, however, was not amused. "All right, everyone, we need to take this seriously. I know these comments are all in fun, but we're here to be educated on how to have the safest, most comfortable and efficient work environment possible. And I know your CFO is *very* interested in efficiency."

I cleared my throat, sobering, and the room quieted down. Essie glanced around for a long moment before turning to me. "Okay, we're going to role-play a situation between me, the boss, and my employee, Mr. Fawkes."

A guy from playtesting snickered before I sent him a sharp glare and he quieted down. "So, here we are. You've just arrived at work."

Essie stepped forward and put her hand on my upper arm. "Hey Mr. Fawkes, how are you today? You are looking really good in those trousers and that shirt." She ran her eyes up and down me like she was checking me out at a singles bar. I'm sure it wasn't the response she wanted from me, but I grinned and straightened my tie. The group laughed again.

Essie's smile faded. "Now clearly this isn't a problem for Mr. Fawkes, but what if Mr. Fawkes is the boss and he says that same thing to an employee? And touches him or her in the same way?"

She glanced around and no one said anything, though people whispered to each other. A few looked incredibly bored. Essie pointed a finger at April. "Miss, didn't you ask about the boss-employee power dynamic before? Could you come up and help out, please?"

April's face went scarlet and she didn't move. "Uh..."

I muttered to Essie. "She's actually really shy."

But that other intern with all the blond hair—what the hell was her name?—started shoving April out of her chair. To keep from falling on the ground, April stood, giving her friend a well-deserved scowl. Essie continued encouraging April to come forward, and she reluctantly moved to stand beside me.

I shifted my weight from one leg to another, trying to distance myself from her without looking like I was distancing myself from her. There was only one word for this situation right here.

Awkward.

April stared at the floor in front of her, self-consciously tucking some strands of her hair behind her ear. I remembered having that delicious lobe in my mouth last night when I'd been engaging in some very *unbusinesslike* behavior with her in the alley behind the martini lounge. The way she'd moaned my name...

I tore my eyes away and scowled at the room as a whole. This wasn't so funny anymore.

"Mr. Fawkes, why don't you make a similar comment to this young lady like I just did to you?"

I cleared my throat and tried hard not to roll my eyes. "Good morning, Miss Weiss," I droned. "You are looking very nice today in your—uh—"

And then I looked at her to see what she was wearing. A pencil skirt and a silky blouse that hugged her curves. *Jesus Christ.* What kind of God up there didn't like me that he gave me a gorgeous intern—one I already knew was hot as a chili pepper in bed, too—that I wasn't allowed to touch? I'd have to continue to fight to keep my hands off of her, and if last night was any indication, it was a losing battle.

No, this was Karma, and she was biting me in the ass right this very minute. This was for every one of the women I'd dated in the past who had told me some day the Universe would get even with me for being a callous asshole.

It took me a second to realize I was standing here gaping at her and had not continued my sentence.

"Go ahead and put your hand on her arm," Essie coached.

Instead, I rested it lightly on her shoulder. I could feel the delicate bra strap through her silky top. It reminded me that last night I'd finally gotten a taste of what was underneath that bra. The memory of her succulent nipple beading in my mouth almost made me sprout wood right then and there. I jerked my hand away as if it had been burned, then took a step back.

April was beet red again, eyes on the floor.

"So, uh, how does his behavior make you feel, Miss Weiss? Do you feel comfortable telling him that he is being inappropriate?"

Self-consciously, she flicked her dark hair over her shoulder. "Mr. Fawkes, you are being inappropriate," she muttered.

Essie nodded her approval. I shoved my hands in my pockets. "Uh, I'm terribly sorry about that, Miss Weiss. It, uh, won't happen again."

"Feel her up!" someone called from the back of the room.

Shocked, my mouth fell open, but before I could say anything, Adam was on his feet, his face flushed red. "All right, I've had enough of this bullshit," he said, his narrowed eyes skimming the group in the room. "I've been through three meetings, and this is by far the worst of the lot. Don't you realize the reason we are here in the first place is because of wildly *inappropriate* employee behavior? Do you think I like wasting my time and yours sitting through stuff you should have learned in grade school? Keep your hands to yourself—one of the basic rules of human behavior. But we're here because someone obviously doesn't have a damn clue how to do that."

My mouth continued to hang open as I watched my friend completely lose his cool. Essie looked extremely uncomfortable, and April—well, she had her head down, her face curtained by swaths of thick, dark hair.

"Someone who works here filmed an intimate moment and then uploaded that to the Internet for the world to see. The moment they did that, they involved this company. And I don't know how *you* feel about your jobs here, but it should offend the hell out of all of you that someone did that. That someone represented *your* company that way. That they had that little respect for the institution to which all of you dedicate a great amount of your time, effort and brainpower. I'll tell you right now, that pisses me off. Because I spend a pretty large chunk of my life to make this a great company, and if I *ever* find out who did this...well, they'll be looking for a new job before they can blink."

The room was silent now, faces down. No one was meeting Adam's gaze and people clearly looked ashamed. However, none of *them* were responsible for the tape.

I should be the one ashamed—and I was. I cast a guilty glance in Adam's direction, once again cursing my thoughtless actions. We'd both worked so hard for this, built this company from nothing in almost five short years. And with one drunken night of hot sex—and apparently poor choice of hot partner—I'd endangered all our hard work.

Thank the gods above we were asked to return to our desks soon after and let out early by a somewhat exasperated and exhausted Essie.

11
APRIL

THE MINUTE THE MEETING LET OUT, I FOUGHT MY WAY OUT the door, ready to bolt back to my desk and huddle into a little ball. In all likelihood, I'd be hard pressed to keep it together until quitting time. That was not to be, however. Cari came up beside me, hooking a hand around my arm.

"Hey, April," she said with that super-fake, sing-songy tone she used. Dread knotted in the pit of my stomach. I had *no* desire to talk to her right now.

"Hey, Cari...sorry, I gotta get running. I have tons of stuff to get done before—"

But as we moved down the hall, she abruptly turned down a side hallway, jerking me along with her. "Ow! What the—"

Cari turned to me, her crazy eyes burning bright. "Did you see how hot he was just now? I am so turned on just hearing him yell at everyone like that. I bet he's so commanding and dominant in bed."

Oh, fucking hell. I had real shit to worry about—like having caused an honest-to-goodness scandal. And here she was still nurturing her

157

unrequited lust for the boss? I jerked my arm out of her grip. "I have a *ton* of work to do right now—"

"Come on, April. You can help me. You've got a position working up front. I'm not going to give up on this. It's the only thing that has kept me going for the last few months—kept my mind off all the crap going on in my life."

I swallowed, genuinely sorry for her. She blinked tears out of her eyes and gave a shivery sigh. I couldn't help it. Cari was bordering on psychopathic obsession with this, but I still felt sorry for her. I wondered what it must be like to lose a sibling, to have that pain constantly. I had siblings, but they were a lot younger and practically strangers. My own fault, really, as the Queen of Avoidance.

"Cari, you're so beautiful. There are *tons* of great guys out there for you. But—"

She jerked back. "I want the best one. I want *him*. Please say you'll help."

I opened my mouth to protest, but what could I say? Adam had already found someone. Someone who made him happy. Cari had no right to horn in on that.

"It would really be a shame..." she began with narrowed eyes.

I frowned but didn't say anything, suddenly feeling a dark premonition. "After hearing him talk like that...I'm sure our upset CEO would be *very* interested to know just who is responsible for that video."

The blood drained from my face.

She saw my reaction, a satisfied smile hovering on her lips. "Your secret's safe with me, April. But you're going to help me, right?"

My fists tightened at my sides. She noticed my silent protest and arched an eyebrow. "Because if you don't—"

She stopped when footsteps approached behind me. I swallowed a knot of fear but didn't dare look over my shoulder. Cari looked up at whoever it was—whoever must have heard our conversation. Her eyes widened.

"Oh...hey, Jordan. How are you?"

I took a deep breath and let it go, unable to turn and look at him.

"I was doing just great until I overheard someone threatening *my* assistant with what sounded a lot like blackmail." His voice was even, clipped, low, probably to prevent someone else eavesdropping on us. But I could tell he was ragingly pissed off. And for once, I wasn't the target of his anger.

Cari's eyes grew impossibly wider, clearly shocked at this transformation in the typically joking, devil-may-care CFO. She glanced quickly from him to me and back again. "Oh...well, maybe you misheard that. I wasn't—"

"Yes, you were. I know exactly what I heard."

Her mouth dropped. She turned her gaze on me, as if expecting me to intervene. "I wasn't threatening you, was I, April?"

I opened my mouth to answer, hesitating because I knew I had to play this carefully so that Cari wouldn't fly off the handle.

"Don't answer her, Weiss," Jordan interrupted. "Now Miss..." When Cari opened her mouth to supply her last name, he waved her off. "It doesn't matter. What matters is that I don't tolerate that sort of behavior in this office. Especially from an *intern*."

Cari's features went scarlet and she shot me a look of pure fury. "What if I knew who the person was responsible for that video? I'm sure Adam would *really* want to know that little bit of information, wouldn't he?"

"Despite what he may have said in there, he already knows. And so do I. So you have no leg to stand on. The only thing you'd accomplish by denouncing a colleague is to make yourself—and this company—look bad. So unless you'd like me to pick up my phone and make a call to Dr. Tretham—that's your advisor at the university, right? I have his number on my on my phone right here. We speak regularly about the intern exchange between the university and this company." I detected a movement behind me, presumably Jordan producing his cell phone and holding it up.

Cari's jaw dropped. "Please don't do that...."

"Why shouldn't I? Were you not standing here blackmailing my assistant with some bullshit accusation?"

Cari sent me a pleading look but I said nothing, folding my arms tightly across my chest. I was shaking so hard I was certain she could see it. He probably could, too.

"Now, if I hear one word that you are speaking to anybody—anybody—about this matter, I will have security escort you out of here so quickly it will make your head spin. Do you understand?"

Cari shook her massive amounts of hair. "But—"

"Do. You. Understand?" he repeated between clenched teeth.

She visibly swallowed. "Y—yes."

"I can assure you that if you speak of this to anyone or go to any of the other officers with this, you will wish you never set foot in this building. You signed an NDA when you came to work here, and if you violate it, you will be prosecuted to the full extent of the law. Is that clear?"

Cari's lips disappeared inside her mouth, and she looked as if she was about to start crying.

"Weiss," Jordan said.

I cocked my head toward him, but I couldn't meet his eyes. "You are to stay away from this young woman, do you hear me? And she's not allowed near you either. If you see her in the atrium, phone security and have her escorted out of the building. Now get back to your desk."

"Yes, sir," I croaked, and without looking at Cari, I turned and fled.

***

I have no idea what else he said to Cari after I left, but Jordan didn't show up at the atrium for another ten minutes. Ten minutes that I tried valiantly to keep it together and not cry. I sniffed. I blinked. Susan pretended not to notice. I kept my face down and attempted—and failed—to continue with my work.

I was proofreading a document that someone on Jordan's team had prepared for him, penciling in corrections through blurry vision, when a shadow appeared across my desk. I jumped even though I knew who it was. I didn't look up and was well aware that I looked hunched and miserable.

"Weiss," he began in a low voice. "I need to speak to you in my office. Now, please." Where had the "please" come from?

I swallowed, and without a word, I got up and preceded him into the office. Susan cast a concerned glance at me, but I didn't hold her gaze for longer than a second. The minute I walked through the door, the tears sprang from my eyes so instead of stopping to face him, I headed straight for his private bathroom. He followed me in, despite the fact that I was certain he knew I was upset. I turned toward the wall, away from the mirror's reflection. It was the second time in two days that he'd caught me losing it. Just great.

When I'd regained control of myself, I squared my shoulders and then turned to face him. It was time to inform him that I was ready to end this now.

It was time for me to take my lumps. I almost felt relieved about it.

12
JORDAN

I GAVE HER A MOMENT TO COLLECT HERSELF, BUT IT WAS MORE
for me than it was for her. Crying women always made me
uneasy. They often brought out that old misplaced sense of
chivalry in me—like I was somehow responsible for the crying and it
fell on me to stop it.

I'd made a woman or three cry in my lifetime. Sometimes I felt
guilty about it. More often, I didn't. But this one was shaking me more
than I'd anticipated. I rubbed my jaw and watched her quietly pull
herself together, straighten her shoulders and turn to face me.

Her blue eyes were clouded with uncertainty, self-questioning. I'd
wanted to crack her cool façade, but this wasn't what I had in mind.
April was tender and vulnerable inside. The thickness of the walls
she'd built to protect herself didn't change that.

I took a breath and let it go. "Are you okay?"

She pressed her hands to her cheeks and shook her head.

I sighed and looked away. "She's not going to say anything now
that I've put the fear of God into her."

163

She shook her head again, apparently still too emotional to speak.

I clenched my teeth, annoyed at how much it was bothering me to see her this way. "Weiss. You need to take a deep breath and calm down. You don't have anything to be scared about."

"I—I'm not scared. I'm guilty. I'm a horrible person. I—"

"You aren't a horrible person. Stop it."

"Everyone had to do all that because of me. Because of what *I* did. I don't even know why you are covering for me like this. You—"

"Because you're part of my team and I protect my own. I'm the only one who has the right to torment you and make your life hell, got it? She's not—"

"But *why?*" Her dark brows scrunched, and she scanned my face as if she were trying to solve a puzzle. "Why are you letting me stay on your team? You could have let me go on the first day. I know you lied to her just now, about the fact that Adam knows it's me. He doesn't know it's me. But he *should.*"

That worried me. I shook my head. "Calm down. You don't even know what you're saying."

She straightened, lifting her chin. "I'm going to end this."

I did not like the sound of that. *At all.* "What do you mean?"

"I'm going to talk to Adam and tell him that I'm responsible for the video, explain it was an accident, and then I'm going to apologize and resign on the spot."

My entire body tensed and my gut tightened. "And what will that solve?"

She turned, grabbed a tissue and dried her face. "It will get Cari off my case and make me feel better."

"Cari is already off your case. And how will it make you feel better to be dismissed from your internship in disgrace, with no chance of getting a recommendation for business school?"

She looked away, her bottom lip trembling. "So, you know how...how I was the one who made the video? And you know that question you asked Essie...about one of the people not knowing they were being recorded?"

I blinked and swallowed, suddenly feeling more than a little guilty. I didn't say anything though, and she took that as a prompt to continue talking—even if I preferred that she drop it.

"Well, you were right. He didn't know...the guy, I mean. It was so stupid. I was drunk and feeling pretty high on the whole experience. I'd never done anything like that before and...well, it was a bit of a fantasy, I have to admit. So, on an impulse, I pulled out the phone to record it. I figured I'd erase it right away. But..." She took in a deep breath and let it go. "I had no idea I was committing a crime. I feel wretched. And the poor guy, he had no idea. I need to find him. I need to apologize."

"Hold the phone. Just calm down, all right? He's fine. He's safe. Nobody knows who he is. He has no reason to want to come after you and put you in jail. The sexual harassment stuff, well, all companies have to do that sort of training by law anyway. So yeah, there's been extra inconvenience brought about by what you did, but I've got it handled, okay? No need to go throwing yourself on a sword in self-sacrifice. Nobody needs that kind of drama."

She huffed. "I didn't want it to be about *drama*. I'm just...I'm trying to do the right thing."

"Sometimes it's best not to. That's another thing you need to learn about business. Ethics are slippery things." And God, wouldn't I know about that? This would have been an appropriate time to let her know that I knew all about her partner in the video because it was *me*.

It occurred to me—it honestly did. But the less she knew, the better. At least that was the lie I told myself so as to not hate what I was doing. It would be for her own good.

And yeah, it helped that it was for *my* own good as well.

She sniffed and then looked at me—*really* looked at me—with a gaze that seemed to penetrate my own façade. I almost drew back, startled.

"Why are you doing this, Jordan? Why do you care so much?"

I blinked. Her question took me totally by surprise. *Why do you care so much?* Good question. I had no idea. I wasn't supposed to care. I'd told myself a long time ago that I wasn't going to ever care again. It had hurt too much, that once.

But this woman was doing something…something she didn't even know she was doing.

And I was allowing it to happen.

I rubbed a hand over my mouth and shrugged. "I care about this company. I care about the IPO being successful. I care about you keeping your nose clean and getting out of here without upsetting more than you have already. *That's* what I care about."

Her brows drew together and I stepped back. I didn't want to feel her near me again, didn't want to smell her. I didn't want to care. So, I wouldn't. That was it. I'd flip it off, like a switch. I was good at that. I could do that.

I had to.

But there was still a thing or two that I wanted to know. "Why didn't you speak up for yourself with Cari? Why'd you let her trample all over you like that?"

She shrugged.

"That's not an answer and you aren't four," I ground out. "Somewhere along the line, you learned that you aren't worth standing up for. That other people's feelings and opinions are more valuable than your own. You keep those feelings inside and show the world a brave face."

She looked at me like I'd slapped her. "And there's something wrong with that?"

I nodded. "In the process of trying to save everyone else's feelings, you give no value to your own. Because you're too *nice*. That will get you nowhere. I learned a long time ago that nice guys finish last. Do you want to finish last?"

"Is this some kind of race?"

I stared at her. "It's life. And it's passing you by because all of those jackasses who walk all over you are doing just that to get ahead of you. And you are letting them."

She blinked. "So that explains why you're an asshole."

I sent her a wicked grin. "And damn proud of it."

She wasn't smiling in return. Instead, she was watching me with those perceptive blue eyes. Even in the semi-darkness of the bathroom, I could see them, glued to my face, inspecting every inch— maybe even seeing things I didn't want her to see.

I stepped out of the bathroom, breaking the moment. "I'll, uh, let you get yourself together."

While she tidied up, I packed up my stuff, ready to finish this godforsaken day. When she came out, she quietly leaned on the edge of the doorway, tilting her head and watching me again. This time, her face was easier to read as her eyes slipped down my body, warming parts of me I'd like her hands touching instead. She licked her lips when her gaze met mine again.

Fuck. I was in trouble with this one. Deep, deep trouble. I knew that and yet I allowed myself to get pulled into dangerous waters again and again, either oblivious or willingly ignorant to the pull she had on me. And any good surfer knew you avoided a riptide whenever you could. They were nothing but danger—a massive expense of energy to escape with your life intact.

"Quitting time," I said, because I honestly had nothing else to say. And I was trying not to remember the taste of her from last night. Trying to push my way out of that dangerous current that was my attraction to her.

"So I actually get to go home on time?" Her dark brows rose hopefully.

"Don't get cocky. It's only because you have to be back here before dawn."

She drew back. "Say what? I don't do 'before dawn.'"

"Well," I said, slipping my shoulder strap on and hefting the weight of the laptop bag. "You do now. I need you here at six."

"A.M.?" she said, alarmed. "What for?"

"I have a meeting with a banker in Santa Barbara tomorrow morning. You're coming with. Wear a business suit. These assholes are conservative as hell."

She opened her mouth and then shut it.

I turned to walk out the door, calling over my shoulder. "Knock off the fish face."

As much as I didn't relish the idea of being alone in a car with her for hours, I needed to make sure she wasn't here at the complex and not under my watchful eye, that she wouldn't go running to Adam with her confession the first chance she got.

I had to hedge my bets. And besides, I was safe with her in the car as long as I was driving. What could possibly happen?

13
APRIL

I THOUGHT ABOUT THOSE THINGS HE TOLD ME ALL THE WAY HOME. I thought about them as I logged onto Dragon Epoch, and I thought about them the entire time I played. I thought about them as I lay in bed at two in the morning, unable to sleep, in spite of the fact that I had to be up at 4:30.

I couldn't *stop* thinking about them. *Somewhere along the line you learned that you aren't worth standing up for.* I struggled against those words, resisted them. Told myself, what the hell does he know? He hardly knew anything about me. But the more I thought about them, the more I decided they were true.

About me. About how I dealt with my friends, my parents. *Especially* my parents. When I was upset with them, I avoided them until it was impossible to no longer do that. But I never told them what I was thinking. *Other people's feelings and opinions are more valuable than your own.* Because I didn't want to hurt their feelings or make them feel bad, I allowed myself to continue feeling bad instead.

But how…how had he done that? How on *earth* had he seen what I couldn't see myself? *You keep those feelings inside and show the world a brave face.*

I tossed and turned all night, haunted by his words. And because of my freakin' insane notion that I needed to be at work earlier than expected, I was actually wandering the halls of Draco Multimedia *before* six in the morning on less than two hours' sleep.

The light filtering in from outside was watery and dim—as dim as I felt, actually. I went to the cafeteria for some much-needed coffee, which was about all they served at this hour. I was surprised to see other early risers there, too, sitting at some of the dozen or so round tables in the breakroom.

As I grabbed my coffee and fixed it up with some cream and sweetener, I noticed a couple of people seated nearby, laughing and talking and sounding *far* too perky for this early in the morning. On a second glance, I noticed it was Mia and Adam's cousin, William, whom I'd met in the alley behind Le Chat Noir a few nights before. He looked over my way and Mia followed his gaze. When she saw me, the smile melted off her face and she turned her gaze away, stirring her coffee. I waved at William and smiled. He smiled back briefly.

Seeing Mia again reminded me of the blown chance at an apology. I'd perfected that thing in my mind since then, running it through different variations. I'd been waiting for another chance, but too afraid to force the issue.

But Jordan's words yesterday…I hadn't stopped thinking about them. The more they'd sunk in, the more they'd marinated my thoughts.

I'd let Cari railroad my one chance at talking to Mia and apologizing for my past rude behavior. I could make up for that now—

if I didn't chicken out. I could at least make *this* right even if I could never right the wrong I had done to Falco.

So with a deep breath, I screwed up my courage and walked over to the table.

"Morning, Mia, William..."

They both looked up at me, surprised. "Good morning," William said.

"Why is anyone in their right mind here this early?" I asked.

"This is our morning to have breakfast together," William explained. He didn't look at me. He didn't look at Mia, either.

Mia cleared her throat and spoke up. "It was a little bit of a tradition for us to have lunch together when I worked here. But I'm starting school soon, so I won't be able to do it much longer unless we meet really early before class. We're trying it out to get used to it."

"Good to know somebody's here voluntarily. I'm just being dragged along on a meeting with the Beast."

Mia almost spit out her coffee and William glanced at me out of the corner of his eyes, smiling. I sank down in the seat across from him. "Mind if I sit for a minute before he gets here?"

"Sure. William was telling me about the incident at the bar."

My face flushed hot. "Uh, what incident?"

"About how Jordan thought it would be a great idea to 'educate' William in how to meet women at a bar."

I cracked a smile. "Oh, is that what he was doing?" I turned to William. "Did he give you any good pointers?"

William scowled. "I should have known better than to ask Jordan to take anything seriously."

Mia laughed. "Yeah, what were you even thinking by asking him? Especially when it comes to women. He's *never* had a serious relationship. He just wants hookups with hot models."

I blinked, thinking about what happened at his house and at the bar the other night. Was that all it had been with me, too? Had he just been bored or horny or both? I tried not to think about that. Plus, I wasn't here about Jordan anyway.

"I hate to intrude on your time together," I said quietly. "But, I was wondering if...I was wondering if..."

They both looked at me as if I were having some kind of seizure. It felt like I was.

I cleared my throat. "Mia, could I talk to you for a minute?"

Mia's features registered slight surprise and she glanced at William. He frowned and looked at his watch. "We have five more minutes of our breakfast..." he began.

"Oh, I don't want to cut things short." I tried to disguise my disappointment.

Mia pushed an opened box toward Adam's cousin. It had fruit and yogurt and a pastry in it. "William, could you do me a favor and spend those last five minutes putting this on Adam's desk? He's going to be in soon. I left before him so he wouldn't think I was following him on that damn motorcycle, even though I wanted to."

William shook his head. "I still don't understand why he bought it."

"Neither do I." She sighed. "If he's already made it here in one piece, tell him I'll be over in a few."

William rose, picked up his trash and disposed of it. Then he took the box of food and said goodbye to Mia.

Mia sent me a curious glance as I watched William go and then straightened in her seat. I bit my lip and turned to her. My heart was pounding so hard it felt like it was going to lift out of my chest and fly away.

I briefly relived that moment three months ago. We were at a charity event at Adam's house, and Cari and I had stood on the porch scoping out Adam—her favorite activity—remarking how he was chatting up a swimsuit model when his girlfriend was nowhere to be seen.

Come to find out, Mia had been inside, probably trying to find the courage to make an appearance. At that point, no one had seen much of her since she'd gotten sick and she was probably self-conscious about her looks. Our thoughtless remarks had only made the situation worse, I imagined.

"Uh..."

"I know what you're going to say," Mia said.

"You—you do?"

She nodded. "You don't need to."

"I *do* need to. I've felt like crap since the day of that party..."

She folded her arms across her chest. "Because I overheard you?"

I blinked. "Yes. That was part of it. But also because it made me feel really crappy to say those things."

Her mouth quirked. "Makes sense. I assume people who talk like that are doing so because of their own issues." She held up a hand. "I'm not perfect, either. I've done my fair share of hating."

"Mia, I'm really sorry. You were so sick, and—it just wasn't right for us to be talking like that."

Her mouth thinned. "Apology accepted. You don't have to feel bad anymore."

I took a deep breath and let it go, somewhat but not fully relieved.

"I want you to know... well, sometimes it's really hard to stand up to that crowd, you know?"

She nodded knowingly. "Cari is a bit of a force of nature."

"She honestly scares the crap out of me."

Mia laughed. "I think she scares the crap out of everyone."

I smiled and then sobered. "It's always been hard for me to stand up to people. When I was younger, *I* was the one people picked on. I know how that feels. I'm—I'm sorry. I'm sorry that it felt easier for me to go along with them instead of going with what felt good in my gut."

Mia tilted her head, looking at me as if noticing something new and different. "Huh, and all this time I thought you were just like her."

My face heated and I shrugged a shoulder, looking away. "You had a right to. That's how I was acting."

Mia frowned. "Don't be down on yourself. Chalk it up as a lesson learned. Yeah, it was a shitty thing to say, and yeah, you girls ogling Adam twenty-four-seven was annoying, but I know you can't help yourselves. He is damn hot." She ended with a smirk.

I laughed. "He is hot. But he's yours. So no more ogling from me. I can't speak for the others though."

"Yeah, you shouldn't speak for them." She grinned. "And you shouldn't let them speak for *you* anymore."

I remembered Jordan's words and was emboldened. This warm feeling burned in the middle of my chest. I felt strong. "I know."

"Women are stronger when we stand together rather than constantly trying to tear each other down."

I took a breath and let it out. Boy, did I know *that* well. Mia didn't know the mother I had. If she did, she'd probably understand me better.

Every time I'd shop with her, I was either too short or too fat or my coloring was wrong because I wasn't the tall, willowy blonde that she was. *Your father's looks and my brains—talk about getting the short end of the stick in the gene pool.*

"I hope we're good now..." I said, raising my eyebrows in question.

Mia nodded. "Yeah, we're good. Just be careful of Cari, okay?"

I was amazed at how accurate her warning was, despite it coming too late for me. "Thanks. I've been trying to steer clear."

"That's probably the wisest thing to do."

I shifted and smiled again. "Can I ask you a favor?"

She raised her brows, nodding.

"Jordan has assigned me a project and I'm hoping he approves it. I want to document what it's like for a non-gamer to get into a game like Dragon Epoch—like what gets them interested initially and what keeps them playing. I'm the test subject, obviously... And I know you're a gamer so I'd like your perspective."

She smiled. "Sure." She whipped out a piece of paper from her bag and wrote on it. "Send me an email and ask away."

I took the paper. "Thank you. Just—thanks for everything."

She shifted in her seat to gather her stuff. "You're on your way out of here, I think," she nodded toward the entrance of the cafeteria where Jordan loomed like a thundercloud—tall and sinfully handsome in a charcoal gray suit with an amber tie the only splash of color. Three-piece, no less, with a vest that hugged his trim, solid build.

I actually found myself catching my breath as my heart skipped a beat. He raised his brows at me expectantly. I stood, threw out the rest of my coffee—that stuff from the cafeteria really was crap—and thanked Mia. We walked toward the exit together.

"There you are," he said when I made it to him.

Mia flashed him a thumbs-up, and he waved to her as she passed by on her way out of the cafeteria.

"What was that all about?" he asked while we walked out to the parking lot together.

I shrugged. "Just some unfinished business I had."

He said nothing and I studied his handsome profile out of the corner of my eyes, that same warm feeling coming over me. I was proud of myself, but also grateful for his words that had given me the courage to apologize. I felt relieved and light as air. And if I didn't think he'd give me some kind of snide reaction, I might have thanked him.

But I swallowed that notion. Not yet. We had a long drive ahead of us and it wouldn't do to start it out with awkwardness. It was two and a half hours from here to Santa Barbara, good traffic willing.

We made our way to his parking space at the front of the lot, where—sure enough—there was a vintage-looking motorcycle in the CEO's spot right next to his. Jordan's car was a shiny new silver Range Rover with every extra feature known to mankind. It was a wonder it didn't drive itself.

We stopped at a drive-thru Starbucks near the freeway on-ramp to fuel up on caffeine. I sipped at my double latte with an extra shot, no sugar. The strong, bitter taste, along with the mega dose of caffeine, helped to keep me awake.

We discussed my project for a few minutes, and he approved of me documenting my journey from "muggle" to full-blown geek, suggesting I give it a marketing angle by providing information on how to attract new players to the game. I took a few notes and then we fell into silence, so I pulled out my phone.

I read the rest of *Pride and Prejudice* as we stopped and started through LA traffic. There was quiet between us as he listened to the business report on the morning news radio show.

But somewhere around Thousand Oaks, as the traffic started to thin, Jordan's phone buzzed with a text.

"Check that, will you? I want to make sure it's not the asshole banker backing out on our meeting."

Gingerly, I picked up his phone and saw the text that popped up on the notification screen. My brows climbed sky high as I read it.

"It's not the banker," I said.

"Oh? Who is it?"

"Uh…well, you have her in your contacts as Sexilicious Sondra."

He snorted, but didn't seem to want to know the contents of the text message. I provided them anyway. Because they were too juicy not to share.

"She wants to know if she left her pink fuzzy handcuffs at your place last time she was there."

I enjoyed the slow creep of color up his neck from the collar of his dress shirt. Without looking at me, he reached up and held out his hand for the phone. I slipped it into his palm.

"You shouldn't read it while you're driving."

"I'm not going to." He set it down in its own little cubby specially designed to hold it.

"Sure you don't want me to reply? You can just unlock it with your thumbprint, and I'll let her know whether you still have her handcuffs or not. And I can tell her where she left her vibrator while I'm at it." My cheeks started to hurt from the grin I was wearing.

"That's okay," he said between clenched teeth.

"It also showed that you had five other unread texts, but they had scrolled off—"

"All right, Weiss. I get it. You're amused. Can we move on?"

"Well, you don't want to keep your lady friends waiting. I'm very concerned that they might feel neglected."

In truth, the idea of him with another woman made more than a little heat rise under my own collar. I clenched my jaw at that thought. Was I...was I jealous? I promptly told myself I was being silly and forced myself to ignore it.

"And in what way does that concern you?"

I shrugged, trying not to feel the sting those words caused. "It is in my best interests. If you have a lack of regular...*companionship*, you might get even grumpier than you already are."

His jaw worked, but he kept his eyes on the road. "I liked it better when you were reading your book."

I shrugged. "Okay. I'll go back to reading, then."

"You read a lot." It was a statement, not a question. He glanced at me before returning his eyes to the road.

"Was that an observation or an insult?"

"What all do you read? Novels?"

"Sometimes novels. Sometimes non-fiction. I've been on an economics theory kick lately."

"*Freakonomics?*"

"I love that one."

"It figures."

"What is *that* supposed to mean?"

"Econ theory lovers are head games people."

I shrugged because I had no real reply to that. Hell, I had no idea what he even meant by it. Did he mean playing head games on others? Or maybe I fooled myself with my own head games?

We rode on in silence for a few more miles, passing the city of Ventura. The highway turned and paralleled the ocean on our left. I found myself gazing out his side of the windshield at the sunlight reflecting on the water. The early morning coastal fog had begun to burn off, and it was going to be another glorious, sunny Southern California day.

And here I was, stuck in a car with the Grumpiest Boss on Earth. The hot, grumpy boss with hands more magical than anything JK Rowling could dream up in any of her *Harry Potter* books. *Orgasmo Patronum.* He hadn't even needed a chant...just those hands. The thought of his hands brought back that fluttery feeling in the pit of my stomach.

My eyes dropped from gazing at the ocean to watching his hands on the steering wheel. They were big, with a light dusting of hair and prominent veins. I remembered what those hands felt like, threading through my hair, holding my head in place while he kissed me.

I flushed hot, and almost as if he could read my thoughts, his head turned. "Are you warm? Do you need the air on?"

He reached out and cut the heater on my seat.

I shook my head, shot him a glance and then turned toward my window, away from him, watching the scrubby coastal hills out the right side of the car.

"So, uh, should we talk about what happened the other night in the alley?" I finally heard myself ask. It was a question that had been nagging at me ever since it had happened. But I hadn't overtly planned on uttering it out loud.

He was silent for another stretch of time while the Range Rover ate up the miles with its smooth glide along the highway. I didn't dare look at him, nor did I even move. I was too afraid he'd snap my head off.

Finally, he let out a sigh. "It shouldn't have happened and it won't happen again. I apologize."

I frowned. That wasn't what I'd wanted him to say. Maybe something like, "*You're so hot and sexy I couldn't keep my hands off you*" Or, "*I hate you because you are beautiful.*" Or, "*In vain I have struggled, it will not do. My feelings will not be repressed...You must allow me to tell you how ardently I want to fuck you.*" My mouth quirked at my modern take on Mr. Darcy's classic words. Yes, those would do nicely.

Instead, I'd gotten a curt apology. Like he had belched in my presence instead of hand delivering an amazing orgasm. That thought made me laugh. And when the laugh bubbled up, it could not be repressed—much like Mr. Darcy's feelings. The laugh gurgled up and over like lava spilling from a volcano.

Soon, I was laughing so hard I was crying, and the more my hilarity increased, the grumpier he got. It started with a frown, then he squeezed the steering wheel, shifting in his seat. Meanwhile, I was wiping tears from my eyes with the back of my hand. By the time I managed to calm down, he'd affected a full-blown scowl.

"So that's what I get for my apology?"

"Oh, that was an apology? '*Sorry, ma'am, for the orgasm. It won't happen again.*' Is that your usual MO? Did Sexilicious Sondra get an apology from you after you cuffed her to the bed and made her scream your name?"

Now he was red-faced and shooting me a glare out of the corner of his eyes. "That is *not* what I meant. I meant that it wasn't appropriate given our professional relationship."

"Yes, Mr. Fawkes, you are very inappropriate. And now, thanks to Essie's training, I know how to tell you that."

"We're here. Thank God."

I glanced up and saw the sign for the Santa Barbara exits, then bit my lip before I started laughing again.

"What now?" he said as he flipped on the signal to change lanes.

"You still have to sit in the car with me all the way home. Maybe you'll get some more text messages that I can read to you."

I stared out the window again, attempting to control my laughter. Santa Barbara was a picturesque little city curved around a sparkling blue bay. Houses climbed toward the back hills, called "morrows" here. It was cultured, sophisticated and a great place for the city-bound to get away for the weekend. But we weren't here for a romantic getaway, as much as the idea of doing something like that with the car's other occupant might have had me feeling warm and fuzzy inside.

No, we were here for a stuffy business meeting.

Minutes later, we were in the parking lot of the investment banker's office. Jordan got out and procured his suit jacket from where it hung on a hook in the back seat so it wouldn't wrinkle. He proceeded to slip it on his broad shoulders and button it up, straightening his tie.

"Should I wait in the car or...?"

He made a face like I'd suggested I go dance around on the curb like one of those human billboards. "No. You're coming inside as my assistant. Do you want to learn this shit, or are you just some trust fund brat going through the motions 'til Daddy delivers you a fat wad of cash to live on?"

My eyes narrowed at him and my cheeks flamed. That was below the belt. His lips curved in a slight smile, as if he were satisfied with himself that he'd baited me. I'd let my feelings show that time. I was usually better at hiding them, but he seemed to bring out the worst in me—and what's worse, he did it almost effortlessly.

I swallowed the irritation and glared heat-seeking missiles—daggers would not suffice—into his back as I followed him through the glass doors.

Within minutes, Jordan was introducing me to the banker, Wallace Holden, one of the team of bankers who would fund the initial set of shares for Draco's IPO. As I took my seat, I watched Jordan smoothly sit down and unbutton his coat in one fluid motion. I pulled out my notebook and poised my pen over a blank page, ready to take notes or create a bulleted action list or do something that might make me appear more like an official assistant.

Despite his formal dress, Jordan affected a casual posture, sitting back and resting an ankle across his opposite knee. With a grin, he began to chat up Wallace—whom he called Wally.

"So I saw that your boy's baseball team made State. He must be over the moon. Are the scouts coming around for a possible scholarship? Heard he's got an amazing arm."

Jordan knew stuff about Wally's kids, his wife—even his last golf game. I watched him under my lashes. He was a smooth operator. They spent twenty minutes talking about Wally and his life, and Jordan seemed intensely interested in all of it. In the end, they only spent ten minutes on business.

"So what's the status on your initial public offering?" Wally finally asked.

"We're a go," Jordan beamed. "My CEO couldn't be more excited."

Wally's brows twitched in surprise. "I've heard your CEO is a little...tight on the reins. Is he going to give us anything more than a tiny slice of the shares to list with?"

Jordan waved his hands. "Adam is thrilled about the IPO and can't wait. He's got big plans. *Amazing* plans. The kid is a genius, and not just because he lets me take care of the business side of things," he said with a wink. "He's a visionary and, let me tell you, he's light-years ahead of the rest of us."

As I watched him ease the banker's ruffled feathers, I couldn't help but wonder if his smooth reputation with women wasn't based on the same principles with which he conducted business. Telling people what they wanted to hear could be as much an art as anything else.

In the end, Wally's fears seemed allayed and we walked out after shaking hands and exchanging pleasantries. In the parking lot, Jordan took off his coat, rehung it and pulled off his tie, unbuttoning his collar.

I watched him with a frown. He stopped and quirked a brow at me. "What?"

"How'd you know all that stuff about him? His kids—family?"

He shrugged. "Social media. And I have some people..." He glanced away. "Collecting info in this day and age is not difficult. But I'm no cyberstalker."

"You have *people*, do you?" He sounded like my dad, and I was a little uneasy about that comparison. The less I thought about my dad these days, the better.

He gave me a canny smile and opened the door, sliding into his seat. I slid in beside him, turned and folded my arms across my chest. "Did you collect information on me?"

That glib smile froze and his eyes looked a little panicked for a split second before he turned back toward the wheel, laughing it off.

"You did, didn't you?"

"You are the creator of a PR situation for my company, Weiss. Does that surprise you?"

Biting my bottom lip, I shrugged. "I'm sure you didn't find out much, considering I'm rather boring. I'm one hundred percent positive it wasn't worth the effort it took."

A brief frown crossed his features before he glanced at the time and sighed. "Well, that was a huge pain in the ass drive to shoot the shit with a skittish banker for thirty minutes. Sometimes I hate this job."

"You could have taken the train up and had a driver bring you over from the train station. Then you could have gotten some work done."

He scowled at me. "Last I checked, this is California. We drive everywhere ourselves. Even when we are rich enough to have drivers. It's part of our culture. Plus, I needed to get my ass out of the office. And I needed to get *your* ass out of the office, too."

"*My* ass? Why would you—?" I cut myself off as understanding dawned. "Oh...you were afraid I was going to confess to Adam while you were gone."

He touched his nose and winked at me.

"We have another stop to make before heading back down south. I'd planned on this before I knew I was bringing you. So you are just going to have to humor me because if I back out, there will be hell to pay."

I raised my brow. Was he checking in with one of his ladyloves? Because if so, I wanted no part of *that*.

My stomach growled. He laughed. "And lunch is included."

We headed into the city and through the quaint downtown before driving to a middle-class residential area on the outskirts. Soon, we'd pulled into the driveway of a modest-looking bungalow-style house. I puzzled this one out as I slipped out of my seat and followed him to the front door.

He knocked loudly and then turned the knob, calling into the house, "Pop? It's Jordan."

There was a call from the back of the house, and Jordan opened the door for me to precede him. The house was decorated in an understated style that was a little outdated and had a feminine, homey touch to it. I glanced around, taking in the large, pastel lampshades, an art deco-style mirror, a few antique pieces, and a big, overstuffed suede couch.

A tall, thin man appeared. He looked like a sixty or seventy-year-old version of Jordan, wearing a sweater and corduroy pants. He immediately clasped Jordan in a bear hug.

"Well, it's about time you got up here to see me," he said. The older man caught sight of me over Jordan's shoulder and his eyes widened. "You didn't tell me you were bringing a lovely lady with you."

Jordan stepped back and turned toward me, appearing embarrassed. "She's my assistant, Pop. April, this is my grandpa, Reverend Gerald Fawkes."

Reverend? Jordan's grandpa was a minister? How...strange and ironic that was. I wondered if he had any idea what a tomcat his grandson was. I stepped forward and gave him my biggest smile as I shook his hand. "Pleasure to meet you, sir. I'm April Weiss."

"Are you hungry, Miss April? Because I made lunch and it's a lot of food, even for Jordan."

"I'm not sixteen anymore. I don't eat like I used to."

"Not even my homemade shepherd's pie?"

Jordan grinned. "Okay, you might have me there. I think I'm drooling."

"Give me a few minutes. Sit down at the table. And be a gentleman, please, and pull out the chair for Miss April."

Jordan rolled his eyes and his grandfather scoffed. The older man was adorable, and I giggled as Jordan did exactly as his grandfather asked with a long-suffering sigh. "So your grandpa lives here? Susan said you grew up in San Luis Obispo."

"I did. My parents are still in SLO. My grandpa had his ministry here until he retired." He pronounced SLO like "slow"—as many from the area referred to it.

"What a pretty place to live and work. What denomination did he minister for?"

"Methodist. And I swear if you crack any jokes about it, Weiss—" He had a playful smile on his sexy lips.

I kept my face as straight as I could manage. "Does that mean I can't ask about his beliefs regarding fornication involving pink fuzzy handcuffs? My spiritual education is at stake."

He only narrowed his eyes, but I could tell that he was trying to keep from laughing.

"It's all right. You can laugh. You won't spoil your reputation as Grumpiest Boss on Earth. But don't think I'm not going to try and get some dirt on you from your grandpa."

He shook his head. "You won't get anywhere."

"Ah, but I *am* half Jewish. We have our ways of wheedling the truth out of the most unlikely places." Not that I was in tune with my Jewish half at all. It was pretty much the entirety of what I had in common with that part of my family.

I couldn't deny the slight twinge I felt when I'd watched him hug his grandpa. Or when I watched other people connect with their family members. I had no real idea how that felt. So I joked about Jewish stereotypes instead and laughed it off, because putting the other person at ease was more important than my own feelings.

I stole a glance at him. Now that his words were in my head, they seemed to color my perception of all my interactions. I took a deep breath and met his gaze. *Get out of my head, would you?*

Jordan hopped up to help his grandpa bring in the plates and food. He soon reappeared carrying a fragrant casserole dish and placed it on the waiting trivet.

The shepherd's pie—a casserole of meat, potatoes and cheese—was delicious, and the company, given that his grandpa's presence had a mellowing effect on Jordan, was pleasant. Reverend Fawkes mentioned that it was an old family recipe, passed down from England. Legend had it that they were descendants of the infamous Guy Fawkes of the Gunpowder Plot. The man who'd tried to blow up Parliament hundreds of years ago.

Jordan rolled his eyes to the sky when his grandfather brought it up.

The Reverend turned to me. "Don't pay any attention to him. He doesn't like being reminded that he's named after him."

"What?"

Jordan grimaced. "My middle name is Guy. My father's idea of a sick joke."

"Don't they burn Guy Fawkes in effigy in the UK?" I asked, thankful I'd been paying attention during my European studies class.

"Every November fifth," Reverend Fawkes said. Then he leaned toward me conspiratorially. "It happens to be his birthday."

I leaned back, laughing, and Jordan's face clouded. "Okay, you have to admit, having the name Fawkes and being born on November fifth...I can totally see why your dad thought that was a sign."

Jordan scowled and I remembered Susan's words. *Except the dad. There's something up with his dad.*

That joking reference had brought him some sort of unwanted feeling or memory. I wanted to reach out and touch his arm, but I stopped myself, my hand twitching atop the table.

The Reverend seemed to sense the sudden change in mood. "Let me get the pitcher of iced tea for refills." He stood and went into the kitchen.

I smiled, trying to cheer him up. "You should have thought twice before bringing me to visit your grandpa. I'll have all your secrets out of him soon."

He opened his mouth to reply when the doorbell rang. Jordan's grandpa called out to ask Jordan to get the door. He slid out of his seat, but before he could get there, the door opened. "Pop, we're here!" a young lady called.

Jordan froze and they met each other's gaze. She was about eighteen, tall and willowy with long, light brown hair and a pretty face. Upon seeing Jordan, she shrieked and leapt at him. "What are you doing here? I was wondering whose shiny new car that was!"

Jordan stiffened, gazing at the doorway she had left open. He wrapped an arm around her while she kissed his cheek. "Who's *we*? Who are you here with?" he snapped.

She took a breath and stepped back, frowning. "Well, hello to you too, big bro. I'm with Mom and Dad, but no one said you were going to be here." She flicked a curious glance my way before Jordan turned on his heel and stormed off to the kitchen.

We were stuck staring at each other for a long, awkward moment before I stood and walked around the table. "Hi, I'm April Weiss. I'm Jordan's assistant."

She and I both turned and gazed at the closed kitchen door where Jordan's raised voice could be easily heard. Poor grandpa.

"I'm Hannah Fawkes. Little sister to the moody man. And I'm betting that my grandpa didn't know you were coming or he would never have tried to pull this off."

I opened my mouth to ask the question when two more people came through the open front door. I recognized them from the family photo on his desk as Jordan's parents. His mom was slim, of medium height, with red hair that was cut short. Jordan's dad looked like him— or vice versa, as I reminded myself. He had that distinguished thing going for him, and I was caught by the strong family resemblance of the three generations of Fawkes men. It was like looking at Jordan twenty-five years into the future and beyond.

Hannah waved toward them. "These are my parents," she said. Then she turned to her dad. "Jordan's here."

The man scowled. "That explains the gas-guzzling, global-warming machine in the driveway," he muttered.

Jordan had reentered on the tail end of that and tossed a glance at his dad before snapping up his keys. "Nice to see you, too." Then he turned to me. "We're going."

I stood rooted to my spot, uncomfortable at being caught in the middle of the family drama. Jordan strode to the door without further acknowledging his father. His mom spun and went after him, catching his arm just inside the still open door. Reverend Fawkes reemerged from the kitchen with a ginormous chocolate cake on a glass cake stand and set it in the middle of the table.

"You want to explain this little stunt to me?" Jordan's dad asked his grandfather.

"Simmer down and have a seat," the Reverend replied affably. "All of you sit down. Maybe Carol can coax Jordan back to the table."

My eyes flew to where Jordan and his mother were conversing in tense voices near the front door. Jordan's body language was rigid, his hands in his pockets. His mother still had a hand on his arm, the other one gesturing to emphasize her point. I half wondered whether she and the grandfather had colluded to get father and son together in the same room. Maybe this was like a drug intervention or something.

And here I was, smack dab in the middle of a dysfunctional family reunion. Like I didn't have enough family dysfunction in my own life.

I hurriedly gathered up the dirty lunch dishes and utensils from the table and took them to the kitchen. I paused for a moment before spotting a stack of dessert plates and forks. I grabbed them and carried them to the table.

The sooner the cake was cut and served, the sooner we could excuse ourselves, if necessary. Or maybe Jordan and his dad would be able to talk to each other. Maybe.

Most of the people were seated and now Jordan was slowly, reluctantly coming back to the table with a dark look on his face. The Reverend cut the cake as if nothing unusual had happened. Likely he was going through the motions to establish some semblance of normalcy. A family rift like this was painful for more than merely the two involved. It tore apart an entire family. Given the glares Jordan was now aiming at his grandfather, the man had risked a lot—and had likely lost.

We ate our cake in strained silence for a few minutes. Then, when people could no longer tolerate the tension, they started on a safe subject—*me*, apparently.

"So April, how long have you been working at Draco?" the Reverend began.

"Oh, well I spent six months in marketing and now I've been working as Jordan's assistant for a month."

Hannah frowned. "That's a long internship. Are you there for the work experience or are you trying to get a job with the company?"

I smiled. "I'm headed to business school, I hope. Barring that, I'm really interested in theoretic economics."

Jordan's father—who I learned was named Grant Fawkes— snorted. "The world doesn't need more corporate drones. You'd be better off studying theory and writing papers about it that no one will read."

Jordan looked up from his cake long enough to glower at his father. Wow, these two really could not stand each other. What was the story there?

"So what do you do, Mr. Fawkes?" I asked to veer clear of whatever collision course those two were on.

"It's Dr. Fawkes. I'm an associate professor of environmental engineering at Cal Poly, and I run a consulting firm on the side."

That explained the 'global-warming machine' comment he'd made. I took a breath and released it.

"Where did you attend school, April?" Jordan's mother asked.

"I just graduated from UCI last June. I want to go to UCLA for graduate school." We fell into silence again and I picked at my chocolate cake. It was delicious but overly rich, and I'd had my fill of it after the first few bites. "So, uh...you must all be really proud of Jordan, that he's speaking at the TED conference."

All of their heads shot up, faces turned to the man in question. His fork froze in the process of bringing the next bite of cake to his mouth.

"You're speaking at TED?" his mother asked first. "When?"

He took a deep breath, let it out and then shot me a look that could kill.

"In a few weeks," I said when Jordan did not supply the answer. I was shocked that they didn't know.

Hannah cleared her throat. "That's awesome, bro. You'll be like, famous and all that. What are you speaking on?"

"How to be a shallow, materialistic mega-consumer, I'd imagine," said his dad.

"Actually, how to live your life singularly to spite your own parent," Jordan inserted without pause.

Awkward.

"Will we be able to watch the speech?" his mom asked as if neither had spoken.

When Jordan didn't answer, I did. "It live streams on the Internet with a slight delay, I think. You'll be able to see it the day he delivers it. I'm sure the schedule is on the website."

"And here I thought you were all wrapped up in your Wall Street money-grab," said his dad with a sardonic smile.

"Grant," the Reverend began. "Enough."

Jordan's father's face flushed as he turned to the Reverend. "What did you expect from this little maneuver of yours, Dad? Happy unicorns dancing in the woods farting rainbows and butterflies?"

"Yeah," Jordan snorted. "There's no reasoning with fanatics."

Grant's head whipped around and he gave his son a dirty look. "The fanatic label is just a fence-sitter's way of justifying his own cowardice."

"There's no fence-sitting over here. You and I are clearly on opposite sides of a very tall fence," Jordan growled in return.

Oh, dear. I tried to think of an excuse that would get me out of this room as quickly as possible. The full frontal confrontation was making my nerves dance with flashbacks of my parents screaming at each other during practically every exchange I'd ever heard between them.

With a shaky breath, I stood and grabbed my plate, heading once again for the kitchen. I'd hide in there until it was over. A minute later, Jordan's mother was standing beside me at the sink with her plate.

"I'm sorry about that. Neither of us figured that Jordan would bring someone with him." Ah, so she was in on it too. "It wasn't fair to catch you in the crossfire like that."

I cleared my throat. "That must get *really* old during family gatherings for the holidays."

She nodded. "They're too much alike and both very stubborn. They've always butted heads, but it's been particularly bad since—well, you probably don't care about all the family dynamics."

"I've got a lot of dynamics of my own to deal with."

"You're just up here doing your job and stepped into family drama, completely unaware." She put a hand on my shoulder. "I'm really sorry. I hope that he's being a good boss to you?"

"Uh. Yeah. He's teaching me a lot. There's—"

I was cut off when the door to the kitchen opened. With that same perpetual scowl, Jordan stalked into the kitchen straight toward me. "We're going now."

"Jordan," his mom began.

"Not now, okay? We can talk later."

"You're upset."

Jordan rubbed at his jaw. "I'm pretty pissed, yeah."

"I'm, uh, gonna give you two a minute. I'll be out in the car," I said.

I left the room, then said my goodbyes to Jordan's other family members. The Reverend walked me to the door and I promptly fled to the safety of Jordan's shiny new SUV, not giving a shit about the fact that it guzzled gas and caused global warming.

14
JORDAN

W E WERE BACK ON THE ROAD IN TIME FOR RUSH-HOUR
traffic. We hit it through Santa Barbara, then again in
Ventura, until finally running into the giant parking
lot that was the San Fernando Valley. I made sure to play music the
whole way. I was *not* in the mood to talk about that hot mess of a
family reunion that only lacked my brother, Seth, to make it complete.
Since he was in college three states away, I guess that wasn't
convenient. But apparently, embarrassing the hell out of me in front
of my assistant *was* convenient.

April spent much of the time on her phone, reading a book,
presumably. But at one point, she leaned back in her seat and closed
her eyes. The sunlight was starting to disappear and the traffic was
slow going. I stole glimpses of her in between brooding and feeling
sorry for myself. And embarrassment. There was that too.

Soon, she'd gravitated to my shoulder to rest her head as she
continued to doze. At first, I was tempted to push her away, but her
smell—that intoxicating honey scent that did weird things to my self-

control—had me taking a nice long whiff every so often. Each time was like getting a head rush.

The combination of her smell and those cute little noises she made while sleeping was making it hard to concentrate on the road—or on anything else but her. It reminded me of the sounds she made when she climaxed, and that thought brought a rush of heat in all the right places. It was all too tempting to drive her home to my place and take her to bed.

I blinked at that thought, sobering. I *really* wanted to take her to bed. And it wasn't because I felt deprived from my self-inflicted period of celibacy, either. I was horny enough these days that I'd probably screw just about anyone. Okay, not *anyone*. But with *this* particular young lady, I had to fight with myself hourly to keep my hands off of her.

No, the less contact between us, the better. She had a little over a month to go until her internship was done. Just a little more than a month of purgatory, and then...then...

I sometimes thought about what would happen if I told her I was Falco from Comic-Con. How would she react? Would she be surprised, angry, turned on? Would it change how things were between us? Did she have good memories of that encounter now that it had been sullied by the viral video? She *had* admitted under nervous duress that it was the best sex of her life. I'd mentally high-fived myself when she'd let that one slip. Jordan Fawkes never, *ever* turned down an opportunity to massage his own ego.

I concluded that it was a good thing she didn't know it was me—that she should *never* find out that it was me. And I couldn't take her to bed under these circumstances. So the sheer fact of her not knowing protected her—and me—from doing something that we would probably end up regretting. I shouldn't even have been *considering* taking her to bed. Those very thoughts should not have been rolling through my mind—but a man had his limits. As long as they only remained thoughts and desires, I was good. She was safe.

Although it would help if she didn't currently have her head on my shoulder, her long-lashed eyes closed, her fragrant hair draped over my arm. I turned to sniff it again and stopped when my gaze met her open eyes.

She frowned, and I returned my eyes quickly to the road. I felt the weight of her head slip from my shoulder, accompanied by a slight pang of loss. I wouldn't have minded if she'd slept there for another hour.

She stretched beside me, arching her back, pushing those lovely breasts against her silk blouse. I looked—for longer than I should have, dammit. Friar Jordan, the would-be monk, was not doing very well with his new vow of celibacy.

"Did I fall asleep on you? I'm sorry." She put her hand to her mouth. "I hope I didn't drool."

"Nope, no drool." Just that amazing smell...

She craned her neck as if to figure out where we were—almost through LA and less than an hour home on the Santa Ana Freeway. The brightly lit Citadel outlets loomed on our left, just outside of the City of Commerce.

"I should be the one apologizing to you," I said, knowing it needed to be said. No time like the present, I supposed.

She turned to me with a frown. "For what?"

"For my fucked-up family. I guess my mom and grandpa were in cahoots on that little ambush."

"At least your mom cares. Be grateful for that."

"Hard to be grateful when all I can feel right now is embarrassment."

She threw me a sidelong glance, folding her arms across her chest. "Because of me? Don't be. My family is way more fucked-up than yours, I guarantee that."

"I heard your dad is a nice guy. Adam likes him, anyway."

"Everybody who works with my dad likes him. He's a hard-ass, but he cares about his people. His work people are more his family than..." Her voice died off and then she shrugged, glancing out the side window.

"Than his own family?"

"He has one of those, too. A shiny new family."

I blinked. "And where do you fit in?"

"I don't."

I looked at her and saw that her features were completely blank. From what I knew of April—and what my social media info guy had collected for me—Daddy was pretty damn loaded and more than generous. She drove a compact, sporty Lexus, wore designer clothes and lived in a condo paid for and furnished by him. But she didn't seem the spoiled rotten type—at least what I knew of her.

"He's not a bad person at all. He just...I just...We just don't get each other, I guess."

"That sounds familiar."

She cocked a head at me. "So your dad's annoyed that you don't follow his ideologies?"

I let out a breath. "Let's just say I'm his big disappointment. He did everything he could to raise a young version of himself and got me instead."

"So that's why he's so pissed at you? Because you grew up to become your own person?" She shook her head.

I felt a twinge of guilt that she had jumped to that conclusion—with my help—when that wasn't exactly the case.

"Some of it is justified and some of it is his bullshit. I lied to him and it pissed him off."

"I take it it was a pretty huge lie?"

I clenched my teeth. That same guilt...my dad's rant on my graduation day, my mom's tears. He wouldn't have attended had it not been for her begging. My chest tightened. "Yeah."

April was watching me, and when I looked up from the road, I saw that she had that deep thing going on with those eyes of hers—like she was studying me.

"It takes two to hold onto a bitter family grudge like that...I hope it doesn't carry over to your mom and grandpa."

"What do you mean by that?"

"I mean that I can't blame them for trying what they did if it's that hard for them to get the two of you to sit down at the same table."

I clenched my jaw and didn't say anything. Easy for her to say. She hadn't had to live through all of my dad's BS.

"Sorry, I didn't mean to offend you."

"I'd have to care about the situation in order to be offended."

Silence. She knew I was lying.

She turned and looked out the windshield at the road ahead.

"A running feud between two people in a family affects far more than those two people, you know. It's kind of like divorced parents who can't stand each other and can't get along, even for the sake of the kids. I know all about what that feels like."

I blinked and kept my eyes on the sea of red brake lights in front of me. I had no answer for that, because she was right. I was more than a little astonished that I'd never looked at it that way. All I could see and hear whenever I thought of my stand off with Dad was his constant criticism, his continuous disapproval, his lip curling as he stated on my college graduation day, "*You're a disappointment.*"

Heat seared under my collar at that remembered insult, but I couldn't tell if I was angrier at him for his harsh words or myself, for having disappointed him. I swallowed.

She was watching me again. Under her scrutiny, I felt sort of itchy. Like she was getting under my skin. And I didn't like that feeling at all.

"Maybe you should pay more attention to your own life and fuck-ups rather than being so quick to point at others," I let out in a tight voice.

With a quick intake of breath, she sat back. I took a fortifying breath but didn't look at her. I felt like shit inside for saying it. But it was safer this way. I could not afford to let her under my skin. Or anywhere else, for that matter.

She folded her arms tightly against her chest and turned her head to gaze out the passenger window. She was fuming, hurt. That much was obvious. The scariest part was that I knew exactly what buttons to push to get that reaction from her. It was a talent of mine.

And she wouldn't speak up for herself. I knew that too. So she'd sit there in the dark and fume and feel like shit, like I'd counted on.

Sometimes I made myself sick.

I dropped her off at her car at work a little after dinnertime. She grabbed her bag and her jacket and muttered a halfhearted 'thank you.'

I didn't reply and I drove home.

So... No sex. No alcohol. My two favorite ways to cope were closed off to me. I hadn't lit up in ages, but I had to admit I was tempted to fire up a joint. Instead, I changed clothes, went to the gym and worked out for hours until I was numb and ready to fall down from exhaustion.

15
APRIL

I STEPPED INTO THE APARTMENT FEELING DEFLATED. IT HAD BEEN a long day, and for all the good cheer and humor with which it had started out...it sure ended on a sour note. Jordan had said little else after lashing out at me. I'd gotten too close—I saw that now. His defenses were quick and impenetrable, and when he detected that I'd seen a weakness, he shoved me far away.

Just when I thought we'd started to make some sort of headway to...whatever this was. Boss/employee? Mutual co-lusters? Friends who kiss each other and hand out the occasional orgasm? Or maybe merely my unrequited crush on the surly man.

I knew I should try my best to keep it strictly professional. Reminded myself yet again to keep my distance.

And I must not...*definitely* must not remember how it had felt to wake up with my head on his shoulder. His hard, solid, wonderful-smelling shoulder.

I gulped. I was in a pool of crap and headed toward the deep end.

I walked into our bedroom to find Sid in bed, her iPad propped on her knees, FaceTiming one of her many relatives who lived on the other coast.

I pulled off my clothes and changed for bed.

After finishing her conversation, she set her iPad aside. "Hey...looks like you had a long day. Are you hungry?"

I sighed. "No, not really. I want to play some DE. Did I tell you I'm almost level five?"

She laughed. "Only about five times." She tossed her pillow at me. "Newb!"

I stuck out my tongue and blew a raspberry.

"How was Santa Barbara?"

"Ugh. Too damn far away." I tried to ignore the sting I still felt from Jordan's tongue-lashing. I knew I shouldn't take it personally. His family had ambushed him, and he'd been upset and embarrassed. But he was so prickly and unpredictable sometimes. It rankled.

"So, I gotta tell you. I'm still trying to solve the mystery of how your video got uploaded to the Internet."

I plopped down onto my bed and stared at her. "That may never be solved. I think we have to chalk it up to my blatant stupidity."

"Can you lend me your phone tomorrow? I want to take a look at all the ins and outs, see if I can reproduce what happened."

"God, no! Why would you want to reproduce what happened?"

"Not with your lurid porn video, stupid. With a blank dummy video. I want to recreate the conditions in which it occurred. I made a blank demo tape of approximately the same length."

My brows furrowed. "That's a very scientific approach."

"Well, I *am* a scientist—or hope to be, if I make it through this semester. But I just have this gut feeling that this wasn't an accident."

I frowned. "You mean that someone hacked me?"

She shrugged. "I don't know. I want to see what I can find out."

"Okay...I'll leave it on the charger. Do *not* answer it if anyone calls me."

Her brows twitched. "Still avoiding Mommy Dearest?"

"Hell, yes."

She stifled a yawn and cleared her bed of books and her tablet. "I'm crashing."

"Mind if I play on the game for a bit? I'm not tired."

She snickered. "You are so hooked."

"Am not. It's research."

"Are too. How close are you to your next level?"

I sighed, holding up my thumb and forefinger together. "I'm *this* close."

"You're an addict. It only gets worse from here on out."

Her light went off, and I plugged in my ear buds and entered the world of Yondareth yet again. My Beast achieved level five quickly, and I told myself just a few more minutes...a few more minutes.

I finally ran out of minutes at three in the morning.

This was getting ridiculous.

At least this time when I went to sleep I didn't lay awake for hours thinking about *him*. Because I was so exhausted, I fell asleep quickly.

The next morning, I was red-eyed and coffee-fueled. My hair looked horrible, so I'd quickly braided it to keep it out of my face. I wore a dark blue dress to work because I hadn't had time to do laundry last weekend.

After finishing a quick lunch at my desk, I was struggling with a fuzzy brain and a whole lot of work to wade through. Sighing and complaining under my breath, I had my arms full of reports and was on my way to the copy machine when, in a rush, I almost collided with two men approaching from the opposite direction. Just my luck, it happened to be my boss and his boss. Half the files slipped out of my hold, and I fought to recover them before they went spilling all over the floor.

"Whoa—need a hand?" Adam said, reaching out to steady the top of the files. Jordan made no such move to help me. My gaze briefly touched his before jerking away. I felt a punch of something in my chest, a blow, like I'd been hit.

"Sorry, guys. I was in a bit of a hurry I, um, seem to be overloaded today."

Jordan raised a brow but said nothing.

Adam threw him a glance. "Cracking the whip again?"

"Oh, it's just me," I intervened before Jordan could reply. "Moving kind of slow today. Very little sleep last night." *Because of your damn addictive game,* I almost added.

I had a level five character in Dragon Epoch who was now *this close* to level six. So close I could smell it. One, maybe two more quests and he'd be at his next level. Strangely enough, as I thought about it, I was more and more excited to get back into the game. No wonder players often referred to the game as Dragon Addiction.

"Sorry you're so tired," Adam said with a small smile. "Maybe you could call on your woodland creatures for help."

I frowned as I got a better grip on my folders, not missing when Jordan and Adam exchanged a look before I turned to leave. They seemed to be sharing some private joke at my expense. My cheeks flamed and I swallowed the irritation, pushing past them to the copy room. Jordan had not addressed or even looked at me directly.

He had barely spoken to me all day, telling me tersely to get my task list from Susan. He was too busy, apparently.

When I got back to my desk, Susan hung up her phone and pulled her chair over to my desk to sit beside me.

"You look as bad as I feel today," she said. Today, oversized golden autumn leaves bobbed from her earlobes with every movement of her head.

"Given that you are pregnant and I'm not, that says a lot. I'm just tired."

"I like your hair like that...all braided up. And that dress...you look like an innocent forest maiden."

I frowned. "What do you need me to do?"

A weak smile touched her lips. "I'm being rather transparent, I guess. I have a huge favor to ask you."

I braced myself, envisioning some monstrous task I had no desire whatsoever to do. Something that might prevent me from working on my own project.

"Uh, well. Have you ever been to Vancouver?"

"In Canada?" My stomach dropped and my eyes flew to the closed door of Jordan's office. He had that TED talk in two weeks. TED stood for Technology, Entertainment and Design. It was a prestigious global conference that served as a gathering of great minds. That Jordan had been invited to present at TED, a CFO of his young age, was a feather in his cap and also gave the company big bragging rights.

The main TED conference took place in Vancouver, British Columbia. Sudden realization dawned. Go to Vancouver with Jordan the way things were between us now? Uh, no. No way. I was supposed to keep my distance. I shook my head.

"*Please*, April. You're my only hope."

"Uh, why?"

Susan rubbed her stomach, though she was hardly showing. "I had a miscarriage last year. We've been trying for about ten months now, and though the doctor says there's no reason to believe I'm at risk again…I just can't stand the thought of getting on an airplane, traveling long hours, working with jet lag—"

"It's the same time zone as us."

Susan pleaded with her eyes.

I sighed. "What would I have to do?"

"You're there as his assistant. Run his schedule. Facilitate his meetings, be the go-between for him and the conference coordinators. Aid him with whatever he needs."

I looked away, a blush staining my cheeks, unwilling to go there in my mind. But apparently, I already had, given that my entire body was heating at the thought of assisting with *all* of his needs—and vice-versa.

"What do you say?"

I shook my head. "I highly doubt he'd go for it, Susan. I'm just an intern, and he thinks I'm a fuck-up."

She looked at me like I'd told her that clouds are made out of marshmallows and the moon of green cheese. "In what universe has he ever said that? I only hear good stuff from him about you. He *is* typically skimpy on praise, mind you, so I can see why you'd think he hasn't noticed. But he has."

I swallowed a lump in my throat. "I don't think he wants me going to Vancouver with him."

"I asked him and he said if I could get you to agree to do it, he'd let me off the hook. *Please*, April. For my baby?" She rubbed her stomach again. She didn't even have a goddamn baby bump and already she was exploiting the kid for her own gain.

I let out a long sigh and looked away. "How long is it?"

"Four days. And you get a room in the penthouse suite at the Fairmont Pacific Rim. It's an *amazing* hotel. I have the website—"

I held up a hand, waving it, mildly uncomfortable and simultaneously aflame at the thought of sharing a suite—no matter how big—with Jordan for four days.

I wanted to say no. Or rather, I wanted to *want* to say no. But I didn't really *want* to say no. Because even though he'd snapped at me and was completely unpredictable, I still thought about him all the time. And it was driving me crazy. I could *not* have a crush on my boss. I could *never* be one of those women who slept with their boss!

I would *never, ever* be.

***

Days passed. Things were quiet. Sid continued with her investigation, not having reached anything conclusive when she'd examined my phone. Jordan and I studiously avoided each other, only minimally discussing the plans to go to Vancouver. Every time I had a question, he quickly directed me to Susan without even meeting my gaze.

It stung, but it was also a relief. Things may have continued that way had it not been for that fateful morning—less than a day before we were to depart for Vancouver.

Then, everything changed.

Since it was a Monday, the morning arrived with its usual brand of grossness. Again, I'd been up too late playing on the game. I swore the typical amount before getting enough coffee in me for my brain to function as I got ready for work.

I fixed my hair and makeup as usual, choosing to put it up in a messy bun and letting dark tendrils of hair hang around my face. I chose eyeliner to match my blue eyes, trying not to question myself too closely as to why I was paying special attention to my looks for work.

In my head, I may have wanted to avoid him, but deep down—and in other places—I was desperate for him to notice me again.

It was stupid, since he'd probably hooked up with some hot model in the meantime and I was likely nothing in comparison. I swallowed the lump that rose at that thought and finished my preparations.

I arrived at the office a few minutes late with Jordan's extra-hot lava flow in my gloved hand. I made sure to change out of my sneakers as quickly as I could before sweeping into his office. He'd left the door ajar, a signal that he preferred people to just come in. When it was closed, it was best to knock or quietly tiptoe away. I usually chose to do the latter when I could get away with it.

He didn't even look up from his computer screen when I set the coffee down. "You're late," he grunted.

"There was a line at Starbucks. I'm—" The apology hung from my lips, half spoken, when he looked up, spearing me with those lovely green-brown eyes.

"I need today's financial reports."

I froze. "Uh. Sure. Gimme a few."

"You don't *have* a few. You spent those 'few' in line at the coffee shop."

I opened my mouth, feeling heat flush to my face, and quickly snapped it closed again. Who the hell had peed in his Cheerios today?

It was like the last few weeks had never happened. His eyes were on my face and they had a challenge in them. He seemed to be daring me to react, with an expectant curl at the end of his lip.

I swallowed. "Yes, sir."

Returning to my desk, I muttered under my breath everything I wished I could say to him. *I don't care if you have gorgeous abs, Mr. Fawkes, or an amazing set of shoulders or a handsome face or that you kiss like a fucking Greek god. Or that you make me want to call you Mr. Fox instead of Mr. Fawkes. I don't care.*

You're still a colossal asshole.

Someone loudly—and rudely—cleared his or her throat, and I looked up to find Charles standing at my desk. I had no idea how long he'd be standing there.

All I knew was that I didn't have time for his condescending ass. "Sorry. I've already been to Starbucks and now the boss is on the warpath."

Charles smirked and ran his eyes down me again. I pretended not to notice. He'd become a little too obvious with his ogling, and his weird way of flirting was obnoxious. Hadn't he sat through that stupid-ass sexual harassment training like the rest of us? What made him the special snowflake?

"So, how about lunch again today?"

I pulled the stack of papers out of the printer and stood. Instead of telling him the truth—that I wasn't interested—I made up a wimpy excuse instead. "Uh, I have plans to eat...with the other interns in marketing."

"Oh...okay. Well, if you need anything, let me know."

Sure thing, I mentally sneered. *Your smug ass will be the first one I think of when I'm in a pinch!*

I grinned wide. "Thank you. That's very nice." As usual, April the coward never said what was *really* on her mind. She just grinned and bore it.

I held my breath when I walked back into the lair of the Beast. He glanced up at me again, this time giving me a longer look, as if he noticed my extra efforts at prettying myself—*not* for him, of course. I set the reports down on his desk. "Here you go. All in order, NYSE on top."

"As it should be."

I turned at the same time he picked up his coffee to make room for his reports, which he usually spread out across the desktop so he could cross-reference them quickly. As if in slow motion, I watched as the top of the cup popped off when he grabbed it and the coffee sprayed all over the desk—and him.

I froze, putting my hand to my mouth, and watched, eyes wide with horror, as coffee stains bloomed on his shirt and pants.

"Motherfucker!" he shouted, shooting out of his chair.

"Oh crap!" I said at the same time. "Let me get some towels." I bee-lined it around his desk into his private bathroom and grabbed a stack of clean hand towels from the cabinet. Rushing back into the office, I saw that he'd already peeled off his dress shirt and was now yanking off his undershirt.

Was I was about to get yet another glimpse of that magnificent chest? Someone up there was getting back at me for something bad I'd done.

I handed him a towel, which he proceeded to dab over his moist, shiny skin. "You aren't burned? With the white-hot temperature you want that coffee, I'm surprised you aren't blistering by now."

He was red in spots, but it appeared as if he'd pulled off his shirt in time.

He shook his head. "How the hell did this happen? Was that lid on properly?"

I paused from where I was mopping up spilled coffee from the desktop. Was he going to pin the blame on me?

"The top was secure when I gave it to you," I said in an even, firm voice. I picked up each paper and wiped droplets of coffee off before setting it back down.

"Well, obviously it *wasn't* on there properly because how else would it just pop off like that? I didn't pull it off and pop it back on. Why would I?"

"I don't know. Maybe you were checking to see if I'd screwed up the order so you could yell at me about it? Or perhaps you had your thermometer out ready to check if it was ten degrees short of screaming molten fusion!"

He raised his brows at me, clearly surprised that I'd snapped back at him. Up until this moment, I'd quietly taken every bit of shit he'd dished out at me. But not anymore. I'd had enough!

I folded my arms across my chest, ready for his onslaught...but it didn't come. I tried to force my eyes away from his chest, his bulging arm muscles, that sexy-as-hell tattoo. God, he was just too yummy to be real. Was it a requirement to have hot male-model looks in order to run this damn company? And be filthy rich and brilliantly intelligent on top of it?

Oh, and to be so perfect that he was arrogantly and insufferably full of himself. I reminded myself not to forget *that*.

Jordan was talking and I was only half paying attention, watching as he dabbed at his chest with the soft, white towel. "—need you to grab me a new shirt, undershirt and suit. I've got a lunch meeting at noon."

I shook my head. "Um...what?"

He snapped his fingers two inches from my face and I blinked. "Earth to Weiss...there's no intelligent life down here...beam me up!"

I clenched my teeth and glared at him. *Fuck you*, my brain wanted to scream.

"I need you to swing by my house and grab me new clothes."

"Uh. Are you sure you don't just want to drive home and change?"

"I'm absolutely sure, since I have a phone call in half an hour with an underwriter and another with the IPO attorney after that. And I have that important lunch meeting that I can't show up to with coffee all over myself. So I need you to take my keys, go into my closet and grab a new shirt, tie and suit. You remember where my room is?"

"Uh, sure." I gulped, remembering the last time I'd been in his room—and had been caught snooping by him. I shoved that thought aside in my annoyance.

He hurriedly scrawled down some numbers and gave me instructions for how to disarm the alarm. I took his keys and marched toward the door, barely managing to keep the epithets unspoken.

"Oh, and Weiss—" he called out, catching me right before I exited. I spun around and waited for the other shoe to drop. "Get me another cup of coffee on the way in, too."

I couldn't trust myself to reply, so I clenched my fists at my side and turned, furious that he'd blamed me for this.

Reminding myself to take deep breaths and push fantasies of violent murder out of my mind, I raced out of the building and through the parking lot to my car.

I floored it all the way to his house, risking traffic violations to get there as quickly as I could. It felt weird letting myself into his place. However, being there brought to mind that night I'd been held captive a few weeks before. That night he'd kissed me—and more—on his couch...

Ignoring the lightning strikes of fresh pleasure at those remembered touches, I swallowed and went about my business. I bolted up the stairs, out of breath by the time I got to his room. In a panic, I went to his closet, threw open the doors and quickly selected a white shirt—that part was easy. Then I located the hangers that held ties, pulling them off the rack and laying them carefully on the bed. I had to think this through clearly and not grab just any tie, or he'd rip me a new asshole. Should I get a light brown one or a green one to match the color of his eyes? *Were* they actually green or brown? Or maybe brown with green and gold flecks. Or green with brown flecks.

Sometimes when I looked at them, they looked like two miniature globes as seen from space—all blue and green and brown... They were as beautiful as the rest of him.

I shook my head—*earth to Weiss,* indeed—deciding instead to match the tie with the suit. Turning back to the closet, I took in the line-up: some dark brown, some lighter, some in practically every shade of gray. There were even some black ones, which I judged would be too severe with his coloring. His hair was too light a shade of brown to look good with a black suit.

I pondered over it far too long, imagining him carrying on that phone conference in his skivvies, checking his watch and fuming.

I sifted through his entire wardrobe, even the stuff it was clear he hadn't worn in a while. I was about to select a nice coffee-brown suit, which would look great with a dark red tie, when my hand landed on some shiny spandex material.

I jerked back in surprise. Did he have a Superman suit in there or something? Or maybe some crazy role-playing outfit for when he had his models over for orgies. I had to admit that curiosity got the best of me, so I yanked the thing out by the hanger to look it over.

And promptly dropped it on the floor in shock. I'd seen that costume before. Stretched across the broad shoulders and solid form of Falco the Bounty Hunter.

What. The. Fuck?

I frantically pushed clothes aside in the closet to get a look at what was on the shelves, and there it was—shoved in the corner. Falco's helmet. The infamous helmet.

Stumbling, I fell back against the bed, not even caring that I was now wrinkling his clothes. That costume was not merchandised. It wasn't something you could go down to the corner drugstore to buy for Halloween or click a button to order off Amazon. It was custom made specifically for cosplay. And I'd only seen one Falco at Comic-Con. *My* Falco.

Jordan had attended Comic-Con, too. I'd seen him often enough at the bar of the hotel we'd stayed at with a swarm of women around him, living it up like a playboy. But the day of the costume party, I had no idea what he'd worn.

Apparently, it was a Falco costume.

But no. This must have been an old costume, probably from the year before or from the Draco company convention the previous November? He'd loaned it out to a friend, surely. The friend who I'd...

But if that were the case, if Jordan had ever been seen in the Falco costume, then people would know that he was the owner of the now infamous ensemble as seen in the unintentional geek porn video.

My head hurt and throbbed with the possibilities.

Because the only one that made sense was that Jordan had worn the costume to Comic-Con for the first and only time, and had done so completely unbeknownst to any other employees there. It was common—even famous actors and other geek celebrities got away with wandering through Comic-Con unrecognizable beneath a mask. Or helmet.

The only explanation that made sense was that Jordan and Falco were one and the same. And all this time...he'd let me believe...

Things were clicking into place now. The real reason he hadn't fired me wasn't out of the goodness of his heart; it was to keep an eye on me, to ensure I wouldn't put two and two together and expose him. And, oh God—that comment I'd made about it being the best sex of my life—he'd *really* seemed to enjoy *that*. I'd been stroking his ginormous ego every time the subject came up.

Oh. Holy. Shit. That horrible fucker!

My breath caught. Actually...not so horrible fucker.

A pretty amazing fucker, if I remembered right. My eyes squeezed shut and now I considered myself a complete idiot for not having figured it out sooner. The way he'd touched me, both on his couch and the night at the bar. How incredible it had felt. And it hadn't been the first time!

And he knew. He'd known it all along...

But what to do now? My first inclination was to go running home and bury myself under pillows and cry. Forget I'd ever worked at a place called Draco or ever met a dickhead named Jordan Fawkes.

I was very tempted by the thought of leaving him there in his underwear, twiddling his thumbs and wondering where I'd vanished to.

I grabbed the shirt, the suit and the first tie I could reach off the rack—an ugly dark pink one with bright, multi-colored polka dots. It still had the price tag on it and I assumed it was a gag gift. Well, it served him right. Let him go chat up his investment banker wearing a Skittles tie.

My mind raced as I went through the motions of locking up.

Should I confront him?

I wanted to. I *really* wanted to. But that streak of cowardice rose up again. I'd have to think about this…maybe find a time or way to get him back.

I shoved the clothes into the hatchback of my car, abusing them soundly. I gripped the steering wheel all the way back and seethed, wondering how long it would take me to muster up the courage to do it.

Or would I chicken out again?

No. I'd do it later today after his meeting. At the Starbucks, I dumped a cup of ice into his fucking coffee. And if he dared say anything about it… Or if he waved that recommendation in my face… I'd—I'd…well, I wasn't sure what I'd do, but I'd make sure it was good.

I arrived at the office with his clothes inside a garment bag draped over my shoulder and his coffee cup in my other hand. I pushed inside the door without bothering to knock.

Jordan was sitting at the desk in his stained undershirt. He stood when I came in.

I was so furious I couldn't even look at him. Instead, I laid the garment bag across his desk and set down the coffee.

Before I could make my getaway, he unzipped the bag and said, "Took you long enough. At least you got things right this time. That's my favorite suit."

"Oh really? *This* is your favorite suit?" And I lost it. The rage was too much. I couldn't take another moment. I felt like a volcano at the moment right before it erupted. Mt. Vesuvius had nothing on me.

I grabbed his shitty cup of coffee, popped off the lid and drenched the goddamn suit with it. Guess I wasn't waiting until later after all.

He jumped back in shock. I tossed the coffee cup on the floor and stormed to the doorway.

But he was too fast for me. I got it open a half inch before he pushed it shut again, holding it closed over my head. I yanked on the knob, but it didn't budge.

"What do you think you are doing?" he ground out between clenched teeth.

"Going home. I quit."

"Take a deep breath and calm down, Weiss. You aren't going home."

"If you'd get your giant manpaws off this door, I'd be gone already."

"Manpaws?"

He leaned against the door, blocking me, and I backed away, avoiding looking into his face. He folded his arms across his chest. I had to force myself to ignore the way his stained undershirt tightened over his muscular build.

He took a deep breath and let it out. "So that's it? You're just going to flounce out of here and not speak up for yourself?"

I folded my arms, mirroring his action, and squared my shoulders, saying between clenched teeth, "Open the fucking door, Jordan."

"No."

I hissed. "I want to leave."

"You're not going to leave. Don't just run away. Say something. Don't leave me in the dark."

My arms dropped, fists tightening at my sides. I'd never before had the desire to commit murder like I did at this moment.

"*I'm* the one who's been in the dark." I jerked my chin at him. "You've known exactly what's going on."

He blinked. Our eyes locked, and I could tell the moment he figured out what I was referring to because there was a spark of fear there that I'd never seen before.

In spite of that, he tilted his head at a cocky angle, giving a half shrug. "Well then, spit it out."

"Fuck you, Jordan!" I ground out between my teeth. "Or should I say, *Falco?*"

He didn't move. Didn't say a word. I bit my lip and experienced a moment of self-doubt. Maybe I was mistaken? Maybe he really wasn't Falco. The thought brought a simultaneous rush of relief and regret that I didn't want to question.

"What do you have to say for yourself?" I said stupidly.

"I don't have to say anything."

My face heated again and I charged, grabbing at the doorknob in spite of the fact that he was firmly planted against the door like a big, hulking oak tree.

"Let. Me. Out!"

He wouldn't budge so I got violent, pounding a fist against his huge chest. He hardly flinched. Didn't even blink. That infuriated me more, so I took another swing at him.

It was like hitting a brick wall.

Soon, I was treating him like a punching bag and he appeared to not even feel it. Damn it! With frustration, I let out a growl and continued pummeling him with my fists. He raised a brow, mildly amused. "Honestly, it's like being attacked by a gnat."

Punch. "You suck!" Punch. "I hate you." Punch. "You're disgusting." Punch.

Then he laughed. "That's not what you were saying that night at Comic-Con."

"*You...*" My knee zeroed in on his crotch. I snagged him in the upper thigh instead. I hated being so short.

His eyes widened, alarmed. *That* had gotten his attention.

"Whoa, there. Calm down."

Ohhh, I wanted to kick the crap out of him! I was not a violent person, but this... My knee jerked up again, this time striking much closer to the mark.

He pushed off the door, true anger crossing his features. I stepped back, suddenly intimidated and realizing that he was a *lot* bigger than me.

"Knock it off, Weiss."

"I'd rather knock *you* off. If I could figure out a way to hide the body, I'd be plotting your death this very minute."

He raised his brows. With him distracted and away from the door, I lunged for it. Before I could even get close, his arm snaked out, catching me around the waist. He pulled me back against him and I elbowed him in the stomach.

Which did nothing at all because it was like elbowing the aforementioned brick wall. Suddenly, he pushed forward and I found myself pressed against the floor-to-ceiling glass windows that overlooked a private, pretty little courtyard. Jordan had me pinned against the window, my back to his front. I could barely manage a wriggle.

His hot breath singed the back of my neck.

"I'm going to scream," I said, knowing full well there was little else I could do at this point.

"Really? And when people come running, are you going to explain what you're so pissed about?"

I had nothing to say to that, so I kept quiet.

After a few minutes, he slowly loosened his grip on me. "Take a minute and calm down, please, so we can talk about this."

"I have nothing to talk about with you. Bastard."

"It's rat bastard, actually."

"Do I look like I'm in the mood for joking around? I'm not. So get your big, giant gorilla body off of me."

"That—"

"If you say that's not what I said that night at Comic-Con, then you'd better kiss your balls goodbye."

His body shook against mine. He was laughing.

"It's not fucking funny, Jordan."

He kept laughing. "If you say so."

I clenched my fists and my jaw and waited. Slowly, he let up, but he didn't back away. I turned around and faced him—

And wished I hadn't. His face was only inches from mine, and my heart was reacting accordingly. His smell, his gorgeous eyes, the feel of his body... Apparently, my body was nothing short of happy to be *this close* to the best sex of my life again.

But my brain was still beyond pissed off at him.

"Are you ready to talk about this yet?" he asked.

"I'm not sure if I will *ever* be ready. And you've got your goddamn meeting in thirty minutes. I plan on torching your office while you're gone."

"Mmm. That might make things difficult for you to get your recommendation."

I stiffened. "If you hold that over my head *one* more time, I'll—"

"What will you do, April? Record me having sex with you and upload it to the Internet?"

My mouth twisted in frustration. Okay, he had a point. I was still the one responsible for the cosplay porn being broadcast to anyone with Internet. But a goddamn *decent* person would have let me know he was the other person weeks ago.

But I was learning that Jordan Fawkes was not a decent person.

He was, however, still inches from my face. With each breath I exhaled, he inhaled, and the cloud of air between us grew steaming hot in seconds, our chests rising and falling. The tension between us thickened.

I was in trouble. So much trouble. Because I'd vowed I'd never, *ever* be the girl who slept with her boss.

And I'd had every intention of holding to that. Until the moment when I found out I'd already slept with him—one thrilling night of not-so-anonymous sex. Now the rug had been yanked out from underneath me and I was in danger of forgetting that very important vow.

16
JORDAN

I WATCHED AS THE COLOR DRAINED FROM HER FACE, HER EYES shifting. My gaze dropped to her hands. They knotted and unknotted before repeating the pattern again. She was a study in anxiety and fear.

If I were a better person, I might have done something to help alleviate that. But I'd be the first to admit that I wasn't a better person. And, hot night of sex or not, sweet-smelling, soft skin and irresistible curves or not, she still had done me a terrible wrong.

"It was an accident. I told you."

My jaw tightened. "What part of it was an accident? Uploading it for the whole world to see, or pressing record on your video app and pointing the camera at us when I had no idea?"

She gulped, eyes widening. "I—I'm sorry."

I straightened, pulling away from her heady scent. I'd had about enough of smelling her and knowing how soft her skin was and not being able to touch it. For the past few days, I'd made a valiant effort to avoid her presence at work and keep her out of my mind.

At this moment, my body wasn't fully on board with that plan.

"But you shouldn't have been torturing me for the past month, either, holding this shit over my head."

"Really? You're going to go there? Should I be happily skipping for joy that your little *oops* has threatened something I've been working for years?"

She paled, her eyes squeezing shut. Instead of answering, she shook her head.

I tensed, waited for her to talk. When she finally did, I wished she hadn't. "This isn't worth it, Jordan. You should just let me go."

I should. I really should.

But I didn't want to.

I rubbed at the back of my neck. "What on earth possessed you to do it?"

"Record it or upload it?"

"Both."

She looked away, flattening herself against the window. There were people milling around the courtyard right outside, but they couldn't see us thanks to the one-way privacy glass. Her eyes returned to me.

"I was caught up in the moment and my judgment was impaired," she said in a shaky voice with wide eyes pleading for me to believe her.

The same bullshit answer she'd given me before. I wondered if she also blamed her *impaired* judgment for sleeping with me.

But I didn't give a shit if she regretted it. It had been a damn hot fuck for both of us—a damn hot fuck that could have stayed safely in the past had she kept her phone in her pocket where it belonged.

As if she sensed my irritation, she reached a hand toward me before letting it fall. "I'm not going to go into the ancient, fucked-up history of why I'm a giant bag of insecurities, but if you must know, I thought it would prove something to myself." She looked away again, blinking, and I felt it in my chest when I saw how sad she was. "That didn't end up happening. The uploading was a complete accident."

I softened my tone. "How does a video go viral without you realizing it?"

"I must have fucked it up somehow. I'm not some kind of techie genius like everyone else here. But please believe me when I say that no one will ever know it's you. I'll walk out of here today, and no one will even know why I've quit. This can all be wrapped up neatly."

I snorted. "There's no '*neatly*' about it, at this point. And you know what? I'm not going to let you walk out of here and take the easy way out. You need to be here and face this every single goddamn day, just like I have to."

She let out a breath of air like I'd punched her in the stomach. "That's not what I was trying to do. I feel bad—"

"Then feel bad. You should. But do it here while you get your job done."

We watched each other and the tension thickened between us. I finally took a step back, forcing some distance between us.

"Who else knows it's you in the video besides the blonde?" I asked.

Her gaze fell. "My roommate knows because it was her elf costume. But no one has any idea who you were. No one knew it was you in the Falco costume. I didn't either, until just now…"

A stupid fucking mistake on my part. I swallowed, half wondering if subconsciously I'd sent her for the clothes so she would find the costume. Somewhere deep down, I guessed I still had a conscience, though I managed to keep it gagged and bound most of the time.

I flicked my wrist to glance at my watch. I had to be out the door in ten minutes or I'd be late for the lunch appointment. My eyes shifted to the desk, now covered by my suit and pools of coffee.

"We have to continue this later. I have to go."

Every muscle in her body visibly relaxed. I could feel the relief coming off of her in waves. "I'm going to see if the ticket can be transferred to Charles. I'm sure he'll jump at the chance."

"What?" I snapped as I grabbed the tie I'd been wearing this morning—fortunately, it was dark brown so I wouldn't have to wear that pink monstrosity.

"We have twenty-four hours before the flight. I think that's enough time to change everything." She sounded less sure of herself than before.

"I already told you that you are not quitting."

She stepped forward, surveying the damage from her caffeinated assault with a grimace. "I won't quit. I'm just talking about the trip to Vancouver. I think I can sweet-talk Charles into going in my place."

First of all, the thought of her "sweet-talking" that little twerp into anything made my blood boil, and second of all, what made her think she was off the hook for Vancouver? I wanted her where I could keep an eye on her. That had been the plan all along and nothing had changed in that regard. I was still aware that her conscience might get the best of her, and at any given moment she could be in the CEO's office, ready to confess all her sins and beg for penitence.

My eyes trailed after her as she disappeared into the bathroom while I grabbed my stained dress shirt. It was still damp, but I'd managed to rinse out most of the mess. But what to do about the suit... Fuck! I had a spare sport coat hanging in my closet. It wasn't normal banker attire but better than nothing. If I'd only remembered it in the first place, we wouldn't be in this mess. April would still be happily ignorant, which would have been better for both of us.

She returned from the bathroom and started sponging up the excess coffee with white hand towels.

"You're still going to Vancouver," I declared as I looped the tie around my neck and collar.

Her eyes shot to mine and then danced away nervously. "Umm. Under the circumstances—"

"No. There are no circumstances. The only thing that has changed is that you have information you didn't previously have. Nothing else has changed. You're still going."

She froze, watching as I knotted my tie quickly without looking in the mirror. Something about that action appeared to fascinate her—hadn't she ever seen a man put on a tie before? Then her blue eyes slid down my body with obvious admiration. I averted mine and tried to think about something else. I knew what was going through her head. She was thinking about that night we were together at Comic-Con.

Well, that made two of us because I was finding it pretty damn difficult to forget that night, too. I grabbed my wallet and sunglasses. "I'm out for the rest of the day, Weiss. After this lunch meeting, I'm going to have to go hide my face in shame for being seen in public like this. Be packed and ready to go tomorrow."

She rolled her eyes and I turned to leave.

"Wait. You have a loose string," she said, moving behind me. I paused without turning toward her, then I felt her brush the top of my back. Her hands rested on my shoulders, and even through the coat, the pressure of her touch was turning me on.

I turned back to her, eyebrows raised.

"I'll go to Vancouver," she finally said after clearing her throat. "But that doesn't mean I have to be nice to you."

"Then, by all means, don't. Now get your work done," I muttered before pulling the door open and leaving.

***

The next day, we boarded our early afternoon flight from Orange County to Vancouver. April had refused to speak to me at the office and during the short ride to the airport. When I'd asked her questions, she answered in monosyllables and refused to look at me, still visibly pissed.

Oh well, I shrugged. She'd have to deal, wouldn't she? Like I'd had to deal those first few days after discovering that my night of hot cosplay sex was on the Internet for all to see.

Since then—pain-in-the-ass work issues aside—I've come to think of it in a more philosophical light. At least the poor lonely geeks that could never get any were able to obtain some sort of education on how things worked. Whether or not any of them could ever get with a girl as hot as April was another question altogether.

I sat in first class enjoying my preflight drink—mineral water. I was still in my own private prohibition hell, or self-flagellation, depending on the day. As the rest of the passengers filed onto the plane, a pretty flight attendant was making chitchat with me. She had a beautiful smile and laughed at everything I said, funny or not. I eyed her for a moment, thinking about how long it had been since I'd inducted another member into my own personal mile-high club, but my thoughts immediately flashed to visions of being tangled up with April inside a cramped lavatory.

The flight attendant flashed her wide, baby blue eyes, but I was distracted by the thought of serious, darker blue eyes that hid all kinds of deep thoughts and secrets. Eventually, April filed past on her way to her seat back in the economy section. She overtly assessed the airline employee before meeting me with her frosty gaze.

I winked at her. I couldn't resist. Her gaze glanced off mine like a stone skipping across a glassy lake. She readjusted her hand on the strap of her carry-on bag, her middle finger poking out, as she had done that night at the martini lounge.

I laughed before taking a deep breath and looking away. I tried to suppress the feeling of guilt that had added itself to the complex soup of emotions I felt regarding this woman. So she was angry. Well, so was I. But at the same time, I also wanted her, yet I had to remind myself that I was her boss and therefore couldn't have her.

Goddamn, it would be easier when her internship was finished and she left the company. Only a few weeks to go...

But I had to hand it to her, she'd taken everything I'd dished out to her with quiet dignity and only lost it once—yesterday. Oh, and how glorious that little meltdown had been, too. I'd known there was fire under that serene surface, and part of me, the reckless part of me, wanted to see it again. And again.

An even more foolhardy part of me wanted to take the fire I knew was there, harness it and hold it in my hands. Just the abstract thought of it—of *her*—was making me hard again.

Shit. I was in trouble. I either needed to find some self-control *fast* or stay the hell away from her before I shredded every last bit that remained.

***

In less than three short hours, we touched down at Vancouver International Airport. We made it through Customs and were sitting together in the back seat of a town car while the driver took us to our hotel, located on the city waterfront near the convention center. Upon arrival, we were checked in by the concierge.

The Owner's Suite occupied the entire top floor of one of the towers of the hotel. The suite itself was two stories of floor-to-ceiling glass windows that gave a 360-degree view of the city, from Coal Harbour and English Bay to the North Shore Mountains, to Stanley Park, to the modern, lit glass and steel of downtown Vancouver—as pointed out to us by the concierge.

April listened to his entire spiel with interest but didn't say much as she followed his directions. He escorted her to a small room off the hallway on the lower floor of the suite. It was set aside especially for an assistant of the occupant of the Owner's Suite. It adjoined the penthouse but was not part of it, and appeared to be nothing more than an ordinary hotel room.

Before I could say a word, she disappeared into the clearly subpar room—when compared with mine, anyway. I spent at least five minutes arguing with myself whether or not to go talk to her and point out that there was another room in the suite. Maybe it would be best, though...the more walls and locks between us during this stay, the better.

Because I really, *really* had no idea how I was going to keep my hands off her. And if she stayed pissed off at me, even better. That much more of a barrier between us would be a good deterrent. But it felt wrong to let her hole up in there when I had this huge place to myself.

I sighed. Against my better judgment, I lightly rapped on her door, and after a long pause she quietly called for me to come in. I opened the door but remained standing in the doorway—she and I alone in a bedroom together would not lead to good things.

Well... good things, certainly, but not the right things.

I looked around her room and my eyes zeroed in on a suitcase on its stand. I caught a glimpse of some silk and lacy underthings peeking out, like they were winking at me, tormenting me. I met her gaze.

"Yes?" she snapped. "May I help you?"

I sighed. "You don't need to stay in here, you know. There's another room on the top floor." The one right next to mine. Why not? I was a glutton for punishment.

"That's okay. This is where the help goes, and I'm well aware of my place."

She turned to tuck a sweater into the drawer by the bed. As she bent, flaunting her fine ass in my direction, the first thought inside my head was, *Yeah, your place is naked and sweating underneath me.*

With a huff of frustration, I tore my eyes away before she could turn back to me.

"Can we call a truce, please? We're both here in a foreign country. We don't know anyone..."

She scoffed. "Canada is hardly a foreign country."

"It's close. They talk funny here. I feel lonesome already. Please be my friend and fellow American?"

She clenched her jaw and released it, folding her arms across her chest. I forced myself not to remember how those tits had tasted. Fuck. What the hell was wrong with me? I was randier than a fifteen-year-old boy who'd been forbidden to whack off.

I backed away from the door. "Come on...let's go check out the view. And aren't you hungry? Come on, Weiss. Loosen up and cut me a break."

Her eyes narrowed, but her mouth curved into a smile. "I'd like to cut you... or break something."

"Very funny. I'll be sure to sleep with one eye open tonight. Now come on." I spun, hoping she would follow me. But deep down I knew it was in both our best interests if she didn't.

17
APRIL

I FOLLOWED THAT SINFULLY HOT—ER—EVIL MAN DOWN THE hallway, through the suite and toward the back patio, which was at the top of one of the towers.

He turned to me, his face split into a heart-arresting smile. His cheeks were rough from the lack of shaving, and I wondered if he was going for some kind of hipster look for his speech. My cheeks burned and I looked away. If it were possible for him to be any more fucking gorgeous than he already was, he'd added scruff to the equation. Scruff was like my catnip. It made me weak-kneed. Oh lordy. I had to keep my thoughts clean and focused on how much I hated him, but the scruff wasn't helping.

It was making my hated but hot boss, who was the most amazing lover I'd ever had, even hotter. I blinked. It had been thirty-six hours since I'd discovered the identity of Falco the sex god of Comic-Con, and I'd been reliving that night ever since. But when I thought about sitting across his hard thighs, my own legs open to him, his hands squeezing my hips, I now saw Jordan's handsome face instead of Falco's helmeted head.

And when I thought about how he'd laid me on the bed then pressed down on top of me with his hard, solid body, I remembered the smell of him as Jordan's smell. And when I thought about Falco's sizable cock moving inside me—

"Let's order some dinner." Jordan stopped by the phone where the room service menu was propped up on display.

Oh yeah, dinner. That'd be good.

He handed me the menu and I picked out what I wanted—a Chinese chicken salad. Jordan ordered a steak and potato. So predictable I almost yawned.

While we waited for the food to show up, I opened the sliding glass door and walked out onto a shiny marble patio, where there was a private pool and Jacuzzi, a sauna and an outdoor fireplace. I glanced up at the sky, gray with darkened clouds. The forecast called for rain, unsurprisingly enough. The Pacific Northwest was known for its profuse greenery for a reason. Fortunately, it was September, so the weather wasn't too cold yet. A soak in the Jacuzzi might be fun, provided I didn't freeze my ass off during the run indoors.

After a few minutes, Jordan trailed after me, standing a little distance away, hands stuffed inside his pockets. I tried not to notice how that made his jeans hug his hard ass. Ugh. I had to stop looking at him and most *definitely* had to stop lusting after him.

I was probably a blip on his radar now. The man bedded women left and right—actresses, models, socialites. I, on the other hand, had been told that I was boring in bed. And Jordan hardly seemed affected by my presence.

Sure, he'd kissed me at his house and had done some other naughty things at the martini bar. But I figured it was because he was bored, and he damn well hadn't tried anything since.

I took a breath and spoke to break the awkward silence. I was still pissed, but I figured it wouldn't hurt to be civil to the bastard. "So have you been practicing your speech? Are you ready for your eighteen minutes of fame?"

He shrugged a big shoulder. "I've *been* ready. I've recited the goddamn thing to myself in my sleep for the past three weeks."

"So you don't need to rehearse again?" I looked out over the view. Vancouver really was a lovely city, situated on a wide bay—all lights and ocean and dark green patches of lush forest.

"I need to go over the slides before the rehearsal tomorrow. But not tonight. I'm too tired."

Our dinner arrived soon after and we sat down at the dining room table. We ate in silence for a while, facing each other across the table. The only sound was the clanking of his silverware as he cut into his steak and me crunching the greenery of my salad.

Jordan eyed my salad suspiciously. "You aren't very hungry?"

"I'm fine. I've never been the best flyer. Makes me a little queasy."

"Hmm. Maybe you can order something later if you're hungrier then."

"The salad's good. It's not your grandpa's Shepherd's Pie, but it's good."

Jordan smiled at the reference. "That's my favorite thing he makes. My grandma is the one who made it all the time, and he started doing it after she passed away."

My mouth thinned and I looked down. "He's such a kind man. Hopefully, you won't hold what happened at his house against him too long."

He shifted in his seat, appearing uneasy that I'd brought it up. He opened his mouth to reply, but his phone dinged and he picked it up. A smile crept across his sexy lips and he typed a message back before setting it down. He glanced up at me, noting that I was watching him.

"What?"

I shrugged. "Nothing. Just wondering if that was more supermodel sexting. Maybe a photo this time? If you get lonely tonight, you'll have some new material to wank off to."

He shot me a dirty look. "It was my baby sister wishing me good luck with my talk and saying she was going to tune in and watch it on the Internet as soon as it's posted."

I grimaced. "Oh." I cleared my throat and then chewed a few more bites of lettuce and tangy tangerine slices coated with ginger dressing. "She really is a sweetheart. You're lucky."

"You don't have a sister?"

I took a deep breath and let it go. "I do. A half sister, anyway. My dad's daughter with his second wife. They have a son, too. Like I said, the perfect family unit. Even the two-point-five children. I'm the 'point five.'"

"They're a lot younger than you?"

"My brother, Daniel, is six, and my sister, Sarah, is nine."

He frowned and then cut into his steak, appearing deep in thought.

"What?" I asked.

"Just wondering...so your dad moved on and got remarried after your parents divorced. What about your mom?"

I tried not to make a face at the reminder of *her* existence. I'd been trying to erase it for the past month. She'd been texting and calling and sending emails and messages on social media practically every day. I'd refused to acknowledge any of them. I had nothing to say to her and her new *hubby*.

I frowned, picking at my lettuce leaves about as carefully as I was picking my words. The silence stretched and then grew awkward.

"Sorry, didn't mean to pry," he said.

I took a deep breath. "My parents got married on a whim and they were completely wrong for each other. He was already successful, and she was young and pretty. The marriage was a disaster from day one. She screwed around on him while he worked all the time. I was so young when they divorced that I don't ever remember them being together, actually."

"Ah, so your mom's not the marrying kind."

I laughed. "Oh, she's the marrying kind, all right. She's just not the *stay*-married kind. She's on husband number four at the moment."

"So who did you grow up with?"

I grimaced at him. "What is this, the 'fifty questions about April' hour? If you want answers out of me, you should cough up some of your own."

He stopped chewing for a moment and watched me with those studious eyes. They looked more brown than green at the moment.

"Hmm. Okay. Ask me something then."

I continued picking at my lettuce leaves. I knew exactly what I wanted to ask him, but I couldn't blurt it out like I'd been wanting to do in the weeks that followed our Santa Barbara trip. I had to at least make it appear like I was searching for something to ask him.

"It's about that comment you made about your dad...that he's angry at you because you lied to him. What did you lie about?"

He rolled his eyes. "It's a long-ass story."

"Well, if you want any more answers out of me, you're going to have to pony up the long-ass story."

His eyes narrowed. I could tell he was deciding what to say and how to say it. He took a deep breath and let it go. "Grant Fawkes is obsessed with his legacy and passing on his vast amounts of wisdom and knowledge to future generations. And he was very careful about shaping his offspring..."

I nursed my water and watched him over the rim of my glass. This was getting interesting. Jordan and his daddy issues. I'd wanted a piece of this ever since that whacked-out family reunion.

He continued, "We were homeschooled. I finished high school at sixteen, started college before I turned seventeen—"

"Wow. I knew you were a brainiac, but that's over the top."

He pushed his plate aside and shrugged. "Not all it's cracked up to be. I was way too young to be starting college. And he should have known that."

I nodded, completely understanding what it felt like to be wiser than my own parent. Knowing how it felt to be at their mercy when they should have been watching out for you. A brief memory flitted through my mind of my mom's second husband, Cliff, backhanding me across the face when I'd accidently broken his prized golf trophy. I was eight years old and went to live with my dad full-time for years after that. My mom hadn't said a thing—hadn't wanted to disrupt her cozy living situation or the promise of future alimony.

Yes, I understood what it was like for a parent to look out for their own best interests over that of their child's.

"He probably did know that," I finally said. "But his goals were more important to him."

He tilted his head, looking at me as if trying to size me up from a different angle. "Yeah…he had me earmarked to become an environmental engineer, like him. As far as he saw it, it was my entire purpose in life."

"That's a lot of pressure at a very young age."

He clenched his jaw and then released it. "That's why I went to Caltech to study. He footed the bill for my tuition and it wasn't cheap. He had to sacrifice a lot, even with my partial scholarship. I was too young and scared to tell him I didn't want his vision for my future. So eventually… I changed my major without telling him."

I traced a finger along the edge of my drinking glass, afraid to look up because it might break the spell and he'd stop talking.

He fiddled with his plate as if it was the most interesting thing in the world. "As you can imagine, he was pissed when I announced a week before graduation that I'd be walking the stage with the Business and Economics Management department instead of the Engineering class."

I let out a long breath. "That must have been a hell of an explosion."

"My dad's non-confrontational and passive-aggressive. He holds grudges. It's a slow burn."

"So he's held this grudge since you graduated? You're twenty-five now… how long ago did you graduate?"

"It's been five years."

Ah yes, Jordan and Adam, the Draco wunderkinder who achieved so much at such young ages. Their bios and impossibly gorgeous faces were about to be spread across the covers of every business magazine now that the IPO was almost a reality. They were young, hot, brilliant, and soon to be even more incredibly rich than they were now. The world was their oyster.

"That's a long time to hold a grudge..."

"Yep. There's other stuff too, though." He seemed about to say more and then shrugged. "We haven't seen eye to eye for a long time."

Sounded like something straight out of a Steinbeck novel to me...

He reached for his glass and swirled the liquid within. "Jesus, this water just isn't cutting it..."

"Still teetotalling?"

"Yeah, you?"

"Hell, yes. I lose all functioning brain cells when I'm drunk."

Something about that seemed to trouble him. But he looked away and then back to me. "So about you..."

I raised a brow. "What do you want to know?"

"Your parents. If they split when you were a baby, where were you growing up?"

"My parents had fifty-fifty custody for a while, so I bounced back and forth between them. Then my mom found another sugar daddy and couldn't be bothered with having me around. After that, I lived with my dad and a nanny, and sometimes my grandma."

"But you said you and your dad aren't close... yet you spent most of your time with him growing up?"

"Well...there was my stepmom." I sipped more water.

Understanding dawned on his features—probably the wrong understanding. It's not like I was some fairytale princess with the requisite evil stepmother. Nope, no Cinderella here.

"It's not what you think. My stepmom is generally a nice lady, but I was a preteen when she married my dad and she's only fourteen years older than me. I wasn't the easiest person to get along with. By that time, my mom was back in the picture because she wanted someone to shop with and go get mani-pedis. I was more interesting to her then, especially since she was between men.

"Rebekah, my stepmom, was ready to start her own family with my dad and was at a loss for what to do with me. Plus, she's pretty religious and I wasn't interested in any of that. She tried, though, but the Gentile ways bred too strongly in me, or something like that. So that's about the time I went away to school."

"Damn, and here I thought you really *were* Snow White, evil stepmother and all."

I narrowed my eyes at him. "What?"

His grin widened. "You have to promise not to tell him, but when Adam didn't know your name, he called you Snow White."

My brows knit. "And why would he do that?"

Jordan looked at me like I was an idiot. "Uh, because you look like her?"

"Do not."

"Do too."

Then I remembered that comment Adam had made about calling on the woodland creatures for help, and it all became clear. "Jeez, is that what everyone calls me?"

He laughed. "No, just him."

I raised my brows. "Not you?"

The smirk immediately dropped off his sexy lips, and he suddenly became *very* focused on his nearly empty plate. I watched him while sipping on my water again.

He sat back with a sigh and rubbed at his scruffy jaw. The whiskers really did complement his already over-the-top sex appeal, providing a deep gold dusting along his strongly defined jaw. My eyelids drooped for a moment as I imagined what it would feel like to have that scruff graze my cheeks and my neck as he kissed me. His mouth moving lower on my body, the feel of that rough sandpaper on my chest, my stomach, my—

I gulped. My panties were starting to feel damp. I had to stop fantasizing about him like this. I was still supposed to be pissed at him! Why was he making it so hard to stay angry?

He'd stopped shifting in his chair and was now watching me. Actually, he was looking at my cleavage, his eyes slowly climbing up my neck, narrowing as my throat bobbed where I swallowed. Either the temperature or the sexual tension meter had been dialed up a few too many notches for my comfort level.

I stood. "I, uh...I have a bit of planning for your schedule tomorrow and some other work to get done. You have your meeting with the speaking coach, then the director and the dress rehearsal, too."

He didn't get up.

"It's nine p.m. Don't tell me you go to bed this early."

I cleared my throat. The dangers of sleeping under the same roof as him had not occurred to me until that moment, and I blushed when I realized it.

I gave a nonchalant toss of my head to cover for it. "I'm not going to stay up 'til midnight. Apparently, I'm Snow White, not Cinderella."

He stood and threw his napkin aside. "Come on, Weiss, live a little. We have a Jacuzzi."

Oh no...no. Him and me in a Jacuzzi together, wearing nothing more than bathing suits? And with those abs of his? No, just no. I could not be trusted. I'd start guzzling booze and licking him as my dessert in ten seconds flat.

"Or this nice, cozy fireplace." He walked over to the wall and flicked a switch. The entire far wall lit up within a giant freestanding frame of wood, gas fire appearing over painted rocks. It was spectacular.

I gasped. "This is awesome."

He beamed a smile at me. "Sit down...make yourself comfortable. Stay a while."

I twisted my mouth, making a face. "I've got my own place. The butler's pantry."

He plopped down on the couch and looked at me expectantly. With a sigh, I settled into a chair near the couch. I leaned back into it and turned to stare at the flames. It was better than watching the flames dance in his beautiful eyes. I started to think naughty thoughts when I dwelled on those too long.

"Now, I want you to admit the real reason you want to go back to your room so badly," he said in a low voice.

Against my better judgment, I turned and looked at him. "Oh, and what is that?" I couldn't wait to hear the ego-fest spew about to come out of his mouth—about how I found him so irresistibly sexy that the mere thought of kissing that scruffy mouth made the floor underneath me buckle. Made my throat dry. Made me shift uneasily in my seat due to the funny feeling down in my lady parts.

"You're hooked on the game, aren't you?"

"What?"

"I logged in to check on that key code I gave you. You have a nineteenth-level character already."

I took a deep breath, relief washing over me. "Yeah, I guess you caught me. That game is damn addictive. Now I know why you boys are so filthy rich."

He grinned. "And it seems you aren't the only one who's been named after a character in a fairy tale."

Heat washed over me and I looked away. Shit. He'd figured out that I'd modeled the Beast after him. And I knew for a fact he'd overheard me refer to him as "Beast" at least once.

"Well, you're beastly *most* of the time."

He sank back, stretched his muscular arms across the back of the sofa beside him and, with a grin dancing on his lips, gazed into the fire. "I've been called worse."

"Did you deserve it?"

He smirked, still staring into the fire. "Yeah, a good part of the time." His eyes wandered back to me. They were the color of molten amber in the firelight. "Like I've said before, nice guys finish last. I learned the hard way, being a reformed nice guy and all."

I watched him as I rubbed a hand over my arm. "Hmm. So there truly is no kind heart buried under the beastly exterior?"

His eyes narrowed at the fire. "I had that organ removed years ago."

Now *here* was a story. At least it seemed so. Or maybe I hoped that he was more than just a brilliant kid who made a lot of money and exploited both his wealth and good looks to live a rock star's life, a different woman in his bed every week. And it occurred to me, as it had been about a month now since our anonymous tryst at Comic-Con...had he been dating his bevy of models and actresses in the meantime? And sleeping with them?

I already knew they sent him sexy texts at all hours of the day. The thought of them—whoever they were—made my blood boil, even as I reminded myself that I had no claim to him. We'd hooked up once, and it had been out of this world amazing but likely he regretted it.

Well, that made two of us. I regretted it too. Sometimes.

"Is that why you don't date women for very long?"

Those eyes shifted to me. "What's this, more true confession time?"

"I think you owe me a few answers for all the ones I gave you."

"I'm not talking about my social life."

"Oh? Why not?"

"Because I don't want to."

I raised my brows. This was only making me more determined to pursue the subject.

"Okay, then I have another burning question," I said.

"Shoot."

"Did you know who I was at Comic-Con that night we went back to my room?"

His mouth set and he didn't look at me. The silence almost rang in the air between us, thickening it with that same tension as before. After a few minutes, it became clear he wasn't going to answer me, nor even acknowledge that I'd ever asked the question.

And that, quite frankly, pissed me off. I popped out of my seat and his laser intense eyes found mine. With a shrug, I moved past him toward my servant's quarters. "Well, if you don't have the balls to answer me...I'll be going."

I turned and walked down the hall, aware of the fact that he'd gotten up from the couch and followed me. Before grabbing the doorknob, I turned to him. His face was inches away, eyes blazing into mine.

And I couldn't breathe. He took another step forward until I was backed against my door and his hot breath was searing my cheeks. Those eyes burned with white-hot emotion—anger, passion, even hunger. I couldn't force myself to tear my gaze away from his. I was like a cornered animal, staring my predator down, the adrenaline coursing through me.

Jordan placed a hand on the wall on either side of my head. That smell...suede and sage. He leaned in close and my chest tightened. My heart pounded a thready beat in my throat.

"Yes," he finally said.

I raised my brows, both unsurprised by the answer—I'd suspected it the moment he refused to answer me—and angry at yet another betrayal.

"I knew it was you," he continued. "And I knew you were going to be my intern assistant."

Fury stiffened every muscle. "Well. That's just wonderful. This gets better and better."

I had to fight which way my emotions were swaying, noting peripherally that there was little difference between anger and desire. They were both strong emotions that took hold of you, threatening to command your every thought and action—and not necessarily in your own best interests.

"It was poor judgment. I shouldn't have done it. I'm sorry."

"You're sorry you had sex with me?"

He shook his head, his eyes trailing to my lips.

"I'm not sorry about the sex. I am sorry that I didn't tell you sooner that it was me."

I swallowed, trying to decide how to take this information, unable to think of anything to say or even determine how I felt about it.

"I still don't regret it, though. I make it a habit of never regretting hot sex."

"You thought it was hot?" Here I went again, desperately seeking validation. Had my past left me that much of a wreck?

He seemed shocked by the question. "Of course."

My gaze dropped to his mouth and I licked my lips. Something flared in his eyes. The seconds stretched and he didn't move. I tilted my head, bringing my mouth closer to his. God, I wanted to feel that scruff grazing across my skin. "Well, you already know how I feel about it..."

His eyelids drooped. I reached up and slipped my fingers through his hair like I'd been aching to do for days now. With the pad of my thumb, I traced the outline of his ear. His eyes snapped shut and he took in a shaky breath.

"I should...probably go..." he whispered.

The following few seconds were a little blurry. I couldn't, for the life of me, say who leaned in first, but next thing I knew my arms were hooked around his neck and his lips were pressed to mine, devouring me. His fingers wound through my hair, which he used to pull me flush against him. His tongue darted frantically in and out of my mouth, and my hands moved to his hard chest, grasping at his shirtfront.

Beneath the shirt, his body felt like granite. God, he felt so good, smelled amazing, tasted delectable. I wanted to start peeling my own clothes off for him. His sharp whiskers grazed my skin as he kissed me—across my face, my earlobes, my neck. His mouth travelled lower, settling in my cleavage.

"You are so goddamn beautiful," he muttered, and a surge of something rose inside me that I couldn't quite explain—power? *Joy?* I couldn't catch my next breath. My fingers threaded through his hair so that it stood up in a messily attractive way. Was there anything about this man that wasn't smoking hot? I bet he woke up looking disgustingly sexy first thing in the morning. A burst of heat surged between my legs at the thought of waking up beside him, our bodies clothed only in the bed sheets, the memory of those whiskers scraping across my skin.

"Jordan," I whispered.

His hand went to the back of my neck, gathering my hair at the nape. I felt his fingers close into a fist and then he pulled my hair tight. The slight jolt of pain made me suck in my breath, even as my desire surged. With a tug, my head tipped back, exposing more of my neck to his delicious sandpaper kisses. The feel of his rough cheeks against my skin was driving me mad.

"I can't get that night out of my mind," he ground out as he kissed his way all over my neck and exposed chest. "I think about it all the time." His fist tightened again in my hair as if with renewed frustration. "How hot it was to fuck you. All I can think about is how much I want to do it again."

My lips found his earlobe and sucked it inside my mouth, grazing it with my teeth. He let out a tight breath. His hand dipped under my shirt, smoothing over my stomach, painting a swath of fire in its wake. His mouth dropped to my chest and immediately clamped over my nipple through my shirt. My back muscles tightened and I arched, pushing against him, hot desire zinging through me, burning hotter than that gas fire in the living room.

Every nerve ending on every square inch of my skin was alive and aching for his touch. But I couldn't—we couldn't.

His mouth was now at the base of my neck, biting and sucking, and his hands were underneath my shirt, holding me against him. Mine were pressed against his hard chest, and the feel of his taut muscles made my eyes roll back into my head. I was delirious with desire for him. And yet—

"Jordan..."

He continued to slide that spellbinding mouth across my collarbone. Over my bra, his thumbs rubbed my nipples, bringing them to pebbled, aching points.

"What?" he finally answered.

"We need to stop."

He pressed his large erection against the scorching heat between my legs. "Your body doesn't agree with that statement."

I moaned as the pressure of his touch on my nipples intensified. "No, it doesn't," I breathed. "It definitely wants you to fuck me again." He groaned in response to that heated admission. "But I'm still pissed off at you."

He stiffened against me then pulled his hands out from under my shirt. We remained pressed up against one other, breathing hard but not able to meet each other's gaze. My eyes fluttered closed. I wanted him so badly it literally *ached*.

He stepped back, pulling away. The look on his face could most easily be described as...confusion. With each second, I saw a new emotion swirling in the mix—desire, reluctance, ambivalence.

"You're right. We can't do this." He sounded more like he was trying to convince himself, not me. He began to rub his jaw with the palm of his hand, appearing deep in thought.

I drew in a long breath and let it go, proud that I'd spoken up for myself despite being so turned on. But all at once, those old insecurities surfaced in my thoughts, and I could practically still hear the backlash whenever I'd spoken up in the past. *To be honest, it's no big deal to me. The sex was never very exciting*, Gunnar had said, months before hopping into bed with my mother.

My breath caught. *April, you should make sure you get a man while you're young and still on your dad's bankroll. I always had my looks to get by on, but you're lucky—you don't have to worry about that.*

My mom and her smarmy, condescending advice on how to catch and keep a man. As always, she seemed to harbor resentment toward me for still having access to my dad's money when she didn't.

All those other gremlins in my head—even Cari at Comic-Con. *You're just a goody-goody, April. You'd never take a big chance and be adventurous.*

Suddenly, I was feeling sick to my stomach.

And Jordan watched it all. He frowned and brought a hand up to caress my cheek. I turned my face away from his touch, closing my eyes, not wanting to see the pity.

"Hey. What kind of head game are you playing in there?"

I shook my head and laughed at myself, blinking to prevent tears of humiliation. "No more than the usual." I turned to go into my room. He stopped me, grabbing my arm.

"I'm sorry I started that. And I'm sorry you're still angry with me. But you did the right thing. I got carried away. I just don't want to take advantage—any more than I already have."

In spite of myself, a smile tugged at the corners of my mouth. "I'm a big girl. I can judge when I'm being taken advantage of."

He rubbed at the back of his neck, looking away. "Good night, April."

We avoided each other's gaze and tried to ignore the heavy tension in the air between us that, if it were a blanket, would have smothered us both.

I cleared my throat and spoke again. "So, uh, remember you've got the orientation, a one-on-one meeting with the speaking coach in the morning and then the dress rehearsal. I'll be with you at that one." I was proud of the way I'd managed to make my voice switch to business mode without even the slightest tremble. I'd heard my dad affect that tone enough to easily be able to imitate it.

Retreating into my room, I quickly shut the door and hustled through my bedtime routine. I tried to ignore the fact that my body was still on fire from his kisses, the firm, sure touch of his hands, and the scrape of those whiskers across my skin.

His sorcery had drawn me in without effort, and under his charm, I was hopelessly captivated.

I had to get my act together quickly or I'd be as entrapped as Rapunzel in the tower, unable to ever escape.

18
JORDAN

I HAD TO ADMIT IT WAS HARD TO SLEEP THAT NIGHT. OBSESSING over someone will do that to you. Her scent, still in my nostrils, was lush and enticing—like how you'd imagine a princess like Snow White to smell. How you'd imagine her to taste. Sweet, soft, succulent. I wanted to taste more of her. And those thoughts ran endlessly through my mind until the wee hours.

The raging hard-on was not helping, either.

At this point, I had too much dignity to crawl off into a corner and start jerking off. So I suffered through it, and thus insomnia ensued. I hadn't had sex in a while and going cold turkey was kicking my ass.

I'd come too close—*way* too close—to shattering all my good-intentioned resolve. Until she'd put on the brakes and brought me back to my senses.

At least she'd spoken up for herself. It was hard, I could tell. Even when she'd been furious at me the day before when she'd found out that I was her anonymous hookup, she'd fought to leave instead of confront me. Because she was always afraid to stand up for herself. And why? That I'd like to know.

I wanted to smack the crap out of whoever had done that to her, made her feel like she wasn't worthy of standing up for herself. Because whoever did it was a bastard, son-of-a-bitch or an asshole. Possibly all of the above. I stayed up long hours thinking about it— thinking about *her*—until I pulled out my tablet and queued up a movie to watch. Sometime around three a.m., I finally passed out.

The wake-up call came too early the next morning, and I washed the sleep out of my eyes and got ready. The next time I saw her was in a room backstage as other speakers went through their spiels. She was wearing a sheer white blouse that clung to her curves and a pair of form-fitting black pants that made her look as alluring as ever. Forcing myself to focus, I opened up my laptop, preparing to hand it over to the AV guy who would copy my file onto the presentation computer so they could display my slides.

But when I fired up the presentation, my stomach dropped. "Motherfucker," I muttered.

She was at my side in an instant, and I was assailed with the scent of honey. "What? What's wrong?"

I slammed my laptop shut so she wouldn't see. "I copied the wrong slides."

She frowned, her eyes still on my laptop. "Wrong slides? What do you mean?"

"My placeholders—for brainstorming and stuff. It's an earlier copy of the same presentation."

She shrugged and peered up at me. "It's the dress rehearsal. We can get the real slides copied over later once we log into the Draco VPN from the hotel room."

"I can't use these slides."

"You already know what you're going to say, right? Just use the placeholders."

I blew out a breath and ran a hand through my hair. Then, by way of explanation, I opened my laptop and gestured to the screen.

It flickered back to life and the first slide came up.

Her eyes grew round. She straightened, throwing glances around the room. "Why do you have pictures of naked women on your placeholder slides?"

I gritted my teeth. "It was for brainstorming purposes. It helps me think."

There was a brief moment when she looked like she was about to bust a gut laughing, but she contained it. "I'm sure all the guys here would *love* those slides. Are these your ladyloves?"

I glared at her. "No."

"So where is the real presentation stored on the Draco Network?"

"In my work folder."

"You mean, the same one I've been saving all that crap work you've been giving me to do?"

"Yeah, that one. But I left the dongle with the code to be able to log into the VPN at the hotel."

Her eyes narrowed. "You know what you could use?"

"Besides a fifth of Jack?"

She smiled and reached into her bag. "No. A *really* smart assistant who preemptively copies your work folder over from the company network before you travel in case you do something stupid like bring porn slides for the rehearsal." She triumphantly brandished a flash drive in her hand and presented it to me.

The tightness in my chest loosened in relief. "I could kiss you."

Something flashed in those beautiful blue eyes, but her mouth thinned. "Mr. Fawkes, you are being inappropriate." She smirked at me and I was reminded of that godawful sexual harassment seminar. Our own private little joke, then.

"How about a raise?"

"I'm an unpaid intern," she deadpanned.

"Exactly." I grinned. "It won't cost me anything." She grimaced and playfully mimed an uppercut punch to my gut. "Try a sucker punch to the kidneys, Weiss. Much more effective."

I plugged the flash drive into the USB port to open the files. She bent over the computer right beside me—standing far too close for my comfort or equilibrium. I was beginning month two of Friar Jordan's New Law of Celibacy, which meant I was horny as hell and focused on all the stunning physical attributes of every woman I came into contact with, particularly *this* woman.

I noticed that she was silently laughing beside me.

"You keep laughing at my misfortunes, Weiss, and I'll make you pay for that later."

Her dark blue eyes cut to mine and there was something there...heat, maybe? "Promises, promises," she said in a low voice. Yup, definitely heat.

I slid my eyes with forceful purpose back to the computer screen, calling up the correct file off her flash drive and then copying it onto my computer. She was goading me. Easy to recognize, easy to dismiss. *Usually.*

As if I didn't already want it so badly I could scream. And below the belt, my body was shouting, *"Challenge accepted."* I took a deep breath—through my mouth so I wouldn't keep smelling her—and let it out, opened the file and then handed the laptop off to the audiovisual guy to copy it onto his equipment.

Minutes after that, I was called on stage to deliver my talk. Just like when the real deal would go down tomorrow, a countdown clock starting at 18:00 flipped numbers backward. I had that time—and *only* that amount of time—to deliver my "ideas worth spreading."

I closed out my remarks with less than thirty seconds to spare. Given the near tragic mishap with the slides, it ended up being a surprisingly smooth rehearsal. When I stepped out of the room, April tagged behind me as we made our way out into the hallway.

"That was really good," she said in a hushed voice.

I adjusted the laptop case on my shoulder and slipped my hands into my pockets. "But...?"

"No 'buts.' It was a fascinating talk." I glanced at her, as if to verify she wasn't mocking me. She wasn't. Her brows were knit, indicating intense interest. "So Dragon Epoch has a virtual economy that behaves exactly like real-world economies?"

"Most of these types of games do. And the best ones employ economic experts to advise as to how it should work in the game."

She shook her head. "That's amazing. And beyond that, I'm surprised that economists can study how economics work in a game and actually learn things about theoretic economics."

Several people coming toward us in the narrow hallway were on a direct collision course, so engrossed in their own conversation that they weren't paying attention. I wrapped my hand around April's arm and tugged her out of the way, causing her to almost collide with me. She put her hand against my waist to steady herself, and even that touch had my body perking up and wanting more. Hell, a stiff wind would perk it up these days. My eyes slid over the beautiful bone structure of her face, the perfect, porcelain skin that resembled a certain Disney princess and the slight build that still managed to boast curves in all the right places. April was far more interesting than a stiff wind.

"Thanks," she muttered as she sluggishly pulled away from me. I swallowed, checking my watch. "What else do we have going on today?"

"You're on your own for dinner, but there's that cocktail mixer with the press tonight. I don't have to be there, but I was going to show up in case any scheduling needs arise. I have a feeling that after your rehearsal today, you are going to be a pretty popular interview subject."

I raised my brows. I thought it had been a competent delivery of a decent speech, but she seemed far more impressed with it than I could have hoped.

"And then, of course, you need to get a good night's sleep. They suggest practicing your speech before you go to bed, when you wake up, and again in the green room before you are on."

"Well, the less we discuss this, the less nervous I'll feel. Let's go get some dinner."

"You—ah—want me to come with you?"

"Why not? You can ask me more about my talk if you want, and I can ask you why you are going to business school when theoretic economics is obviously what gets you giddy."

She darted a glance at me, then put her head down and continued walking in silence. I arranged for a driver to take us to one of the nicest restaurants in Vancouver, hoping she liked Hong Kong fusion cuisine. It was original, delicious and she obviously enjoyed it, though she refused the wine pairings with each dish as they were suggested.

We ate while we talked, enjoying ourselves, and she appeared fascinated as she continued to pepper me with questions about my speech.

"What made you decide on business school if you enjoy economic theory so much?"

She shrugged. "It seems more practical."

"The idea of being able to tap into a virtual economy like the one in Dragon Epoch doesn't get you hot and bothered? If you studied theoretical economics, you could do your entire thesis on DE's economy."

She took a spoonful of her desert—vanilla bean mousse. She eyed me for a moment before answering. "There are a lot of things that get me hot and bothered." Her dark pink tongue snaked out to lick her spoon.

I wasn't wearing a tie, but if I was, I would have had to loosen it. That familiar knot of desire was tightening, twisting and making everything below the belt feel heavy and a little achy.

I cleared my throat and looked at my watch. "Well, let's get this cocktail shindig over with."

"We have enough time to get back to the hotel and change clothes. The reception is at the hotel."

I smiled. "Even better then. If it's boring, I can just bow out."

"Or you can pull that move where you get the hot babe's room key." Her blue eyes glittered. "I won't wait up."

I already have the hot babe's room key...and it's the same as mine. I fought saying it but, oh, I thought it. April didn't know about Friar Jordan's New Law of Celibacy, so she threw out the occasional, sexy little snark bomb.

Two could play at that game, though. "Well, ya know, I've got condoms in my pocket at all times...just in case."

I hadn't brought condoms. Too tempting to carry them around. With those suckers handy, I'd know there was always a chance I could use them. Not having them accessible would help me stay on the straight and narrow.

"Of course you do." She primly wiped her mouth with her napkin and stood.

Forty-five minutes later, I was pouring myself a mineral water from the minibar in the hotel room when April stepped out of her cubbyhole, fully dressed. She paused when she saw me, running her eyes over me from head to toe. I tried to ignore how much it turned me on when she looked at me like that. And, of course, she looked elegant and regal in her party attire.

She wore a light blue cocktail dress that came to just above her knees. It had a strap over one shoulder and fell down in waves around her breasts and hips like a Roman toga, only artfully tailored to show her feminine curves. She wore silver high-heeled sandals and jewelry to match. Her long hair was brushed out, shining around her shoulders and down her back. She looked like a million bucks, and I could have a lot of fun spending every dime of *that*.

I took a deep breath and jerked my attention away, taking a long gulp of my drink before I actually started drooling.

"You look very dashing," she said.

"Thanks," I grunted. She was probably waiting for a compliment in return, but I didn't want to chance it. I already wanted to slip that toga off her shoulder and taste every inch that it covered. *Shit.* Even the thought of it was getting me hard. I didn't even have to look at her. Goddamn it. Friar Jordan was struggling.

"Well, let's get this bullshit over with," I said and April nodded, tucking her phone into her sparkly clutch purse. "You need to be back before midnight or your carriage will turn into a pumpkin."

She darted a look at me out of the corner of her eyes before slipping out the front door ahead of me. "Wrong princess. I'm supposed to eat an apple and fall into a death coma 'til my prince comes around and wakes me up with a kiss."

"It's always a kiss that wakes them up...did you notice that? Snow White. Sleeping Beauty. Why a kiss?"

"Because the right kiss from the right person can wake anyone up." She pressed the button for the elevator to take us down to the ballroom level where the reception was being held. "A touch of lips is such a simple thing...but 'where heart, and soul and sense, in concert move, and the blood's lava and the pulse ablaze, each kiss is a heart-quake.'"

I watched *her* lips, those full, ripe lips as she recited each and every word. "Is that from one of your books?"

"*Don Juan.* A poem," she said simply, as if everyone should know that.

When we entered the reception room, April encouraged me to mingle, though I was reluctant to leave her side. I knew it was expected of me to mix with conference attendees, TED employees and journalists, but I had no real desire tonight. Plus, this was hardly my kind of scene. Too sedate.

There was no shortage of beautiful women, though—I did notice that. A few gravitated to me rather quickly and struck up conversations, but the minute April peeled off from my shoulder and went to stand at the edge of the room, I found myself seeking her out regularly, no matter who I was talking to, no matter what was said.

266 | BRENNA AUBREY

I refused the glasses of wine and cocktails being passed out on trays and did my duty while resisting the urge to look at my watch. What I couldn't resist was watching April, who had found a group of people to stand with, one of whom seemed to be having the same problem I was.

And I couldn't even get mad at the guy who was chatting her up, stroking her generously with his gaze. Because who could blame him? That ice blue dress, her shiny dark hair, those full, pink lips—she was a knockout.

And the surface was pleasing to the eye, sure, but what was hopelessly drawing me in was that undertow. Just like standing in coastal waters when a wave was about to break, that deeper current underneath that threatened to sweep you off your balance was more formidable than the flashy whitewater bathing your shoulders. That undertow could drag you under and not let you up until it was too late.

April was like that—what was deeper was more alluring. And I had to remind myself of it over and over again, because otherwise, as with any powerful undertow, I was in danger of being sucked under and drowned by it—by *her*.

19
APRIL

FROM THE EDGE OF THE ROOM, I WATCHED JORDAN AS HE engaged with people, particularly the ladies, not spending too much time in any one place. I also happened to notice an overt exchange of cards, which he tucked into the pocket of his charcoal gray suit jacket. I took another few minutes to admire him again. When I'd come out of my butler's pantry and saw him pouring some water for himself, he'd looked so gorgeous in that perfectly tailored suit that he'd taken my breath away.

And that scruff...that delicious scruff was driving me insane. He was now on his third day of whisker growth, and he looked so yummy I wanted to eat him. I wasn't the only one. Practically every other woman in this room had followed him with hungry gazes, and it made me want to bitch-slap each and every one of them.

I was so involved in watching him, I kept forgetting to take the time to mingle myself. Who, after all, would be there to speak to me? I was making small talk with another assistant when a woman stepped forward, attempting to get my attention.

"Excuse me," she said. I turned to her. She was pretty, if a little ragged looking, as if she looked older than she actually was, even though I had no idea how old she really was. I judged maybe a few years older than me. She had pale blond hair with a fairly dark tan that obviously wasn't natural, especially for someone who lived in a place like British Columbia—and according to her badge, Vancouver was listed as her hometown.

"Hey there. I'm April Weiss, Jordan Fawkes's assistant. May I help you?"

"Cynthia Nolan, TED assistant media coordinator. I have a couple of journalists here who would like to schedule an interview with Mr. Fawkes."

"Certainly. I can take care of that. Would you like me to introduce them now? Then we can coordinate a time later."

Her eyes widened and she darted a glance in Jordan's direction. "Uh…"

The woman beside her, with a badge noting that she was a journalist from *USA Home Weekly*, perked up. "That would be wonderful, thanks."

With a wave of my hand, I escorted the small group toward where Jordan was now conversing with another guy in a business suit, a TED badge hanging from his lanyard. He was an assistant speaking director for the conference.

"Mr. Fawkes, I have some people here who'd like to meet briefly with you tomorrow. I thought I'd make introductions and then schedule some interview time for them after your talk?"

Jordan nodded and I began, drawing his attention to the assistant media coordinator. "This is Cynthia—"

"Cyndi?" Jordan said, his eyes widening. At that same moment, I noticed that Cynthia was wearing a short-sleeved dress. Around the top of her arm, just peeking out from one of the sleeves, was a band tattoo that looked *very* familiar—a stylized wave pattern in three different shades of blue. I'd seen an identical version of it around Jordan's left arm. This one was on Cynthia's right.

By the way these two had locked gazes, it was obvious they knew each other. Cynthia went white underneath her tan, but she smiled, her lips curving tremulously.

"Hey, Jordan. So good to see you."

Jordan visibly swallowed. It took a minute for him to recover from his surprise, and by the look of him, it wasn't the good kind of surprise. So I intervened. "These are the journalists from *USA Home Weekly* who would like to meet with you tomorrow. Will that work?"

Jordan was still staring at the blonde. "Uh, yeah. That sounds great." His eyes finally drifted toward mine and they had a desperate edge to them. A server with a drink tray passed near us and Jordan waved him over, immediately grabbing a glass of wine and downing it in one gulp.

"Uh—how's your mom?" Jordan asked her.

Cynthia, who looked as uncomfortable as he did, nodded and said, "She's doing all right, considering. And your parents? I saw them last year...last time I was down."

I turned to the journalists, motioning them back toward the edge of the room where we'd stood before, extracting my phone from my purse. "What time would you like to speak with Mr. Fawkes? He's free from three o'clock on."

My eyes cut to Jordan, who now had his head bent toward the blonde, peering at her through narrow eyes as if deep in concentration. He grabbed another drink off the tray, replacing his empty glass. I continued to watch them as I set up an appointment with the journalists and then waited patiently for the awkward-appearing conversation to end. When Jordan placed a hand on the woman's arm—below the tattoo that matched his—she gestured toward him with her free arm and nodded. He smiled and pulled away.

Their conversation appeared to have been pleasant, if uncomfortable. He stepped away. His stiff smile evaporated the moment his back was turned, and he headed straight for me.

"We're all done here," he muttered as he walked past me. Cynthia watched Jordan go, a look of deep regret in her eyes. *What the hell was that?*

I spun and followed Jordan out the ballroom door, struggling to catch up to him as he took long strides toward the elevator.

"Hold up," I called.

Without looking at me, he held an arm out to keep the elevator doors open until I stepped inside. He followed after me and pressed the button for the penthouse. As soon as the doors slid shut, he let out a breath and slumped against the back wall, running a hand through his hair and watching the numbers climb as we ascended. I watched him.

"You okay? You look a little shaken up."

His cheek bulged where he clenched his jaw. He stuffed his hands in his pockets but said nothing to me, like I hadn't asked him a thing.

Frowning, I turned back to face the door. Clearly, he didn't want to talk about it. Fine. He could be that way. He was the Beast, after all. And flirty, gorgeous and charming or not, you never knew when a beast would turn on you. I vowed I wouldn't become collateral damage for whatever eruption was about to take place.

The elevator dinged and then opened. I preceded him to our door, fumbling in my clutch for the card key. He came up beside me and swiped his instead.

I walked past him but hesitated near the door. Maybe I should hang out to make sure he was all right and then go barricade myself in my room. I'd never seen him this out of sorts before, except for maybe my first day working for him—the day all the shit had hit the fan with the sex video.

Jordan strode in past me with purpose and headed straight for the mini-bar. He didn't even hesitate before opening a bottle of Jack Daniels and pouring it into a glass. Whiskey neat. Oh shit.

"Jordan..." I said as he lifted the glass of amber liquid to his lips. His eyes darted to mine and he paused with the glass at his lips. "You wanna talk about this?"

He hesitated only a minute before slamming the untouched glass down on the nearest table and moving to the living room, where he shoved his hands in his pockets and paced.

"No, not really."

"Okay. Do you want to practice your talk?"

"No, not really," he repeated in that same monotone. He stood there staring at the glass as if it held the answers to all of the world's problems.

"Drinking that probably isn't going to help. Not really."

His brow went up. "Yeah, it actually will. And after, I want to chase it down with another one."

Slowly, I walked toward him as he watched me with brooding eyes. "But you vowed no alcohol. And so did I. And I'd really like a drink right now, too."

"Christ, we sound like we're at an AA meeting. I also vowed I wasn't going to be a serial manwhore, but all these vows are getting me is way too sober and sexually frustrated."

I felt a rush inside my chest—a surge of happiness, perhaps—to hear about Jordan's vow. I'd been wondering if he'd followed through on those sexts that he'd received. Or the Snapchat propositions, or any of the other ways in which women did not hesitate to throw themselves at him. It must have taken a lot of willpower and determination on his part to turn them down.

I frowned.

"What?" he said.

"Just curious about your vows of sobriety and chastity. Are you trying to join a monk order or something?"

He clenched his jaw. "Feels like it sometimes."

He strode over and snatched up the glass of whiskey, then flipped on the fireplace switch and sank onto the couch. Silence hung in the air, but I didn't want to pester him with another question. I didn't want to let him off the hook, either.

He held the glass of whiskey between his open knees, swirling it and watching the play of light on the liquid. Slowly, I approached and settled beside him.

He didn't look up but took a deep breath and started talking. "After the fuck-up with the video, I just had this epiphany, I guess. That and—well, it's actually kind of weird, and if you ever breathe a word of this to him, I will utterly deny it. But watching everything Adam went through with Mia was a learning experience for me. It changed him. I think it was a good change." He took another breath and then tilted his head with a shrug. "I didn't like her at first. She reminded me of...someone."

"Cynthia?" I supplied.

He darted a look at me out of the corner of his eyes and shakily raised the glass to his lips. He appeared to take a long sniff but didn't drink before once again lowering the glass. His eyes, glaring into the firelight, were the color of butterscotch.

"Nice girls don't stay nice girls. They do shitty things..." he muttered. I'd heard him make similar comments before but had no idea what to make of it. I kicked off my strappy heels and leaned back on the couch, tucking my feet underneath me.

"You two must have been pretty serious. You guys have matching tattoos."

Tense silence. More whiskey swirling. I could hear nothing but the hiss of the gas fireplace and the distant, ever-present hum of the appliances in the penthouse. It was quiet and dark except for our tiny amber bubble of light.

Jordan was the epitome of tension, his broad shoulders stiff with it. He continued to fiddle with the glass. "I have known her my entire life. We grew up together," he began in a hushed voice. "Our parents were friends—they still are, actually. We did everything together. School. Surfing. Hanging out at the beach. Homework. *Everything.*" He shook his head. "We were a lot of firsts for each other—first kiss, first girlfriend, first..." His voice died out and then he shrugged. "I hadn't seen her for years. Had a vague idea that she had moved up north somewhere."

I cleared my throat. "What happened?"

He rolled his shoulders, as if forcing them to relax. "I asked her to marry me before I left for college. We're the same age but I'd finished a year and a half early due to the parental homeschooling indoctrination. The old man had pushed me into that engineering program he wanted me to start so badly. Christ, I was sixteen fucking years old. What did I know? She said yes, of course, and I left her behind. Drove back to SLO every chance I got...every weekend practically. And when she started at UCLA, I was ecstatic. We were only thirty minutes away from each other."

"Then you met someone else?"

His features chilled and slowly, deliberately he placed the glass on the coffee table in front of him. His free hand clenched into a fist. "You assume it was me that cheated, hmm?"

I swallowed, my face flushing. "Oh, sorry. I thought that, given your proclivities and the text-harem..."

"That's just great, Weiss. So because I'm the man, naturally I was the cheater."

"Guess that was a sexist assumption on my part."

"Yup."

"Well, to be fair, it wasn't just because you are a man. Your behavior toward her tonight was a little...I don't know...kind of like you feel guilty."

Those eyes found mine, the look in them so intense I found myself holding my breath. "I am—I do. I have a lot to feel guilty for when it comes to Cyndi. But I didn't cheat on her. No, I surprised her one Friday afternoon at her dorm to take her out. Came through her door and found a tatted-up piece of shit biker dude on top of her in bed."

"Oh, dear God," I said, falling back against the couch. "Fuck, I'm so sorry."

He winced and looked away. Scooting to the edge of the couch, he sloughed off his jacket and removed his tie. "It was six years ago. Ancient history." He unbuttoned his cuffs and rolled up his sleeves. I could barely take my eyes off his powerful forearms, the strong veins lining them under his skin.

"But ancient history has a way of sticking with you...coming back to haunt you."

"Yeah?" he bit out. His voice held a bitter edge. "What would *you* know about it? Did your fraternity boyfriend make out with your BFF?"

"No, he didn't, fuck you very much. He married my mother."

He let out a long breath that evolved into a shaky laugh. But when his eyes landed on my face, he could tell I wasn't joking. He immediately sobered. "For real?"

"It's okay. You can laugh. I know it's fucked up and dysfunctional. My mom loves only one person in her whole world—herself. So I'm sure Gunnar is only husband number four in a string of eight or nine, maybe even a baker's dozen."

He frowned. "This happened recently?"

My eyes darted away from his to fixate on the fire. "Right before Comic-Con."

"So your cougar mom swooped in and stole your boyfriend?"

"We'd been broken up. As far as I know, he didn't sleep with her until after I broke it off with him. She flirted with all my boyfriends, so who knows? Apparently, I bored him in bed."

Jordan blinked. "*What?*"

"That's what he said when I broke up with him."

"He's a fuckin' liar, Weiss. I hope you didn't believe that shit."

I shrugged, staring into the fire. I had to admit that I *had* believed it. But Jordan's reaction was somewhat encouraging.

He shifted to face me, reaching out a hand. The back of his fingers skimmed along my jaw. The touch sizzled right through me—as it did *every* time this man touched me. I swallowed. He grasped my chin and turned my face toward his. "If he really thought that, then he's the dimmest man on the planet. For real. Or maybe *he* bored *you*."

My eyes held fast to his, which appeared darker since most of his face was in shadow now. I licked my lips. His eyes followed the movement and I saw his Adam's apple bob. But instead of removing his hand, he brushed it along my cheek, pushing a strand of my hair behind my ear. I couldn't control the shiver that trickled down my spine.

"So...so you didn't think I was boring?" My voice was barely above a whisper.

Slowly, he shook his head, his eyes never leaving mine. I was enthralled by every move, every gesture. His fingers slid along my jaw again, his thumb caressing my cheek. Every breath in my chest was checked by a band of tension tightening around me, and each inhalation seemed harder to grasp than the last one.

The pad of his thumb smoothed over my bottom lip. The touch was light, slow, deliberate. Torturously erotic. I felt every ridge of that thumbprint smooth over my skin, permanently marking me.

"You were the complete opposite of boring," he breathed in a voice so quiet I had to strain my ears to hear. His thumb pushed again and I pursed my lips, kissing it.

His eyes darkened, the thumb slipped between my lips and I caught it lightly in my teeth. "It was so not boring that I fight with myself to try to forget." The tip of my tongue snaked out and molded around his invading thumb. His head moved, his face inches from mine, so close I could not see him clearly. "You don't fight fair, Weiss."

My lips closed around him and I sucked. There was a new feeling all over my body—fire on my skin and a cold, cold ache inside. I was an empty bowl, and I needed him to fill me up.

I drew back so I could speak. "Because I don't want to fight it anymore," I said.

His lips were on mine in an instant.

He tasted a little like the wine he had downed at the reception, but other than that, he tasted just as he had the night before. His warm lips covered mine, melded with them, our tongues uniting at the same time. His hand hooked around my neck, holding my head to his. He needn't have bothered. It wasn't like I was going anywhere.

I wanted this too much.

After minutes of our mouths pressed together, I felt like I had to remind myself to breathe. My eyes fluttered closed and I could barely think of anything but the feel of his lips traveling across my jaw, the scrape of whiskers against my cheek and neck. Now I was breathing too fast and I was too mindless to draw it back under my control.

My lips found the pulse on his sandpapery neck, and I sucked and licked him there. "You're making this very difficult, Weiss," he said.

"So are you."

His mouth traveled down my neck, kissing along the low scoop of my neckline. I shivered. His hand that gripped my upper arm tightened. "I really want to peel you out of this dress."

My hands laced through his soft hair as he kissed his way toward my cleavage, each touch of his mouth striking me like an arrow clear down to my core. God, the ache was so ferocious now, I was almost whimpering with it.

"I wouldn't mind at all if you did that."

"But I can't—I shouldn't. You're the forbidden fruit." His tongue dipped between my breasts, licking his way up my breastbone. I gasped. "But damned if you don't taste so fucking good. What I really want to do is strip you naked and spread you out underneath me."

"Also something I wouldn't object to." My voice trembled. The tension inside was building to near epic pressure levels. His mouth and hands were conjuring wicked, sinful spells, entrancing me willingly. He was far too good at this.

And I was forgetting every bit of sense I was born with. He was my boss. My business school recommendation depended on him. If anyone found out this was happening, he could lose his job.

"We shouldn't be doing this," he said, as if reading my thoughts. But at the same time, his fingers were dipping below the edge of the back of my dress.

Despite the alert in my brain that we should stop, my hand snaked up to unbutton his shirt. We both seemed to be having the problem of our hands and bodies functioning independently of our brains. I slipped my hand inside his shirt, smoothing across that hard, sculpted chest. He felt so good I could—

In seconds, his hand closed around my wrist, wrenching it out of his shirt. The other hand found my other wrist. The next second, he had abruptly pushed me back on the couch so that I was lying flat on my back and he was pinning me down with his body, my hands restrained above my head.

"If this goes any further, I won't be able to stop. We aren't just fooling around now," he hissed between his teeth, his eyes flashing with both irritation and lust. "I want to fuck you so badly I can taste it—I can taste *you*. And fuck it all, I can't taste anything else *but* you."

I swallowed tightly. He wanted me to give him the out. He wanted me to talk sense into him. And he had a point. He was feeling vulnerable right now, and to seduce him like this was taking advantage. The thought seemed ludicrous because I doubted Jordan had ever been seduced against his will.

But...maybe I had a little power to shift his judgment. Maybe I had a responsibility to be the one to keep my wits about me.

"We shouldn't because...we work together. It might threaten your job." My voice hardly sounded committed to this, but shakily I continued. "Um. Maybe...maybe you regretted last time."

His grip around my wrists tightened. "Stop it," he groaned, his head lowering so that his forehead rested against mine. "The only thing I regretted was your goddamn video."

I swallowed. "Maybe you don't really want this."

He shifted, pressing the large, hard bulge in his pants against my thigh. "Does it *feel* like I don't really want this?"

My breath was quickening again. I wanted him inside me so badly that my thoughts and sense were now swirling around inside my head, roiling and bubbling over like a storybook cauldron. Lust burned through every synapse, every vein, every sinew. My hips shifted and I ground them against him.

"Jordan," I breathed. "I want you."

His mouth was on me again, his tongue tangling with mine. He clasped me so fiercely around the wrists that I was starting to lose feeling in my hands. Suddenly, he pulled back and sat straight up, releasing me.

Shit.

I wanted to scream at his sudden bout of self-control. The look he was giving me, though, was anything but controlled. He looked like a wild animal, his chest rising and falling.

His jaw set. "Stand up, April."

I was one hundred percent certain I would not like whatever he was going to say. I sat up slowly and faced him.

"Stand," he repeated, reaching to help me up. He rose along with me. "There are a number of indecent things I want to do to you right now—and in several different ways—but, despite what I said earlier, I didn't bring condoms with me."

I frowned. "That's unfortunate."

"Quite."

"Perhaps it's too much of a temptation, then, to inform you that condoms came in the suite's hospitality basket." I pointed over to the counter where the basket sat, untouched, since I'd glanced through it the day before.

He gazed at the basket, all the breath hissing out of his chest. He scrubbed his hands over his face. "Fuck, Weiss. You weren't supposed to tell me that."

We stared at each other for a long, tense minute. I tried to regulate my breathing. His eyes dropped to my chest, likely noting the aforementioned difficulty with drawing air into my lungs.

Abruptly, he spun and strode over to the bar, where he pulled out a bottle of water, uncapped it and took a long pull. With a deep breath, I turned my back on him and faced the fire. I wasn't ready for this to be over yet. However, it took two to waltz and my dance partner was fleeing the ball. I blinked, frustrated.

But could I blame him? There were so many reasons—some that I hadn't even named—that he shouldn't be into me. Number one, that virus video from Hell. Number two, I was his intern and he loved his job. Number three, he should be preparing for his talk in the morning with practice and a good night's sleep. Number four... I frowned, rubbing my forehead between my eyebrows. I couldn't imagine what number four would be. I was sure there had to be a number four.

Then I heard him behind me and I froze. His body was so near, so warm—warmer than the heat of the fire in front of me because he was inches—maybe even millimeters—away. And there was something else...kind of like having a compass pointing toward the source of magnetism, I felt a mystical pull between my two shoulder blades. He was drawing me under his enchantment again, simply by standing close.

When I felt his warm breath on the back of my neck, shivers scurried down my spine. His strong fingers brushed my hair away, and slowly—ever so slowly—his lips touched at the juncture of my neck and back. With that scruff and those smooth, smooth lips, he brushed along the top of my shoulder. I gasped, unable to control myself.

One of his hands pressed against my belly, pulling me back against his chest while he kissed me. It was driving me wild with expectation. Yet another spell in his arsenal of sorcery.

My breathing froze and I was keenly aware of my heartbeat—everywhere—especially on that spot at the back of my neck where his lips were connecting with the sensitive skin.

"Well, well, lovely Snow White. Looks like the Big Bad Wolf is here to eat you all up," he muttered against my flesh, his mouth simulating his words.

"Wrong fairytale," I shakily replied.

"Well, I sure as hell am not Prince Charming, because I doubt he ever did to her what I am going to do to you," he groaned.

His fingers slid through my hair then curled, and with a quick tug, my head jerked to the side, making more of my neck available to him. His hand tightened and his breath came fast. My scalp prickled with the pain that only served to turn me on even more. The only sound was the unzipping of my dress with one swift, determined tug.

"Yeah?" I asked. "And what are you going to do to me?"

"Nothing you aren't going to thoroughly enjoy."

That ache was growing, radiating from my center but increasing with each passing minute that he carefully wove his charm. With one quick flick of my wrist, I let the dress fall into an ice-blue puddle at my feet. I felt like the goddess rising from the waters in Botticelli's famous painting, *The Birth of Venus*. And Jordan, with his lips of fire trailing across my skin, was a worshipper at my altar.

"I've been wanting to see you naked for months."

I knew the feeling well. I faced him and his hand dropped from my hair. I stepped out of my dress and he bent to pick it up, then draped it over the back of a chair. I waited until he turned back to me to reach around and unhook my strapless bra. When it fell loose, I flung it so it landed on that same chair. Then, before I could lose my nerve, I slipped off my underwear and kicked it in the same direction. Now I was clothed only in the reflection of the fireplace flames and his hot gaze that slid over me.

Jordan, on the other hand, was still completely clothed. His partially unbuttoned white shirt, his suit pants—complete with taut bulge at the front. Even his shoes. As if reading my mind, he slid them off. Then he finished unbuttoning his shirt and dropped it on top of my discarded clothing on the chair. His biceps bulged with the action and the planes of his chest gleamed in the amber glow. I imagined feeling that hard, bare chest against mine. Skin rubbing on skin. My nipples hardened to points, and though his hand had dropped to his belt, he came over to me instead, pulling me firmly against him.

"You are so fucking beautiful," he said. My hands went up to his chest, feeling every hard muscle, tracing every crease. My head dipped to do what I'd been craving ever since I'd seen him in the doorway of his beach house wearing nothing but a pair of swim trunks. I licked him, my mouth tracing the line of his collarbone, and he hissed out a breath. I felt him surge against my stomach and my hand dropped to his belt.

"I don't want you to regret this..." he whispered.

I almost laughed at him. *As if.* The only thing I'd regret tonight was *not* having an orgasm. And I was pretty sure he wouldn't let that happen.

"Fuck no," I said. Right now I was so tightly wound that I was about ready to snap if he didn't go through with this.

"But April...this can only be a one-time thing...we can't continue this beyond tonight."

I swallowed a sudden lump in my throat. I wasn't thrilled about it, but I understood why it had to be. Jordan was giving himself an out, letting me know this was just about sex.

"I understand." I unbuckled his belt and ran my hand down his fly, caressing him through the sleek material of his suit pants. His cock leapt under my touch and I grasped him. "I want you inside me again, Jordan."

In an instant, he had us against the wall, his pants and his boxers pushed down. He was naked but standing too close for me to properly admire him. He had the necessary foil packet in his hand, courtesy of the hotel. I'd have to write a thank-you note to housekeeping for being so considerate.

With hardly any effort at all, he lifted me and pressed me against the cold wall so that our faces were level with each other. My legs locked around his waist and his tongue invaded my mouth with such ferocity that I could hardly breathe. I writhed against him and he came up for air, gasping before dipping his head and sucking my nipple into his mouth. Fucking hell, it felt so good. My fingernails dug into his shoulders, my eyes rolling back into my head.

His tongue and teeth were kneading the sensitive point of my nipple, driving me straight into ecstatic oblivion. I ground my hips against him and he grunted in response, switching to the other nipple.

"Oh my God, you are driving me insane," I gasped.

"Nice to finally return the favor. You've been driving me insane for over a month."

"You've just been making me hate you," I said as I raked my nails down his shoulders and chest.

"Hmm—so mean of me. I should make up for that." Slowly, he let me slide down the wall until I was on my feet again, but he kept sinking until he was on his knees and then sitting on the rug. I moved to go down with him, but he held my hips in place. He began applying those magical, heavenly, scruff-filled kisses to the tender skin on the inside of my thighs. I leaned back against the wall, opening my legs at his nudging, closing my eyes to savor the feel of him there. His hot mouth traveled up one thigh, then switched to the other, repeating its path. He gently pulled, prompting me to shift my weight to the other leg so I could drape one over his shoulder, opening myself to him.

"I can't wait to find out what you taste like, Weiss."

I gulped. None of my boyfriends had ever performed oral sex on me. They either had never offered or a few times my high school boyfriend's efforts had been so awkward, I'd stopped him before he'd begun. I almost wanted to stop Jordan now. I'd never had this experience before and wasn't sure this should be the first time, but I had no time to think or react before his mouth was at the juncture of my thighs, his fingers spreading me open to his attention.

His tongue slipped out to connect with my clit, and I had to bite the inside of my cheek to keep from yelping. The minute I could breathe, I let out a long moan and his shoulder tensed underneath my leg. He leaned forward, applying more pressure, and I was lost to him and the intoxicating movements of his tongue against my flesh. Each flick of his tongue felt like it was drawing every cell in my body tighter and tighter together. Soon he was sucking me into his mouth, consuming me, as he'd threatened to. And with that scruff and those muscles, I could easily picture him as the Big Bad Wolf, devouring me.

Every nerve ending in my body was alive and lusting for more attention from him and his bewitching mouth. He must have judged I was close, because his mouth pushed harder against me, his movements coming faster. Then a finger slipped inside me, pushing deep and curving upward, pressing against my most sensitive spot, as if it was an 'on' button and that was all I'd been waiting for.

In moments, I was climaxing in mind-blowing waves of pure screaming pleasure. I couldn't hold back anymore. My one leg buckled and Jordan held me up as he continued to suck—every last drop of tension wringing from me until I was so sensitive it started to hurt.

"Please," I gasped, pushing him away. "Oh God..."

Slowly, he let up as I fought to recover. He unhooked my leg from his shoulder, releasing my hips. My eyes were closed and my entire body was covered in perspiration. I tingled everywhere. Instead of satisfying me, that orgasm had made me hungry for more. I wanted to feel him moving inside me, filling me up. I wanted to hear him groan with his own need, taking his pleasure from my body.

When I opened my eyes, he was lying flat on his back, looking up at me with predatory eyes. I gingerly sank down on the carpet beside him, peppering his chest with hungry kisses.

"You are so unbelievably hot," he muttered.

"I was just going to say that about you."

Our mouths connected and when he pulled back, he muttered, "If I'm not inside you in the next two minutes, I'm going to fucking lose it."

He grabbed the packet off the ground beside him and tore the foil, then slipped on the condom. This was the first chance I'd had to see him naked and he was beautiful—sculpted, lean, muscular legs from years of balancing on a surfboard, his firm abdomen, the ridge above his hips. I also got my first glimpse of his cock, and it was as magnificent as the rest of him. And large, just as I remembered—if I'd known what I'd been getting into last time, I might have run screaming.

"You really should be practicing your talk, you know," I teased when he'd finished slipping on the condom.

"I'll have time for that after I've used these condoms." He rolled on his side and reached for me. I went willingly.

"I didn't count…how many of them came in the basket?"

He grinned like the wolf he had likened himself to. "You'll find out."

With a gentle nudge, we both rolled and he pinned me down with his wide chest. A hand slipped down to press my knees apart and I opened to him.

He slipped in between my legs, and in one swift movement pushed himself inside me. I was slick, wet, ready for him, and though he was big, his entry was easy enough. I held my breath, enjoying the feel of him there, of his weight pushing me down into the carpet. He bent forward, pressed his mouth to my neck and began to move.

He found his rhythm quickly, resting on his elbows, holding my head in his hands as he continued to feast on my neck. I locked my legs around his swiveling hips, pulling him into me tight and not letting go.

"Jesus, Weiss, you're killing me," he muttered in a hoarse voice.

"Fuck me hard, Jordan."

With a growl, he pushed up on his arms and did just that, slamming into me with rushed, quick strokes. The force of it took my breath away and almost hurt, but it also felt intensely good. Abruptly, he shifted the tempo and the angle at which he entered me, and I sucked in a breath, my body arching underneath him. He watched me closely, likely trying to gauge how close I was. I could barely catch my breath. It must have been pretty obvious I was close.

"Come on, April," he ground out. "Come again."

I closed my eyes, concentrating on nothing else but the feel of him moving inside me and against me, the friction of his solid chest rubbing against my nipples, the feel of his hands digging into my hips, his hot breath on my face and neck. All at once, I was up and over the edge, coming in breath-stealing gasps, completely shocked that I had come again so quickly.

But then I remembered... that night, the night of the video. I'd orgasmed more than once too. It had been the first time that had ever happened, and all because I'd been under the hands of a very skilled lover. Under Jordan's hands.

He was still moving on top of me, his breath becoming more ragged until I felt him stiffen against me with one final push deep inside.

Behind my closed eyes, I was still seeing stars. That had been fan-fucking-tastic. Every bit as hot as the night of Comic-Con—no, even better. This time I could look into his handsome face and see his desire for me. I could feel his hot mouth moving over my neck, my face.

Holy shit.

As I floated back down to earth, I began to dread his words from earlier. *April...this can only be a one-time thing...we can't continue this beyond tonight.*

A feeling of cold emptiness washed over me and I suppressed a shiver, an ache of loss.

Because already I was addicted.

20
JORDAN

INSTEAD OF PRACTICING FOR MY TED TALK AND REMINDING myself about Friar Jordan's New Law of Celibacy, I spent half the night fucking my hot intern. And though it blew all those newfound ideals out of the water, there was no way in hell I was going to regret it.

After the first time on the floor in front of the fireplace, I carried her upstairs to my room. I had another condom and I intended to use it. If this was a one-night-only thing—as it really *had* to be—then I was going to make the most of it.

After two orgasms, she appeared fatigued, a sheen of sweat making her porcelain skin glow in an otherworldly beautiful way. There was another fireplace in my bedroom, so instead of turning on the lights, I flipped the switch for the fireplace instead. Then, I laid her gently on the bed and she smiled up at me with sated eyes that I couldn't resist. I bent to take that mouth with mine again, kissing those plump, pink lips that reminded me of a fairytale princess. A very naughty fairytale princess.

"You thirsty? Hungry?"

With a smile, she shook her head then scooted over on the bed, patting the place beside her.

I ducked into the bathroom before joining her. She had rolled onto her stomach, having tucked a pillow under her chin, and was watching the fire intently from the foot of the bed. I lay on my back and admired the curves of her gorgeous ass and thighs.

Her body was different from the women I dated nowadays. Most were models, so they were tall, lean, and lanky. All firm, toned muscle and few curves. They were beautiful women, no doubt, but there was something about this one...

"Your body is beautiful," I said, running a hand over her soft skin, cupping her ass.

She turned her head to look at me, a frown creasing her dark brows. It was clear she didn't believe me. "Weren't you dating a Victoria's Secret model last year? And the actresses...I hardly compare to any of them."

My hand paused only momentarily in its exploration of her skin, her ass, her legs. I was already getting hard just from touching her. And I wanted inside her again—soon. Hopefully, the second time would be enough for tonight because the condom count would be zero after this. Though I could call room service for more if I became desperate enough.

"You shouldn't compare yourself to any of them. You're different. You feel like a woman. A real woman. It's their job to look like that so the clothes look good on them," I shrugged. "But I wouldn't kick any of them out of bed for eating crackers..."

She scowled.

"I might kick *you* out of bed, though. So I could fuck you on the floor again, of course."

"Wow, the things you tell a woman just to get in her pants..."

My hand stopped on her arm and closed around it—a little too tightly, I realized, when she sucked in her breath. I let up on my hold and she turned, our eyes fastening on each other. "I don't lie to a woman. Ever. Not to you. Not to any of them."

"I could make you lie to me."

I narrowed my eyes at her, but it didn't have the intended effect. She smiled craftily.

"How many lovers have you had?"

I hesitated, pulling back. "I'm not going to tell you that."

She raised her head off the pillow and looked at me. "What if I told you how many I've had?"

"Tell me, then."

"Let's see... I was seventeen my first time—junior prom. That was my high school boyfriend—"

The thought of her with other men was annoying me for some reason, even if it was ancient history. "Just a number, Weiss, not a complete sexual history."

She shrugged. "You're number six."

I lay back on my pillow and watched her, running my hand down her leg again.

"Well?" she said after a minute. "Come on...tell me your number."

"The truth?" I sighed. "I have no idea."

Her brows shot up. "What?"

I shrugged. "It's not like I count."

"Okay, but...*could* you count if you sat down and thought about it?"

I stared at the ceiling, avoiding her eyes—and the question. She was probably disgusted.

"Are we talking dozens, scores, *hundreds?* Ballpark it."

A sly smile spread across my lips. "Definitely less than a ballpark."

She smacked the back of my arm and laughed. "Jackass."

I laughed and shrugged. "But it's just a number anyway. I actually think sex gets hotter the longer you are with someone. You get to know them better, their body, what they like..."

My hand smoothed over her again. Had I ever touched skin this soft before? And even after all that sweating she'd done from our scorching encounter downstairs, she still smelled amazing.

Her eyes widened. "Wow, that's so not something I expected to come out of the playboy millionaire's mouth."

Yeah, if I kept talking like that, I stood to damage my reputation. But I'd already started to feel jaded about all that anyway.

And seeing Cyndi tonight had reminded me of that emptiness. Of how I probably would never be satisfied if I kept hooking up in those shallow, unfulfilling liaisons. Sure, it was fun to get my rocks off in the moment. But at the end of the day, I went home alone. The chick might not even be someone I'd want to sit around and watch movies with or have a meal or long conversation.

I hadn't had any of that in a long time, until... My hand stilled on top of April's weird tattoo at the small of her back, right at the curve above her ass that drove me crazy. I rose up on one elbow to get a better look at it, running my hand over it again.

"So here it is, the damning tattoo."

She tensed under my hand. "You mean my brand of shame? My scarlet letter?"

"Your what?"

She turned her head and looked at me. "Oh, please don't tell me you've never read the novel. *The Scarlet Letter?* Nathaniel Hawthorne?"

"I was homeschooled. My mom didn't like classic literature. I saw the movie, though. Some Puritan chick got pregnant out of wedlock and they made her put a red 'A' on all her clothes."

She got that same dreamy look on her face she always did when she talked about books. "Hester Prynne. She was an amazing woman. They tried to shame her, but she rose above their jeers and taunts. She bore the brunt of their horrible treatment, stood up on the scaffold and faced the humiliation in front of everyone in the village. The scarlet letter was meant to be her brand of shame. Eventually it became her badge of honor."

I traced the skull and snake tattoo at the small of her back. "And this is your brand of shame?"

She shrugged. "Sometimes it feels like that."

"What on earth possessed you to get this, Weiss?"

"What possessed me to do just about all of the stupid things I've done in my short life? A combination of my parents, a steep nose-dive in self-esteem and a lot of alcohol."

"So your mother did something to piss you off?"

She shook her head. "No, that one was my dad. I was sixteen. We had a big fight. I wanted to leave the boarding school I was at because I hated it there and was having a hard time. He blew me off. I went out with some questionable friends, got drunk using a fake ID and woke up the next morning with the tat. It was basically a symbolic slap in the face to him. And he *was* hurt when he found out about me getting a tattoo—though he never saw it. I want to get it removed someday."

"Until then, it's damning evidence of your bout with cosplay stardom," I said, laughing.

She turned to me with intensity in her eyes, and I knew I wasn't going to like what she had to say. "Speaking of damning evidence, I do believe you have a tattoo that proves you were once madly in love with someone."

I swallowed hard and looked away. That same fresh hurt rose up and stabbed me in the chest. So weird that after all these years, you'd think you were over something—someone. But tonight...looking into her face again, seeing her so much older now. And a far cry from that smiling, carefree surfer girl I grew up with... The woman who basically shattered my trust in all women forever. Because if I couldn't trust her, who the hell could I trust?

I rubbed the bridge of my nose. I didn't want to talk about Cyndi. Not now...not ever. But I doubted April would let me off the hook, and she was starting to tread into uncomfortable territory. So I leaned forward and kissed her on the shoulder, smoothing my hand down her back. Although this was a classic distraction tactic, I really was ready to go again. I nibbled on her ear and she drew away from me to catch my gaze with those beautiful dark blue eyes. I took a breath and let it go with a sigh.

Her serious expression smoothed into a smile and then a laugh. "Hmm. You know, you *really* should be practicing that speech and getting a good night's sleep."

"Thank you, ladies and gentlemen, for the opportunity to address you this afternoon," I began without hesitation, pushing her long hair away from her neck. That hair...that neck. Angling for taste, I dipped my head, opening my mouth and sucking her soft, fragrant skin into my mouth. She gasped and wavered against me.

Rolling so that I was on top of her, her curvy ass pressing into my groin, I reached under her to grope those full, firm breasts as I kissed my way down her back.

"And...?" she prompted with a breathy voice.

"For decades, the integration of video games and education have revolutionized the way we teach and learn..." With my leg, I pushed her thighs open. My hand dropped from her breast and scooted between her body and the mattress to find her already wet and ready for me. *Oh, hell yes.* I pressed my cock against her opening and she gasped.

"I'm going to fuck you, Weiss. This time it's going to take a long time and it's going to feel so good."

"It felt pretty damn good last time."

"I'm going to see how many times I can make you come in one night." I tore the foil wrapper with my teeth and slipped the condom on. Fuck yes, I was going to make this last shot count.

"I'm not opposed to that plan."

"Are you willing to let go and let me take you there?"

With the hand underneath, I pulled her toward me and entered her with a quick, smooth thrust. One of my favorite moves. I'd wanted her to cry out, maybe even scream—at least gasp loudly or groan. Instead, she sucked in her breath. Before I was done pounding her, I vowed to have her weeping. This girl needed to let go and I was going to make that happen.

But for this moment, I savored the feel of her closing around me, gripping me tight—so tight I could barely breathe. I buried my nose in her fragrant hair, covering her body with mine, and I began to move. I reared back on my knees, pulling her up with me, and slammed into her with quick momentum. She held herself up on the baseboard of the bed, and with one hand, I gathered her hair and carefully tugged, pulling her head back. She rewarded me with a grunt.

My other hand slipped underneath her to rub against her clit. She felt so damn good, but she was too quiet this time. After a few minutes, I bent over her to place my mouth at her ear. "Do you like that, April?"

She was breathing heavily, at least. "Yes."

"I want to hear how good it feels." I gave her hair another tug and pounded into her.

This time the grunt was accompanied by a moan.

She shifted her hands on the baseboard, pushing back against me as I rose and fell over her. My lust surged. "That's right." I quickened my pace.

"Oh, God," she moaned. I got that a lot. With a growl, I bent forward, and finding the base of her neck with my mouth, I sank my teeth in. She jerked in response.

"You like that."

"Yes," she grunted, sounding feral.

"You want more?" She didn't reply. I slowed down, giving only short, shallow thrusts. "Tell me, April." She pushed back against me again, as if in protest, and I grabbed her hips and held her still. "I want to hear you lose control."

"Go faster," she pleaded.

"I told you I was taking my time." I stilled and continued to rub her sweet spot. She tried to thrust back against me and I stopped her, waiting until she was close again. I used my free hand to palm her breast, rubbing over her nipple over and over until she was gasping and coming, gripping me with her climax. I relished the feel of her around me, tight and hot.

Pushing into her again a few times, I waited until she came down from that. Then I pulled out and rolled her over.

"That's three."

She gazed up at me with satisfied eyes. "You count orgasms but not partners?"

I lowered my mouth to hers, about ready to climb on for more when she pressed against my chest, shoving me away.

"What?"

She grinned wickedly as she pushed me again and I slid off her. "My turn to ride high," she said as she rolled me onto my back and straddled me.

Oh. God, yes. My hands glided from her hips, across her waist to cup her breasts as she shifted her hips and I entered her again. With a thrust, I slid home, pushing in deep. This time, instead of a reserved intake of breath, she moaned, her eyes widening in surprise.

"Slowly, April," I warned as she began to move, but there was a challenge in her eyes. She licked her lips and shifted quickly against me. I pinched her nipples hard. She threw her head back and yelped, her nails digging into my skin.

I brought my hands up to her head and cradled her face in my hands. She continued to move and I thrust against her. I pulled her face down to mine, both to kiss her and to slow her down. Her breasts rubbed against my chest and it felt incredible. *She* felt incredible, surrounding me, gripping me tight.

"Open your eyes," I commanded. She complied as she continued to move against me. Her long silky hair splayed across my body felt like heaven. But when her gaze drifted away, I pulled her head closer. "Look at me. Don't look away."

As we stared into each other's eyes, we slowly climbed again. Each movement brought a sweet, high-pitched moan from her. And each moan did something to me deep inside. But it was her eyes holding mine that penetrated a layer I didn't even know existed. It was far more intimate than I had imagined. At one point, I was the one who wanted to look away, afraid she would see too much of me.

Before long she was gasping with another orgasm, her back arching. I sat up and sucked her nipple into my mouth as she writhed and whimpered against me. Her slick body was stuck to mine and I rolled us over, pushing into her again and again until I was coming, the hot release pulsing from my body. Her mouth was on my neck, her nails in my back, her legs clamped around my hips, pulling me flush against her.

Holy. Fuck. It was minutes before I could even think again, let alone talk or even remember how to breathe. The last time had been amazing. This time had blown it—and just about every other good roll I'd ever had—right out of the water.

I pulled back and looked into her glowing, flushed face. What the hell was this woman doing to me?

Feeling uncomfortable and more than a little exposed, I rolled off of her and went to the bathroom to clean up. She was still lying on her back staring up at the ceiling when I came back into the room. I plopped onto the bed and pulled her against me. Her body was cold from the sweat so I curled up around her back, spooning her. She turned and kissed my arm.

"I do believe that final count was four," I said.

"Six, if you count yours..."

"We're only counting yours. I could shoot for making it an even half-dozen."

She laughed. "I'll be passed out long before that. Mmm, that was good. And I am now a firm believer in scruff."

"You like the scruff?"

She raised her palm to my cheek, rubbing her hand across my whiskers. "'Like' is an understatement. Especially when you are kissing me and rubbing it all over my body."

I indulged her by kissing her shoulder and giving her a nice, healthy chin rub, which made her laugh. Then I pulled her back and she settled against my chest. It felt good. Half of me wished I had another condom. The other half was telling me to calm the fuck down and get some sleep. I felt good, sated. For now, anyway.

"So, um..." she began timidly.

I traced a hand over her round hip. "Yes?"

"Just checking to make sure things with you are...better. You weren't doing so hot when we got back here from the reception."

My hand stilled on her soft skin and I planted my nose in her hair, inhaling liberally. She angled her head toward me so she could see my face, then ran her hand over the scruff on my jaw.

"You definitely made me feel better. Much better than Jack would have." I smirked.

She laughed, then rolled around to face me. "I just mean...well, it shook you up pretty badly to see her again. But I don't understand something that you said. That you feel guilty toward her. If she's the one who cheated on you, why is that the case?"

I tensed and tried to ignore the old feelings of agitation that arose whenever I thought of Cyndi. "I told you that nice guys finish last. I was a nice guy and I got fucked over—literally. So that was my last day of being a nice guy. I decided that anyone who screwed with me would live to regret it."

She swallowed, fingering the tattoo on my arm. "So you got some kind of revenge on her?"

I clenched my jaw and then released it. Lying back, I stared at the ceiling, that same guilt taking hold of me. Christ.

"I'm not proud of it now, but it sure felt damn good when I did it. I know people. They do stuff for me...that's not a new thing. It was the case in college too. I found out who the guy was that she was fucking and threw a hot redhead his way. Didn't take long before he was fucking her, too. And...well, Cyndi ended up getting a taste of her own medicine. I ended up ruining him, too, after the fact."

Silence. I held my breath and let it go slowly. Then I chanced a look at her. She was staring off into space, appearing deep in thought. She was a thinker, I'd noticed. She lived in her head a lot.

Finally, she spoke. "I screwed you over, too, with that video, even if it was on accident. Does that mean you're going to get revenge on me?"

I turned toward her, propping myself up on an arm. "I think after tonight, you can consider yourself thoroughly screwed." I smiled wolfishly. "But in a much more pleasant way."

When she looked at me, there was more than desire in her eyes, there was a little fear, too. And damn if it didn't turn me on a little to see it there. Maybe I'd have to call down to room service for another condom after all.

I tugged on her shoulder to roll her onto her back and then took her mouth with mine, possessing it fiercely. I claimed her with my lips, teeth and tongue until she was gasping for air.

"You'd think after two times I would have had enough," I mumbled against her neck. "I just want you more now."

"Oh, God, you always know how to say the right thing."

"It's not bullshit, April."

Her soft hands slid down my back and fresh desire surged.

She pulled away and looked at me, and those deep blue eyes seemed to scour my soul. "You should talk to her."

I recoiled. "What? Who?"

"Cynthia."

I took a deep breath and looked away. Wow, she really knew how to kill a moment.

"I mean...if the guilt is getting to you."

I tensed. "I have no idea what I would say to her."

"Tell her you're sorry. It will make you feel better."

"What will make me feel better is if we forget we saw each other and go on with our lives."

She looked away, shrugging a shoulder. "It's just a suggestion, Jordan. You don't have to listen to the lowly little intern if you don't want to."

I didn't reply. I had nothing to say—even to correct her about her lowly intern remark. So I let it hang there between us.

April pressed her mouth to my chest, murmuring, "God, you are beautiful." She settled in next to me between my arm and my chest. Exhaustion fell over me like a blanket.

My eyes drifted closed, and I sifted my fingers through her soft hair. The agitation over discussing Cyndi was fading again. This felt...comforting. "You're lucky I didn't sleep well last night or I'd be all over you again," I mumbled.

"Promises, promises," she said, tracing an idle finger across my stomach.

We lay like that for a long time. I drifted off to that no man's land between sleep and wakefulness, where I was aware of her skin against mine, her smell, her soft hair. In my happy place, I felt her shift, sit up and pull a blanket over me.

I cracked an eye open when I realized she was getting up to leave.

"Where are you going?"

She bent to kiss my forehead. My eyes zeroed in on the way her breasts swung along with the motion of her body.

"I'm going back to my room," she whispered.

I snaked a hand up and caught her around the waist, pulling her down on me. "No, you're not. You're sleeping here."

With a tired laugh, she only halfheartedly struggled to be free of my tight hold. "The Beast has declared his will."

"Yes, I have. The Beast needs his Beauty to lie down right here and sleep beside him."

"So I'm Beauty, now?"

"Always," I muttered, snuggling her against me. Then I drifted off to sleep with visions of fairytale princesses in my head, and each one had the face of the girl lying in my arms.

21
APRIL

I WOKE UP BEFORE JORDAN THE NEXT MORNING AND HIGHTAILED it out of bed before we had to deal with the inevitable awkwardness of would-we or wouldn't-we again. Apparently, there were no more condoms in the room anyway. And while I would have liked more of what we'd done last night, he'd been clear—this was a one-night-only thing.

And it had to be that way, but I wasn't pleased about it.

I studied him in the gray morning light. He was naked, tangled in the sheets, his hard, beautiful male body all planes and angles. As tormented as his sleep had been—I'd had to give him a wide berth during the night—his face was one of peace. I wished I knew what he was dreaming about.

I went downstairs, showered, dressed and ordered breakfast from room service all before I heard him moving around upstairs. He had the opening workshop to attend this morning and then his speech came just after lunch.

He appeared downstairs in jeans and a t-shirt that stretched across his broad chest. His eyes traveled over the fare—a dish of scrambled eggs, bacon, a plate of pastries and fresh, hot coffee. Without a word, he poured himself a cup, hot and black. I watched as he raised it to his lips, blew on the surface and then sipped carefully.

His eyes drifted over to mine. "Morning," he finally said in a gruff voice. "Sleep well?"

If sleeping next to a human hurricane meant sleeping well... "Sure," I said unconvincingly.

"Was I that bad?"

"Uh, the sleeping or the other part?"

He laughed. "Sleeping."

"Well, let's just say I could tell you were nervous about today. You, um, mumbled parts of your talk in your sleep."

"You're lying."

I grinned. "Nope. Honest to God. I got to hear all about videogame micro-economy, even if it was mumbled and slurred a bit."

He smiled, walked over to the window and looked out on the overcast day, sipping his coffee again. I stole glimpses of his magnificent butt in those jeans. *A very nice view indeed.*

"You dreamed about her, too," I said quietly.

He stiffened, tilted his head back and finished off his coffee. Turning, his eyes slid over me, cold and hard. "Well, what are you sitting there for? Don't you have some assistanting to do? Sorting my schedule or something?"

My eyebrows shot up toward my hairline. Business as usual. Well...I'd been warned, hadn't I?

"Sure, whatever you say, *boss.*" I cleared my throat and stood from the table, then brushed crumbs off my fingers while avoiding his gaze as he watched me tidy up and turn to leave.

An hour later, we were ready to go. He had on a dove gray blazer over those jeans and a black Polo shirt. With that dusting of growth on his face and a bit of product run through his hair so that it was artfully askew, he looked yummy enough to eat.

I gulped and pulled out my phone, ignoring how his eyes traveled over me in my dark green sweater set. "Um, we need to be at the convention center in twenty minutes."

He gestured toward the doorway. "Lead the way."

The morning continued about the same way it had started. Jordan didn't say much to me. I wasn't sure if he was still angry about the comment I made at breakfast or if he was trying to distance himself, to reinforce that our one-night fling would stay just that.

One night. He'd probably had lots of one-night stands among the *countless* women he'd been with. He likely thought nothing of this...except for the awkward fact that we still had to go on working with each other for another month. Maybe he didn't feel that the sex between us had been mind-blowing on two separate occasions, but I was finding it difficult to ignore that fact.

The minute we'd finished, I'd started craving it again with an ever-increasing need. Even sitting next to him in the auditorium, feeling the heat of his arm near mine...hell, even his smell was torture. I wanted to climb into his strong, hard lap for a cuddle—maybe some other things too.

What the hell was wrong with me? Why was I letting him affect me like this—every touch, every reminder of his presence was an instant flashback to the electricity generated by our sweaty, naked bodies moving against each other.

Jordan didn't eat much for lunch and retreated to the green room shortly after a few bites and another cup of coffee. I told myself that his cool behavior was because he was nervous. I tried not to feel hurt. I tried not to care so much.

But damn it, warning or not, it did hurt. And I was already starting to care too much—about the demons that haunted him so much he couldn't get a good night's sleep, about who he was underneath the delicious, perfect exterior.

Yeah, he was a cocky jerk on the surface. An insufferable, cocky jerk. But underneath? Underneath that arrogant exterior was something elusive, golden, rare. Something he kept hidden except in moments when he couldn't, like when I was staring straight into his soul during sex.

Oh shit. This situation got stickier the more time we spent together.

I stood backstage in a separate room, watching his speech on a monitor while he delivered it to a darkened auditorium filled with people. Though I knew he was nervous, very little of that showed in his presentation. He looked sufficiently scholarly yet also hip, the scruff and blazer lending some credence to his youth. And he was both articulate and intelligent. To me, that only made his physical beauty all the sexier.

Not long into his introduction, I became aware of a presence standing at my shoulder. Glancing over, I saw that it was Cynthia, her eyes glued to the screen. She wore a long-sleeved blouse today, the incriminating tattoo that linked her to Jordan now hidden.

She glanced at me with a smile and nodded to the screen. "He's brilliant. I knew he would be a great match for TED. That's what I told the committee when I suggested him as a speaker."

I looked at her, wondering if Jordan knew that she was the one responsible for his invitation to speak. "Would you..." I began.

She looked around and then stepped a little closer to me, indicating for me to lower my voice. "Would you like the chance to speak to him? Alone?"

She drew back a little, a frown creasing her brow. She tucked a strand of blond hair behind her ear and hedged, "I don't really think he'd want that."

"But if he did...would *you* want that?"

She pressed her lips together and then shook her head. "He wouldn't want that," she repeated. "Jordan believes in his own form of karma."

I'm sure she meant that cryptically, but I understood nevertheless. She knew about Jordan's payback for her cheating. I wondered if Jordan knew that.

We stared at the monitor for the rest of his allotted eighteen minutes. He smoothly wrapped up his subject with a charismatic, self-deprecating smile and a gleam in his eyes that could make panties melt. Mine were definitely feeling warmer than normal.

Cynthia turned to go just as I saw Jordan exit the stage to widespread applause. I stopped her, asking her about the meeting with the journalists who wanted to speak with him in a few hours. By the time she answered me, Jordan had walked into the room, confident and grinning. He opened his mouth to say something to me before catching sight of Cynthia, who had frozen at my shoulder. The smile slid off his face.

I walked up to him. "Hey there," I said. "You have an appointment in an hour with the *USA Home Weekly* journalist. Until then, you're, uh...on your own," I said with a pointed glance at Cynthia.

His eyes narrowed and he swallowed but didn't say anything as I walked out of the room. He'd probably be pissed at me, but when else would he have a chance to clear the air with her, if not now?

I could tell it had been bugging him since last night when he'd seen her. Likely it had been bugging him a lot longer than that. I couldn't get the image out of my head of him staring pensively into that glass of whiskey. I was convinced I'd done a good deed and that he'd understand and probably thank me for it. Hopefully. Eventually.

But when I heard from him a few hours later...yeah, not so much.

He was pissed. His face looked like a thundercloud when he made it back to the penthouse. He said nothing before hitting the stairs, and I knew enough from what I saw that I immediately hightailed it into my little butler's pantry. I'd put on my pajamas and cuddle under a blanket with one of my favorite books. Maybe he'd wander out again. Since avoidance was my method of coping, I was good at it.

I had my top and bra off, about to go grab my nightie, when there was a knock at the door. Before I could call out that I wasn't dressed, he'd pushed the door open. I covered up with what I had at my disposal—my hands.

Jordan had changed into a sweatshirt and jacket with leather logger boots on his feet. He still wore those jeans that stretched across his muscular thighs.

"Uh, excuse me!" I huffed, cupping my breasts in my hands.

His eyes dropped to my chest, lingered for a moment, then met mine again. "Weiss, I had my hands and mouth all over those last night. What's the problem?"

My skin flushed and prickled with the heated memory and how good it had felt.

I tossed my head. "You didn't have the murderous gleam in your eye last night that you have right now."

His jaw clenched. "Get dressed in something warm and meet me by the elevator in five minutes."

I would have mock saluted him, but he'd already turned his back and pulled the door shut. Not to mention I was still using my hands to cover myself up.

I pulled on a pair of jeans, my Doc Martens, a sweater, scarf and a light jacket, which was all I'd brought other than business attire. I hadn't thought I'd be getting out much, and my idea of British Columbia in the fall had apparently been vastly different from reality. Because I'd lived in Southern California all my life, I wasn't prepared for wintery weather in September. But apparently, September in Vancouver was along the lines of winter at home.

Jordan was silent, austere and refused to answer me when I asked him where we were going. Down at the valet parking, he picked up the keys to an SUV that had been dropped off by a local rental company. It was a Land Rover, though not as nice as the one he drove at home.

There were blankets and a box in the back seat. In minutes he was on a highway headed north—the Sea-to-Sky Highway, it was labeled.

"Are you taking us out of town so it will be easier to hide my body?"

He smiled grimly but didn't answer, instead fiddling with the GPS. He'd set the destination for some place called Porteau Cove Provincial Park, which looked to be on the road to Whistler, about an hour north of the city.

We drove along the inlet out of West Vancouver, along Horseshoe Bay and its massive ferry port and the dark, looming shapes of big islands off the coast. The tension between us was thick, and it didn't help that Jordan made no effort to start a conversation. I stared out the window and drummed my fingers, wondering why the heck he was taking us out into the pitch-black night.

An hour into our drive, he followed the GPS directions to turn off the road into the benighted park. We crossed over railroad tracks and into a mostly empty but large parking lot that overlooked the sound. There wasn't a single light along the coastline, and with the moon just a thin sliver, all we had to light our way were the stars.

So many stars. I'd never seen this many at once before. I leaned forward, peering out the windshield, my mouth agape. Out of the corner of my eye, I saw his head turn, watching me. I was uneasy. There was no one out here but us. A long pier stretched out over the quiet, dark bay. According to the signs, it was for a ferry that apparently visited sometimes but was currently missing. He could easily strangle me and then dump me over the side of that pier…

I turned to him.

His eyes glittered in the dim light. "Come."

I folded my arms across my chest and huffed at him. "How do I know you aren't going to ditch me out here like an unwanted dog or something?"

With a gruff laugh, Jordan got out and slammed his door shut. As reluctant as I was to follow the command that sounded much like something he'd say to the aforementioned dog, I followed him. He was walking toward the pier, and I trotted to catch up with him. It was chilly out here. Even through my quilted jacket and fashionable wool infinity scarf, the evening nipped at my cheeks.

"Are you pissed at me?"

"What do you think?" he asked in a flat, even voice.

"Why did you bring me out here if you're so angry?"

"Because I planned this before you pulled your shitty little stunt."

I was silent for a moment, struggling to keep up with him, as he was making no effort whatsoever to make his pace manageable for me. He took one stride for every three of mine. Abruptly, he came to a halt and veered to the railing at the side of the pier, where I joined him. We were about halfway down its length, just before hitting the slope of the loading ramp.

His hands were in his jacket pockets, his eyes on the ground in front of him. A cool breeze tugged at my hair, bringing tears to my eyes. He pulled out a knit beanie and gloves, handing them to me. I thanked him and slipped them on.

At that moment, my eyes caught on something along the horizon. A band of greenish fog had risen up. It was lovely. But... green fog?

"What the hell is that? The zombie apocalypse?"

"Aurora Borealis," Jordan muttered.

"Northern lights? You can see them this far south?"

"Sometimes. I saw the forecast for them tonight, so I asked the concierge for a good place to go see them. Some place dark enough and away from the city. He got me the rental."

I watched as, slowly, the green light arced upward from the horizon, like fingers grasping at twinkling celestial jewels. The streaks of light grew into emerald tendrils curving across the dome of stars, transforming everything into a giant cathedral of light that stretched into eternity. They moved like distant phantoms, reflected on the still water of the sound.

"So beautiful."

Jordan bent forward, resting his elbows on the railing without taking his eyes off the beautiful vision in front of him. "It's like...magic really does exist," he said reverently.

I was comforted by his demeanor, relieved that he appeared to not be as angry as he claimed. I took a deep breath and decided to take a chance. Reaching out, I placed my hand on top of his. "I really shouldn't have done that."

"There're a lot of things you shouldn't have done," he said between clenched teeth, jerking his hand away. That action hurt and I swallowed the feeling, knowing that I probably I deserved it.

"Would it help if I said I was sorry?"

"Maybe. But only if you were actually sorry, which you aren't."

"Was it that bad?"

He stiffened but didn't answer me. In the silent night, there was only the gentle lap of the bay water against the shore.

"Do...do you still love her?"

He huffed out a laugh, a faint cloud of vapor escaping his lips. "Don't be idiotic, please."

"Then—"

"She deserved what I did. Got it? She destroyed me. You have no idea. There was not another person on this planet that I trusted more than her. "

I watched him carefully. "So I take it you had nothing to say to each other?"

He rubbed his forehead. "No, that's not what that means."

"I didn't do it to hurt you...I hope you know that. I was trying to help—"

"You have no fucking idea what will help and what won't. Keep your nose out of it from now on."

His words hurt. Of course they did. But I couldn't take my eyes off the way he was white-knuckling the railing of the pier. Something about that confrontation with her had deeply distressed him. Either because of what he'd said or what he hadn't said.

"I see. So no one is allowed to care. Not your grandpa. Not your mom. Not me."

"I never asked you to care."

I craned my head to get a look at him. "You didn't have to ask me."

He bent down to get in my face. "Don't do it, Weiss. It was sex. It was good. Don't fool yourself into thinking it was anything more than that. You're not my girlfriend. You're not even my friend. Got it?"

Tears sprang to my eyes and I jerked back. A slap across the face would have felt better. That was beyond harsh. But he didn't care. I huffed at him. "Reading you loud and clear. No one is allowed to care."

"*You're* not allowed to care. You're just another one who's fucked me over."

I blinked. Now he was referring to the video. My mind raced to things he'd said before...about how he wasn't a nice guy. He'd told me he got back at people who screwed him over.

"I see. So that's what last night was about? Revenge?"

"Last night was about sex. I already told you that."

"How many ways can I explain to you that uploading the video was an accident?"

His eyes blazed into mine. "Why should I believe it? You've got me over a barrel, don't you? If I don't write that glowing recommendation, you can go to my boss and—"

I gasped and held up my hand to stop him. "Don't even finish that sentence. I've never threatened you and I never will."

"You didn't have to. You had me by the balls before you were ever my assistant."

It made no sense for him to think that. Until two days ago, I had no idea he was even Falco! But he was so wound up right now, he clearly couldn't think straight.

"No wonder you're afraid of people getting too close. Believe it or not, Jordan, we don't all think and act like you do. Some of us refuse to let that darkness poison us."

"So now you're the Dalai Lama? Stop acting like you know anything about me, because you don't know *shit*. About me or about how the real world out there works."

His words pelted me like rocks in the middle of my chest. My first instinct was to throw some right back at him. But I didn't. "This world is a mighty dark, disturbing place, the way you see it. If everybody's out to screw you, then you're on your own, because the only person you'll trust is yourself. You're going to end up being very lonely."

He said nothing, just shook his head and let out a scornful laugh. Tears were starting to fall now, and I angrily scrubbed them away when he wasn't looking.

He had a point. It was my own fault that I cared. But it wasn't like I was a machine. I couldn't turn that off.

"I feel sorry for you."

He spun, his face twisted, angry. "Feel sorry for me all you want. People shit on me, I get them back—twice over. I'm *proud* of that. You want to know the real reason my father won't look at me? Because I went after the fucker who screwed *him* over. His partner, and, I might add, a family friend, cheated my dad out of millions. *I* got him because Grant Fawkes was too much of a coward to stick up for himself. So when I got the dirt on that asshole and got him to cough up the money, the old man wouldn't touch it. Said it was dirty." He huffed out a bitter laugh. "I took his fucking dirty money and invested it in my company. *His* loss, my gain. Karma is for pussies. I make my own."

I gasped at his words that closely echoed Cynthia's. She was right. I backed away from him, hugging myself in the chilly air but feeling even colder inside. I didn't want him to see my emotional reaction. Why was I letting him get to me like this? I spun on my booted heel and headed back to the car.

A few seconds later, I heard the sound of his quick footsteps bearing down on me. I sped up, knowing I could never outrun him but hoping to clue him in that I had no interest in continuing this conversation. I wasn't going to be his punching bag.

I headed around the side of the SUV in order to get in when his arm hooked around my waist, stopping me. He pulled me back against his hard body. Once again, the air was sucked out of my chest and I could barely swallow because my heartbeat in my throat felt so big and intrusive.

He pressed his face against my hair and then muttered harshly, "Who the fuck do you think you are, my conscience?"

"I'm just a person who cares..." I whispered.

"Don't do that. You are not allowed to care." His voice was hard, like rocks grinding together.

"I can't help it."

"Yes, you can."

"Not everyone in this world is out to get you."

"What is it you want, Weiss? You want to fix me? Good luck with that. Work on fixing yourself first." He wound his fingers through my hair, holding my head still.

I swallowed. "You're a bastard."

"But I'm the bastard you want." He pressed his lips to the back of my neck, and I would have jerked away at the contact had he not held me immobilized.

"As long as it's *just sex*," I ground out sarcastically.

"That pulse in your neck says one of two things." He ignored what I said—as usual. "Either you want me or you are scared shitless of me. Which is it?"

I struggled to inhale. "Both."

His breath warmed my hair, my ear, the back of my neck, sending shivers of anticipation down my spine. "Good."

Even if he hadn't done anything else, his words were enough to cause all the breath to escape my lungs. His mouth pressed against my ear while his hand slid beneath my jacket, under my sweatshirt and smoothed across my stomach. He angled us toward the front bumper of the car as his mouth landed on my neck, making the world spin around me. His hands on me were harsh, kneading my breasts. His mouth pressed against me, nipping and sucking. Hot desire flooded my every sense, and I was filled with a hyper-awareness of him. The way his hard erection pressed against my butt through my jeans, the way his hands cupped and rubbed me, the way they slipped under my bra, pushing it up and away from my breasts to free them for his pleasure.

Soon he had us bent over the hood, one hand working furiously at the button on my jeans. Was I going to let him use me for sex? Hell, why did I even think about it like that? *He* was the one who had insisted it was just sex—out-of-this-world amazing sex. I could use him for sex, too. Sex was as good an outlet for anger as it was for desire.

"Jordan—"

"What?" he asked as he tugged my zipper down, wasting no time burying a hand inside my panties. His fingers curled upward, finding me even in the tight confines of my jeans. I gasped, as his fingers worked against me. "You are so goddamn wet for me. You gonna tell me you don't want it? Because I know it's a lie. "

"I'm pissed at you," I panted, angry at myself over my automatic, intense reaction to him. "I don't like you very much right now."

"You don't have to like me. Just as long as you like what I'm doing to you."

My eyes slammed closed and I squeezed them tight as his hand started to move, sliding over my clit. "That depends on how good you are."

"Oh, I think you already know how good I am. But if you don't want it, then tell me. Otherwise I'm going to fuck you hard and fast, just the way you want it. You want it that way, don't you, April?"

I gasped again, the pleasure of his fingers pressing against the bundle of nerves at my center painting warm pleasure over my stomach, my thighs. With each stroke, he gained more command of my body. He was casting his spell again, reeling me in to do his will. And it felt. So. Damn. Good.

"Mr. Fawkes," I breathed. "You are being inappropriate."

One of his hands palmed my breast, the other continued to push me closer to orgasm. He pressed his mouth to my ear. "You love it when I'm inappropriate."

I was close—so close. Everything in me tightened when he stopped and pulled his hand out of my pants. With a quick tug, my jeans and panties were around my knees. I shivered. Jordan pulled off his jacket and laid it against the car in front of me. It was warm with his body heat, and I sank into it even as I heard him unzip his jeans and fiddle with the packaging of another condom—courtesy of the concierge, I presumed.

I didn't care, as long as he had one and as long as he used it as well as he had last night.

"Well, that wasn't impressive," I said after he pushed into me with a fierce thrust. "You could have at least let me come."

"Tough shit," he said, hooking a thick arm around my hips while he braced the other against the hood of the car. "You'll get your orgasm. When I think you deserve it."

"Asshole."

"That's right. I'm the asshole whose cock is owning you. Right now."

He pushed into me again, then slammed into me repeatedly with a ferocity he hadn't shown the night before. The car rocked with our movements.

Inside me, he felt so good. He was big, stretching me with every thrust, sinking deeper inside me, and soon I was moaning and panting for more. My moans echoed into the dark night and seemed to drive him harder.

With one hand between my legs again, the other had my hair in his grip. In a voice thick with lust, he said, "Brace yourself. God, you feel so good."

I did as he said and soon he increased the rhythm with which he was pounding into me, his hand tightening in my hair, pulling my head back so he could press his mouth against my temple and whisper dirty things in my ear about how good it felt to be inside me and how he wanted to fuck me senseless.

He was close to getting his wish. The world seemed to turn around us, but I couldn't make sense of anything except the way he was making my body feel at that moment.

Until I saw a bright light flashing from underneath my closed eyelids. At that same moment, Jordan froze. I opened my eyes to see a vehicle circling the large parking lot. As we were at the front of the car, we were hidden from view, but from the way the driver was shining a spotlight, it looked as if it were a ranger checking on things. As he made another circuit, I could see emergency lights on top of his truck.

"Shit," I breathed.

"Don't move. Don't say a thing. He'll be gone in a minute."

Jordan may have stopped moving, but his hand hadn't. He still stroked my clit and the touch was maddening. I clamped my hand around his wrist.

"Stop," I said. "I can't concentrate."

"Shhh," he said as the truck slowed down. Goddamn it. He was going to get out, and I was going to get caught with my pants down— *literally.*

I clamped my mouth shut as Jordan continued to stimulate me. I squeezed my eyes closed. He pressed his mouth to my ear. "Shh," he said again. As if he had to remind me.

Jordan's hand moved faster against me and I stifled a whimper, biting my lip hard. He was watching the truck as it slowly continued its circuit, finally moving away from us. My heartbeat was drumming against my chest like I'd just run for my life to escape a serial killer in the woods. The thrill was intoxicating, and as I watched the truck drive away, I was close to coming. Thankfully, instead of being a jerk and stopping like he did last time, Jordan started to move again.

And I don't know if it was the danger of getting caught, the ferocity with which he was taking me or just the fact that we were getting to know each other's bodies better, but the orgasm that followed was beyond incredible. My head dropped back and I let out a little shout that echoed all around us as every muscle in my body tightened. I was coming in air-stealing waves, not even able to gasp my next breath. The stars may have started twirling overhead, too...mingling and swirling with those Northern Lights like a giant kaleidoscope in the night sky.

I fell against the hood of the truck trying to catch my next breath, the pleasure wrung forcibly from my body. I was still coming even as he moved gently inside me, as if he wanted to savor the feeling too.

"Oh God, that was... fuck yeah," I gasped.

"Fuck yeah is right," he said tightly, and then he began pounding against me again. I locked my elbows, bracing against the car as he groaned behind me. "Fuck yeah," he breathed just before he stilled, stiffening against me. He let out a long breath as I felt the pulses of his orgasm deep inside. Pressing a flushed cheek to the cold hood of the car, I let out a low moan, loving the feel of him inside me.

For a long time, he didn't move, just stood there holding me as his hoarse breathing normalized. Slowly, carefully, he released me from his tight hold and pulled out of me. I missed the feel of him already.

I heard him remove the condom and shove it inside what sounded like a plastic bag.

After buttoning himself up, he bent and pulled my underwear and pants up my legs, landing a kiss on my hip. I quickly zipped and buttoned my jeans, then turned around to face him. He took my shoulders in his hands.

"That was a lot more fun than arguing," he murmured.

"That was almost an international incident. I don't even have my passport with me."

"Oh, chill... Bears do it in the woods. Why can't we?"

I slapped his chest. "I'm not kidding. What if Mr. Canadian Mountie had gotten out of the truck?"

"What if he had?" He shrugged. "Besides, I can't think of a better reason to go to jail. And it's Canada. How bad could their jail even be? *Sorry I had to arrest you, sir. That was pretty impolite of me, eh?*" he mocked in a faux Canadian accent. I couldn't help but snicker.

He pulled away and opened the passenger door for me. I slid inside and watched as he came around the front and climbed into his side. I shivered on the cold leather seat.

"Here, take the blanket." He grabbed it off the box in the back and handed it to me. I tucked it around myself. "The concierge packed some food. Are you hungry?"

"I don't know. Did you poison it?"

"Only the apples." He winked and smiled that devilishly handsome smile.

I reached back and pulled out a package of cheese and crackers, handing it to him, then grabbed one for myself.

"So much for the 'one-night thing,' huh?" I cocked a brow at him.

"Technically, all three times have occurred within a twenty-four-hour period."

"Ah," I said, rolling my eyes. "I guess we are safe, then."

His gaze cut to mine. "You're not safe, Weiss. Take my word for it."

I set down the slice of cheese I was about to eat. "The cheese is poisoned, too?"

"The cheese is fine. But the Big Bad Wolf is hungry for more than food." His eyes roamed my face.

"What if I still don't like you?"

"You don't have to like me. You just have to like what I want to do to you."

I swallowed, thrilled again by his words. "Well...we are out of the country. Maybe it doesn't count if we're across international borders."

"I like how you think. I think we should make the most of our Canadian carte blanche."

I snacked on my cheese and crackers and watched through the windshield as the Northern Lights continued to dance across the inky sky.

Our differences had not been resolved—not by a long shot—but we silently agreed to table it.

And we did table it, quite literally. We had sex on the dining room table when we got back to the penthouse. Followed by the bed.

Apparently, this was all I was ever going to get. So if I went home walking bowlegged like a cowboy, then so be it. At least we'd enjoyed ourselves.

The only problem was... I wasn't ready for it to end. But I'd be the last person in the world to tell him that. Because, like it or not, he *was* ready.

22
JORDAN

A DRIVER IN A TOWN CAR TOOK US HOME FROM THE AIRPORT. It was late afternoon and we both had to be at work early the next morning. I'd resolved to stick to my guns, meaning no more sexual contact with April once we returned to the country. What happened in Canada stayed in Canada—at least I hoped it would.

I was more than a little worried because I was already starting to crave the smell of her hair, the feel of that soft skin at the small of her back, the taste of her neck and earlobes. The feel of her thighs wrapped around me.

Christ. I watched her as she worked, bent over her laptop. The car inched down the 405 freeway on the drive from LAX in rush-hour traffic. I faked checking my phone. I had a shit-ton of emails to go through, but I couldn't concentrate on work right now.

"It's too bad you couldn't stay to enjoy the rest of the conference," she said without looking up from her screen.

I supposed I could have taken in some of the talks, but I would have loved enjoying *her* for a few more days even more. Because honestly, our time together had been fucking amazing. I couldn't get enough of her. I sure as hell *hadn't* gotten enough of her.

"So, uh..." I said, clearing my throat.

She looked up from her laptop and fixed her dark blue eyes on me. "Yes?"

"Are we cool?"

Her brows pushed together. "You mean, do I know my place? Oh, Mr. Fawkes, I've never forgotten it."

My lips thinned. "That's not what I meant."

"Are you worried I'm going to rat you out? Because—"

I scowled. "I didn't mean *that* either."

She smiled. "Then I guess you'd better tell me what you mean."

"I hope you don't feel used or anything like that...that you understand why..."

She sighed and turned her head, looking out the window at the same time she closed her laptop. "I understand. You don't have to say anything more about it."

"So tomorrow at the office..."

"Business as usual. I've got it."

I swallowed. I didn't particularly like the idea myself. And if circumstances were different... Maybe after her internship, when she was no longer working for me, I'd ask her out. Or had too much dirty water gone under the bridge for that?

We rode along in tense silence before she shifted, leaning toward me conspiratorially. "Don't you think it might be better if..."

"What?"

"Well, I'm just thinking about the video. There's always a danger of our identities getting out, right?"

I said nothing but was quite sure I didn't like the direction she was taking.

"What if we warned Adam about it? Just in case things flare up again? You guys could devise a plan and have it ready to head off a PR situation if it arises. And if you go to Adam, then it might not be as bad as if it came out some other way."

I was silent for a long time. She was feeling guilty. Only natural, and it wasn't like I didn't feel like shit about it, too. Maybe her suggestion made sense on some level, but most of me just wanted to believe that this had died down forever.

"I understand what you are getting at, but you don't know Adam like I do. He'd pop blood vessels if he found out. It would be messy."

"Aren't you afraid that it will get out, though?"

"Not really." I shrugged. It was a total lie. She stared at me with narrowed eyes and I tried not to sweat it.

"I just know in my gut that if he had that info—"

"Let me handle it."

"Does that mean you're going to tell him?"

"No. It means I'm going to handle it. Don't worry about it, okay?"

She frowned. "That's a lot easier said than done. I worry about it all the time."

I couldn't resist. I stroked her soft hair. "Don't. I'll take care of it."

But she still looked doubtful, worried. Suddenly, her head was on my shoulder and it was hard to breathe. This unfamiliar feeling of fierce protectiveness overwhelmed me. I *wanted* to take care of it— take care of *her*. Ridiculous thought, I knew, because she was capable of doing that herself. But...

326 | BRENNA AUBREY

What were these feelings she was drawing out in me? I leaned my head against hers for maybe a second before that feeling just grew heavier and more uncomfortable in my chest. It was too hard to think or feel anything else but her. Slowly, I pulled away, though it was probably one of the hardest things I've ever had to do.

With a shaky breath, I forced myself to turn away from her, to think about something else. Out of the corner of my eye, I saw her straighten, watching me as I sat back and stared out my own window, fiddling with the whiskers on my jaw. I'd finally gotten it looking how I wanted only to have to go back to a clean-shaven look come tomorrow. Those bankers were conservative, and I'd taken out my earring and let the hole close up last year before entering their conventional world. I wondered again why I'd wanted to be a part of this world so badly, this world that wasn't really me.

What was I trying to prove and to whom?

As always, it came back to that shadowy figure—my old man— staring over my shoulder. I huffed and blew off that thought.

When we stopped at April's, I'd already decided that I wouldn't get out and walk her to her door. I'd allowed this to go too far already. But I couldn't resist reassuring her again. "April..." I said before she got out of the car.

She turned back to me, grasping the door handle. Our eyes locked.

"I'll take care of things, all right? Trust me."

The corners of her mouth turned up and her eyes closed, and the expression hurt because I could see that she was torn, reluctant to put that trust in me. She leaned forward and kissed me, an affectionate, innocent kiss.

"I know you'll do your best." She didn't look at me again as she turned to leave.

I watched as the driver helped her with her luggage, taking it to her door. I kind of hated myself for letting her go like that, but I didn't trust myself to go near her place. If I did, I knew I wouldn't want to leave.

Strangely, after spending those days with her, I suddenly felt at a loss and lonelier than ever. I closed my eyes, rubbing them with the palms of my hands. I'd told her not to care. That she wasn't allowed to care. I should have sent the same memo to myself.

I'd only been gone four days, but when I got home the place felt empty. I had to fight the inclination to pick up the phone and send Weiss some teasing text. To get my mind off her once and for all—yeah right—I grabbed my board to catch a few good waves before the sun set for the day. But my heart wasn't in it.

***

The next morning, I was at the office an hour early, ready to take on the day and get to work planning our IPO roadshow. We'd be making a series of presentations in an appeal to large-fund managers across the country. We had a two-week window to put the shiniest, most impressive face on our company to get them interested in taking on our stock. The IPO roadshow had to be perfect, and to that end I'd hired a professional director and camera crew who would interview Adam, me and the other officers.

Today was also the scheduled photo shoot for *Entrepreneur Weekly* magazine, all a part of our big press push for the IPO. I arrived in my second favorite suit with a spare slung over my shoulder in a garment bag, just in case my assistant got a little crazy with the coffee. I smiled a little at that thought.

There was hardly a soul hereabouts. The interns and assistants were filing in slowly, and I noticed that Adam's door was ajar. I knocked and then pushed the door open.

The boss had a woman attached to him at the lips. When they heard me enter, they pulled apart and stared at me, wide-eyed, looking like teenagers caught making out in their parents' bedroom. I almost laughed. Almost.

"Hey, Mia," I said. "A little early for a booty call, isn't it?"

"I was just...swinging by for a little moral support," she said, a blush staining her cheeks.

Adam slipped an arm around his fiancée's waist. They were so cute together it was almost sickening. Scratch that, it *was* sickening. And Adam's obvious bliss didn't help matters.

"It's Mia's first day of school today," he explained. He sounded like he was talking about a kindergartner. I guess Adam liked them really young...

"Oh, right. Medical school. You get your own cadaver to work on and all that gruesome stuff. Dr. Frankenstein, why didn't you make your beau carry your books to class for you, then?"

She rolled her eyes. "Don't give him any ideas. He wanted to drive me there, but we compromised and came here first. I'm taking the car to school and then coming back to get him tonight."

I resisted the urge to smirk. They were commuting together, probably because she was still annoyed with Adam's recent transportation purchase—a sweet, vintage Indian motorcycle. Even I was envious of it.

She turned to me. "That was a great presentation, by the way. I was impressed, even though I didn't understand half the stuff you said."

"Sorry I couldn't make any commentary on the chainmail bikinis the characters wear in the game. I know that's your favorite subject. Plus, I like them and I vote we keep them."

"Of course you do." Grinning, she slipped out of Adam's hold and bent to grab her sweatshirt and purse. "I gotta get going. Don't want to be late on my first day."

Adam walked her to the door, where she paused to kiss him goodbye. "Text me later. Let me know how it's going," he said, hooking an arm around her and pulling her against him. She kissed him again.

"Mmm. You have to stop, or I won't want to leave."

"You've caught on to my evil plan."

God, any more of this and I was going to start making gagging noises right here on the spot. I coughed into my hand, *"Get-a-room."*

Adam glared at me. "We *did* have a room 'til some douchebag decided to barge in on us."

I raised my brows. "She's gonna be late, dude."

He grimaced but let her go, then kissed her again on her cheek. "Good luck. Love you."

"I know." She turned, waving to me as an afterthought, and was gone.

Adam took a minute to watch her go, as if he wasn't going to see her again in months or a year instead of this evening. Something about that irritated me. And yet, underneath that layer of irritation was envy, if I allowed myself to admit it.

I looked away, annoyed at that thought. *Love. Who needed that shit?* I turned back to Adam. "Should I step out? Give you a moment to recover?"

"Go fuck yourself," he said with a good-natured grin, turning to join me by the window.

"She'll be okay. Her docs gave her the okay for school, right?"

"She's fine." He shrugged self-consciously, but I could tell he was still worried.

"She's still not letting you ride the bike?"

He gestured to the suit he wore sans jacket. "Like I was going to ride the bike in this."

"Gotta look pretty for your pictures today."

He rolled his eyes. "Speaking of looking pretty...we watched your TED talk a few times. It was really good. Well done."

I smiled. "Thanks. It went over well. I've got some follow-up interviews to do for some of the newspapers who wanted more."

"We need all the good press we can get. I also have some really good news. I'm bringing in someone who I think is going to be key in the formation of our board of directors." Adam turned to me, his mouth turned up in a self-satisfied smile.

Uh-oh. I knew that smile. He was about to spring something on me. He glanced at his watch. "He should be here any minute. He's stopping by for a few so I can show him around."

"And this person is someone I don't know?"

"You've never met him, but he's been supportive of me and my ventures for a long time. I owe him a lot."

"And his qualifications?" I bit out, trying to hide my irritation but not quite succeeding. "I really wish you would have run this by me first."

"I'm running it by you now. And he has no idea what I'm going to ask him to do. I thought I'd introduce you first. I know that he'll be a good—"

The intercom on Adam's desk buzzed, and his intern's voice came through, "Adam? You have a visitor to see you... Mr. David Weiss?"

Instead of answering the intercom, Adam headed for the door, motioning for me to follow. Upon first hearing the man's name, my stomach had dropped. *Not good. Not good at all.*

I trailed behind Adam by about three or four feet, feeling like a dog being dragged to the washbasin. Adam stopped when he came face to face with a man in his early fifties—medium height, fit build, salt and pepper hair, olive skin. He didn't look anything like April—or rather, she didn't look anything like him.

Adam was enthusiastically pumping his hand. "Hey, David. So great to see you. Glad you could come out."

"Well, thanks for inviting me—*finally.*" He had an East Coast accent—Boston, I guessed.

"I have to be careful letting the competition in here, you know. You signed that NDA, right?" Adam smirked.

David Weiss laughed. "You were always a funny kid."

Adam turned to me. "Let me introduce you to my right-hand man. This is Jordan Fawkes, our CFO. He's running the show on all of the IPO stuff."

"Ah, you're the one who's been putting my little girl through her paces."

My hand almost went limp inside his, and I could feel the sweat starting to form. Oh God, this was awkward. "Nice to meet you, Mr. Weiss. I've enjoyed your daughter—I mean, having her as an assistant. She's very good." *Fuck. Goddamn it. Now was not a good time for a Freudian slip.*

He pulled his hand back with a nonchalant shrug. "Well, she's not going to be an assistant for the rest of her life, so it doesn't really matter if she's good at it."

I laughed. "True enough. She's destined for greater things, for sure."

David looked us both up and down. "So, you two are looking awfully formal for tech geeks." I was grateful for the change in subject. "Those boys at Facebook wear t-shirts to work. And I don't believe I ever saw Adam wear a tie in the two years he worked for me."

"We have a photo op later this afternoon," said Adam. "All the press stuff for the IPO."

David's eyes gleamed shrewdly. "That wouldn't have anything to do with why I'm here, would it?"

Adam looked at me for a minute before turning back to David. "It might." He checked his watch. "I know you've got things going on today, but do you have time for me to show you around?"

"Sure. I'd like that. I'd also like to steal my daughter for lunch, if that's possible. I didn't tell her I was coming and I'd like to surprise her."

As the two men talked, I tried to wrap my head around the ramifications of his presence here. I suspected Adam wanted to make him an interim chairman to organize a new board of directors, which was necessary once we were a publicly traded company. I cursed myself that I was just now seeing this, at the exact moment it was dropped in my lap like a load of bricks. Adam had had his own reasons for moving April into my office—reasons he hadn't cared to share with me.

But I knew now this was all part of his master plan to bring David in to help with our IPO. I sent a heated glare at my best friend, resentment bubbling up. I was pissed that he'd withheld this information from me until now. It was so typical of him to behave this way.

And yet, had I known from the beginning, would it have changed anything? I'd known April was off-limits *before* I'd had my way with her—half a dozen times or so.

Even if I had been tentatively planning on pursuing a relationship with April after her internship, that would now be impossible. As an officer of the company, there was no end to the potential disasters that could occur if I dated—and subsequently broke up with—the board director's daughter. My gut tightened.

But my brain was telling my gut to shut the fuck up. Bringing this guy on was good business. He had experience in the industry and was an executive at a competing company. This opened up possibilities for Adam—and possibly even me—to serve on his board, as quid pro quo was common in business. Beyond that, Adam trusted the man and he had apparently helped him out early on in his career. How could I go against all that?

Putting David Weiss on our board would be a smart business move. I couldn't deny it.

But...

No, there were no buts. This thing between April and me had to be over. *For good.*

Adam and David were discussing where to start the tour when movement at the periphery of my vision caught my attention. April stood at her desk beside Susan staring wide-eyed at Adam and her father. She looked at me and our gazes locked. I swallowed, shaking my head. The color drained from her already pale face. She really was the color of snow—or as close as she could get to it. I let out a breath and motioned for her to join us, but she shook her head stiffly.

David must have seen my gesture because he turned to see who I was motioning to.

"There she is!" he said, walking toward her. She walked around the desk, casting a self-conscious glance at the people around the atrium.

"Dad. What are you doing here?"

"Nice to see you too," he said, landing a peck on her cheek, which, judging from the flash of her blue eyes, she barely tolerated. "How was Canada?"

"Good. I was very busy."

Yeah, busy with me between her luscious, soft legs. I swallowed again, loosening my suddenly tight tie.

Adam watched the two with a frown. When he turned to me, I sent him a pointed glance, hoping we could just get on with this hot mess and get it over with as soon as possible.

"Let's start over in development, maybe?" I said when the uncomfortable father-daughter greeting didn't seem to getting any less awkward. "April, you can come along too. I'm sure your dad would like that."

"I would, thank you." David smiled.

April's eyes, hard and blue as glacial ice, told me a different story, however.

Adam and I led the way while David deliberately hung behind to walk beside his daughter. "Rebekah was wondering why you hadn't answered her last email."

"I told you. I've been busy with work."

I stepped up the pace, feeling like an eavesdropper. Adam followed my lead, but they stayed right behind us. "She wants to know if you're coming down for Yom Kippur."

"I'll, um, let you know. I have a lot of work coming up."

Adam turned his head and said over his shoulder, "You can have that day off, April. It's no problem."

Corporate policy. Of course she'd get that day off if she requested it. But I suspected she didn't want to request it. I peeked and saw April staring at Adam's back with a clenched jaw. "Okay, thanks."

"I'll tell her you're coming, then?"

"We'll see. So why are you here?"

"Adam invited me. I think he's cooking up some kind of plan. He's always got secret plans. Like that time he ditched me to start his own company..."

"Hey," Adam said with a smile. "I do recall you gave me your blessing."

And I suspected that David must have bought in with a fat wad of cash, too, or he was about to. His company, Sony Online, it was rumored, was preparing to be spun off and sold, even as they worked on their "next big thing" that might give us a run for our money if it ever got off the ground. It was sad, because his company had been among the most innovative in the industry, at the forefront of massive multiplayer online role-playing games less than two decades ago.

But time, and progress, stopped for no man—or company. I suspected that David knew the bright new future when he saw it and had probably been following Adam's progress very closely. There could be no other reason why a man would let someone as brilliant and talented as Adam leave to go start up a rival company with his blessing.

Of course, I couldn't approach him about the rumors, and they were just that—rumors. But I read up on the industry every day. This community was not very big and we often exchanged employees. Basically, everybody was all up in everyone else's business.

As if to illustrate that point, David made the quiet allusion, once we were in a private room outside of development, to the forbidden subject. "So, uh, forgive me for asking, but...what's all this about a sex video involving the company?"

Adam's face betrayed nothing, but he did pale a bit. I swallowed and studiously avoided his daughter's gaze. She had frozen beside him.

I spoke up. "A couple employees goofing around, nothing more—" And the minute they escaped my mouth, I wanted to grab those words and shove them back inside. Fuck. Fuck. Fucking fuck.

"We only know that *one* employee was involved, actually," Adam corrected quietly, managing, to his credit, not to throw me one of his dark, correcting glares.

"And this person has been fired, I hope?"

Adam and I locked gazes nervously. "Their identity hasn't yet been discovered," Adam said.

April fidgeted at her father's side but kept her eyes down, saying nothing.

David looked skeptical. "You've got the situation under control, though, right? I've been through this process before and those bankers are a skittish bunch. They'll bolt at their own shadows."

"I have the bankers rounded up and on our side. We've done damage control, and the situation has pretty much blown over," I said.

David seemed to accept that and we concluded our tour without any further mention of it, thank goodness. April seemed to want to avoid her father's invitation for lunch, but, not having much choice, grabbed her purse and, with rounded shoulders, followed him out.

As soon as she was out of my sight, I went back to my office, pulled out my phone and sent her a text message.

Can we talk after work tonight?

An hour later, while I was standing in Adam's office waiting for the photographers to set up their backdrop for the cover shoot, my phone chimed.

Yes.

I heard some weird chatter about the cover story being labeled, *"Tech World's Most Eligible Bachelor Millionaires."* But Adam set them straight and said he wanted none of that—most especially because he wasn't eligible anymore.

I could only imagine Mia's face when she saw an article like that. I hoped to God he wouldn't throw me under the bus to get himself off the hook.

But that was the least of my worries.

I met April outside by her car in the parking lot at five-thirty. She looked tired and pale but not unhappy, and something lit up inside me when I saw her again. I stopped in front of her.

"So, um, we should talk. Want to grab a bite to eat or something?"

She rolled her eyes but smiled. "That sounds suspiciously like a date, Mr. Fawkes."

"No, nuh-uh. If you keep calling me Mr. Fawkes, then it's a business dinner, Ms. Weiss. And I think that after this morning, you can't deny we have a lot of *business* to discuss."

She nodded. "Do you mind if I drop my car at home before we go eat? It's okay if I ride in the back seat of your car. That's still *business-like* and me knowing my place."

I blew out a breath. "Knock it off, Weiss. I'll follow you home."

She lived less than four miles from the complex in an upscale condo in Irvine. After she parked her car and got out, I rolled down my window when she indicated she wanted to say something.

"I need to run up to my place for a minute. Want to come? Strictly *businesslike*, of course." She smirked.

"Whatever. But this better not take long. I'm hungry because I skipped lunch. My intern ditched me to go eat with her daddy."

"Park over there in visitors' parking," she pointed with her middle finger. I laughed and followed her directions.

She waited for me on the curb, her arms folded across her chest, looking down, deep in thought. Inside her head again.

"What's up?"

She shrugged, avoiding my eyes. "Just thinkin'."

"Yeah, I've been doing a lot of that today, too."

She flicked a worried gaze at me. "I suppose this talk we're having has to do with my dad showing up out of the blue?"

"Let's save it for dinner."

She rolled her eyes. "Always good to have a new excuse for indigestion."

She turned to climb up the steps to the second floor. I followed her up. "I'm just going to change really quick and get out of these pantyhose. I promise I won't be more than five minutes."

I leaned against the wall next to the door as she fumbled with the key in the lock. With all the distractions today, I hadn't even had a chance to get a close look at her. She looked as gorgeous as ever, that glossy dark hair, those blue eyes, that elegant, upturned little nose, that graceful white neck.

I enjoyed your daughter. I grimaced with the memory of almost blowing it with her dad while amending that dirty little statement in my head. *I enjoyed her on the living room floor, on the dining table, up against a car and several times in a hotel room bed.*

She opened the door, stepped inside and I followed close behind. Then I crashed right into her as she halted in her steps and gasped.

23
APRIL

I STOOD FROZEN IN SHOCK AND THEN SUDDENLY FOUND MYSELF propelled forward by the force of a six-foot, two-hundred-pound man colliding into me from behind. Strong hands steadied me while a soft voice murmured an apology I barely heard. Because sitting on my living room couch were my mother and her new husband—the asshole formerly known as my ex.

What the hell was this, invasion of the obnoxious parents day? No, that wasn't fair to my dad. He wasn't malicious in his neglect. My mother, on the other hand? Pure evil she-demon from hell. My face immediately flamed and I stiffened.

"What's wrong?" I heard Jordan ask quietly behind me.

"Hey, April-Flower!" My mother popped off the sofa, her arms in the air, her pert body posing like a dancer performing a routine. Even in her mid-forties, my mother was still a beautiful woman. And she knew it. She also used it to her advantage with every breath that she took. I swallowed bile in the back of my throat and tossed my purse and keys on the counter.

"What are you doing here?" I said without preamble, vaguely aware that I'd greeted my dad this morning with those exact same words.

Mom approached me, but her eyes were on the man standing behind me. *Typical.* She flashed Jordan a wide smile, then continued to speak to me in her fake, sing-songy voice. "I wanted to see my daughter. Isn't that enough?"

She swished her long blond hair over her shoulder flirtatiously. The bile threatened to come up again.

"Excuse me," I muttered and turned to walk through the kitchen into the hallway. Sid was standing in our bedroom, chewing on her thumbnail and staring at her phone.

"You couldn't have texted me that they were here?" I asked between clenched teeth.

She jumped and looked up at me. "I just texted you like ten minutes ago. And again just now. They showed up and I had no idea what to do!"

I took a breath and then released it. The text must have come through while I was driving and I hadn't heard the update. "I don't suppose you want to tell her to go fuck off for me?"

Her brows shot up, and I gestured to cut her off before she reminded me that she didn't use those potty words.

I heard voices behind me. Jordan and my mom were talking. Ugh. I spun and headed back to the living room. Mom was chatting up Jordan. Oh, *hell* no.

"So you and April work together?"

Jordan, for what it's worth, was more interested in the jackass sitting on the couch than in my mom's batting eyelashes.

"Mom, leave him alone."

She turned back to me, the smile sliding off her face. "You make it sound like I'm attacking him or something."

I bit my lip. Well, it *was* her typical mode of attack. I mentally counted to five, then took in a deep, cleansing breath. None of that was working.

"I'm just getting to know Jordan, here, a little better," she continued when I didn't say anything. "I didn't realize you were seeing someone. And since you've been avoiding me, I don't know anything about what's going on in your life."

I looked at Jordan in time to see him frown at that statement.

"You used to disappear for months at a time," I reminded her. "And if I recall correctly, before your *latest* wedding, I don't think I'd heard from you for six months. Why are you suddenly so interested in my life?"

My mother glanced over to the couch and exchanged a long look with Gunnar. Then she squared her shoulders and walked over to me. "I'm sorry your feelings are still so hurt. I can't choose who I fall in love with."

Great non-apology. So typical. I blinked away the stinging sensation behind my eyes. Her insensitivity to this entire awkward situation got me every time. And really, that was my own fault. I was always hoping, maybe even expecting that she'd become a better person.

But she was the same one who, when I was fourteen, didn't pick me up from a friend's birthday party, leaving me stranded for hours at a restaurant after everyone had left. Her Hollywood director third husband had forced her to change her plans and she'd never bothered to notify me. My poor stepmom ended up driving hours out of her way to get me. Rebekah hadn't gotten there until after midnight, at which point I'd been sitting alone in the dark for hours.

I'd gotten one of my mom's shruggy non-apologies then, too.

"If you're stopping by just to say hello"—which I highly doubted—"I have to get going. I have some important business to take care of right now."

My mom frowned and then reached up and wiped at something on my face before I batted her hand away. "Have you been getting enough sleep? You look tired and your makeup is all worn off. And that mascara—I taught you better than that." She added another cutesy laugh at the end of her statement and threw another assessing look at Jordan.

"I don't need a makeup tutorial, thankyouverymuch."

"Of course you don't, sweetie." She smiled and alarm bells went off. She wanted something. She never, *ever* called me sweetie or any other term of endearment. "I, uh, actually wanted to ask you something." *I knew it.*

She stepped toward me and put her hand in my face again. I caught the distinct smell of alcohol on her breath. "Jeez, April, this gloppy mascara is annoying the hell out of me."

This time, she poked me in the eye with her thumb.

I jerked back. "Ow, shit! Mother, get your finger out of my face and tell me what the fuck you want."

She did this stupid exaggerated thing where her mouth dropped in horror but she still used her cutesy, fake voice—for Jordan's benefit, I presumed. "Since when do you talk to me like that?"

I rubbed at my injured eyeball. With my other eye, I noticed that Jordan was beginning to look pissed. I turned back to my mom. "Have you been drinking?"

Out of the corner of my eye, I saw Gunnar rise from the couch. He was tall and thin, and I'd once thought him a good-looking guy. But now, standing in the same room as Jordan, he looked like a pre-pubescent teen.

I held up my hand to block out his face. "Stay the hell out of this, Gunnar," I said before he'd even said a word.

"Apologize to your mother," he said, ignoring me.

"Go fuck yourself," I said, turning to him. Without warning, my mother lunged at me.

Almost as if it had been rehearsed, Jordan dove for me and Gunnar grabbed her. "Jen, stop," he said to her.

I grabbed her wrists to prevent the uncharacteristic attack. Her features were twisted with anger and her body was shaking. She appeared to be at the end of her tether. And apparently, under the influence. *What was going on?*

My mom was not a drunk—at least as far as I knew. She struggled against Gunnar's hold, and as he tried to contain her, his elbow slammed into my mouth.

Pain exploded in my lip. I fell back, gasping and holding my mouth, the taste of hot copper filling it. Gunnar had split my lip.

"Shit," Jordan muttered, pulling me into the kitchen.

"April! Shit! I'm sorry," my mom shrieked from the living room. Gunnar was trying to calm her down as she began sobbing—loudly.

Jordan led me to the sink, where I spit out both blood and saliva. I could feel my lip already starting to swell, and it stung like...well, like I'd just been elbowed in the mouth. Jordan handed me a paper towel. "Hold this to your lip and press down, then tell me where your plastic bags are."

I pointed to the drawer and watched as he extracted a baggie before opening up the freezer and pulling out ice cubes. He was at my side in a minute with a bag of ice and a glass of water. He pulled the towel from my mouth.

"Here, let me see."

His head dipped low to inspect the damage, his beautiful face just inches from mine. I wanted him to kiss me, and I wouldn't have given a shit if it hurt. I had this overwhelming desire to be in this man's arms, to be comforted by him.

He scowled. "That miserable little asshole split your lip," he ground out between clenched teeth. "Here, rinse your mouth out with this water and then put the ice on it. Your lip is swollen."

I did as he asked. "Thank you," I murmured from behind the bag of ice.

He reached out and pushed my hair behind my ear, his fingers tickling my earlobe. I involuntarily shivered and his eyes darkened when he noticed. He visibly swallowed, then smoothed his thumb over my cheek and this pang of fierce affection for him flared up. I wanted him to put his arms around me and pull me against him.

"Does she show up drunk very often?" he asked.

"Never. She's stressed out, I think. Something's going on."

He frowned, opening his mouth to speak again when Gunnar walked into the kitchen.

"Heya, April. Can I, uh, can I talk to you alone?"

Jordan stiffened. I had a feeling that even if I wanted him to go, he would refuse to leave me alone with Gunnar. Thank God for that.

"Whatever you have to say to me, you can say in front of him," I said.

Gunnar eyed Jordan a little nervously. "This is family business."

"Funny. You're not my family. What do you want?"

"We, uh...we need to borrow some money."

I raised my eyebrows. What the *what?* That was pretty much the last thing I expected to hear from him. From her, yes, but not from him. Gunnar was the sole heir of a fortune. His dad was the head of his own corporation and his mom was from old money. He had access to a sizeable allowance from his trust fund. He didn't need my money. Plus—

"What happened to the job your dad promised you after graduation?"

He shifted his weight from one leg to the other, eyes on the ground. "That hasn't gone as planned."

I adjusted the bag of ice against my lip. Out of the corner of my eye, I could see that Jordan was watching me carefully.

"And you can't ask your parents for the money because...?"

He scowled. "Same reason. They're upset about the marriage."

I almost laughed. Gunnar's dad adored me and pretty much pegged me as his future daughter-in-law the first night I'd met him. Guess he wasn't as enthusiastic about my mom, because it sounded suspiciously like they'd cut Gunnar off for marrying her.

However, I was so desperate to get Gunnar and Mom out of here without any more fuss, I was willing to fork over some money to do it.

I sighed. "How much do you need?"

"Five thousand."

I drew back, shocked. "*What?* Did you get roughed up by drug dealers or something?"

He rolled his eyes. "It's just rent and groceries for the month."

Jeez. No wonder she was liquored up in there. She'd probably needed the booze to get the nerve to walk in here and ask me for that kind of money. This was an all-time low. It was a pattern for her, to move on to the next rich dude the moment her alimony from the previous divorce expired. And I was certain that if Gunnar had been a penniless pretty boy instead of a rich heir, she would have screwed him and moved on instead of rushing off to Vegas with him.

She obviously hadn't counted on Gunnar's source of wealth drying up. And now it was clear they were panicking.

"I don't have that kind of money sitting around."

He scowled. "Then call your dad."

My mouth dropped. "I can't do that. You, her *husband*, actually expect me to call up her *ex*-husband and ask for money for her? Have some pride and don't be an idiot."

His fists clenched and he stepped forward. "Don't you *dare* call me that."

Jordan pushed partway between us and Gunnar cast a wary glance at him. "C'mon, April, grow a backbone and just call him."

Jordan's hand clenched into a fist at his side.

Gunnar scowled at him. "Chill out. You're just the dude she's fucking this week. I've known her for years."

Jordan took a step toward Gunnar. "Doesn't mean you can insult her."

Gunnar flicked a hard gaze at me. "Trust me, she's not worth the trouble."

Jordan's fist came up. Oh shit. I never thought of Jordan as the combative type. And even though they were almost the same height, Jordan outweighed Gunnar by at least fifty pounds. I'd hung onto those meaty biceps while I'd been in his arms and had a feeling they could do some serious damage.

"Jordan, no. It's not worth it..." I said in a trembling voice.

Gunnar grinned triumphantly. "You see? Even *she* agrees."

Gunnar didn't even know what hit him. Jordan lashed out, his fist connecting with Gunnar's jaw. The little weenie was knocked back, stunned, as his nose gushed like a red fountain.

"That's for splitting her lip and not having the decency to apologize, you fucker."

Gunnar cupped a hand around his nose and straightened. "Jesus Christ! Calm the fuck down! It was an accident."

"*This* isn't." Jordan swung again. Since he was left-handed, Gunnar hadn't been prepared as the left hook came at him, this time clipping him under the eye.

Gunnar fell back against the corner of the counter—which had to have hurt—and he slid to the ground. "I'm calling the cops!"

"*Really?* And what'll happen when I show them her face and tell them you did that to her? I may go to jail, but you're going right along with me."

Gunnar sniffled, blood pouring out of his nose now. My mother came running in and screamed when she saw him. I grabbed the roll of paper towels and threw it to Gunnar. It bounced on the floor before he snatched it up, immediately grabbing a fistful and pressing it to his face.

Jordan shook out his hand and I saw that his knuckles were scraped. He reached into his pocket, pulled out his wallet and removed a wad of hundred-dollar bills, throwing them on the ground in front of Gunnar. They rained down like an orange-green waterfall. "You take that. You go quietly and you don't ever, *ever* mess with her again. Got that?"

My mom's jaw dropped, and I'm pretty sure mine did too. "Who the hell do you think you are? She's *my* daughter. No one can tell me that I can't see my own daughter!"

Jordan's features chilled and he turned to me, taking my arm in his hold. "*She* can." I let him push me toward the bedroom where Sid was cowering on her bed with a pillow clutched to her like a teddy bear. She jumped when we came in, then her eyes widened when she saw Jordan.

He nodded to Sid before turning toward me. "Grab your stuff, April. I'll take you over to my place."

I grabbed some pants, a shirt, my makeup and toothbrush and stuffed them into an empty gym bag. "Sid, I'm so sorry," I said.

"Hi there...I'm Jordan. Do you feel safe if we leave now?"

She nodded at him. "My brother is on his way over here. I already called him to come get me." She turned to me. "Just *go*, Apes. Get the heck out of here. I'm so sorry this happened."

Jordan took my arm again and pointed me toward the door. "Let's go."

"Thank you," I whispered.

He slipped an arm around my shoulders and pulled me against him. "No need to thank me."

When we got out to the living room, Gunnar had his face buried in the paper towels. My mother was huddled on the couch next to him, stroking his hair and crying.

She looked up when I crossed the room and grabbed my purse. "Where are you going?" she asked faintly.

"That doesn't concern you. Please be gone before I get home."

"April," she began in a voice that was half apologetic, half reproachful.

I shook my head in warning. "Not now. I'm going."

Jordan ushered me out the door before she could say anything else.

Fifteen minutes later, we were at his house and he was ordering dinner from a local Italian place that delivered. I didn't feel much like eating, but I didn't want to cheat him out of his pizza. He'd earned it. Jordan did what I wished I could have done a year ago—smacked the crap out of that creep, Gunnar.

While waiting for the food to arrive, we changed out of our work clothes. I made two new ice baggies—one for my swollen lip and one for his hand, which was now bruised in addition to being scraped. He was sitting on the couch reading emails on his phone when I settled in next to him, handing him his bag of ice. He thanked me and pressed it to his knuckles.

All through dinner, Jordan remained quiet, thoughtful. It wasn't long before we reached that awkward moment where I didn't know if he wanted me to stay over or I should ask him to drive me home.

In the uncomfortable silence, he broke out a spare laptop and told me to log onto my character, Beast. Meanwhile, he logged onto a character on the same server, a svelte, sexy elf woman with dark hair named SnowWhite. I didn't say anything but looked at him under my lashes, feeling heat rise to my cheeks at the realization that he'd created that character, thinking about me. Or maybe, like me, he'd just wanted to watch her die over and over again? My mouth quirked. *Hmm.*

We spent an hour playing Dragon Epoch together. He gave me pointers and we defeated hordes of goblins, worked on quests, laughing until I yawned. With that, he reached over and closed my laptop and did the same to his. I figured I'd better give him the out. "Sid texted me earlier. The coast is clear at home."

There was a long pause. "Do you want to go home?"

It was hard to breathe. I turned to him, looked up into his face and shook my head.

He raised his hand to my chin and tilted my head up, then lowered his mouth to press against mine. It was a gentle, tender kiss, and it was obvious he was being careful with my split lip because his touch was feather light. But even that was enough to get my blood pumping, every nerve coming alive. I leaned my head back on the edge of the couch and looked into his eyes, which looked gray-green in this light. I raised my hand to his jaw, now peppered with a sexy five o'clock shadow. "Thank you...no one's ever stuck up for me like that."

My hand stroked along his jaw and his eyes closed, as if savoring the touch. "It wasn't anything more than you deserve, April. I just wish you realized it."

My eyes stung and I blinked, surprising myself with the sudden emotion that rose up, clogging my throat. "Maybe I just needed someone to show me."

He gently shook his head. "It has to come from inside. You've got to know deep in your heart that you are worth sticking up for. But I'm afraid that Snow White has been poisoned for a long time." My breath caught...and not just because he'd finally gotten his fairytales straight.

I knew what he was referring to. The entire time I was growing up, I was taught that my mother's love—if it could even be called "love" at all—came with conditions, and her feelings and needs were more important than mine or anyone else's.

That's why I'd never stood up for myself or expressed my feelings, never let her know how deeply she wounded me. Jordan had only seen a brief glimpse of what it had been like for me, but it had apparently been enough to discern that our dysfunctional relationship was at the root of my problems.

"How could you know me so well in the short amount of time that we've known each other?"

He shrugged and sighed, his warm breath smoothing over my face. "Let's just say I understand you because...I've been there myself."

"Your dad?"

He looked up at the ceiling for a long time before nodding. "Yeah. I was only worth something to him when I was following exactly in his footsteps."

But I had options that he didn't. His family being intact, he still had to try to make things work with his dad. But for me...I didn't have that burden. It was alarming, the similarities in our family situations, though the personalities involved were so very different.

"Don't you find it weird that we both have family members who think nothing of ambushing us? Your mom and grandpa...my mom. Even my dad with that lunch today."

He tilted his head. "Yeah, that is weird. But you ambushed me too..."

I sighed. "You mean with Cynthia...I'm sorry. I had no idea that would go so badly. It's just that it seemed like you both wanted to talk to each other. And you both told me separately that the other person would never want to hear what you had to say. So I just thought..." I shook my head. "It doesn't matter. I shouldn't have meddled."

He watched me with studious eyes, his brows knitting. Then he blinked and looked away as if suddenly uncomfortable, but in that split second I saw something that looked like...gratitude.

He cleared his throat. "At least your dad seems like a cool guy."

I sighed and rested my head against his arm, which stretched across the back of the couch. "My dad is a good guy. Only he barely knows who I am as a person."

"Well, I think that as long as you have one decent parent...maybe you should consider cutting the poison out of your life."

I looked up at him and he held my gaze, strong and steady. I shook my head. "I've never had the guts to do it. To hurt her like that."

"But it's okay if she tramples all over you?"

I bit the inside of my cheek but didn't answer, my eyes drifting away from his.

"April, you're worth more than that—more than how I saw them treat you tonight. They treated you like shit. You have the power to end that."

I swallowed. "I do."

We were silent for a long time and his arm came down to press me against him. It felt so good being in his arms. It made me feel safe...special. It made me feel like I was worth every bit as much as he told me I was. Like I was too good for them. For *her*.

I sat up straight and reached over to the coffee table for my phone.

"What are you doing?"

"Cutting the poison out of my life."

He didn't say anything as I texted my mother, telling her not to contact me again. That I wouldn't respond to her or Gunnar by phone or email, and if she showed up in person again, I would get a restraining order against them both on the basis of her harassment and Gunnar's assault.

Then I snapped a selfie close-up of my face with the prominently displayed bruised and swollen lip. I went into my settings and blocked her phone number and Gunnar's. I did the same with Facebook and email.

"There. It's done." I swallowed, feeling like a brave, grown-up girl. My heart was beating a million miles per second, but it was such a rush and I felt strong for the first time in a long time. Probably ever.

I turned to Jordan to find him watching me with an intensity that I was starting to get used to. I settled into his side again, resting my head on his shoulder. Slowly, slowly, my hand crept across his chest until I had his hard body in my arms. I tilted my head back.

"Better be careful or I might start thinking you care. And that was against your rules, right?"

He didn't stiffen like I expected him to or draw back. Nor did he challenge or contradict me, even with a sarcastic quip. Instead, he ran his hand through my hair then turned to smell it.

"I'm incapable of caring, April. I told you that already."

I didn't agree with that. Not for one second. Every single action today, from the minute I'd set foot on the campus and saw my dad until right now, said that he *did* care. Jordan could choose to delude himself, but he couldn't fool me.

"What happened when you talked to her?"

His hand on my hair stilled and I looked up. He was staring at the far wall, deep in thought.

"I told her I forgave her," he said quietly, not bothering to pretend he didn't know who I was talking about. "And I told her I was sorry."

"Did it make you feel better?"

His eyes closed. "Not really."

I turned toward him, pressing my face into his shoulder. That smell—sage and soap and a hint of salt and garlic from the pizza. But there was another scent underneath it. The smell of his skin that brought back the toe-curling, back-clawing pleasure we'd shared. Without even realizing it, my lips were on his neck. I couldn't help it. I probably shouldn't have. But how the hell could I resist?

I felt his Adam's apple bob under my lips as he swallowed hard. He stiffened in my arms but I pressed the issue, throwing a leg over his lap and straddling him while kissing my way up his neck and along his hard jaw.

"April..." His voice was a hoarse whisper.

My hands flew down the buttons on the front of his shirt. My mouth followed the trail down from his neck, across his collarbone, to his chest. His hands were on my shoulders, squeezing firmly, and my tongue flicked across his nipple. He hissed and pulled me up and away from him.

"We can't," he said. But I could feel his arousal swollen against me. I frowned.

"Please don't stop this, Jordan." I leaned forward, pressing my forehead to his. His eyes snapped shut.

"We stopped it. It has to stay stopped."

My hands caressed his rough cheeks. "For now...but I only have six weeks left. You won't be my boss after that."

My heart beat in my throat, and I died a few times while I waited for his reply. He took a breath and let out a sigh, and a weight inside my stomach dropped as I anticipated his rejection. Reaching down, he put his hands on my hips and scooted me back on his lap. "April..."

My eyes fluttered closed. Here it came...

"You know why your dad was on the campus today, right?"

I frowned and my eyes flicked to his. "He's investing in the company. He's done that before. And since Adam used to work for him and the company is going public..."

His jaw tightened. "It's more than that. Adam brought him in to help form our new board of directors. It means...it means that he'll probably end up being the chairman of the board after the IPO."

My throat tightened and I felt sick, pressure building behind my eyes. This meant that there would be no hope for us, not even in six weeks. If my dad was the chairman of the board at Draco, and the CFO of the company was dating his daughter...

Wait, it wasn't like that was against the law or anything. Unless Jordan was counting on the fact that we wouldn't last...

"It's not impossible." I said, testing my hypothesis, to see if I was right.

"It could cause a lot of problems between your dad and me."

"It *could*, if things don't end well, but why are you assuming that will happen?"

He pressed his lips together. "Because it always does."

I blinked. I knew that his past had messed with his head, but did that honestly mean he had no hope at all?

I absently played with the collar on his shirt and avoided looking into his eyes. "There's...there's a first time for everything. You aren't willing to take that chance?"

He clenched his jaw, eyes narrowing. "It's not really fair of you to ask me that."

It hurt to breathe. My eyes stung from the sudden emotion rising up. I would not let him see me cry. I would *not*.

I quietly slipped off his lap onto the couch beside him.

He ran a hand through his hair. "I'm sorry—"

When I thought my voice would be steady enough, I spoke. "So am I."

There was a pinch of loss deep down in my chest. I'd allowed my foolish heart to get involved when I'd known perfectly well that this wouldn't go anywhere.

"April...come here," he said, pulling me into his arms, pressing me against him. I didn't resist, letting him feel like he was comforting me when he really wasn't. The tears, they were coming. I didn't know how long I could fight them off.

Everything in me hurt. My throat was tight. My gut ached. My skin was hot and flushed, my pulse erratic.

I had either contracted the Ebola virus or I'd fallen in love with Jordan Fawkes.

24
JORDAN

THE NEXT FEW WEEKS BROUGHT LONG, ARDUOUS HOURS AT the office as we prepared for the IPO roadshow. I was here for twelve to fifteen hours a day, arriving at seven in the morning and leaving at nine or ten every night. I'd worked those kinds of hours before, but this was different. It seemed sort of hollow and meaningless, and the harder I worked, the more I realized that my heart wasn't completely in it like it had been.

April was here most of the time, too, which made things all the more difficult. She arrived at her usual start time—I'd noticed in Canada that she wasn't a morning person—but she always stayed late and was one of the last people out of the building each day.

Sometimes Daddy Dearest was here as well, and it was interesting to watch them together. I puzzled at the guarded way with which she dealt with him. I wondered if she counted him among the list of men in her life who had hurt her, who had let her down. I couldn't help but wonder if I was on that list as well.

Her demeanor toward me could best be described as coolly polite. No more joking around, no conveniently placed middle fingers indicating that she wasn't going to take my shit. Even when I tried to get a rise out of her, she gave me the same tight, courteous smile.

And I hated it.

One night, on a particularly late night the week before we were to hit the road, Mia arrived with a stack of take-out from a nearby Mexican place. She wanted us all to sit in the break room and have a decent meal—together. And that *all* included Adam, Mia, David, his daughter, me, and a couple of other officers and their assistants, along with Kat, Mia's friend who worked in playtesting.

The two of them were talking about going down to the warehouse and getting the prototype equipment out to play with it. Mia turned to April, who sat next to me, and said, "You want to come? We'll show you how it works. You could use it for your project."

April hesitated mid-chew, her eyes lighting up. "That would be—"

"I'm sure you've got work to do, right?" her dad interjected. As if he wanted me to confirm it, his dark blue eyes—which were eerily like hers—flicked to me. *Screw that.* As her boss, *I'd* be the judge of what work she needed to get done.

"She's been working hard. She could use a break. Go for it if you want to, Weiss," I said to her.

But April's eyes were on her dad, her features clouding. She blinked and then turned back to Mia. "Maybe if you're still there in an hour or so. I do have to finish up some stuff for Jordan."

Mia nodded, getting up from the table. "Join us whenever you want, April. We'll be there until I can pry this one away from his desk," she said with a wave of her hand in Adam's direction. "Hopefully before midnight."

"Another hour," he said, capturing her hand and kissing the back of it.

"I'll believe it when I see it." She stuck out her tongue at him.

"Care to make it interesting?" He raised his brows at her.

"I *always* make it interesting." With a cheeky grin, she turned to leave.

David watched her and Kat go with a smile. "You've got a winner," he said to Adam with a nod in Mia's direction. "I like her."

Adam smiled but didn't say anything as he forked the last of his Spanish rice into his mouth.

"So when's the happy day?"

"We haven't set a date yet. She just started medical school."

I glanced at April, who was watching her father and Adam with a strange intensity. I wondered what was going through her head at that moment. What was the dynamic of their parent-child relationship? They didn't seem particularly close, but she seemed to desperately want his approval. She'd been about to get up and go play with the girls before her father's comment had stopped her. I wondered what kind of baggage was involved.

Another woman with Daddy issues, like with Cyndi. I seemed to attract those.

Of course, I had my own damn Daddy issues. I guess we all did.

"Smart woman, knows what she wants. Successful. Beautiful, too. You've got the complete package. You need to make that official soon before she figures out she's getting the raw end of the deal," David joked.

Adam threw his head back and laughed. "You were always good at taking me down a few pegs when I was getting too full of myself."

"I was the best boss you ever had, admit it."

Adam stood and wiped his mouth with a napkin before tossing it on the table. "You were the only boss I've ever had."

David and Adam wandered back to his office, still laughing, while April watched them, absently gathering the paper plates and debris from the table and tossing them. I helped her collect the leftovers and put them in the fridge.

"You okay?"

She shrugged. "Yeah."

She looked particularly fetching today in a short black skirt— barely long enough to be called professional attire—that came a few inches above her knees, a white, button-down blouse that hugged her luscious breasts, and shiny black patent Mary Janes with enough of a heel to emphasize the swell of her gorgeous calves.

I tried not to look too closely these days. It was pure torture to stare at what I couldn't have. I supposed I could have called one of my paramours for a night of fun, but to what end?

By default, I guess I was again observing Friar Jordan's New Law even if I'd shattered that fucker all to pieces—and in various different positions and locations in between April's extremely soft and supple thighs.

The hot memory of it had me sporting a semi as we made our way back to my office. It didn't help that she walked ahead of me, giving me no choice but to study the sway of that pleated skirt against the back of her legs. It was so fucking unfair that I couldn't have her again.

"You seem...upset," I said, mostly to distract myself from my wayward thoughts.

She glanced in the direction of Adam's office, where the door was open and Adam and her father were bent over a computer screen having some sort of intense discussion about the business plan.

"No. You're just mistaking my sexual frustration for something else," she quipped as she sauntered into my office. I almost swallowed my own tongue.

I hesitated before following her inside, leaving the door wide open. Just to be on the safe side. Immediately, I got back to my pre-dinner task, which was a frame-by-frame screening of the latest version of the roadshow video while adding my last comments for any edits needed.

April was in the middle of revising my slides for the banker presentation, but she seemed distracted, squirming in her seat and constantly catching my notice by doing so. I could hardly concentrate on what I was doing, too concerned about my damn hard-on and the way her breasts looked in that blouse.

"I'm warm in here, are you?" she finally said in a low voice.

"Huh?" I glanced up in time to see her unfasten two buttons on her blouse. I could now see the top of her lacy bra. *Holy fuck.*

"Maybe if I close the door in here so the warm air doesn't come in from the atrium. I could turn down the thermostat, too." She got up, shut the door and then pressed the lock. *Holy hell.*

Then she strutted—and there was no other way to describe the gait that made that pleated skirt dance against her sexy legs—to the thermostat and fiddled with it for a moment. I swallowed and focused on my computer screen, trying desperately to think about statistical finance or the market cap formula...hell, even baseball stats.

She sashayed back to her seat—thank God—but instead of sitting, she placed a foot on the seat of her chair, giving me a torrid view of the whole length of her leg. *Holy Christ.*

Then she reached under her skirt and tugged on the top of her thigh-high stockings. Edged with white lace, they looked like delicate, delicious cake frosting hugging her lush thighs. She had a dark beauty mark on the inside of her left thigh. I'd tasted it several times while we were in Vancouver. I wanted to taste it again. Without looking at me, she switched legs and did the same with the other one.

And now I was officially in pain from the swelling below the belt, my erect cock straining against my pants. I put my face in my hand, unable to look anymore.

"What's wrong?" she said in a faux-innocent voice. "Do you have a headache?"

Nope, definitely not the location of the aching. Unless she was talking about the head below the belt. I didn't say anything, scrubbing my palm across my eyes, the vision of her curvy legs forever burned in my mind. Why the hell was she torturing me like this? Or maybe this was her enacting a well-thought-out plan of revenge she'd had since the very beginning.

Nice timing. Her father was in the next room, separated by one office wall, for Christ's sake. If she wanted to spell my doom, she couldn't have picked a better opportunity.

When I looked up again, I almost jumped, seeing that she was now sitting on the edge of my desk right beside me, looking down with a knowing smile.

"I know an *excellent* cure for a headache and…that other problem you seem to be having," she said with a meaningful look at my crotch.

I blew out a breath in exasperation. "Are you enjoying this?"

She smiled as she swung a leg back and forth. "I plan to. And I think you will too."

I took a deep breath and let it out. Hard-on, be damned. "No. I am not doing this."

She raised a brow and stuck her bottom lip out. "No? You don't sound very committed to that."

"Jesus, April, your dad—"

"We're not talking about him. He's very busy over there and so is everyone else. And that door is locked." She bent over and ran a hand from my knee up the inside of my thigh, giving me a tentative, questioning glance.

When she reached my cock—now past the point of mere pain—I captured her delicate wrist and yanked her toward me. With a gasp, she stumbled off the desk and fell against my chest. She looked up, her mouth ready to be kissed.

"Miss Weiss, you are being inappropriate."

"You love it when I'm inappropriate."

"Fuck yeah, I do."

Then she kissed me. "Mmm. I thought I'd miss the scruff. But I missed your hot mouth more."

"You don't fight fair."

"Nobody said life was fair." She kissed me again, her sleek tongue darting into my mouth. One hand slid down my stomach to cup my cock through my pants. I hissed against her mouth, threaded my fingers through her glossy hair and yanked her off my lap so that she was on her knees in front of me. *Fuck yeah, indeed.*

April held my gaze for a long time, the shock evaporating like foam seawater off the hard-packed beach sand. Understanding dawned in her ocean-blue eyes and she swallowed, licking those puffy pink lips. I reached out and traced the bottom one with my thumb.

"I want these gorgeous lips wrapped around my cock," I ground out between my teeth.

Her eyes darkened with lust and she nodded, reaching for the fly on my khakis. After she undid my belt and unbuttoned my pants, I leaned back, watching as she dug into my boxers and pulled out my stiff, painful erection. She swallowed again, then ran her thumb up the bottom of my shaft and over the head. Fire crackled through my veins and my heartbeat drummed in my throat.

I was throbbing with need. She looked at me, as if reassuring herself that I was enjoying it. As if she had to be reassured of *that*. The thought almost made me laugh. "You're so beautiful," she muttered. "Every part of you."

Her words had a new, more powerful effect on me, stroking me in places her fingers couldn't reach. I had to have her—*now*. I leaned forward and reached around the back of her head, pulling her closer, pressing my cock to her lips. Her gorgeous mouth opened to take me in, and my chest felt like it was about to explode as her heat enveloped me.

I reached down, groping her breast through her shirt, and she let out a soft, muffled moan. My fingers slipped under her blouse, inside that lacy bra, where I rubbed and rolled her nipple until it came to a beaded, hard point under my attention. My cock surged in her mouth.

With a shudder, my eyes closed and I concentrated on her subtle movements as she slipped lower, taking more of me in. I hadn't had sex in weeks, and working in such close proximity to her made me feel achingly deprived and tense. Now I was so over-the-top turned on, I feared this was going to be over before it even got started.

This moment transported me back to the time I'd first laid eyes on her, late last year during the intern orientation when they'd been brought around on a tour. The group had spent a few minutes in my office, and I distinctly remember her asking a question because my eyes landed on her beautiful face. Right there and then, those luscious lips had given me visions of her on her knees in front of me, pleasuring me just as she was now. She'd flashed that even, white smile that must have cost thousands at the orthodontist. I'd felt something then, a twinge of want, of lust. The interns were off-limits, sure. But it didn't stop me from fantasizing about burying myself inside her every time I saw her.

Now here she was, sucking me off, her eyes never leaving mine as her mouth slid down, taking more of me in before slipping back up again, the suction increasing until I was about to start whimpering with the intensity of it.

Jesus fucking Christ. Where had she learned to do that? I didn't know whether to be grateful to whoever it had been or to hunt him down and kill him for having been there before me. Pure, ice-cold pleasure spread out from my crotch, up my stomach and down my thighs. I was panting, my own breathing out of my control. I was going to come if she continued at this pace.

My hand darted out, holding her head still. "Slow down..." I muttered, and obediently she kept her head in place. But her tongue—that sinful tongue—was sliding all down the underside of my cock and back up again, lavishing it with her hot, wet attention.

All the air rushed out of my chest. With her head still pinned in place, I pressed my hips forward, thrusting into her mouth. She sucked in a breath of surprise through her nose until her breathing was cut off—by me. I froze, watching her, carefully noting if it was too much for her. But those eyes held fast to mine before her lids drooped and her hand thrust into my pants, stroking my balls. Slowly, I pulled back and pushed in again. I was seconds away from coming. I removed my hand to give her a chance to pull away if she wanted.

I really hope she didn't want to.

"I'm going to come," I groaned. A second later, her mouth slid down over me again, taking me in deeper than before. My head fell back and I stared at the ceiling, my eyes shut tight, that familiar pinch gathering at the base of my spine.

"April—fuck!"

Her mouth locked over me, sucking harder than before, and I came in hot, gasping waves. I couldn't breathe, I couldn't think. And all I could feel was the molten pleasure of her mouth on me, sucking. Still sucking.

She held me there until the spasms faded and then slowly pulled away. I opened my heavy eyes, feeling completely wrung out. *Holy shit.*

"That...was fucking incredible."

Without a word, she got up and walked into the bathroom. I heard the drawer open and the faucet turn on. But I still couldn't move, so I sat there with my dick hanging out in the air like an idiot. My body felt relaxed, like I was boneless.

She came back into the office and handed me a washcloth to clean up. I thanked her and then finally got up to take my turn in the bathroom. When I returned, she was in her seat, buttoned up and arranged primly in front of her laptop, back to work as if nothing had happened.

I walked over to the door and unlocked it, but left it closed. When I turned around, she was watching me, a smile hovering on her lips.

"What was that about?" I asked.

Her mouth quirked. "I told you...sexual frustration."

"And did that help?"

A knowing smile. "It helped *you*, didn't it?"

I sighed and scrubbed a hand across my face, then made my way back to the desk and sank into my seat, ready to continue the conversation. Before I could figure out what to say, there was a knock at the door and it opened. Daddy Dearest poked his head in.

Holy Christ. If he'd tried that door five minutes before, it would have been locked and the whole situation would have been extremely suspicious. Had he been able to open the door, he would have found his daughter kneeling in front of me with my cock in her mouth. I went pale and April looked startled.

"April, I'm out for the night. I just wanted to say goodbye. I'll see you down at our house for the weekend? Sarah and Daniel are really excited."

She took a deep breath and let it go, holding her dad's gaze for a long moment before nodding. "Yeah. Uh, sure."

Minutes after he was gone, there was silence between us. I tried to focus on my task at hand while she seemed to be engrossed in her own work. All of a sudden, she burst out laughing.

And I couldn't help it—I started to laugh, too.

When Adam came through the door to say he was locking up and sending everyone home, we were still cracking up and he stared at us like we were insane.

"Don't mind us. We're just giddy with exhaustion," she said.

Adam frowned. "Ohhkay. All the more reason to go home and go to bed."

I mock saluted him and he returned with a salute of his own, of the middle finger variety.

"Your cousin's going to be happy you're getting home at a decent hour." April gave me a strange look. She didn't know about the Adam-Mia cousin connection. I didn't bother to explain.

"Die in a fire," he replied.

After closing up shop, I walked out with the group while humming the tune to "Dueling Banjos." At least Mia thought it was amusing. The boss, not so much.

***

We had four days until the IPO roadshow began. It would be two weeks of whirlwind visits to major cities across the country, presenting our case to the big bankers and investment companies for their backing. In a mere fifteen days, we were going to take Draco Multimedia Entertainment (under the New York Stock Exchange symbol, DME) to the market, and we needed them in our corner when it came time to ring the bell.

That didn't mean I kept my hands off of April, though. The BJ in my office re-opened a sexual Pandora's box that could not be closed, even if we'd wanted to.

The next day, just before lunch, April brought me some reports to glance through. She stood a little too close and smelled a little too good. I looked at the mess on my desk and sighed at the thought of all the work I had to do. She waited for me to say something, and I muttered about how annoyed I was that Charles was over at her desk every five minutes.

"Hmm. You're not...*jealous*, are you?"

I lifted my brow. "*No.* I just don't like how he's distracting you from your work."

"I'm getting my work done. But if you want, I'll tell him that you told me to tell him to stay away."

"I didn't tell you to tell him that."

She leaned against my desk, arms folded. "You seem a little frustrated, Mr. Fawkes. Can I help you with that?"

I clenched my jaw and scowled at her. She reached into her pocket, pulled something out and bent forward, stuffing it into my shirt pocket. "My lunch hour starts at one, and I might be hanging out in that ladies' room off the warehouse that no one ever uses..."

With that, she straightened, pivoted and walked out, my eyes fastened to her ass like glue. When she sat at her desk, she tapped her chest to indicate I should look in my pocket. I did...and wished I hadn't.

That foil wrapper represented everything I shouldn't do but probably would.

I spent my lunch hour considering the possibility of an ice-cold shower in my private bathroom. At one, my phone chimed with a new text. I knew who it was from. I glanced up at her desk anyway and saw that she was, in fact, gone.

Come find me.

That was all it took. I was hard as a rock—again. Goddamn it. I had work to do. A lot of work to do. But I wanted her so badly it hurt.

I found her waiting by the door to the restroom in question. Without a word, we went inside and I spent the next half hour spreading her against the wall and having my way with her.

The ensuing days until I left town were like that. We'd find some place private and knock boots, sometimes twice a day, sometimes in my office when we were able. There was rarely any discussion involved, but the thrill of possibly getting caught was enough to get both our motors revved, much like our little outdoor adventure at the provincial park in Canada.

The night before I departed to start the roadshow, I actually left work early. I'd be flying to the East Coast and working my way back west, sometimes meeting Adam in the cities where more of the bankers were located. I'd be attending all the presentations; he'd be there for the biggest and most important ones.

April brought me dinner and she was my dessert. We still didn't talk about what all the screwing meant—or what it *would* mean once the company went public and David was voted in as chairman of the board.

But regardless whether we discussed what would or wouldn't happen, I was beginning to realize that it was going to be a long two weeks without her.

And it was. But not in the way I'd expected.

It quickly became obvious that she was following my itinerary, starting each day with a text message. Those messages soon became the highlight of my day.

Her: How's Boston treating you?

Me: Not as good as you do.

Her: I'm sure you have some old sexts from former, ahem, "friends" to get you by.

Me: How 'bout some new ones from you?

Her: Hi, how is Chicago?

Me: It sucks. I like my own bed.

Her: I like your bed, too. Preferably with you in it.

Me: Weiss, YABI (Our adopted acronym for "You are being inappropriate.")

Her: Dallas! Woo hoo. Ready for some line dancing?
Me: I was born ready—and horny.
Her: You were born inappropriate.

Her: San Francisco...you're getting warmer.
Me: I'm already hot.
Her: Fawkes, YABI
Me: Of course. And you love it.

Throughout the course of the roadshow, I was hit on a few times by some of the hot underwriters, but to my surprise, I wasn't interested. They didn't tempt me at all. I found myself thinking a lot about April instead, wondering what she was doing. Nonetheless, I fought the urge daily to hit the call button on my phone.

Finally, we emerged triumphant. Friday afternoon, just after close of business in New York, Adam and I touched down at John Wayne airport from Seattle. I got the call from our investment banker that the company had been valued at 8.3 billion USD. Our stock was going to open for a cool thirty-five dollars a share the following Monday morning, and we'd be on the floor of the stock exchange to ring the opening bell. It was going to be a feeding frenzy. And it was also going to be the realization of a long-awaited dream.

Adam and I stood by the baggage carousel high-fiving each other after I gave him the news. He immediately pulled out his phone and called Mia to share it with her. And I realized that the first person I wanted to tell was April...

I pulled out my phone and started keying in a text.

Market cap 8.3 bil. $35/share. Keep it quiet for now.

She replied less than a minute later.

Her: OMG! So happy for you. Deleting your text msg now.
Me: Our driver's on the way, right?
Her: He should already be there.

"Who are you texting?" Adam asked once he hung up with Mia.

"Just making sure our ride is here. I get irritated when I have to wait," I half-lied.

"We've got the company party tomorrow afternoon. We'll keep it quiet until then and announce when we're all together."

"Sure. You going to tell David Weiss ahead of time?"

"Of course. He gets the next phone call."

"How did Mia take the news that her cousin-slash-fiancé is a billionaire now?"

"She wasn't very surprised. Happy for me, and all that."

"Of course she's happy for you. She gets half of it in the divorce." I grinned but didn't bother saying "*JK*"—he already knew I was joking.

He shook his head with a smile as he walked from the baggage area out to the curb. "I don't even know why I tell you anything."

"I know all about the legal particulars. For instance, it's legal to marry your first cousin in California."

"Good to know." Adam approached our usual driver, who was already waiting with the trunk open. He tossed his bag in the back, and I came around and did the same. "Ah c'mon, you're no fun when you aren't telling me to fuck off."

All he did was shoot me a knowing grin. *Killjoy.*

On the way home, I pulled out my phone to check it and found myself sending April another text.

Stay over with me tonight.

She didn't reply for a long time. In fact, the next text I received from her was sent over two hours later.

Sorry, was in the middle of driving to La Jolla. Visiting my Dad's tonight for little sis's b-day. We'll be coming to the party together. I'll see you then.

I couldn't believe the disappointment I felt by that. I wanted to see her. Sure, I wanted to rub myself all over her luscious body, but I also wanted to talk with her, maybe tease her a bit, smell her hair. I'd just assumed she'd be at my beck and call. And after two weeks of no sex, I wanted her at my beck and call, damn it.

***

To burn off some of the sexual frustration, I went out on dawn patrol to catch the waves early the next morning. Conditions were clean, and I caught some awesome A-frame, reef-breaking waves with hardly a soul out there. As it was October, the water was getting cold, so I wore my wetsuit. But after an hour or so, I got bored and headed back in. Then I checked my phone a few times, to see if maybe she'd sent a text. Nothing.

And really, what the hell was happening to me that it mattered so much?

That afternoon, there was a company pool party to celebrate the next step in our quest for gaming market domination. We'd rented out part of an obscenely expensive country club in South County for poolside cocktails and appetizers.

The officers and tentative board members met early for a private luncheon. David Weiss sat between Adam and me at the big round table, and I couldn't help scanning the surrounding area for his daughter. I knew she'd come up with him, but I wasn't *supposed* to know that and I didn't want to be so obvious as to ask.

He was very interested to hear about the details of the road show and we filled him in accordingly. Finally, to my relief, Adam asked him about his daughter.

"Oh, she's here. She's running around with some of your assistants, helping with the details of the company party."

It now became my mission to spot her without looking like I was trying to spot her. It was stupid, really. I could just text her. But she hadn't texted me.

And what was all this stupid shit, anyway? I'd been out of high school almost a decade. Next, I'd be wondering if she'd kiss me under the bleachers at the homecoming dance. Fuck it. I was doing a pretty miserable job of staying uninvolved while being involved in whatever the hell this was. Co-workers with benefits? Very, *very* nice benefits.

After lunch, we went into dressing rooms and changed for the party. Though it was fall, it was still warm enough for a pool party. *Only in Southern California*, I thought, shaking my head.

Fifteen minutes into the party, I caught sight of her on the other side of the pool, speaking with a group of other interns. One of them was that little brat, Cari, who had tried to blackmail her weeks ago. They appeared to be on amicable terms now.

April was wearing a modest, black, one-piece swimsuit trimmed in bright blue. It had a high back, probably to hide the damning tattoo, which everyone here would recognize in an instant.

When she finally looked my way, I caught her eye. She sent me a tentative smile. Something lit up inside me and I smiled.

I shot a meaningful glance at the building, indicating I wanted to meet her there. She frowned and looked away. *What the hell was up?* Now I was pretty sure that she was purposely avoiding me, and that didn't sit well. I thought about sending her a text message, but she'd likely ignore that too.

I skirted the pool and went directly to her and her little flock. She looked up, eyes widening. "Weiss, can I speak with you for a minute, please? I have a couple questions."

"Sure," she mumbled, looking back down. I stepped away while she excused herself, and then she followed me up the steps and toward the building, walking slower the closer we got. I held open the door for her, but she hesitated.

"What did you need to talk to me about?"

I glanced at the door. "Inside."

She took a breath and then let it go. Once inside, I found an empty cabana dressing room and pulled her in with me. Just as she was about to talk, I turned, holding her face in between my hands, and kissed her the way I'd wanted to every night I'd been gone. She responded as if I was breathing new life into her, her body rising up against me, her fingers clutching at the t-shirt I wore with my swim trunks. Her mouth opened for more, as if she'd been starving, and, to be honest, her reaction just made me even hungrier for her.

Minutes later when I pulled back, she was flushed and breathless. The only sound in the silence between us was that of our heavy breathing. As I was bending in for more, she pulled away. "Did you actually have a question or were you pulling me in here to kiss me?"

"Is there a problem with that?"

She took a deep breath and let it go, her eyes hardening. Apparently, there *was* a problem with that.

"I'll only be working for you for two more weeks. I want something real between us—not this sneaking around."

I grinned. "I thought you liked sneaking around." I punctuated that statement with another heated kiss, my tongue sweeping into her hot, delicious mouth. Then I reached around and grabbed her ass, pulling her flush against me.

She put her hands on my chest. "Jordan," she said against my lips.

"Mmm...I missed you."

She tilted her head away, looking up at me, perplexed. "You did?"

I frowned. "Why does that surprise you?"

She shook her head. "Because you're confusing me. I don't know what this is. Is this just about sex or is it more?"

I clenched my jaw and looked away. "It can't be more than this. You know why. I've already told you."

"You aren't willing to take a chance on me—on *us*."

"So I'm supposed to tell your Dad that we aren't really dating, we're just hooking up? Because I don't do relationships—not *real, serious* relationships. So I'll tell him I'm just fucking his daughter. How well will that go over?"

She swallowed. "Jordan..."

"What? Can it be more than that? No, no it can't."

Her lip trembled. "Well, it's more for me, because...because I'm in love with you."

At first I wasn't quite sure I'd heard her right. Then, as understanding dawned, my first reaction was to deny, deny, deny. This wasn't what she thought it was. It couldn't be that. I couldn't breathe. My chest felt tight and there wasn't enough air in this little dressing room. She watched my reaction closely.

The last time a woman had said those words to me, I'd asked her to marry me and then she'd fucked some other guy. I couldn't go there again. I wouldn't go there again. Not now, maybe not ever.

I closed my eyes, scrubbing a hand over my face.

25
APRIL

I WATCHED JORDAN BLANCH AS HE REACTED TO MY DECLARATION of love. He actually looked like he might pass out. Not the response I'd always imagined when telling a guy I loved him. And I didn't say the words lightly. In fact, I'd never said those words to any other man—not even Gunnar. But I'd never felt like this for any other man. I could admit all that to him now, but I knew he didn't want to hear it. His features were shuttering, like a house boarding up in preparation for a hurricane.

"I'm not expecting anything more from you than to just give this a chance," I said into the silence, hating how my voice trembled.

He looked away. "What does that mean exactly?"

Well, this was hopeful. At least he wanted to hear me out. "That...that we date like normal people when I leave Draco."

"I don't know how to date like normal people. Last time I did that, I got my nuts squashed. Not willing to go there again."

"Not now or..."

He shrugged. "Maybe not ever."

I blinked. "So this was all about sneaking around, the thrill of it? After I walk out of here, we're done for good?"

He didn't look happy with that possibility either. I felt nauseous, my stomach tight and knotted. I'd just put all that out there. I'd pulled my heart out of my chest and put it in his hands. Whether he twisted and crushed it or cradled and treasured it was entirely out of my control.

"Jordan..." I scooted up to him, put my palms on his cheeks, splayed out my fingers and gently guided his head so that he would look at me. My eyes met his, and I peered into those murky depths—today, the color of silt and seawater. "Let me tell you something. There's a big difference between the person you see when you look in the mirror and the one I see when I look at you. The one you see was betrayed by a childhood lover, rejected by a father who was angry at you because you didn't live up to *his* dream. But the man I see? He's strong and sensitive. Protective, brilliant, caring. You put yourself out there for me—with the video, when Gunnar was pulling his shit, when Cari was threatening me. You didn't have to do those things, but you did. And I'll be forever grateful. But it's not why I love you. I love you because of who you are when I look at you. Not what I want you to be."

Something in his eyes changed. They were hard. And I still couldn't read him or his face, but his hands slid around my waist to pull me against him into a tight hug.

He didn't say anything, just held me there. I could feel his wild heartbeat beneath mine as our bodies pressed together. I could get lost in this feeling, the security of his arms around me, despite this uncertainty of what his feelings were. I didn't need a label from him right now if he was too afraid to admit the truth. But he couldn't deny it. He *did* care, as he'd shown over and over again with his actions.

He buried his face in my hair, muttering, "What are you doing to me?"

I kissed him where I could reach him at the bottom of his neck, just above the neckline of his t-shirt. His arms tightened and his arousal surged against my stomach. Immediately, his mouth landed on my neck, devouring my ear, my jaw, my lips.

He pushed us back toward the wall in the tiny dressing room and I went with him willingly, our mouths fastened together. My hands slipped under his shirt, across his hard, packed abs. His hand slid to the inside of my thighs, stroking them firmly, and then he slipped his fingers under the crotch of my swimsuit. I whimpered...and that really seemed to get him going.

With a swift yank, one side of my suit was off my shoulder, exposing my breast. He sealed his mouth over my nipple while sliding his fingers under the other side of the suit to roll that nipple between his thumb and forefinger. My lust surged and I arched my back, crying out. He quieted me, putting his mouth back on mine as he tugged on the front of his own swimsuit.

Then, he pulled a condom out of the pocket of his swimsuit, deftly opened the package and slipped it on. There was no dirty talk this time; my confession must have left him speechless. He tugged aside the crotch of my swimsuit again and pressed himself against me.

Our mouths found each other again as he lifted me against the wall, leveraging himself before sliding into me easily. I clung to his strong neck and shoulders as he moved against me, almost frenzied, driving himself relentlessly to orgasm. It would be quick, I could tell. He watched me with lust-glazed eyes. His fingers glided between us and he rubbed my clit. I came—hard—groaning into his mouth. Seconds later, he was coming too. He pushed his hips against me just a few more times as we came down from that high. It had been fast, intense and, like always, hot.

He held me there for a long time, pressed between his hard body and the slightly harder paneled wall behind me. I wanted him to stay inside me forever. I tightened my legs around his slim hips, but he slowly relaxed and pulled away.

We took a moment to clean up and right our clothing. Jordan tossed out the condom, congratulating himself for having the forethought to stuff one in his pocket, "just in case."

He took a deep breath and then released it. "I've always been good at thinking ahead."

I smiled, relaxed against the wall and watched him, my head tilting. Content, but also deeply sad. "For our last time ever, that was pretty amazing."

He blinked. "Uh. What?"

I frowned. "I think it's obvious why this can't continue."

"It's not obvious to me."

"It should be. The most important reason is because of what I just told you. I need to protect my heart. The sneaking around and having sex—it's fun, but I can't do it anymore."

He scowled again and sighed, shaking his head. "You aren't making this very easy for me."

"You aren't making it easy for me, either."

He closed his eyes and then opened them. "Give me some time to think...to figure things out."

Why did I have the feeling he was selling me a line? This feeling sank to the base of my throat, cold and hard. At the back of my head, alarm bells rang,

"Do you want to?" I asked anyway.

He nodded, and with a smile, bent to kiss me again. "I do."

Despite those darker premonitions, a rush of happiness threatened to drown me so that I could hardly catch my next breath. I put my hands on his cheeks. "So do I."

He pulled away, taking my hand and giving it a squeeze. "We'd better get back, in case someone's looking for me. With my luck, it will be Adam with some new bug up his ass about something."

I kissed him. "Then you go first, and I'll wait a few minutes before I leave."

He pushed my hair away from my face and kissed me again. Then he turned and was gone.

I waited a few minutes, using that time to will my heart to quiet, but it wouldn't listen to me. I was on an adrenaline rush, and not just because of the amazing dressing-room sex. He wanted to try! He wanted to see if we could make something work.

I swallowed hard, trying not to feel the hopeful surge that that vision of the future placed in my brain—even though it was only a few weeks into the future. I wondered what going out on a normal date with Jordan would be like...would it be similar to those few idyllic days in Vancouver?

Five minutes later, I emerged from the dressing room and caught sight of the pool below through the huge line of floor-to-ceiling windows. The officers and my dad were gathered together in a group, and people were high-fiving and slapping each other on the back. I suspected they'd just announced the company's market capitalization and opening share price to everyone. As I watched, Jordan and a couple of other big guys, including Adam's handsome cousin, William, grabbed hold of Adam and carried him—under protest—to the edge of the pool. I laughed until a movement at the edge of my vision caught my attention.

Cari sidled up to me and watched, too, as Adam's friends dumped him into the pool.

"There's a whole pile of new millionaires down there," I said to Cari with a nod, hoping our semi-silent truce would continue. I'd avoided her for weeks and hadn't spoken to her alone since our confrontation in the hallway when she'd threatened to expose me. She had remained coolly polite since.

She laughed. "Too bad I'm still hung up on the biggest fish in that pond. He's going to come out of that pool with a wet t-shirt. I should be down there to watch that. Too bad Mia didn't get dumped in there. She's wearing that ridiculous sundress, probably because she's too ashamed to be seen in a bathing suit."

I resisted the urge to shake my head. At this point, I just felt sorry for Cari. I turned to lead the way back to the pool when she grabbed my arm and stopped me. Her eyes were burning with something feverish. "I know what you were doing in that dressing room."

I glanced back in the direction where I'd come from with more than a little guilt. But I wouldn't let her see it. "Jordan needed some information about—"

"Don't lie to me, April. You're fucking him. I wondered how you got him to keep silent about your starring role in the sex video. Now I know, you slut. Screwing your way to the top, huh? I wonder if your daddy knows that."

I yanked my arm out of her hold. "You've lost your mind," I muttered in a strangled voice and then turned to go.

I had to listen to her poison on the way back to the pool, hoping the safety of the crowd would shut her up. "You wouldn't help me get Mia out of the picture because you had a bigger fish to fry. Well, I have news for you. Jordan is using you. He uses women, and everybody knows it."

I stopped and spun, getting in her face. "Leave me the hell alone with your nutball theories. There's nothing you could have done to break up Adam and Mia, okay? They are in love, and they're engaged. I don't care what kind of sick obsession you have with him. It's over and you lost."

"You have a lot more to lose than I do, April."

I moved away from her, my heart hammering against my ribs. She continued. "If you help me, I'll shut up and I won't say a word. We were going to untie the top of her sundress and show everyone how repulsive she is. You're friendly with her. You can get close enough to do it easily and even make it look like an accident."

I gasped and turned to her. We were at the top of the stairs, and no one could hear us over the din of the cheering and taunts leveled at the now sopping wet CEO. He waded out of the pool as Mia, laughing, handed him towels.

"I'm not doing any such thing and neither are you."

Cari's face was murderous as she clamped onto my hand and practically dragged me down the stairs. I lost my balance as I fought her hold, tripped and fell to my knees, stumbling after her. I slipped free from her grip just as we reached the bottom. The group of officers were mere feet away, and I could see what was coming so I turned to climb right back up the stairs. She reached out and grabbed the back of my swimsuit, and I felt it ripping down the back seam. I was halfway up the stairs before I realized I was exposed, and she was already shouting, "Adam, everyone, look! I found out who was in the sex video! Check out the tramp stamp on that tramp's back."

There was silence behind me and everyone gasped or mumbled. I hadn't made it all the way up to freedom yet, but my ass was hanging out in the air for all to see. I spun to hide myself, mortified as I was to face them.

Everyone had frozen. Everyone was staring at me. This horrifying moment almost froze my heart.

I was like Hester Prynne, stuck on the scaffold, standing to face the jeering crowd with her innocent baby in her arms and that gleaming letter A for "adulteress." The blood was rushing out of my head and I saw spots at the edge of my vision as if I was going to faint from the humiliation.

Apparently, I wasn't that lucky.

Slowly, I took a step backward up the stairs, my hands on the railing. My eyes flew to find Jordan in the crowd. Adam was still dripping wet, staring at me with narrowed eyes. Some of the younger employees were laughing, including Charles. I couldn't find Jordan, but my eyes landed on my dad. A sob escaped my lips when I saw the look on his face—utter humiliation.

Oh God. Oh God! Could this have been any worse? I was shamed in front of the company where I'd worked for nearly a year, and on top of that, my dad was here among them—among people *he* would be working with for years to come. My vision blurred and I stumbled on one of the steps, this time landing hard on my knee. I pushed to my feet again.

Someone wrapped a towel around my back. The person was taller than me. All my hopes gathered in one single thought—*Jordan*? I turned. No, not that tall. It was a woman. Short, dark hair. Mia.

She slid her arm around my shoulders and turned, guiding me up the stairs. Before we reached the top, I'd already completely broken down. However, even though I was blinded with tears, I still managed to see a scuffle at the base of the stairs.

"Slut-shaming bitch!" Katya yelled and was on Cari with a mean right hook. The huddle of men broke to pull the women off each other. A tall man bent to yank Katya away from Cari, rescuing her from Kat's attack. I blinked a few times to see who it was—Jordan. He yelled at her to calm down.

And that was it, the final humiliation. Jordan didn't come to *my* rescue. Didn't stand up for me. Instead, he was saving Cari from Katya.

I couldn't look away from him, but he never once looked toward me. Everyone was now watching the scuffle between the two women. Kat was still trying to break free from his hold, hurling insults at Cari, who was cowering behind some of the other guys in hopes of keeping her face intact.

He uses women. Everybody knows that.

Mia jostled my shoulders. "Come on, let's go get you covered up."

We went into the clubhouse and, ironically enough, Mia led us to the exact changing room where Jordan and I had just had sex a half an hour before. I'd walked out of there filled with hope and happiness, and now I was walking back in, disgraced and humiliated.

I slumped onto the bench, still bawling. "I'm s-sorry."

She grabbed some tissue from the small vanity, handed it to me, and then looked around the room. "Where are your clothes? Did you put them in a locker?"

I handed her the key that I had pinned inside the bodice of my swimsuit. In the locker were my purse and the clothes I'd worn over my bathing suit when I'd arrived. Mia grabbed the key and told me she'd be right back with my stuff. Before she could step away, however, both my Dad and Adam could be heard outside the door. I whimpered.

Mia stepped out, closing the door a crack. "She's not decent. I'm going to go get her things."

I heard her footsteps as she walked away, and then I was privy to the heated words on the other side of the door. Dad was pissed. More pissed than I'd ever heard him. Adam sounded like he was trying to talk him off a ledge.

"I can't begin to tell you how mortifying this is," Dad said. "She should be fired immediately. I don't want special exceptions because she's my daughter."

"I'm going to wait until she can talk to us and explain what happened."

"April is going home with me. Now. But I expect you to terminate her. There's no excuse for her behavior."

"David, I appreciate where you're coming from, but she is a grown woman and my employee, so I'm going to speak to her. This—"

"Excuse me," Mia muttered, asking them to move out of the way so she could slide back into the dressing room. When she came in, her face was full of sympathy. She handed me my bag of belongings. Then, she bent down and whispered, "I'll try to distract Adam so you can slip out. Not sure about your dad, though."

I shook my head, slipping my shorts and tank top over my now ruined suit. "I came with him. He's my ride."

Mia bit her lip and looked off to the side, as if thinking.

"I can't avoid him. But thank you for everything."

She gave me a weak smile, and I grabbed my bag and then opened the door. The two men stopped talking. I stepped forward, relieved to see that no one else was here, just the two of them. I swallowed, avoiding my dad's eyes as I turned to Adam. He was still soaked from being tossed in the pool, his hair, t-shirt and board shorts dripping wet.

"I'm sorry," I began, "I wanted to tell you weeks ago, but...I was too scared. I'm really sorry for all the trouble I caused you and the company."

Adam's dark brow creased with concern. Just over his shoulder, I saw the glass door open. Jordan stood there, frozen in his tracks. We locked eyes for an endless moment, but he was too far away for me to read his face. My cheeks flushed hot with humiliation and I tore my gaze away from him. He approached as Adam continued. "April, who was in the video with you? Why was it posted?"

I tensed. "I can't tell you that."

"*Can't* or *won't?*" my father said, reaching up to grip my arm.

"It's another employee, April. I do know that." My gaze found Adam's and his features were deadly serious now. "The badge was an employee's, not an intern's."

I'd forgotten, for maybe about ten seconds, anyway, that Adam was a genius and probably recalled everything he'd ever seen or read. He remembered the color of the badge in the video and immediately concluded that it wasn't mine.

392 | BRENNA AUBREY

Jordan now stood behind Adam. My eyes flashed over to his face, taking in his curiously blank features, before turning my attention back to Adam. I took a deep breath and then let it go. "I'm not going to tell you that. I'm sorry, but I can't. As for why it was posted…it was my fault and it was an accident. I've regretted it ever since…" My voice faded out and I felt the tears blur my eyes again. Maybe Jordan would be offended by that, but at this point, I didn't care. He'd offended *me* enough.

There was a long, tense silence. "April—" Adam began in a tight voice, but Jordan held out a hand.

"Adam, this isn't the right time. We should deal with this later."

Adam shook his head and ignored Jordan. "April, I can't help you if you don't cooperate. If you want to leave Draco on good terms, that's still possible."

Adam was offering me an ultimatum. If I ratted out my co-conspirator, I could still get my recommendation. I looked at Jordan again, but his eyes seemed to bounce off my gaze. He looked everywhere but straight at me.

"I'm sorry, Mr. Drake, Mr. Fawkes. Thank you for the opportunity to work with you at Draco, but I can't…"

"Get in the car," my dad said through his teeth in a voice full of disgust.

I felt like a deflated balloon. I gently pulled away from his hold, and he pressed his car keys into my hand. I did as he said. Behind me, I could hear him continuing his discussion with Adam, their voices fading as I made my way out of the building. I could also hear footsteps. Quick footsteps that sounded as if they were bearing down on me. I glanced over my shoulder to confirm whose they were.

Jordan was coming up behind me quickly, but I didn't stop. I had to keep walking. I found the car, clicked it open and had the door handle in my hand when he hit the parking lot at a run. "April!" he called.

And, stupid me, I hesitated. He came up beside me but kept his distance—I was thankful for that. I pulled the door ajar and looked up at him. "You'd better not be out here when my dad gets done talking with Adam. It will blow all your efforts at CYA out of the water."

He clenched his teeth. "I'm not out here to cover my ass. I want to see if you're okay."

I laughed at him. What a ridiculous thing to say. I may have been laughing, but at the same time, tears were rolling down my cheeks. I wanted to take back everything I'd ever said to him. I especially wanted to take back those three damning words that he didn't deserve. I couldn't, though, because it would be a lie. But right now, I was so angry and *so* disappointed in him. And no matter how hard I tried, I couldn't change what my heart wanted.

"April..." He put a hand on my arm and I wrenched it away from him, pulling the car door open wider so that it created a barrier between us.

"No, Jordan. Don't do that. I'll take your precious secret to the grave. No need to worry. We were just having sex. It's over now."

His face clouded. "That's really not fair—"

"Not fair? *Really?* You're going to tell me what's not fair? You left me up there on the scaffold alone with that blazing scarlet letter for all to mock. You're Dimmesdale, cowering in the shadows, wallowing in your shame. That's not my problem, it's *yours*. But don't ever, *ever* tell me that I'm worth speaking up for myself. You just proved those words were empty. Because you didn't speak up for me."

His face paled then began to redden in anger. "I didn't ask for that little encounter to be recorded and uploaded to the Internet. That's all on you, April."

I nodded. "You're right. That is all on me. But twice—*twice*—I was going to go to Adam, tell him everything and make this right. Who stopped me both times? It didn't have to come to this—it probably wouldn't have. And now, because it wasn't handled earlier, everything is ten times worse." I took a long, painful breath. He was about to speak, but I cut him off. "And this time with everybody watching me, probably taking pictures with their phones. I'm sure my ass will be all over the Internet *again*. This time attached to my name. But hey, you got me back for what I did, didn't you? You got your karma."

His mouth fell open. "April—"

"Don't say anything. Just turn around and walk away." I couldn't have said another word, anyway, because my breath was stolen in shattering sobs. He made a move toward me again but I backed away, holding up my hand.

Through my tears, I saw my dad exiting the building, striding toward the car like a man on a vendetta mission. I nodded my head in his direction and slipped into my seat, sinking into the plush leather. I slammed the car door shut after me. It was hot and stuffy inside, but I didn't want to roll down the window. I wished I could curl up and die.

Jordan hesitated by my door for a few moments longer before drifting away. He crossed paths with my dad on his way back into the building. Dad hesitated for a few seconds, nodding at Jordan with a grim face, his eyes continually fixed on me.

Then Jordan continued to the building without looking back, and I dropped my eyes to the dashboard, folding my arms over my chest protectively. I tried to ignore the sting inside me that came with every beat of my heart.

Dad opened the door, slid into the driver's seat and then slammed the door shut after him. Coolly, I handed him his keys, leaned away from him and stared out the window. He started the car and, without speaking, headed toward the 5 freeway, which would take us back to his house and my car.

However, before he even made it onto the interstate, he pulled over into a strip mall parking lot and turned off the ignition. I didn't look up from where I fiddled with my phone. I'd checked social media and already tweets were starting to appear under the hashtags #ComicConSexGeeks and #assexposed. My name and handle were all over them, along with pictures of my backside in the torn bathing suit.

There were no personal texts on my phone. I was already wishing one would show up. One with two little words, the words he hadn't said to me. *I'm sorry...*

Dad waited for a moment, taking a deep breath. Throughout my childhood, the only time I'd ever heard him yell was at people who worked for him. He'd never yelled at me before, even those times when I wished he had rather than not acknowledge me at all.

But he couldn't just shove me away now. I was the daughter who had publicly disgraced him in front of everyone involved in his exciting new business venture.

"Put your phone away for a minute," he said in a quiet voice.

I held my breath and did as he asked.

"I'm going to be blunt. I'm too angry to get on the freeway right now."

"Do you want me to drive, then?"

"I want you to tell me what the hell was in your head. Why would you do something like this and risk blowing your entire future?"

I straightened, squaring my shoulders, digging deep within myself to find the strength to say the words burning on my tongue. I looked him straight in the eye as I spoke.

"I made a very bad choice. If you can say you've never done the same, then you get the right to judge me for it. But you can't, because I'm living proof of one of the worst choices you've ever made."

He scowled. "So you are going to make this about me and your mother? I've heard this song and dance before...but you aren't a teenager anymore. You're twenty-two years old. You need to grow up."

"You're right. I do. But...isn't that what growing up is all about? Making mistakes and learning from them? Isn't that how *you* learned?"

He ran a hand over his eyes and I noticed he was a little pale. There was a long, tense silence. His phone chimed and he pulled it out, read the text message—likely from Rebekah—and typed something into it. Then he put his phone down.

"You know what hurts me most about this? Beyond any of the embarrassment, it's the fact that you're sabotaging yourself and your future. You're in danger of throwing your life away. You're an intelligent, beautiful woman. You really shouldn't be blaming your poor choices on your parents."

I nodded. "My choices are mine to own..." Then my voice died out and tears sprang to my eyes. I took a deep breath and released it. Even my throat stung. "It's easy to throw things away when you don't think they're very valuable in the first place."

His face clouded. I blinked, trying to keep my tears from spilling over.

"Why would you think that?"

I looked up at him. "You tell me."

His gaze intensified and he rubbed a hand along his jaw. I knew he didn't know what to say to me.

"It's okay. You've got your perfect family waiting for you at home. You don't need to worry about me anymore."

He hissed out a breath like I'd just punched him in the stomach. I looked away, and a lone tear spilled down my cheek. "What do I need to do to show you that I love you, April? I love you every bit as much as Sarah and Daniel. I don't get where this is coming from. I pay—"

"I don't want your bank account. I want *you*. Ever since I was a kid, you were never there for me. You always pawned me off on someone else. Oma or the nanny or my mom, and eventually, Rebekah. But never what I needed. Never *you*."

He looked stunned. "I didn't think I could give you what you needed. I thought a woman—"

"You thought I wouldn't want you because my mom didn't." My fists closed, knotting with the frustration that I felt.

He grimaced. "Your mother and I were a disaster. I never, ever wanted any of that to affect you."

The tears were now flowing freely down my cheeks. How could he be so smart and yet so clueless about the people who loved him most? "But it *did*, Daddy. Because neither one of you wanted me."

Alarm crossed his features and he shook his head. "How could you think that? I've never said—"

My lip trembled, and now I just didn't care if he saw me lose it. I'd found the courage to speak up to my mom. Now it was time to do the same with my dad. Only this was scarier, because I cared far more about losing any relationship I had with my dad than the nominal one I'd had with my mom.

"I tried to call you..." I began faintly.

"When?"

"I was in San Diego at Comic-Con. She called me from Vegas to tell me she'd just married Gunnar."

His features chilled. I'd ended up having to inform him about Gunnar and my mom via email a few weeks later. He hadn't said much. My dad didn't often discuss my mother, likely for fear that he would say something negative about her to me.

"I got your assistant and you never called back."

"I'm sorry. I told you in the email. I didn't realize how urgent the message was. I'm not perfect, April."

"You're not *there*. Period." I shook my head, continuing on. "I needed to talk to someone who would understand. *Anyone*. Because you don't have to put up with her shit anymore, Dad. I do."

He held up a helpless hand. "There is nothing I can do that can change that."

"Yes, there is. You can be there for me."

I sighed, feeling defeated. I didn't want to talk about this anymore. I just wanted him to turn on the ignition and drive. It hurt too much—and like always, I was afraid if I told him how I really felt, I'd lose whatever love he had for me, such as it was.

"You've never told me any of this before."

I wiped my cheeks with the back of my hand. "I was afraid to."

He frowned. "I didn't raise you to think like that—"

"You didn't raise me," I said, my voice low in my throat. My dad flinched, but he said nothing. "Neither did she, and I finally stood up to her. It's time I did the same with you."

"So this is what it's come down to? Some cliché? The slutty girl with daddy issues—"

I held up my hand. "Stop right there. I'm not a slut and I am not ashamed of myself. I made a bad decision—but that has nothing to do with my having sex. If I were your son, you'd be congratulating me for that."

He took a deep breath and closed his eyes, rubbing them with his thumb and forefinger through his lids. "I'm sorry," he said in a voice thick with emotion—more emotion than I'd ever heard from him. "I'm really sorry. I didn't mean that."

"I'm sorry too...I'm sorry you're ashamed of me. But *I'm* not ashamed of me, and that is what's most important. Not what *you* think. Not what Rebekah thinks. And definitely not what my mother thinks."

He opened his eyes and dropped his hand, then looked at me with that hard stare I'd seen him use in business deals when he was going for the jugular.

"I'm not ashamed of you. This situation, however, has humiliated me. I'm not going to lie about that."

I lowered my eyes and ran my hands over the upholstery of my seat, picking at it nervously. I'd spoken up for myself—finally. But it didn't feel as freeing as it had with my mom.

"If I could change that, I would. But I've been going through a pretty rough period in my life, and I had no one to turn to."

He shook his head. "I'm sorry you couldn't get a hold of me. As for your mother—"

"She came to the condo last month. Just showed up out of the blue, sitting in my front room with her boy toy, asking me for money, drunk off her ass." I wiped my wet cheeks with the back of my trembling hand.

He nodded, swallowing, apparently too overwrought to talk. We sat there in silence before he cleared his throat. "Has she bothered you since then?"

I pressed my lips together and shook my head, certain he wouldn't be pleased with the news I was about to give him. "I cut her out of my life, Dad. I had to. I told her I would block her texts and calls. It's a long story, but if she shows up again, I'll get a restraining order."

He took a deep breath and let it out. "That doesn't make me happy, April. But it's not your fault that it came to this. You were right to do it. I just...I hope someday you can forgive. Her...and me."

I couldn't say anything in response. My face lowered and the tears came faster, and I had no idea what to say even if I could even talk. Everything just felt so raw and sore. Every breath stabbed me a little deeper.

When I'd stood up to my mom, it had been easier. Jordan had believed in me—he'd told me I had the courage to do what I needed to do. To cut her out of my life. He certainly could talk a good talk when he wasn't the one in the line of fire. The enormity of the loss of him felt like a hole ripped in my chest. I almost couldn't breathe.

Dad sat quietly for a long stretch, staring out the window.

I cleared my throat to speak again. "I—I'm sorry you're hurt. I'm sorry you're humiliated. But your feelings are not more important than mine. And I've learned that lesson. That I need to speak up for myself."

He didn't react for a minute, then looked at me with wary eyes. "Are you going to cut me out too? Like you did with your mother?"

"No."

His face slackened with relief and that reaction did something to me—showed me that he *did* care. He blinked quickly and then looked away, and I could tell that he was trying not to break down. Seeing my normally stoic dad showing even a hint of emotion cut deep—soul deep. But underneath all that pain was a spark of hope, a glimmer of happiness. My dad loved me enough to break down at the thought of my never wanting to speak to him again. And until this moment, I'd never known that.

He quickly took control of his emotions, though, clearing his throat a few times and sniffing before turning back to the wheel. "We should—uh—Rebekah will be wondering where we are."

He started the car and I leaned against the window, closing my eyes. I tried not to think about this day, tried to close my mind off to the hurt and humiliation. Tried not to envision those faces all staring at me in shock and disgust as I stood on the stairs, fully exposed. It was like a combination of all the worst naked dreams I'd ever had increased exponentially. It was hard to breathe and the occasional tear spilled over onto my cheek through my closed eyes.

A half hour into the drive home, as I faded in and out of consciousness, emotionally exhausted, I felt my dad's hand close over my own where it sat on the console between us. My fingers grasped his and clamped on for dear life. His hold tightened on mine. It was the smallest gesture, but in that moment, we'd communicated more than we had in years.

We arrived at my dad's place after dinner, and Rebekah was getting the kids ready for bed while I gathered up my stuff from my overnight stay and prepared to leave. She'd seen my face—blotchy skin and swollen eyes—but hadn't asked questions. But as I packed up, she wandered into the guest room with some containers.

"I packed some dinner for you. There's enough for a few days. I know you like my vegetable frittata."

I sniffed and took her offering, tucking it alongside my bag. "Thanks."

"Are you okay?"

I nodded but didn't say anything. Rebekah's features sobered as she studied me. She was a pretty woman in her mid-thirties with short, dark hair and brown eyes, and she was about my height. If I were ever to go out into public with both my mom and stepmom—God forbid that ever *really* happen—people would be more likely to think Rebekah was my biological mother. Which was apropos, really. Rebekah had been more of a mother to me than Jennifer ever could be.

"Come down again soon, please? We like seeing you."

I nodded again, my eyes stinging with fresh tears. Rebekah moved forward and—a little awkwardly, because she usually wasn't the hugging type—put her arms around me.

"We care about you, April. I don't know what's going on with you and your dad and I'm going to respect your privacy, but...just remember you've got family here, okay? We love you."

I pressed my hand to Rebekah's back and returned the hug, grateful for her care and concern—and especially her willingness to respect my privacy. "Thank you. Thanks for everything. I know I don't say that much. But thanks."

Dad walked me out and put my bag in the car for me. As I bent to slide into the driver's seat, he stopped me with a hand on my arm.

"April...I just want you to know that I do love you and I do care. I'm sorry I've done a poor job of showing you before this."

"You did the best job you could," I said, clearing my throat. "Just like I did the best job I could. But it wasn't good enough."

"Then we have to do better."

I nodded. "Yeah."

Slowly, as if fearing I'd pull away, he bent and kissed my cheek. "I'm going to be up in Orange County again next week. I want us to spend some time together if you can fit me in."

"I appear to have a lot of free time," I whispered, remembering his words to Adam, insisting he terminate me from the company. It didn't matter. After that utter humiliation, I wouldn't go back of my own free will anyway.

I got in the car and drove the two hours home, all the while thinking about this new shift in my relationship with my dad—and even Rebekah. And though the day had been completely mortifying, I couldn't help but think about the radical change in me. I'd stood up for myself—to Adam and to my dad. And to Jordan. And though I'd royally fucked things up, I was also proud of myself. I felt strong.

But I also felt empty. I'd checked my phone before I started the car—no texts or calls from Jordan. What had I expected? I forced myself not to think about him all the way home.

More often than not, I failed.

It was just before Sid's bedtime when I arrived at our condo. She was dressed in her flannel pajamas while playing Dragon Epoch on her computer. Just the glimpse of the game's graphics on her screen was enough to make me feel nauseous. I walked into our room, tossed my bags down and flopped onto my bed. I was tempted to just roll over and go to sleep like that.

Sid turned around and looked at me. "You look awful."

I rolled my eyes. "Thanks. It's been a crap day, to put it mildly."

She frowned. "I, um, heard. Or saw, rather. I was waiting to hear from you. I would have texted, but...I wasn't sure what state you were in."

My lids closed over sore, aching eyes. Of course she'd heard—her and half the universe. I hadn't even checked since this afternoon to see how the story had undoubtedly grown and mutated across the Internet. I was bloody chum in the dark, shark-infested waters of social media.

"So, uh, I pieced together what happened based on tweets and updates. Does this mean you aren't going to business school?"

I chewed on my bottom lip, covering my face with my hands. I didn't have an answer for that.

She shifted in her chair, which squeaked loudly. "I'm not sure if this is the right time to bring it up, but...I figured out how the video got uploaded."

I turned to her. "How?"

"Well, all this time I'd been trying to scour the Internet for the earliest known source of the video. But that was a crazy way to go about it, because when something like that goes viral so fast, it's almost impossible. It was all over Tumblr and Reddit and 4Chan and Facebook and—"

I held up my hand to cut off her dizzying litany. "All right. All right, I get it."

"Anyway, I didn't realize that I could go to the source and trace it from the weapon itself!"

"Huh?"

"Your phone, Apes. I logged into the cloud backup of your phone, since you gave me the password. And it allowed me to see everything you did with that phone from the moment you made the video to the next day when you emailed said video to this address." She snatched a sticky note off her desk and handed it to me. On it was a cryptic email address to a generic, free email provider.

"I never emailed the video. I'd remember that. And I don't even know how I could have done that by accident."

"Because you didn't do it. Think...did anyone else have access to your phone that weekend? You said no, but..."

I tilted my head, thinking. "Well, I was showing some pictures I'd taken of the Iron Man panel. I'd gotten a front row center view of Robert Downey Jr. and snapped a bunch of pics of him. The girls wanted to see."

"Okay...so you held the phone while they looked at the pics?"

I searched my memory. We'd been in the back of a carpool van riding home from the Con. The girls had been oohing and ahhing about how hot RDJ was. "Well, you know, I handed the phone around..."

Her eyes narrowed. "And the video was in that same group of photos?"

"I guess...I took tons of pictures that weekend." I frowned, trying to remember. "Hell, I was so hungover all weekend, I don't even know if I could remember my name. But my phone locks with my thumbprint. No one had access to it."

Sid raised her dark brows. "You are way too trusting of your *friends*, April. Because someone did find that video and emailed it to themselves from your phone."

My eyes squeezed shut as I froze in panic. "Oh shit. I remember now...Cari wanted to see the photos again. She took the phone out of my hand. But she only had it for like a minute or two."

Sid nodded to the piece of paper she handed me. "That email is an anonymous address, but it's attached to a Twitter and a Tumblr account. I did some Googling, some cross-referencing. It wasn't easy because she covered her tracks as much as she could, but...the accounts are linked to Cari MacFerson's social media. In that two minutes that she had your phone in her hands, she emailed the video to herself from your phone. When she got home, she downloaded it to her computer and then uploaded it to the Internet. After it had been shared around, she deleted the original copy. But by then, it had gone viral."

Shock made it hard to breathe, freezing my insides cold. "Fucking bitch."

"Yeah...that. I'm not even going to argue with your potty mouth."

I couldn't sleep that night. I was exhausted, mentally, physically and emotionally, yet I still couldn't sleep. And it wasn't because of the tumultuous revelations between my dad and me. It wasn't even because of my pure blinding range toward Cari.

It was over *him*.

The way that Jordan had so callously brushed aside what had happened between us. *I didn't ask for that little encounter to be recorded and uploaded to the Internet. That's all on you.*

It was all on me. It was true. But I'd expected something from him. Something more. And maybe that hadn't been fair, either.

Just because I loved him didn't mean those feelings were reciprocated, no matter how much I wanted them to be. I'd told him how I felt. In return, he'd pushed me against the wall and had his way with me. And I'd let him.

It was just sex. He'd told me that over and over again. Why had my stupid heart not listened? Stupid, stupid April. You've fucked up. Yet again. And you can't even blame alcohol for this one.

But somewhere, deep inside, I knew that this, too, would pass. Broken hearts would mend. Sure, it hurt like hell now and I'd need time and distance. Come to think of it, taking a trip to Israel didn't sound so bad right about now. I drifted off to sleep for about an hour or two before dawn with the image of myself standing before the Wailing Wall, atoning for my sins. Maybe Rebekah was right. Maybe I did need to find out more about that part of myself. Maybe the blessing in return would be a healed heart.

And then I could turn my back on all of this and forget.

26
JORDAN

I T WAS JUST AFTER NOON ON SUNDAY IN NEW YORK CITY. THE officers and their respective partners—those of us who had them, anyway— had chartered a private flight from LA early this morning, and we were now at a private affair in an exclusive restaurant that looked out over Central Park. Company officers mingled with potential board members and investment bankers, all celebrating the imminent listing of Draco Multimedia Entertainment. On Monday morning, we'd gather on a special platform at the New York Stock Exchange while the CEO of the newest publicly traded company rang the bell to open trading.

It was the realization of a dream I'd had since the day Adam and I had gotten together over coffee one weekend and he'd told me he wanted to start his own company. He'd asked for my help, and that's exactly what I gave him. I'd worked tirelessly for the past four years so that this day would come to fruition. Everything I'd done, every connection I'd made and every meticulous record I'd kept was geared toward the audits that a board would eventually want, with the sole purpose of taking the company public and thus becoming ridiculously rich.

And here I was, less than a month before my twenty-sixth birthday, about to quadruple my net worth, pushing it up into the nine-figure range. Easily, I would be a billionaire before I turned thirty. I should have been flying high.

In truth, I felt like shit.

I hadn't slept last night at all. Oh, I'd given it the old college try. I lay in bed for hours staring up at the ceiling, but I couldn't stop thinking about *her*.

Especially that look in her eyes when she'd backed away from me at the car before she'd left with her dad. *Betrayal*. I knew that look. I'd worn that same look when I'd been betrayed. I knew how it felt inside. And I swore that I would never let anyone do it to me again. I also swore that I'd never let anyone in close enough for me to do it to.

I let April in, though. I reeled her right in and I didn't let her get away. Even when I knew that she was starting to care too much. I could have ended it in Canada. And nominally, I had.

But I'd been incapable of letting her walk away. So I reeled her back in again and convinced myself that it was just sex for both of us. Even on my subconscious level, I was a rat bastard.

A rat bastard who was in love with her.

Contrary to my normal sociable behavior, I huddled in a corner, planted on a seat near the window, and sipped my third glass of champagne, hoping for a buzz to take the edge off. So much for abstaining from alcohol. It had been a good run while it lasted but no way was I going to get through this day sober.

Someone landed in the seat next to me with a heavy sigh. I could tell it was a woman and hoped it wasn't yet another underwriter trying to pass me her hotel key surreptitiously. I didn't even look or acknowledge my seatmate until she began to speak.

"Penny for your thoughts," Mia said.

"My thoughts are worth at least thirty-five dollars a share."

She laughed. "You okay?" And before I could answer that, she added, "Have you, by any chance, heard from April?"

Lead seemed to clog up my throat and a sliver of pain pierced my breastbone. I downed the last of the champagne in my flute, set it aside and leaned back to look at her.

Adam's fiancée was a very pretty woman with light brown eyes that shone with intelligence. She was as smart as a whip, and I figured I'd have to be as careful with her as I usually was around her one true love. He had a way of figuring things out quickly.

"I haven't heard from April. I don't suppose she wants any reminder about her time at Draco these days." *Especially me,* I thought with a dull ache in my chest.

Her lips thinned. "Can you pass me her number? I'd like to make sure she's okay. She didn't deserve that shit treatment, and it's something I'm going to have to have words with Adam at some point after all this with the IPO dies down. The slut-shaming that goes on when a woman is sexual—and especially if she happens to *enjoy* sex—while a man gets the slaps on the back and the 'atta boys.' It's just not fair."

Alrighty then. I slid my eyes to the greenery out the window. Adam's fiancée was also a rabid, sign-toting feminist. Okay, maybe not that bad. As far as I could tell, she hadn't burned her bra, but issues like this brought out the Susan B. Anthony in her.

"Yeah, I'll...see what I can do."

Mia continued to stare at me. I grabbed her untouched flute of champagne and began to sip it. Fourth time might be the charm? Her eyes narrowed as she watched me.

"You're worried about her."

I clenched my jaw and released it. "Have you ever read *The Scarlet Letter?*" I asked.

Her brow rose at the abrupt change of subject. "Not recently. Everybody has to read that goddamn book in high school, though."

"So you actually read it? You didn't just get the cheat notes? I was homeschooled so I never read it."

"I did actually read it. I never got cheats on books I had to read. I'm a nerd like that, even though I'm not a big fan of the classics. Why?"

"Who's Dimmesdale?"

Now she was frowning. I could tell she was wondering what the hell was going through my head, but she humored me.

"If I remember correctly, he's the guy who got Hester pregnant. He was the reverend of the town. But he kept silent and no one but Hester ever knew he was the father of the baby. So Hester had to endure all the shame and wear the letter. And those same townspeople who all spit on her held him up to be the model of a holy, pure man. He's the epitome of a hypocrite."

You're Dimmesdale, April had said. She was right. My head ached. My chest was tight. And I felt like the lowest of the low, the weight of guilt pulling me down.

I had a few more in me—only enough for a pleasant buzz—before I got up the courage to tell Adam I needed to talk to him alone. He agreed to come to my suite when he could break away from all the congratulations and schmoozing going on around here.

Back in my room, I may have fortified myself with a little single malt Scotch before he got there. When he knocked on the door, I let him in, and then headed straight back to the bar.

"Care for some Johnnie Walker Black Label?" I drawled.

He scowled. He didn't touch hard liquor and I knew that perfectly well.

"What's up, Jordan? You look like shit."

"Thank you. I feel like shit."

"Are you getting sick? Why didn't you tell me? You're going to be up for the bell ringing and trading on the floor, right? They're going to interview us."

"I'm not physically ill, no."

Adam let out a breath, visibly relieved. "Glad to hear that." He shucked his suit coat and found a nearby lounge chair to sit on, immediately yanking on his tie to pull it off and roll it up. I'd already removed my jacket, tie, cufflinks and shoes.

He sat back, resting an ankle on his knee, and waited. I took a sip of Scotch and geared myself up. "Okay, so...I need to talk to you about April Weiss."

Nothing on his face betrayed his thoughts. "Okay. Go ahead."

"You can't fire her for being in the video when there's another employee who participated and is getting off scot-free."

Adam stared at me as if I'd just grown horns. Then he blinked. "Well, you were there. She wouldn't say who it was. And you heard her dad—"

"Screw him. If he'd cared about her, he wouldn't have said that shit. It's not fair. And on top of it, it's sexist." Thanks, Mia, for putting that bug in my ear. I had a vague image of standing next to her at some ritualistic bra-burning ceremony.

"So after that scene she caused at the party yesterday, I'm supposed to take her back?"

"She didn't cause the scene. Someone else did. It's not her fault."

Adam's eyes narrowed. "Two questions. One, how much have you had to drink, and two, why do you care about this so much?"

I braced myself against the edge of the bar with stiff arms. "Two answers. One: not enough. And two: because..." I took a long, deep breath, held it and let it out. I needed more liquid courage for this shit.

"Because?" Adam prompted.

"Because if you fire her, you're going to have to fire me, too."

Adam pushed out of his chair and stalked to the window to look out, brushing his fingers along his jawline.

"Are you going to explain that statement to me, or am I going to have to make some guesses? Because I don't really like the stuff that's popping into my head right this minute."

"Whatever you are thinking is probably not as bad as reality." He turned to me with an expectant look on his face. I cleared my throat. "I had a custom-made costume for this year's Comic-Con. I went as Falco the Bounty Hunter, and no one knew."

Adam's eyes closed and his face flushed a little before he shook his head and looked at me. "And I'm only finding out about this now because...?"

"Well, that's obvious, isn't it? Because I'm a coward. Because I froze like a deer caught in the headlights the day that shit went viral and had no idea how to handle it. So I didn't say anything, hoping it would go away. And the more time passed, the harder it became to dump it on you."

"So not only did you screw an intern, but you videotaped it and put it on the Internet? *Are you insane?*"

I clenched my teeth. "Who videoed and uploaded it isn't the point. The point is that if you fire her, you have to fire me, too."

Adam scowled and he started to pace, his hands opening and closing at his sides. "This relationship, how long has it been going on?"

"It was a one-time thing...until..." He stopped and pinned me down with his signature death glare. "Until Vancouver. Then it started up again and has been pretty much ongoing until yesterday."

"And on the company premises? Did you fuck her in your office?"

I swallowed. "Yeah."

He shook his head, muttered something under his breath and started pacing again. "Screwing an intern in your goddamn office. Who the *fuck* do you think you are, Bill Clinton?"

"That's not—"

"No, it's perfectly accurate," he cut me off, raising his voice. "You're the goddamn CFO of the company. A founder. An officer. You took advantage of her. Even before you sat through that sexual harassment training, you knew better, Jordan."

My throat closed up. I had nothing to say. He was absolutely right. With a shaky hand, I lifted the Scotch to my lips and knocked it back.

He hissed out a breath, shaking his head. "And to make it all that much worse, David will probably be our board chair. Jesus Christ, Jordan, when you fuck up, you fuck up big." He ran a hand through his hair, his lip curling with disgust. "You've lied to me this entire time. From the beginning. And you dug yourself in deeper with more lies. Not only is that disturbing, it's a massive disappointment."

You're a disappointment. I'd heard those words out of the old man's mouth often in my formative years, and I'd hardened myself to their effects. But similar words coming from my best friend...hearing

Adam utter them was like a bludgeon to the chest. I let out a long breath and set down the glass.

Yes, I was a disappointment. To my father. To my best friend. To *her*.

"This is why you have to fire me," I said in a voice that was too shaky for my own comfort.

He shook his head. "I'm not firing you."

"You have to. You fired her. You have to fire me, too. If this got out—"

"It's not going to get out."

"Not from her, no. She wanted to go to you and let you know, prepare you in case this got out. I told her not to. It's not fair to make her pay for what both of us did."

Adam rubbed at the throbbing vein on his forehead, his eyes rolling in exasperation. "Well, you've succeeded in getting my nuts in a vise. Is this the part where you start tightening it?"

"I'm sorry, Adam. I fucked up. Believe me, if I'd known what all would have come from this... I—I wanted her gone first thing, remember? I asked you to move her—"

"But you didn't tell me *why*."

I took a breath and let it go. "No."

"Fucking hell," he said, rubbing his forehead again. "We'll deal with this when we get back to California. I'm not doing this now. We have a company to take to the market. After tomorrow, we'll get on the plane and we'll iron this out at home."

My fists tightened. He was giving me an out. Over and over again he'd offered it to me. It was more than I deserved. "Adam, you have to—"

"I don't *have* to do anything. Do you understand me?" he yelled. "This is *my* company and I'm the goddamn CEO and I'm not firing you!"

"Then I quit."

He froze. We stared at each other for a long stretch of minutes. From the look on his face, I could tell he wanted to reach out with his bare hands and strangle me. I did have his nuts in a vise and I wasn't loosening it. I couldn't...I *wouldn't*.

He shook his head. "Five years. *Five years* we've worked our asses off. Hundreds, *thousands* of hours of time, energy, brainpower. You are throwing that all away, over what exactly? A newfound principle?"

I couldn't answer. All I could think about was April, her pale, beautiful, tear-stained face, that look of betrayal in her dark blue eyes. Those lips uttering that condemnation of me, calling me a hypocrite, even if I didn't know that's what she was saying. As much as Adam's admonition had hurt, disappointing her felt so much worse. Because she'd believed in me.

Until I'd let her down.

"I don't even know who the fuck you are anymore." Adam snatched up his jacket and tie, spun and stormed out of the door.

When it shut, I let out the breath I'd been holding, a little dizzy, more than a little sick over what I'd just done. But also, if I cared to examine the feeling closely enough, relieved.

A few hours later, I made my way through John F. Kennedy airport, bag slung over my arm, on the way to my gate. I had two hours before the red-eye flight I'd managed to book at the last minute. I wandered into a bookstore and went straight to the classics section.

It took some searching because I kept forgetting the name of the author, but a clerk helped me find it. I found an empty seat in the first-class lounge, plugged my phone in to charge and cracked open *The Scarlet Letter*. From the looks of it, I would have it finished by the time the plane touched down.

I could have stayed. I could have been there on the floor of the exchange to answer press questions by Adam's side, but the victory was hollow without her.

I'd watch them ring the bell on the Internet instead.

27
ADAM

B Y THE TIME I'D CLIMBED THE FEW FLOORS FROM JORDAN'S room to our suite, I was more pissed off instead of less. My mind raced, wondering what the hell to do with all the information he'd given me. This was a clusterfuck of epic proportions.

I pulled my card out and keyed into the room. Emilia looked up from her textbook, her highlighter poised in her hand, ready to mark up more passages. Her eyes widened when she saw me.

"What?" I asked, pausing in the entryway.

Her brows rose. "What do you mean, what? Your hair is sticking up like you ran your hands through it a few hundred times, and you usually only do that when you're upset."

Self-consciously, I smoothed my hand over my hair. Then I took a breath, let it out slowly and tossed my jacket on the couch. She capped her pen and set it down. "You okay? Did you get some bad news about the opening tomorrow?"

I sat against the back of the couch, rubbing my jaw, and gave a sharp shake of my head. I pondered how much of this was confidential, how much I should share with her. I closed my eyes. I wanted to tell her everything, like always, but there were professional lines I couldn't cross, weren't there?

"Oh shit, do you have another one of your headaches?" She stood and approached me. I hooked my arm around her waist and pulled her against me, shaking my head again.

"Jordan just quit."

She drew back to look in my face, likely trying to determine if I was joking or not. "*What?* Why?"

"I'm not sure how much I can tell you."

"Company stuff?"

I licked my lips. "It's company stuff but also personal to him. I—" I cut off, staring at the ground and frowning.

She wrapped her arms around my waist. "What does this mean for tomorrow? Is he not coming to the opening of trade? I can't believe that. He's been obsessed with the IPO."

"I don't even know. I was so floored, I didn't ask."

Emilia frowned, slipped down on the couch behind us and patted the cushion next to her. I got up and went to sink down beside her. "I noticed he was acting strangely today at the reception, so I went to talk to him. I think it had to do with all that happened yesterday at the company party. April is his intern, after all, and I think he's really upset about what happened to her."

"Uh, yeah, you've pretty much hit the nail on the head. How did you do that?"

She looked away, her eyes narrowing at some random memory. "I asked him about April because I was concerned, and he got all weird and started asking me about *The Scarlet Letter*."

"You mean the movie with Demi Moore?"

She laughed. "The novel that the movie is based on, silly."

"I may have...watched the movie to get out of reading the novel."

"You and about ninety percent of all high school graduates." She paused, looking thoughtful. "I don't get why he was fixating on that, though, or why he thought to ask me about it when I asked him about April."

Understanding dawned, based on what I knew. I had a feeling it wouldn't take her long to figure it out. Nevertheless, I kept my mouth shut.

"Does it have to do with April being outed for the video? But they don't know who the guy—" She stopped and her eyes widened. And there it was... Not surprising, given her brilliance. "Oh em gee. Jordan was the guy, wasn't he?"

She amazed me every time. All the time. "I don't know how you figured that out. Not sure I want to know." I cocked a brow at her.

She gave me a sly look. "I have super powers, but I would gladly give them up if I could have been a fly on the wall when he told you that."

I grimaced. "Not unless you wanted to see steam coming out my ears."

"Hmm. I've had that same effect on you before. I don't think I'd like to see it again. Did you two argue?"

I reached out, cupped her cheek with my hand and she smiled, leaning into my touch, turning to kiss my palm. Slowly, I calmed down from the yelling match with Jordan. "Yeah. I was pretty pissed at him."

"You're still pretty pissed at him."

"I feel betrayed."

She nodded. "He was probably terrified to tell you."

"Then he should have grown a pair and done it anyway," I ground out between clenched teeth, feeling the heat under my collar rise again.

"Why'd he tell you now?"

I shrugged. "He said I wasn't being fair by firing April and not him."

Her face clouded and she straightened, looking at me. "He's right."

I took a deep breath and released it, letting my hand fall. "He's the CFO of my company. She's just an intern—"

Her jaw dropped. Uh-oh. "*Adam.*"

"What? You don't even like the interns."

"Not your groupie interns, no. But April is not one of those jerks. And saying she's *just* an intern is sexist, especially since Jordan was the one in the position of power."

"I didn't mean it that way. But her dad insisted I terminate her on the spot."

Emilia's eyes narrowed and she flicked a pointed finger toward my chest. "Then *you* should have grown a pair and told him no. Who's in charge of the company, you or him?"

I didn't answer the rhetorical question and she continued. "I'm actually pretty impressed with Jordan...that he put himself out there like that for her. He was just so miserable today..." Her voice died out and she looked off to the side, almost as if she'd forgotten that she was lecturing me.

"What's wrong?"

She shook her head and then looked at me. "I'm going to go out on a limb here and say that... No..."

"What?"

"You've known Jordan for a long time, right?"

"Since I started college at eighteen."

"In nearly ten years, has he ever stuck himself out there for a woman?"

"Not since his surfer girlfriend at UCLA, no. But that was a bad breakup, and it was after that he became a womanizer. And now apparently, a perv who screws his interns," I said, unable to disguise the bitter edge in my voice.

"'Cause you and I never had sex while I was working for you, right?"

I clenched my jaw and released it. She always had a comeback for everything. "We had a relationship before that and we weren't just sleeping together."

"But if he was just sleeping with April, why would he have gone to bat for her with you? He's sacrificing his career for this. It means more to him than just doing the right thing. She means something to him."

"Maybe she gives a really good blowjob." Emilia scowled and I held up a hand. "Don't shoot. I was joking. You're right, though. This isn't how he normally acts."

"I never thought he'd be capable, 'cause it's *Jordan*, but maybe he's in love with her."

"But he finds the whole concept of love utterly repulsive."

"So did you, once."

"Well, so did *you*."

We looked at each other for a minute before she mock-punched my arm. "Okay, so we were dumb, too. But you can't let him walk away from the company like this."

I threw up my hands, exasperated. "Apparently, I don't have a choice. Emilia, he insisted I fire him and I absolutely refused. So he quit."

"But he quit because you won't take April back."

"Her dad—"

She raised her eyebrows at me. "*You're* the boss."

"You usually only say that in bed. I'm getting all hot right now."

She quirked her mouth at me. "I *never* say that to you in bed. Maybe in your dirty dreams. But seriously…I think what's bugging you about all this is that you already know what you have to do to make this right."

I sighed. "The timing couldn't be shittier, and I really still am pissed as hell at him. He didn't come forward and tell me before. And not only did he keep it a secret this entire time, but he covered it up."

"So you're going to trash a ten-year friendship and a meaningful business relationship because your feelings are hurt?"

I sighed, throwing my head back. "Stop making such good points, please."

She snuggled up beside me, laying her head on my shoulder and tilting it to kiss me on the neck. I closed my eyes.

Her mouth found my ear. "You're the boss," she murmured, devouring my lobe, sending a nice zing right down to my center.

"That's right. Say it again."

"You're. The. Boss…" she drawled, laughing.

"Mmm. That's what I like to hear," I said, pushing her down on the couch beneath me. I pressed my body over hers, kissing her. I didn't want to think about anything but this.

I didn't want to think about going down on the stock exchange floor alone without Jordan tomorrow or not having him as my right-hand man from this day forward. And I definitely didn't want to focus on that heavy feeling in the pit of my stomach that indicated what the right thing to do really was.

Emilia was helping me forget, at least for a little while.

28
APRIL

THE DOORBELL RANG AT OH DARK HUNDRED. NATURALLY, SID was already awake, quietly puttering around the apartment while I moaned and rolled over to face the wall, hoping to forget I was still alive.

That persistent ache in my chest, that feeling of loss and rejection, it was still there like a giant hole that could very well take ages to heal. And my eyes were sore from crying all day yesterday. I'd checked my text messages constantly. Nothing from him. *Nothing.*

I'd also checked social media against Sid's advice. Tons of people had tagged me in their unflattering posts and tweets, of course. *How thoughtful of them.*

Jordan's profile displayed a picture he'd taken in Times Square yesterday, mentioning his excitement for the impending IPO. But that was it. I had no other inkling of what was going on with him and I couldn't exactly ask Susan for an update, since I was now persona non grata at Draco.

She'd be back at her desk today. It was Monday morning, business as usual, at the company. It wasn't like I could sneak into the office and clean out my desk. Maybe Mia would take pity on me and do it when she got back from New York City tomorrow. As soon as I found some shred of dignity, I'd email and ask her.

My mind continued to race, even though I willed it to shut the fuck up. I wished I could fall back asleep, since I hadn't been able to even close my eyes before one a.m. I was exhausted enough to sleep until noon, *if* I could just fall back to sleep. I stuffed my pillow over my head with a groan. Sid was speaking to someone at the front door, but they were quiet enough that I could muffle out the sound with my pillow.

A few minutes later, just as I was trying to turn off my thoughts so I could doze in blissful oblivion, Sid came back into the bedroom and sat down at the edge of my bed.

"Go away," I mumbled from under my pillow.

She tugged at the pillow and I clutched it tighter to my face.

"Sid! Do you really want me to tear you a new one? Please let me sleep."

"But I want to talk to you," came the reply. Not Sid's voice. A man's voice. Not my dad.

I froze, my heart thumping wildly at the base of my throat. I was certain I was having audible hallucinations. Could a person hallucinate a voice?

The weight on the bed shifted as if he was turning toward me. He tugged the pillow again, and this time I allowed it to be removed from my face. He set it down by my leg and turned to look at me, his face serious. His hazel eyes scoured my features. He was taking in my puffy eyes ringed with dark circles, the chafed skin around my nose where

I'd frequently blown it. I'd seen myself in the mirror the night before. I knew how bad the damage was. And it was probably even worse this morning with the additional swelling that troubled sleep had brought.

I looked at him, my eyes widening then flying to the clock on the dresser. It was five thirty in the morning and Jordan was dressed in rumpled clothing—like he'd slept in his clothes. I sat up to face him.

"What are you doing here? The stock exchange opens at six."

"I came here to watch the opening with you. Can you livestream it to your TV?"

My jaw dropped. "Why the hell aren't you in New York?"

"Because I didn't want to be in New York. I wanted to be here. With you."

I rubbed my forehead, looking down. "I don't understand. You're supposed to be on the platform with the other officers so you all can ring the opening bell."

"Well...I'm not."

I pushed myself out of bed and stood, crossing my arms across my chest. I was wearing a short, thin nightie because it had been a warm night. Jordan's eyes slid over me like a warm caress. I got goose bumps just from the touch of his gaze. Which pissed me off. I was supposed to be mad at him. I was supposed to hate him.

It was five forty. "I'll be right back."

In the bathroom, I brushed my teeth, splashed cold water on my face and found a thin robe to slip over my shoulders. Quickly determining that I had no time for an emergency makeup session, I stiffened my spine and went back into the bedroom. He'd grabbed my laptop off my desk and had it sitting on the bed, unopened. I blinked.

"Can we watch the livestream? It's almost nine there. The bell rings in ten minutes."

With a shrug, I settled beside him on the bed—not too close, since I still wasn't sure what the hell he was doing here—and leaned against the wall. Jordan scooted next to me so he could look closely at the screen. I keyed in my password and quickly closed the social media and news sites I'd been using to track my name smeared across the whole world, along with pictures of my ass and tattoo. Jordan didn't react to those as I opened a new browser window and typed a Google search to get the livestream for the NYSE. By the time this was all accomplished, we were five minutes from the opening of the floor and the ringing of the bell.

The platform that looked out over the trading floor was a white gabled balcony. Across the front hung a banner with the Draco logo and lettering. My former bosses and their significant others crowded the platform around the CEO. Adam stood talking to the chief executive officer of the Stock Exchange, likely receiving the last of the instructions. Mia stood at his shoulder, a wide smile on her face. The operating officer, Cheryl Waltman, whom everybody called "Walt," and her husband and all the others stood behind and around them.

But there was a noticeable empty space at Adam's other side, where Jordan should have been standing.

Adam looked tense. But whether it was because of the hoopla surrounding the initial public offering or because of Jordan's absence, I couldn't tell. America's soon-to-be newest billionaire stepped up to the podium and, at the exact stroke of nine, pressed the button that set off a cacophony of bell-ringing while everyone around him beamed and applauded. Then he picked up the gavel and handed it to Mia, who, with a shocked smile, hit it against the sounding block. Then they embraced.

I turned to watch Jordan as he took in the goings-on. His face was an unreadable mask, his eyes hooded. It was his dream to be up on that platform when the company listed on the market. He'd been working hard for *years* to that end. But he'd left. He was here, sitting on my bed, watching it on a twelve-inch laptop screen instead.

My throat closed up, but I didn't want to interrupt his moment. Just after the live feed cut, we went to the trading page to follow the price of the shares opening at thirty-five dollars and watched them rise steadily. Jordan remained silent and didn't tear his eyes away from the screen.

Finally, I leaned back against the wall and sighed. "Are you going to tell me why you aren't there with the rest of your colleagues?"

His gaze flicked to me before skirting away. "I no longer work at Draco."

All breath left me in a sudden rush and my jaw slackened. I blinked, my mind racing and my mouth unable to find the words— any words—to say. Jordan spoke for me.

"I told Adam he needed to fire me, and when he refused, I quit."

"*Why?*"

"Because—because I didn't want to be a hypocrite."

My mouth worked for a moment, my throat dry. "That's...that's so stupid."

His brows shot up. "Excuse me?"

"There's no reason to share this humiliation...it's not like doing that is going to make this any better for me. In fact, it will make it worse."

He frowned but didn't say anything. My fist tightened.

"You need to tell him you want your job back."

"I won't do that."

My face flushed and I pounded my fist on the bed between us. "Jordan! Could you be any dumber? I was going to end my internship in two weeks anyway. It was so not worth it!"

He scowled, his eyes narrowing. "I really hate it when you say that. Because it's not true."

In exasperation, I set the laptop aside and stood. I needed a minute. This nausea and anger and...and...this stew of emotions simmering inside my chest made it hard to breathe. I was almost out of my room before he caught my arm and closed the door. He pulled me around to face him.

"Why is it so hard for you to see?" he asked in a voice steeped with emotion.

That simmering stew was boiling over. Tears sprang from my eyes and my chest tightened. I couldn't talk so I shook my head.

"April," he said quietly, placing his hands on both of my cheeks, holding my head still. I squeezed my eyes shut. Who would have thought I'd have more tears to shed than I already had?

"Go away," I whispered. "I've already decided that I need to hate you."

"Really?" he said in an equally quiet voice. His thumb smoothed over my cheek, and he moved so close I could feel the tendrils of his warm breath skate across my skin. My throat tightened and those damn tears kept coming.

"It's my only defense right now. You need to go."

Slowly, his hands dropped away from my face, but he didn't move. I shuddered a little, already aching with the loss of him. I didn't want to open my eyes. I didn't want to see his beautiful face staring into mine. It hurt too much. But I didn't want him to walk away, either.

"Let me tell you something, and then I'll go away if you really want me to."

I didn't say anything but nodded my silent permission.

"It really pisses me off when you say that you aren't worth it. You say that over and over, and I honestly think you believe it."

"It's just an expression—"

"No. It's an ideology. You firmly believe it. You think it's not worth it for me to step in to defend you with your shithead ex-boyfriend or your dad or whoever. It's not worth it, you think, for me to put myself out there for you. But you know what? It's not *enough*. Giving up that job was nothing compared to what you mean to me."

Those words. Those words did something to me physically. They pierced me with a needle-like pain while joy burned white-hot inside my chest.

"We were just fooling around..." I said faintly, almost hoping he would confirm that. I needed to stay angry at him. I needed those walls to protect my tender and battered heart.

"I've wanted you since the moment I first laid eyes on you. And yeah, I wanted that in my way, on my terms. I wanted your body. I thought you were beautiful. I knew who you were at Comic-Con, and I thought being drunk would be a great excuse to be one and done with you, get you out of my system."

He blew out a breath and reached up to rub the back of his neck. "But it didn't work out that way. I couldn't get the taste of you out of my mind and it just made me want you more."

He had no idea that his words were doing the opposite of whatever his intent was. Because they were only confirming what I'd suspected all along. "Yes. We had fun, but—"

"I'm not finished." I raised my brows and folded my arms across my chest, leaning back against the door to allow him to continue. "The sex was good. *Really* good. I thought—I thought that was all it was. Just really good, hot sex." I opened my mouth to interrupt him, but he held up a hand to stop me.

"But then I realized there were other feelings involved and that I was putting the cart before the horse. I thought that the sex being so amazing was leading me to confuse that for deeper feelings...until I started thinking about stuff yesterday on the plane and in New York. I couldn't stop thinking about everything that had gone on and how I felt like shit because of it. And then it occurred to me that the reason the sex was so good was because I *already* cared. Deeper than I ever thought I could. Than I ever even wanted to."

"You didn't want to?"

He looked away and then back at me. "No."

"What—what made you change your mind?"

"I never changed my mind, April. *You* changed my heart." My eyes slipped from his even as my own heart skipped beats. First one, then two. Then it tripped all over itself as his words registered.

"I wish...I wish you had said something to me on Saturday at the party. But you didn't. You left me there, standing in front of everyone."

He closed his eyes, his jaw working. "I'm completely ashamed of that. And if I could change it, I would. Everything happened so fast. I have no excuse for how I behaved. It was cowardly. I'm so sorry, April. I should have stood up there with you."

He opened his eyes and met my gaze again. Then he took a deep breath.

"Those last two weeks while I was on the road, I missed you. A lot. I thought about you all the time, wondered what you were doing. I picked up the phone to text you at least a hundred times a day. I had to restrain myself. Any funny thing that happened, any iffy joke I heard, I wanted to send to you. I wanted you to tell me I was being inappropriate. I love being inappropriate with you."

I took my own deep breath and let it go. He smiled, and reaching out, he took a strand of my hair and wound it around his index finger. "I love *you*, April Weiss. My very own fairytale princess."

Tears immediately pricked my eyes, and I covered my mouth and nose with my hands. Jordan watched me carefully but still made no further move to touch me. I leapt forward and threw my arms around him, pulling him to me.

His arms snaked around my waist, tightening. It felt so good. So damn good. He buried his face in my hair, kissing my neck, and I kissed him everywhere I could reach…his neck, his jaw, his cheek.

"Who would have thought a beast could say such pretty words?"

He turned his head and caught my mouth with his. My heart surged in my chest, like it had grown too big or my chest cavity was too small to contain it. It felt full, painful even. And there was too much love here for it to hold.

"I told you, I'm the Big Bad Wolf. And later, I'm going to eat you all up."

I smiled and nipped at his neck with my teeth. "Yes, please."

He held me for a long time, his hands on my back, his face in my hair, his head against mine. I could have stood like that all day, it felt so good.

"Come on, get dressed and grab some stuff. I want you to stay over at my place with me. I'm exhausted and you don't look much better."

I huffed at him with mock indignation and he smiled, tapping my nose. "We can go take a nap and wake up at one p.m. to see what the stock closed at."

"And after that?"

He smiled. "I'll teach you how to surf."

I quickly pulled on some jeans and crammed enough clothes and toiletries in my bag to last me a few days. Then I grabbed my laptop and purse and told Sid what we were up to. She had a huge grin on her face when we walked out, hand in hand.

We fell asleep on a day bed on his covered back patio with the cool sea breeze blowing through the screen walls and the sound of waves mercilessly pounding the sand. He was warm and hard and—unlike the first night we'd slept together in Vancouver—a peaceful sleeper.

He lay so still, I used him as a pillow, my head rising and falling with his gentle breathing. His heavy arm draped across my back, holding me close to him. It took me a while to fall asleep because I spent a long time watching him sleep. Then finally, I snuggled into the nook between his body and his arm, pressed my head to his shoulder and dozed off.

We woke up to the sound of his phone beeping incessantly. It took us both a minute of stretching and blinking—the bright early afternoon sunlight streaming in through the screen blinding us.

As if suddenly remembering, he sat up, turned off his alarm and opened the stock app on his phone.

"DME, come on…DME, where are you? Ah! Holy *shit!*"

I sat up beside him, rubbing sleep from my eyes, trying to get a glimpse over his shoulder. "Was that a good *holy shit* or a bad *holy shit?*"

His arm wrapped around my shoulders to pull me to him, and he kissed my hair. "That was a good *holy shit*. A very, very good *holy shit*. Closing price is just over forty-one dollars a share."

"Holy shit!"

"I know, right?"

"That's amazing."

"Yep. Time for me to buy my tropical island and retire."

I laughed, looking up into his face. He appeared pleased, but there was something else. His great victory had come at a high cost.

I cleared my throat and he looked up from his phone. "So, uh, what does this all mean? You're unemployed. Does this mean I have to quit grad school to go to work and support you?" I joked. It was worded lightly, but there was still that issue of him having sacrificed his entire career because of me.

He smoothed a thumb over my cheek. "Don't worry about the job. Depending on how trading continues, as soon as I'm vested in my shares, I might not need to work again for a long time, if ever."

I pressed my lips together. "But it's not just about the money. You're not going to become an aimless beach bum at twenty-six years of age. We joke about it, but...that was a pretty huge sacrifice you made."

"Do you still think it was stupid?"

I shook my head. "I think you believe I'm worth it."

His eyes glowed with something—admiration, maybe?

"You are."

That indescribable feeling filled my throat now and I could hardly swallow. I reached up and ran my hand over his delicious scruff.

"Then we'll figure it out...we'll find a new dream to work on together."

He grinned. "Maybe I'll go back to grad school and we could be classmates."

He bent down and we kissed. It was a slow, sweet kiss. We'd rarely shared those kinds in the weeks we'd been frantically stealing time to hook up. But this was different, because now we knew...there was a future for us, and we didn't have to cram every spare amount of passion, desire and lust into the few minutes we could pilfer from a work day.

"I don't know...royalty hardly need to go to school," I said, sticking my nose in the air with faux haughtiness. "And I think that, as a princess, I need to make my first royal decree."

A slow smile formed on his lips. "And what is that, Your Highness?"

"You must have scruff at all times. Just the right amount of scruff. Not a full beard and not smooth shaven."

He laughed. "Well, that will tricky. Keeping just the right amount of scruff is an art, you know."

I laughed. "On the days you have scruff, you can kiss me as much as you want, wherever you want."

His eyes darkened. "Well, talk about incentivizing. That's talking like a true economic theorist. And I'll take you up on that right after I have something to eat. I'm starving."

"So am I."

We ate. We spent the rest of the day together, walking along the beach, talking, joking, watching the recorded interviews from the floor of the stock exchange. There was wild energy out there, and we soaked it all up hours after the fact and from three thousand miles away.

Later that night, after watching a movie on his widescreen TV and dining on pizza and a little wine, we snuck out to the beach and made love on the packed sand under a big blanket. It felt daring and risky and fun, not unlike the other times we've had sex.

But *unlike* those other times, we weren't filled with that rushed urgency to do as much as we could while we could. This time, there was a promise of a future—and oh, what a difference that made.

29
JORDAN

IN MY DREAM, SOMEONE WAS KNOCKING AT THE DOOR. IT started out as a gentle knock, and after a few minutes progressed into pounding. At the same time, my phone chimed with a text message.

April sat up first, shockingly, and jostled my shoulder. "Some dickhead is pounding on your door."

"Mmm."

"It's probably whoever is texting you."

I sat up. *What the hell?*

"Maybe Sexilicious Sondra is demanding her handcuffs back. She's had enough of the waiting," she said, stretching lithely. The sheet fell away from the upper half of her body and my eyes fixed on her luscious bare breasts. Nothing downstairs was compelling enough to pull me away from this gorgeous, naked woman in my bed and the promise of morning sex...

The doorbell began to ring—at five-second intervals, no less—and I'd finally had enough. I slipped out of bed and went looking for my jeans on the floor, not bothering with underwear or a shirt. Whoever it was would have to deal.

April flopped back on the bed. "You wore me out last night with all that sex. I'm going back to sleep."

"Get your strength up. I plan on wearing you out again when I get back upstairs."

"Mmm," she muttered as I left the room. I flew down the stairs, yelling that I was on my way. The pounding stopped.

When I whipped open the door, ready to tear somebody a new one, I stopped short.

"You look like hell," I said. Adam hadn't shaved and appeared as if he'd been on a red-eye and slept in his clothes. Not unlike me just twenty-four hours ago, in fact.

"You, on the other hand, look like fresh morning dew."

I laughed and stepped back to let him in, combing a hand through my hair, which I was sure was sticking up in eighty different directions.

"I would have said you look like a million bucks, but that's now chump change for you. It's actually more like forty-one, thirty-two a share."

He broke into a grin. "I'm still in shock about that."

"Congrats, man. You are the first official billionaire that I have ever been friends with..." If we were, indeed, still friends.

Adam walked into the living room and looked out onto the beach through the sliding glass door. He folded his arms across his chest.

"Sit down. Can I get you something? I can start some coffee..."

"I'm good," he said, turning around to look at me. "I've been sitting down a lot lately. I'd rather stand."

That meant he wasn't staying long. "Where's Mia at?"

"She had to go straight to school this morning. It was hard enough for her to miss the one day."

"So, umm. I just wanted to say again that I'm sorry—"

He held his hand up. "Don't. You don't need to say it. I'm sorry, too. I didn't handle that well at all."

My eyebrow twitched as I tried to hide my surprise. Getting an apology from Adam was about as rare as a gamer nerd at a frat party.

I shrugged. "I dropped a bomb on you out of nowhere. It's understandable."

"And I am still pissed about that. Mostly because it sucked being on the stock exchange floor without you. This was supposed to be our crowning moment. Our first huge milestone."

I looked away, shifting my weight from one leg to the other. "It sucked not being there, man. But I watched it all on the Internet."

"I don't want to do the rest of this without you, Jordan. The company needs you too much. I need you too much."

"But you get why I had to, right?"

"No, I'm still not getting that part." He frowned. "Can you just...explain again?"

"About it being unfair to punish just her?"

"But would you have done this for anyone else? Why her?"

I jammed my fists in my pockets. "Because she's..."

He folded his arms across his chest. "Go on..."

"Because I'm...."

"Yes?"

"It's different with her man. I'm—ah hell, I love her."

Adam sucked his lips into his mouth for approximately two seconds before he burst out laughing. "Shit!" he said. "Emilia's going to be so pissed she didn't hear that straight out of the horse's mouth."

I grimaced. "Sorry to disappoint."

"So yeah, we already figured that out. It was just fun getting you to admit it. Damn, I should have recorded it on my phone."

"Fuck you."

He whipped out his phone and pressed the record button. "Can you say it again so I can send it to her?"

"You'll have to beat it out of me, dude."

"That can be arranged." He tucked his phone back into his pocket and sobered. "So, after I leave here, I'm going to contact April and offer to let her finish her internship. Then you're going to have to figure out a way to dodge the bullets after you tell David that you despoiled his daughter on camera."

I gulped.

"And then, you are going to have to get your lazy son of a bitch ass dressed and into the office before I have to fire you."

"So about David..."

Adam glanced away for a minute, clearly uncomfortable. "I have no idea how David will take this, to be honest. That's going to be on you—and on her. I had Walt's team track down the people at the company party who tweeted and posted those photos of her. They've been asked to look elsewhere for jobs. There were five, and three of them were interns. Cari, the one who tore April's swimsuit, was already dismissed with no recommendation." He paused, shifting. His gaze flicked away from mine. "I think it would be appropriate to inform the officers of what happened. That's not going to be easy for you..."

I took a deep breath and let it go. "I'll take my lumps. It's only fair."

He smiled. "And, of course, I'll have to document all this humiliation so I can savor it for years to come..."

"That's out of the question," I said, grinning. "No deal."

He paused, almost at a loss for what to say, and then met my gaze again. "So we're good?"

"Yeah, except you don't have to go anywhere if you want to speak to April."

His brow went up and he threw a glance at the stairway. "You want to get her down here so I can talk to her, then? And for God's sake, put a shirt on."

It took me a little time to quickly explain to April what had happened and then convince her she looked decent enough to go downstairs. She washed the sleep from her face, got dressed and pulled her hair back, but still mumbled about how she looked terrible. Impossible, in my opinion.

Finally, she came downstairs. By this time, Adam and I were both drinking fresh cups of coffee in the kitchen. April was pale—more so than usual—and looked sheepish, but quietly congratulated Adam on the successful IPO. He thanked her and explained that he wanted to offer her the chance to finish her internship at Draco.

She took a deep breath and let it out, stirring her coffee while appearing deep in thought. Then, she looked up. "Thank you for the offer. And thank you for taking Jordan back. He shouldn't lose his job over what was basically my fault." Adam's eyes widened and I frowned, about to open my mouth to object. She stopped me, holding up her hand. "I hit record on my phone without his knowledge. He would never have done something that stupid."

"I've done stupid shit before. We all have. Adam has too." Adam rolled his eyes at me and returned his attention to April.

"How did it end up on the Internet?" he asked.

April straightened and looked at me. "Well, even Jordan doesn't know this because I just found out. I'd always thought it was an accident. Just so you know, I'm probably the most non-tech-savvy person you have ever employed. But my roommate traced what happened using my phone and figured out that one of the other interns—Cari—found the video on my phone when I showed her some pictures, and she sent a copy to herself and uploaded it." She turned to me when I reacted to this news with a curse. "With everything going on yesterday, I forgot to tell you. Sid figured it out the night before."

Well, now *I* was really pissed. Adam rubbed his forehead, taking that in. "Wow, she ended up being a real troublemaker. Wish I'd known that six months ago."

April sighed. "I wish I'd had the guts to tell you sooner...but I should warn you now that she has a thing for you and it's a bit obsessive." Adam colored but didn't look the least bit surprised. Then April licked her lips and squared her shoulders. "When she started plotting to try to get Mia out of the picture, I finally figured she'd lost it. She was trying to pressure me and others to do her dirty work for her."

Adam and I both straightened and looked at her, alarmed. *Hell no.* I was about to speak, but Adam cut me off. "She was planning to do something to Mia?"

April looked down into her coffee, coloring. "At the party, Cari wanted me to tear Mia's dress and pull it down, saying she would expose me if I didn't. When I refused, she grabbed my swimsuit and did it to me instead."

I exchanged a look with Adam. Wow...that was some crazy shit. I knew the girl had been a bit touched when I'd caught her threatening

April, and now I regretted not letting her go on the spot. But I'd been more concerned about covering my own ass so that none of this came out...

I watched April while she looked at Adam with no small amount of fear. Adam's jaw tightened. "Well, thanks for letting me know. I'll handle this, and you don't need to worry about her anymore."

Her shoulders rounded with relief. I knew it had taken a lot to tell him all of that. But I was glad that she didn't need to be reminded to speak up for herself.

She blinked and looked out the window, her chin held high. "I have to be honest. I'm not brave enough to walk back into Draco after what happened on Saturday. But I'm grateful for what you did on my behalf—dismissing the people who posted the pictures and all of that."

I frowned, disappointed, but could I blame her? I cleared my throat to get her attention. "I'm going to butt in here and say that I think you *do* have the guts to go back in there. I know you do."

She shook her head. "That's easy for you to say. They don't all know it's you in the video."

I nodded. "You're right. That's why I'm going to tell them."

She straightened, eyes locking on mine again. "Jordan—"

I held my hand up. "We can talk about it later. I'm not going to force you to go back there if you don't want to, but...I sure could use your moral support when *I* go back."

Adam glanced between the two of us and pushed his coffee mug aside. "I'm going to get going. I at least need to show *my* face over there before I go home and crash."

I walked Adam out, and before he left, put my hand on his shoulder. "Thanks, man."

He shook his head. "It's what friends do." And he was gone.

When I went back inside, April hugged me around the waist, holding me close for a long time, her head pressed to my shoulder. I ran my hand down her silky hair. "We'll figure it—"

"I'll do it. I'll go with you. I was almost done with my project, anyway."

I kissed the top of her head, something like pride glowing in my chest. "You're sure?"

She tilted her head to look up at me. "Yes. Now kiss me before I change my mind."

I did just that. Long, slow and deep, our lips and arms locked. I was reminded of that morning sex I'd been deprived of… But there was still some ground we needed to cover.

"You know…when I'm *really* going to need you is when I talk to your dad."

Her mouth twisted at the thought. "I might throw you under the bus on that one."

I laughed. "As long as he isn't a firearms enthusiast or trained assassin. He's not, right?"

She laughed. "My dad won't even kill house spiders. I think you're good. He might get my grandma to level a curse upon your head, though."

"I might be tempting fate by saying this, but I'm curse-proof. Those young ladies of my previous acquaintance who may have, at one time or another, cursed me that certain vital organs would shrivel up and fall off, would attest to it."

Her eyes widened. "It had *better* not shrivel up and fall off, or I'd have to dump you. The only reason I plan on keeping you around is for the hot sex."

"And the scruff. Don't forget the scruff."

She broke into a smile. "For sure."

And with that, I kissed her, taking her up on her royal decree to kiss her whenever and *wherever* I wanted. She was tingling with scruff burns for days.

30
APRIL

TO SAY THAT MY DAD DIDN'T TAKE THE NEWS WELL WAS AN understatement of epic proportions. Jordan and I had decided to tell him before informing the employees at Draco, so we arranged to meet for lunch at a neutral location—a private room in a nearby restaurant.

Dad had his elbow on the table, pinching the bridge of his nose, his eyes closed. Jordan and I exchanged a long look and my throat closed up in fear. That same flight instinct raced through my veins, making me want to bolt for the door and let Jordan deal with the consequences alone.

"So, let me get this straight—you recorded yourself having sex with him—but you didn't know it was him."

I worried my lip between my teeth. "Yeah..."

His hand dropped, eyes opening. He locked eyes with me, and though I really wanted to look away, I held his gaze. "This story gets more and more bizarre. I feel like I've stepped into some weird alternate universe, and you…" He shook his head. "What the hell were you thinking, April?"

I shifted in my chair. "We've already been over this—where my mind was at when I made those choices. The only difference now is that you know who the other person in the video was."

Dad's cheek bulged where he clenched his jaw. He hadn't so much as looked Jordan's way since we broke the news. "That is a rather important detail you left out. But"—he flicked a brief look in Jordan's direction—"he also could have filled me in."

Jordan straightened in his chair. "April and I both made some big mistakes, David. I'm not going to deny that—"

"You can call me Mr. Weiss," he bit out. "And really, is there any point in denying it now?"

Jordan hesitated, shaking his head, clearly flummoxed.

Dad's eyes snapped back to me. "April, I don't want you to take this the wrong way, but…your choice of boyfriends in the past has not been great. Starting with that idiot who took you out to get that tattoo right up through this last jackass who ended up marrying your mother."

Ouch. That hurt.

"And don't think I haven't heard the office gossip about this one." He turned back to Jordan, his nostrils flaring. "The parties, the boozing, the women… Every pimply geek at that place reveres you like some kind of womanizing god. I know you're a natural-born charmer…so it looks like you've pulled the wool over my daughter's eyes for the moment. To say I'm not happy that you've set your sights on her is an understatement."

Jordan took a deep breath, having flushed a little during my dad's rant. "Mr. Weiss, it's not like that. I know we're in a difficult situation, given our work relationship. But I have nothing but the best intentions when it comes to April. I'm not stupid enough to lie to you about this. I know there is a lot riding on it if things go south. But...I love her."

Dad paused for a beat, scowling at Jordan, appearing completely unmoved by his speech. "I'm going to assume you don't have any children—that you know of, anyway." Jordan flinched slightly. "But you do have a sister, right?" He jutted his chin toward Jordan. "How'd you feel about some player taking her for a ride? Hmm? Your little sister, hooking up with someone who's bedded—I don't know, dozens? Hundreds? You think I should be happy about that? Would *you* be happy about that?"

Jordan's leg bounced up and down in place, and his hands tightened on the tabletop. "No. I wouldn't be happy at all. But there wouldn't be a whole lot I could do about it. My sister is an adult. The decision is hers. However, I'd do exactly what you are doing now and warn her away from someone like me. But ultimately...it would be out of my hands." For the first time since my dad had engaged with him, Jordan looked over at me. My mouth turned up in a small smile of encouragement.

"I care about April. I want to start a future with her. We love each other. My past is my past. I can't change that. Everyone has done things that they regret. It doesn't mean I have to stop living at the age of almost twenty-six because I've suddenly woken up and realized that the lifestyle I was living no longer does it for me."

"There's a saying—a leopard can't change its spots—"

"Enough, Dad." I scooted up in my chair and put my hand over his on the table. "It's my decision. I'm an adult, and I love him. I want him.

And I want you—and Rebekah and Sarah and Daniel. I want to be a part of your family. But you need to accept that I want Jordan, too."

Dad's eyes cut to Jordan, sharp as blades swiping through the air. "You're right. I have no say. But don't think I'm not going to watch you like a hawk. If you hurt her..."

"I understand. You love her, too. But I want you to know that I'd rather stab myself in the eye than hurt your daughter."

"Dad, *please*. Please let us give this a chance."

"So I assume he's giving you your recommendation to business school?"

I looked over at Jordan again. "I've been having second thoughts about business school. Remember how I was telling you that I love studying theory?"

His forehead creased with a frown. "You're going to study theoretical economics? And what the hell are you going to do with that?"

"I don't know...maybe work as a consultant—like on a game. Or develop new models, or teach."

Dad's phone chimed and he checked it. "We can talk more about this later. I'm not opposed to that idea, as long as you are sure that's what you want to do." He stood and took us both in again. Those nervous jitters were back in full force. I didn't need Dad's approval—but I really, *really* wanted it.

He rubbed his jaw and sighed. "I'm going to be honest and tell you that I don't have a good feeling about this—especially considering how things started. But you're a woman. You're my beautiful daughter and I'm proud of you, and I really hope that I'm wrong about him."

Well...that was as good as it was going to get, I guessed. I stood and hooked my arms around his neck, pulling him in for a hug, then kissed his cheek. "Thanks, Daddy."

He patted my back, eyes widening in surprise. "Love you, April. Please...just be careful, okay? That's all I ask."

I pulled back and looked him in the face, nodding. "I will. If he hurts me, you can fire him and kick him out on the street."

He laughed, but at the edge of my vision, I caught Jordan fidgeting. To let him off the hook, I sent him a sly smile and he narrowed his eyes at me before returning the smile. Dad turned to go when Jordan stepped forward, putting out his hand for a handshake.

Dad waved him off. "I'm not quite ready for that yet. Give me a few. I'm an old man. But..." I almost busted out laughing when he pointed two fingers toward his eyes and then turned to point them at Jordan in the universal symbol of *'I've got my eyes on you.'*

"See you soon, sweetheart." Then he turned and left.

Jordan expelled a long breath, and I suddenly realized how nervous he must have been. He'd hidden it well. "Shit, that was rough," he said.

"Were you expecting a picnic?"

He shook his head and approached me, holding out his arms. I slipped into them and he pulled me against him, kissing my cheek. "Thanks for speaking up for me," he said. "I was *this* close to bailing when he started playing hardball."

I pulled back to give him a dirty look and saw he was smiling, clearly teasing me. "Well... I *guess* it was worth it." A slow smile crept across my face.

His arm around my waist tightened. "How about I make it worth your while? I don't have to be back to work 'til tomorrow, so we have a whole day to burn, my naughty fairytale princess..."

I grinned. "What was it Snow White kept singing about? *Someday my prince will come...*"

His mouth twisted. "*Someday?* Your prince plans on coming tonight—more than once." I burst out laughing and he waggled his eyebrows. "Just so you know, I'm in this for the win. And I can be pretty goddamn stubborn when I set my mind to something...so no bailing, no balking, no running away."

"Hmm. But inappropriate behavior, that's okay?"

He grinned. "Fuck yeah. It's *required.*"

31
WILLIAM

I HATE BEING IN THE WAREHOUSE. EVERY SOUND ECHOES AND bounces off the floor, the walls, the high ceiling. It's not a *bad* place, but everything here is strong. The lights are brighter, the sounds are louder, the smells—I *really* don't like the smells—are oily and plastic. Synthetic and overpowering.

But I find that if I breathe through my mouth slowly, it helps. So I stand at the back of the crowd and fold my arms tightly over my chest. When I start to feel agitated, I tense them suddenly. The pressure helps keep me calm. Just like clenching my jaw helps or squeezing my eyes so tightly I can see spots behind them.

These are tricks I've taught myself to deal with the loud, strong, brightness of places like this. It's either that or my sketchpad, and I left that on my desk because I had no warning about this meeting.

That's another thing that makes me itchy and agitated. I tense my arms again just at the thought that the whole routine for the day has been thrown off by this announcement the officers want to make. I suppose that Adam would let me stay at my desk if I tell him how much I dislike it. I actually have told him before and he understood—or at least he said he did. But this time, I have a thing or two to say to his annoying best friend. And *he's* here too, standing next to April Weiss.

Adam has just finished with the announcement regarding the stock prices and release dates on vesting shares owned by employees. He's also declared that Draco will be acquiring a company to make the hardware for the new virtual reality equipment. This means more work for me as I am on the team to create the three-dimensional modeling for the new interface.

I blink. I don't know what to think about that and I try not to, but I squint as Adam announces that Jordan has something he wants to talk about now. I saw him outside in the parking lot this morning, holding hands with April Weiss when he thought no one could see. He gets all the girls to fall in love with him.

And yet all of his advice is pure bullshit.

Maybe he lies so that no one else will compete with him. Maybe his techniques are secrets. The look on his face means he is nervous, I think. He is already talking, and I'm in my own thoughts so I've missed what he's said. He is standing about fifty-three feet away and there are a lot of people between us...because in crowds, I never stand in the middle. Always on the outer edge. It's easier to breathe there.

"If you care about the welfare of this company, know that it's expected that what we talk about here is internal company business only," he's saying. I have to scrunch my brow and narrow my eyes and really focus to follow him. He's far away, and the noise—feet shuffling, people whispering, echoes of every little thing. "The incident at the pool party in which one of our interns was wrongly humiliated should not have happened. What's worse, it should not have been shared with the outside world via social media. But the most shameful thing about it is that she was left to face that humiliation all alone. I want to make that right. On behalf of the company and myself, I'd like to apologize to April Weiss for the behavior she had to endure at the party. I also think it's right to let you know that I was the other party involved in the video."

Everything is a lot quieter now. No one is moving. Some eyes are growing rounder, postures are changing, mouths are dropping. Surprise. They are surprised. Unpleasantly so.

"I also owe you, my fellow employees, an apology..." But I'm not listening now. I'm feeling tense, my fists are tight. I'm angry. I don't like Jordan. I used to like him, but today I don't like him.

And I'm going to tell him...just...just as soon as these people go away and it's not so crowded. So I focus my attention inward, trying to use my tricks to think about not being in this room with these bright lights and this noise.

I spend time thinking about *her*. How her hair is so pale that it is almost white. Pale blonde. Sometimes she pulls it away from her face. The way it forms tiny curls around her neck. I like her wrists. They are delicate. Thin. Elegant. Even her wrists are beautiful. And her eyes. So soft a blue that if I were painting them, I'd have to mix white with the cerulean oil paint. Maybe two parts white to one part blue.

She reminds me of a Raphael angel.

It's thirteen minutes before they start clearing out. I wait until then to step forward and speak with Jordan. He is walking beside Adam and April, and when they are nearby, I wave to catch his attention.

The three of them stop. My cousin says, "Hey Liam, everything all right?"

I take a breath, remind myself not to be irritated. Only family members call me 'Liam.' I tolerate it from three people only—Dad, Adam and my sister, Britt. Oh, there's my new stepmother, too. Sometimes she slips and calls me 'Liam' because the others do and she forgets that I don't like it.

"I need to speak with Jordan." I point at him.

Jordan's facial expression changes. His eyebrows scrunch together. Adam says something to him and then turns back to me. "Okay. See you later." He keeps walking. April follows Adam after a little hesitation.

"I am angry with you," I say to Jordan.

He sighs and his eyes look into mine. I jerk my eyes away. I don't like staring in people's eyes. I clench my fists, trying to calm myself.

"The advice you gave me was very bad."

Jordan tilts his head to the side. "I'm sorry. Did it not work out?"

"You said to invite Jenna out in a big group of friends. I invited her to my medieval reenactment society, along with Alex, Heath, Connor and Katya."

Jordan blinks a couple times. "Okay... I take it she didn't like that?"

"She likes it a lot. She keeps coming back."

His feet scuff loudly on the floor. I hate the way his feet sound on the warehouse floor. He's not wearing sneakers today. Those are much quieter.

"Isn't that a good thing? Don't you want her to keep coming back so you can see more of her?"

My fists clench again. I want to swing one of them at him. "No, it's not a good thing. Because that first night she met Doug Callihan. He's one of the chief knights of our organization."

My hands ball up and then relax over and over again—another thing I do to calm down. I take a few more deep breaths, because I still really want to hit Jordan.

"Okay…and what happened when she met him?"

"He asked her on a date. And now they are boyfriend and girlfriend."

Jordan's mouth gets round, like he's shocked. "Oh man. I'm sorry…but that doesn't mean it's over. You can still swing this. I'll—"

I hold up my shaking hand. "I don't want to swing. I want Jenna. I don't want more advice because I don't like your advice. You said that if I asked her out in a group that we would get more comfortable with each other, and then we could become boyfriend and girlfriend. You were wrong."

Jordan holds his hands up, palms out. "I'm sorry, dude. My advice doesn't come with a guarantee. But let me see if I can—"

"No!" I shout. I don't like to shout, but I'm so angry that the choices are either hitting Jordan or shouting. I turn and start to walk away from him. I need to leave this warehouse.

"Whoa, William, wait up." Jordan speeds up his steps to walk beside me. "Let me see if I can fix this."

"I'm going to do that myself. Doug is my foe. My rival. My arch enemy. I've already challenged him to one-on-one combat."

Jordan stops walking and stares at me. I pick up speed and run from the warehouse, and I don't stop even though Jordan is calling my name.

I have to prepare for a duel.

ABOUT THE AUTHOR

Brenna Aubrey is an author of New Adult contemporary romance stories that center on geek culture. She has always sought comfort in good books and the long, involved stories she weaves in her head.

Brenna is a city girl with a nature-lover's heart. She therefore finds herself out in green open spaces any chance she can get. A mommy to two little kids and teacher to many more older kids, she juggles schedules to find time to pursue her love of storycrafting.

She currently resides on the west coast with her husband, two children, two adorable golden retriever pups, two birds and some fish.

43220243R00278

Made in the USA
Charleston, SC
21 June 2015